CAPE'S SIDE BAY

JAMES RASILE

Published by Inkshares, Inc., Oakland, California
www.inkshares.com

Edited by Matt Harry and Sarah Nivala
Cover design by Tim Barber

ISBN: 9781947848733
e-ISBN: 9781947848740
LCCN: 2023939867

First edition

Printed in the United States of America

For My Family, who always supports me,
regardless of how many crazy projects I take on.

To Erin, for making me go camping
not knowing it would lead to this book.

And for Selena, you can't read yet,
but when you can, read Dickens instead.

PROLOGUE

IT WAS EARLY September in the town of Hillsbury.

Labor Day weekend, the final long weekend of the summer. The weekend before students returned to their schools and summer tourists departed for the year, was the busiest for the town. Hillsbury was cottage country; families would travel upward of ten hours to stay in their wood cabins or the luxurious campsites that had recently been upgraded with electricity and fresh-stained picnic tables for the summer months.

Hillsbury liked to think of itself as a tight-knit community. To say that it was, though, would be a lie. Most locals knew each other, and most tourists knew the locals. But does anyone really ever truly know a person? The cost of living, for groceries, land, and the houses on that land—grew exponentially over the years. What was once a town where couples could comfortably afford to buy a house and raise a family, turned into one for the wealthy. The locals rarely sold their properties. They felt the town was theirs, and while they approved of the summer crowd spending money on local shops and merchants, the tourists were looked down upon. The façade was working. Hillsbury remained an ideal place to raise a family.

The locals (of which there were few) were all friendly with each other, and the tourists (most of whom liked to refer to themselves as the true locals of Hillsbury) got along with them just fine. Since practically everyone knew everyone else, committing a crime there was much easier said than done. There were barely any crimes or strange happenings on record at all. Except one.

Seven years ago, Jill Carter and her lover, Marcia Richter, went on what was meant to be a short fishing trip. After months of dating in secret, the couple had finally come out to their families and close friends; after relieving themselves of that particular burden, the women decided to spend a day unwinding with a fishing trip. Lately, fish had been swimming to Cape's Side Bay in droves. What you could typically catch in a month could be caught in mere hours. Neither Jill nor Marcia had fished before. This seemed like a perfect place to start.

So, the night before, they began packing for their trip. Jill borrowed equipment from her brother, Henry, whose job as head park ranger made him a fountain of knowledge regarding pretty much any outdoor activity in Hillsbury or Cape's Side Bay. Marcia went to the general store and asked for fishing advice from her friend, Jett, who ran the place. Jett—who'd had a crush on Marcia before learning of her preference—recommended the right type of fishing rod and bait. Armed with all the right equipment and knowledge, the girls departed for their fishing trip at six o'clock the following morning. At six forty-five, they stopped at Thomas O'Leary's Donuts for a coffee. Marcia ordered a vanilla dip donut and a medium coffee, one cream, two sugars. Jill ordered a tea and a cranberry scone. At six fifty-seven the ladies left Thomas O'Leary's and were never heard from again.

Within hours of when they were meant to return home, Henry (having heard nothing from either of them), used his connections to make as many phone calls as possible, inquiring on their whereabouts. Turns out there was no sign of either of the women at Cape's Side Bay: no car, no tire tracks, no fishing gear . . . nothing. The bay hadn't been visited by anyone that day. A missing person investigation was opened, but—before Henry knew it—it was closed. The search had yielded no results. Jill and Marcia were gone.

The locals began putting their theories out there, suggesting that Hillsbury's predominantly Christian population were offended by the lesbian couple's coming out, so perhaps they decided it was best to drive somewhere more urban—more metropolitan—where they could live away from the gaze of judgmental eyes. Henry Carter, however, knew his sister better than anyone, and he knew it was unlike her to have just vanished without at least telling him. And if they were truly planning on disappearing, why would Marcia pay full price for a brand-new fishing rod from Jett? And why would they stop for breakfast at Thomas O'Leary's, an establishment run by the father of one of Marcia's closest childhood friends?

The people (and the police) chalked it all up to their wanting to create a ruse, and the best way to convince the world of a lie is to live the lie to its fullest. So, to Henry's utter amazement and grief, the book was closed on the disappearance of Jill Carter and Marcia Richter.

Time passed, the strange disappearance became a distant memory, and everyone moved on. Henry was still frequently haunted by the thought of something terrible happening to his sister, but even he made do with envisioning her living a happier life somewhere else with Marcia. Maybe they'd gotten married and adopted a child or two. The thought of being an uncle always brought a wide smile to his face. His wife of twenty-six years, Rachel, would smile back and remind him that he is a father of two and doesn't need to worry about his possible nieces or nephews. She knew he only imagined this scenario to keep from thinking the worst, but she encouraged him to remember that he had a family of his own, in the here and now, who needed and loved him very much.

Eventually, the amount of fish in Cape's Side Bay diminished until there were hardly any left at all. Tourists were already showing signs of packing up and leaving. So, Mayor Tremblay decided that the town would close the summer off with a bang—their annual fireworks festival with the works: beer tents, candy trucks, maybe a few carnival rides. The festival was in its fifth year, and each one had been a bigger success than the last. The mayor told Henry that no expense would be spared this time, that this was to be the festival to end all festivals, the event that would finally put Cape's Side Bay on the map.

It was the Thursday before Labor Day weekend. The day had been mostly cloudy. Most people either stayed inside or lounged on their decks. There was a strange, unsettling feeling in the air. It was humid but dark, with a sky that promised rain but gave none at all. Hillsbury Park was rather quiet: some dog walkers, couples, a few kids playing tag, but otherwise empty. As day turned to night, activity began to pick up in the park. Nothing was scheduled this particular evening, no bonfire, no fireworks, and no fair to speak of. The park was cold and damp; a mist began to fill the night air.

Four boys snuck out of their homes just after nine o'clock and made their way to the wooded area of the park, just north of Cape's Side Bay.

Joel Liman, David Curtis, and Mitchell Rooney were the local kids. Chris Randall's parents owned a summer home in Hillsbury and had visited the town every summer for the past five years. All four boys were thirteen, and they harbored a shared disappointment that the summer holidays were about to come to an end. The boys settled beneath a large tree and formed a circle around each other. Mitchell Rooney removed an object from his pocket; it was wrapped in cloth. He looked around at his friends and asked who wanted to touch it first.

The boys looked at one another, no one willing to take it. Joel grabbed the object from Mitchell's hand. He quickly removed the cloth and saw that he was holding *a gun*.

"Holy shit, where'd you get it?" Chris Randall shouted.

Mitchell snatched the gun back from Joel's hands. "Shut up, someone'll hear you!" Mitchell stared thoughtfully at the gun, with a small grin on his face.

"But, seriously, dude, where'd you get it?" Chris continued.

"My stepdad. Keeps it locked up in the liquor cabinet. I found the key."

Joel glanced at Mitchel, confused. "What're we gonna do with it?"

"Hunt," Mitchell said.

"Hunt what?" chimed David Curtis, the quietest of the group.

"Animals. What do you think, dumbass? We're men! My stepdad hunts all the time, and what is he?" He didn't wait for a response from his friends before offering it up. "A man. And what do men do?" This time Mitchell waited for a response;

unfortunately for him, none of the other boys offered one up. "Hunt!" Mitchell raised his voice in frustration.

"It's getting dark. Aren't all the animals sleeping?" David asked in his quiet voice.

Mitchell just looked at David and laughed. "You're such a child. Come on, don't be a pussy. Let's kill something!"

The boys looked at one another again. Joel was the first to reluctantly nod, followed by Chris. David stayed still. He was unwilling to participate in these shenanigans, though he was afraid it was only a matter of time before the others talked (or forced) him into it.

"Come on, David, let's be men!" Joel egged him on.

Mitchell placed the gun in David's hands and said, "Man up."

There it was. The moment David feared would come. Things like this always happened to him, it seemed. It was the curse of being quiet: other people tended to use their own voices to speak for you. He couldn't back away now. So, sighing heavily, David joined them on their quest to find a living creature and end its life.

The boys walked softly through the woods toward Cape's Side Bay. The water—which over the past seven years had begun to dry up and now resembled more of a swamp—was covered with fog.

Not far from the shoreline, a fallen tree lay limp across the water. Mitchell placed an empty can of pork and beans atop the log and nodded to David. David was in no way a violent boy, but he *was* extraordinarily impressionable. David was slave to Mitchell's commands. He did not possess the backbone to stand up for himself, and if Mitchell Rooney handed him a gun and demanded he fire it at an empty can, David would do so. It wasn't even that David respected Mitchell; quite the opposite, in fact. David almost despised Mitchell. He wished he could just hang out with Joel and Chris. Unfortunately, David had also known Mitchell the longest. On many occasions, Mitchell had even referred to David as his own (sort-of) brother. Mitchell made David uncomfortable, but David had settled into an uneasy acceptance that the two of them were stuck with each other.

The only weapon David had ever so much as touched was a water pistol, and not a particularly good water pistol either. It was a cheap off-brand one that his father had gotten for him when they were at a flea market one Saturday morning three years earlier. It had broken after a few days' use, and now the trigger (without a spring to support it) simply flopped back and forth at the whims of gravity. David hated that water pistol. But he'd much rather be wielding that piece of cheap, painted plastic than have to contend with this.

With the real thing . . .

He could feel the eyes of the other three boys boring into the back of his skull. Nervous, David lifted the gun, closed his left eye like he'd seen the guys in old Westerns do, and took aim. As he pulled the trigger, he closed both eyes and . . . Nothing. Nothing happened. No bang. No feeling of unlimited power at his fingertips. No anything. Mitchell snatched the gun from his grip.

"You gotta take the safety off, dummy," he said. He switched off the safety and shoved the gun back into David's chest.

David swallowed. Despite the relative chill of the night, sweat was beginning to trickle down his forehead. He began to think the absolute worst; what if he misfired and hit one of his friends by accident? What if the bullet ricocheted off the can and hit him? Guns weren't safe for kids . . . hell, they were barely safe for adults! That's what his mother used to tell him. But the pressure from his friends surrounded him, suffocating him, drowning him like quicksand. The more he struggled, the more he fought, the deeper he'd sink.

His index finger pulled back and the gun fired. The bullet missed the can. In fact, if someone had witnessed the shooting and not known he was aiming at the can, they would not know it was his intended target. Mitchell chuckled as David calmed himself with deep breaths. Firing a gun was an exhilarating feeling. So much power and force tucked between his fingers and thumb! It was remarkable! He was embarrassed that he'd missed, but he also had to admit that he'd liked it.

Mitchell took the gun from David and handed it to Joel. Joel's mother was the town librarian; her family had lived in Hillsbury for seventy years. Her father was the town mayor before passing away of a rare liver disease. She often cautioned her son to stay away from Cape's Side Bay, even before the women went missing all those years earlier. She would tell Joel stories of her childhood, of bears living in the area. At the east end of Cape's Side Bay there was a cave, roughly seventy feet above sea level, and local kids used to tell stories of a bear living there high above the water. This was, of course, later confirmed to be nothing but an urban legend. Even still, Patty Liman believed there was a bear in Cape's Side Bay, something she had warned her only child of on a constant basis. Naturally, this made the idea of sneaking out into the park and bay after dark all the more intriguing to Joel. He loved his mother and had never once gone out against her wishes.

Not until this very night.

Joel's father passed away before he was born, leaving his grandfather to act as a father figure. Orville Liman was a no-nonsense individual. The straightest of shooters, and quite possibly the most noble and only honest politician the world had ever seen. The town loved him, and if it were not for the terrible illness that took his life, many believed he would have served as mayor for much longer than the three years he'd held on to the reins. Orville was raised by a hunter and, in return, *became* a hunter, though he never enjoyed it as a sport. He would hunt deer or duck and serve the meat for Christmas or Thanksgiving dinners. At certain times, he would donate the meat to a homeless shelter just outside of town. Orville was a rare kind of selfless, the kind Hillsbury feared they'd never see again.

Joel was comfortable with a gun. Though he had never handled a live weapon, his grandfather had taught him how to hold a pistol properly, how to aim, and most importantly, how to respect it. Joel's eyes focused on the can. Mitchell leaned in closer to him. Joel could feel his breath on his neck and swatted Mitchell away.

"Oh, he's so serious!" Mitchell laughed.

The others took a step back and waited, breath held, for what would happen next. Joel's finger pulled the trigger ever so gently and the bullet launched out of the gun, grazing the empty can just enough to spin it around three times over. Joel was visibly disappointed he had missed. His shoulders sagged, and he handed the gun to Chris. As Joel made his way over to the tree stump to take a seat, the boys heard a sound that would change all of their lives forever.

A roar.

It was so ferocious, it shook the surrounding trees. The only animal the boys figured could make such a sound was a bear, and a big one at that. Joel stood and looked around. Mitchell grabbed the gun from Chris.

"What the hell was that?" Chris asked.

"The bear," Mitchell said with a grin.

"There's no bear," Chris retorted.

"Bullshit. Joel, didn't your mom always tell you stories about the bear in Cape's Side Bay?"

Joel nodded. She hadn't done so, since it was ruled out as an urban legend. His mother had no interest in being known as the "town loon," and so she kept whatever thoughts she had of the bear to herself. But she still believed the bear existed.

Mitchell began to walk closer to the bay. "What're you doing?" Chris asked, still unsettled by the roar.

"Gonna check it out. What does it look like?" Mitchell held his gun up.

"Are you nuts?" yelled Chris, who looked like he had no interest in sticking around.

"Here's an idea: Why don't you stop being such a pussy and come for a walk with me? It's not like we're not armed!"

"And it's not like any of us have any aim," Chris fought back.

Mitchell, not saying a word, turned and fired his gun at the can, hitting it right in the center. The others stared, slack-jawed. Mitchell turned to leave again, and this time Joel followed him.

"Where are you going?" David asked.

"We can't let him go alone," Joel said over his shoulder. The other two boys hesitated, then followed. Chris was swearing under his breath. David's mouth was a thin line of worry.

By now the fog had completely covered the bay. The water was barely visible and the only things they could see were the tree trunks looming around them in the darkness. The boys walked carefully through the woods of Hillsbury Park until they were standing directly on the shoreline of Cape's Side Bay. Mitchell commented on the fog being bad. David tried to use it as an excuse for them to leave, but Mitchell pressed on, regardless. Walking over rocks, they made their way to the area of the bay that sat directly below the cave. David slipped on the rocks twice; lucky for him, Chris was following close behind and was able to keep him from spilling into the swampy bay water.

As they stood under the cave, they remained silent, all with the same thought in their minds. Joel was the first to say it aloud. "Now what?"

Nobody moved, nobody reacted, and nobody answered, because none of the boys had an answer. Mitchell was the first to attempt to scale the rocky wall but could not find decent enough footing.

"Why don't we just go home? We can come back another day with a rope or something?" David spoke softly, hoping that "another day" would never actually come to pass.

"Rope? You need more than a rope to scale that wall," Joel responded.

"Dude, shut up!" Mitchel was visibly upset.

Joel, on the other hand, sided with David. As much as he wanted to get to that cave and as much as he wanted to prove his mother right, he also knew they didn't have the resources to make the trek up there. He voiced his concerns to Mitchell, who begrudgingly agreed. The boys started on their retreat, walking back across the rocks. David slipped three more times, and when they reached the shore, he had them stop so he could let the water out of his shoes.

The fog was everywhere now. What little the boys had been able to see was now surrounded in a thick gray mist. The fact that most of them were locals helped immensely when they tried to get their bearings. David finished draining his shoe and put it back on. "I hate wet socks." He grumbled. He stood up to continue walking, but Mitchell raised his hand to stop him. He squinted his eyes, hoping to see through the thick night fog.

"What is it?" Chris asked.

Mitchell had no intention of answering; he heard the rustling of leaves in the distance. He turned and whispered to Joel, "You hear anything?" Joel simply shook his head. Mitchell lowered his arm and moved slowly through the woods.

Joel hurried to catch up. "What're you thinking?"

"I'm figuring it was a rabbit or deer or something."

"Me too, but—"

Mitchell had put a hand on Joel's shoulder to stop him. "Stay here," he said. Then Mitchell walked into the fog. Joel watched until his friend's form vanished into the mist.

"Where did he go? Where'd Mitchell go?" David asked in a panic.

"It's all right; he'll be back in a second."

The three boys all stood in the middle of the misty woods waiting for their friend to return. After several minutes, Joel was about to open his mouth and suggest they follow Mitchell into the woods, when suddenly they heard a gunshot.

Terrified, the boys looked at each other, one by one. "Go GO GO!" Joel yelled.

The boys all took off like a flash through the thick air. As the boys got farther and farther out, they heard another loud roar, followed by a second gunshot.

Silence.

Nothing else. No rustling, no gunshots, no roaring, just complete and utter silence. The boys stopped to catch their breath.

"Come on, let's get going," Joel said after a moment.

David and Chris were concerned for Mitchell, but they were more concerned with getting themselves to safety. If there was a bear in the park, they had no interest in sticking around to meet it.

As the boys hurried on, the fog began to feel as if it were gripping at their bodies. They felt heaviness around their limbs and throats, as if the fog were intending to strangle them.

"Mitchell will be okay. Heck, Mitchell's probably already home," Chris mumbled.

"Absolutely," Joel said as he moved a branch from his vision. Then the ground from beneath him vanished.

The boys were on a cliff. Chris seized Joel's shoulder and pulled him back. They looked down and saw the dark waters of Cape's Side Bay. Directly across from them, about a hundred yards out, was the cave.

"How did we get here?" Joel had been in these woods hundreds of times, but he had never made it to this high point of the park.

"How did we go up? We never went up!" David cried out.

"We went straight," Joel said in an almost whisper.

David wiped his glasses clean and looked across at the cave. He could see an object, just slightly out of his range of vision, lying on the ground. "Guys, what is that?" Joel squinted as hard as he could to see the object. None of the boys could make it out.

After a few seconds, the mysterious thing rolled over and David got the sense it was staring right at him. "I think it looked at us."

"Don't be—"

Joel couldn't finish his sentence. The thing across the bay locked eyes with him. It looked oddly human and was covered in what looked like blood.

Joel gasped, staggering backward. "Oh my God . . ."

"Is that?" Chris tried to lean in closer but almost lost his footing.

"Holy shit, I think that's Mitchell!" David spoke out.

"Yeah," Joel agreed. "Me too."

Joel leaned forward and called out Mitchell's name. The bloody shape across from them didn't budge. Joel grimaced and cried out Mitchell's name once again.

This time, the object rolled over to the edge of the cave and looked up again. There was no mistaking it now: it was definitely Mitchell. He looked like he was trying to catch his breath as Joel screamed his name again.

With all of his energy, Mitchell let out an awful scream. "RUN!"

Blood was dripping from Mitchell's eyes. He cried and wept in terror. The boys stood frozen in fear before Joel pushed them back the way they came. They ran as fast as they could into the belly of the woods. Joel was at least two strides ahead of the others. Huffing and puffing, David brought up the rear.

"Faster, David, faster!" Chris pleaded.

David, near tears, was running out of energy. He had spent the entire afternoon walking uphill through the blistering heat with his family. He simply had no energy left in his legs. He could feel himself slowing down with every step . . .

"You're doing good; we're almost there." Chris looked back to check on his friend. But David was nowhere to be seen. Chris stopped running.

"David! David?" His mind was spinning. *What the hell is going on?*

Joel continued to run as fast as he could. Ahead of him, about two hundred yards away, was a bright light. He had never been so happy to see a streetlight. Joel ran and ran. A second wind kept his feet moving. As he got closer and closer to the light, an eerie feeling came over him, as if he wasn't alone. He looked to either side, but nothing was there. He ignored it and kept going. He was so close now. But as he got closer, the light seemed like it was getting *farther*. But how was that possible? Joel was starting to tire now. Each leap became a step, and then each step became a crawl. He was done. He slumped against a tree in the middle of the woods and looked around.

His friends were gone. All he could see was fog. No trees, no shore, no streetlights, no night sky. Simply fog.

Exhausted, Joel passed out.

FRIDAY MORNING

LABOR DAY WEEKEND was about to begin, and the sun had never looked so beautiful. Banners were raised throughout the town, reminding visitors of the grand fireworks display scheduled for Sunday evening. *Bigger and better than ever!* The tagline for the festival screamed from every banner, a giant, inescapable invitation for one and all.

Hillsbury was not very large; it housed a total of 3,500 permanent residents. The town was eleven miles from the park, which was the "hub of the town," as the locals described it.

The town was situated along the Great Wildebeest Trail, which extends a whopping 127 kilometers along cottage country. The final destination of the trail was Cape's Side Bay. The bay was located at the far end of Hillsbury Park. If the park was the great gathering spot for the town, the bay was the destination. Located at the far end of the park, through a kilometer of forest, the bay crept around the surrounding land. No sand, just grass until the water hit. At one point there was a makeshift dock, but when tourists complained and the police department discovered there was no permit or owner they could find, it was torn down. The far end of the bay was a rocky exterior, with the cave looming high above. Many teenagers and tourists alike attempted to scale the wall to reach the cave; none were successful. Locals knew better.

The farmers market, located in the library parking lot, was booming with business. O'Leary's was full of early birds looking for Thomas's famous cup of coffee (even though its owner had retired last season and left the shop in the care of his son-in-law, Edward Sleen). The final weekend of the summer was always bittersweet for the town. Though it was nice to see so many faces making the most of their time and enjoying it, the locals still knew they'd be saying goodbye to new and old friends for another year. Business was never quite the same during winter months. The majority of campers at Hillsbury Park were awake bright and early, cooking breakfast over their campfires and swimming in the lake. The campgrounds were directly opposite Cape's Side Bay, and so campers wouldn't hear most of the activity happening in the bay. Several people that morning did claim they'd heard something akin to a bear's roar and gunshots during the night. But since recycling bins all across the park were overflowing with empty beer cans, most campers chalked these stories up to delusions.

At six fifteen that morning, Henry Carter woke up.

The sun was already shining over a gorgeous blue sky, enhancing the emerald hue of the cottage country's acres of grass. Henry stared at his reflection as he brushed his teeth. He had planned on growing a mustache that summer, but his wife, Rachel, was not a big fan of how it itched when they kissed. He found a few new wrinkles over his brow he was sure hadn't been there at the beginning of summer. He recalled Father's Day weekend in June, when a teenage boy and his father took a fishing boat out in the lake with no permit. They'd brought beers with them, and after a short period of time, their boat tipped. Not only were the two charged with drinking and driving a motorized vehicle but also with fishing without a license and the consumption of alcohol by a minor. The teenager and his father decided to turn around and sue the county. The case was still ongoing, and Henry was certain it was the cause for more than a few of those wrinkles.

Another gray, he thought as he combed his hair. He was beginning to see more gray than the healthy brown he once knew.

Rachel flipped a couple pancakes over the stove. Behind her, their seven-year-old daughter, Sarah, sat at the table, sucking strawberry milk through a straw. Sarah had recently discovered the sheer joy of blowing bubbles in her milk, a habit neither Rachel nor Henry were fans of. Whenever Rachel flipped a pancake, Sarah would stealthily blow a bubble. When Rachel turned around, Sarah would always have a giant, innocent smile plastered across her face.

"If I see one bubble in that milk, you won't be getting any pancakes, you hear?" Rachel knew it was an empty threat. She just hoped Sarah *didn't.*

Labor Day weekend pancakes were a staple in the Carter household. The tradition began the Labor Day before the birth of their firstborn son, Jeffrey, sixteen years ago. Back then, it was Henry who made the pancakes for his pregnant wife, who often craved pancakes topped with peanut butter, banana, and sometimes (to Henry's revulsion) sardines. With Sarah, Rachel's cravings evolved into half-pound burgers with oregano. Henry fulfilled her odd requests, acknowledging that he was probably never going to understand how the appetites of pregnant women worked.

Knowing that Labor Day was Henry's busiest (and final) weekend of the year, and with no other pregnancies to concern herself over, Rachel volunteered to assume duty as pancake chef.

Henry entered the kitchen, buttoning the last two buttons on his shirt before Rachel rushed over to him and straightened his collar. She gave him a gentle kiss on the cheek as he made his way to the table.

"Jeffrey up?" he asked as Rachel brought him his morning coffee.

"Not yet."

Henry checked his watch. He had hired his own son to work in the park this summer, even though there were only three openings. This led to a great deal of townsfolk muttering behind his back about nepotism, even though Henry assured everyone (including the mayor) that he'd made his decisions based on the best-qualified applicants.

It *was* nepotism, of course. Henry wanted his son to work, and he wanted him to work in an honest field, one where Henry understood all the ins and outs and could keep an eye on his son whenever possible. Jeffrey, on the other hand, was not so thrilled to fill the position. He was his father's son in many ways, but an interest in parks and nature was not something they shared. Jeffrey spent his days dreaming of living in a city like New York or Chicago, somewhere far from Hillsbury Park and Cape's Side Bay.

If Jeffrey wasn't dreaming about a life in the limelight, he was dreaming of his crush, Claudia Burton. She was a year older than him. He knew her brother, Morgan, and would often eat dinner at their house. The truth was, Jeffrey didn't care much for Morgan; he wasn't into the same hobbies or the same movies. Morgan was more of a book nerd and into nature. Jeffrey saw to it that Morgan was hired alongside himself as a junior park ranger for the summer, hoping he could spend more time with Morgan and subsequently, Claudia. The plan ultimately backfired: Claudia went away to a summer camp with several of her friends. She'd been gone three and a half weeks. There'd been only one instance all summer when Claudia drove Morgan and Jeffrey home after work. Thoughts of Claudia spending the summer, alone in a cabin with another man would rush through Jeffrey's head from time to time. It would keep him up at night, breaking into cold sweats and shuddering. Some days his jealous rage would get so bad he would be short with Morgan and make sure his father assigned him trash duties for the day. As if Morgan had anything to do with what Claudia did at camp.

Henry sipped his coffee and watched Rachel serve him pancakes. He picked up a glass jar of syrup that he couldn't remember seeing before. "What's this?"

"Maple syrup, fresh from Judy Beene. Her and Marty went on a trip to Vermont last fall and gave us three jars for Christmas. Don't you remember?"

Henry shook his head; he did not remember and frankly did not care. He liked his fake, sugary syrup. Nevertheless, Henry spread it over his pancakes and took a bite.

"How is it?" Rachel curiously questioned her husband.

The look on Henry's face made it clear that this was not the finest syrup he had ever had. "You mean you haven't tried it yet?" he asked, grimacing.

Rachel shook her head. "I can't sit and enjoy them myself till I've made everyone else's.

Henry swallowed his mouthful of food, gazing into the glass jar of thick syrup. "I think it's gone bad . . ."

"I don't think so," said Rachel.

Before Henry could respond, Jeffrey entered the kitchen, fully dressed in his ranger attire.

"Well, look who decided to show," Henry teased.

Jeffrey rolled his eyes and sat at the table. Rachel gently placed a stack of pancakes in front of him. Henry slid the bottle of syrup over to Jeffrey, who glowered at it with a disgusted expression.

"What is this?" he asked his father.

"Syrup. Natural. You'll like it."

Jeffrey grabbed the bottle and let it slowly drip over his pancakes. He cut a piece and placed it in his mouth. He immediately opened and let the chewed pancake fall onto his plate.

"What the hell?"

"Jeffery, what are you doing? Don't act like a child in front of your sister!" Henry said, only half joking.

Jeffrey blinked quizzically at his father, who burst into laughter and turned to Rachel.

"Told ya it went bad!"

Rachel hefted the bottle, removed the lid, and took a sniff. "Ugh. I think you may be right."

Henry slammed his hand down on the table and laughed. Rachel hated to admit when Henry was right; he usually never let her live it down. This time, however, Henry had enough on his mind that this would not be the case. He slid a napkin across his mouth and stood up, giving Rachel a kiss on the cheek.

"Gonna be late." He turned to Jeffrey, pointing to his plate of pancakes soaked with expired syrup. "You can bring that with you if you want."

"Yeah, no thanks." Jeffrey left the table.

"Go get your shoes on. I'll meet you in the car."

Rachel watched as Jeffrey grabbed his shoes. "Be careful out there," she said to her son.

"Yeah, yeah," he mumbled back to her.

He had heard the same thing from her all summer. What danger could he possibly get into when his father assigned him simple duties like sweeping, mopping, and cleaning up loose leaves from trails? He grabbed his junior ranger hat and exited the house.

Rachel glanced at Sarah. "Just you and me, kiddo."

"Can I go play at Tammy's?" Sarah asked in a high, innocent voice.

Rachel's arms dropped. "Sure." She headed to the phone to call Tammy's parents. As soon as her back was turned, she heard the unmistakable sound of bubbles being blown through a straw.

The Jeep was a year older than Jeffrey. Henry bought it for himself as an early birthday present. Rachel wasn't too keen on it; she'd heard they tipped over easily during sharp turns, but Henry convinced her it was best for living in Hillsbury. "The perfect off-roading vehicle," he called it. Of course, he was lying. After the first three and a half months, it was barely even an *on*-road vehicle. Henry had purchased it not knowing it was a standard transmission, and he'd had no idea how to drive stick. Of course, after all these years, he'd gotten the hang of it. Now he couldn't imagine going back to an automatic transmission. Especially since their other family vehicle, a five-year-old minivan, didn't exactly paint the same rugged, outdoorsy image of head park ranger that his Jeep did. Henry gladly let Rachel have free reign over the minivan.

At Jeffrey's request, Henry had a satellite radio installed at the start of summer. Jeffrey loved riding shotgun and picking the station. Henry, on the other hand, had a love-hate relationship with that satellite radio. Even with hundreds upon hundreds of music stations at his disposal, he still couldn't find a song he was in the mood for.

As they drove toward the park, Henry noticed something on the side of the road. He pulled over and told Jeffrey to stay in the car. Jeffrey, of course, ignored these instructions at once. Henry walked about fifteen feet down the ditch toward the object that had caught his attention. He knelt down in front of it, using a branch to lift it from the grass.

It was the front breast of a plaid shirt. The pocket was still intact, but the rest was missing. As he spun it around to examine it further, he could see a small drop of blood, long since dried, and a white foamy liquid that must have hardened over time.

This was . . . interesting, but not unheard of. In the heat of summer, in an isolated area like this, it was common for teenagers to have a few drinks and then move on to other, more enjoyable nighttime pursuits. When this happened, clothing was removed in a hurry, and sometimes things were ripped and left behind. Still, the single drop of blood gave Henry cause for concern. Something about it felt wrong.

Henry opened the Jeep door, tossed the object in a Ziploc bag, and placed it in the trunk. He got back into the front with Jeffrey and drove off without saying a word. As he continued to drive, Henry looked over at his son, who was actively swiping away at something on his cell phone.

"I heard Claudia Burton's back in town," Henry said, trying to keep the mood light while still mulling over his grim find. He watched as Jeffrey's eyes widened for just a moment before they returned to scanning the screen, feigning nonchalance.

"Oh, ya?" Jeffrey shrugged it off as if it were nothing.

"Yeah, she got in last night." Jeffrey had no follow-up. He just continued swiping away at his phone. "What is that? What're you swiping there?" Henry asked.

Annoyed, Jeffrey responded, "An app."

Thanks for clearing that up! Henry thought. "An app for what?" Jeffrey turned his phone off and put it into his pocket without saying another word. "Okay." Henry sighed, and he continued to drive in silence.

"When did she get back? Claudia?" Jeffrey suddenly asked in a very soft voice, as if he hadn't heard the answer the first time.

"Last night or the day before. Can't remember. I was speaking to Mr. Burton over at O'Leary's, and he told me he was going to pick her up. Wouldn't be surprised if she came around the park later today." Henry watched Jeffrey from his peripheral vision and saw a slight smile form on his son's face. He was at that age when girls would begin to rule his life and inform his every decision. The thought of this managed to make Henry simultaneously proud, excited, and terrified.

As they pulled up to the staff parking lot (which after yesterday's rainfall was essentially a pool of mud), Henry noticed a shiny new Lincoln Town Car parked at an angle, taking up two spots.

"Well, who's *this* dick?" he wondered aloud before spotting the license plate: *Mayor1*.

Henry stopped his car and parked. "Jesus, what does he want?"

"Maybe the weekend's been cancelled?" Jeffrey joked.

"With our luck, he'll extend the fireworks to all three days."

Jeffrey smacked his head against the window.

Ava Trillium was the assistant park ranger. She just turned thirty and had initially studied to be a lawyer, but her love for nature and wildlife took center stage, and eventually she changed her major. In truth, she'd initially opted for marine biology, but when no clear career opportunities arose, she once again changed her life goal, and here she was: assistant park ranger. At the time, she had no idea that one of her many, many duties in the role would involve calming an absolutely terrified mother.

When Henry entered the rangers' office, he saw Ava trying to console Patty Liman, Joel's mother, while the mayor sat rather impatiently in the waiting room. Henry took Ava by the arm and pulled her into his office.

"You mind telling me what the mayor's doing sitting in the waiting room while you chat with Patty Liman?"

"Mayor wants to talk fireworks," she responded.

"Okay. And Patty?"

Ava lowered both her head and her voice. "Her boy's missing."

The words seemed to hit Henry like a punch to the gut. "Missing?"

Ava nodded. "He and some friends went out into the woods last night. All the other boys came back, except Joel."

Henry sank into his chair. "Get Patty whatever she needs. Bring me the mayor. I'll try and get him out of here as soon as possible." Ava nodded and left. Henry straightened a few items on his desk before booting up his computer. It gave a little chime as it powered on, coinciding with the mayor's entrance. Henry glanced up. "Mayor Tremblay, please come in. Come in. Have a seat." The mayor removed his hat and sat across from Henry. "What's up?" Henry asked.

Mayor Tremblay removed a cigar from his breast pocket. "You have a lighter?"

Henry smiled and shook his head. "No. Also, no smoking indoors. Sorry, sir."

The mayor begrudgingly placed the cigar back into his pocket. "You know I'm up for reelection in the fall. I don't have to tell you that." Henry nodded. "Good, good. Tourism, Henry . . . tourism was down thirty-six percent this summer. Two family-owned shops had to close their doors for good, and I don't have to remind you about the fishing fiasco we had in June."

Henry shuddered at the thought. Still, right now, all he cared about was getting the mayor out of there so he could talk to Patty Liman about her boy. "What is it you want, sir?"

"We need the fireworks display to eclipse all others. But, we need more."

"More?"

"Yes!" The mayor nodded with a childlike grin on his face. "More spectacle! More puzzah!"

Henry combed his fingers through his hair. "Uh . . .what 'puzzah' are you looking for, exactly? We have the beachfront, we have the fireworks, and we have popcorn, ice cream, hot dogs . . . same as every year. What else do you want?"

"Well, that's just it, Henry," the mayor began. "It's the same thing every year, isn't it? People are looking for change. People are looking for something spectacular!"

Henry had no idea what to say. Thankfully, the mayor said it for him. "A carnival! A full carnival, with petting zoos and coasters and what have you. Some of that three-dimensional crap the kids are so into. Everything! That, Henry, is puzzah!"

Henry leaned back in his chair. For the first time in his career, he wished he had taken a sick day. "Mayor Tremblay, you're looking at a stack of permits, not to mention a location. Where do you plan on having all of this?"

"Cape's Side Bay, naturally."

"Cape's Side Bay is a swamp. It's unwanted land. You'd need a team of hundreds to clean it up and have it ready for Sunday."

"Sunday? I'm moving the fireworks to Monday." The mayor rolled the cigar in his hands.

"Monday?" Henry couldn't believe what he was hearing. "But most of the tourists are on the road by then. You'll have a dozen people at max out there!"

The mayor took to the offensive. "We promise to deliver the biggest party of the year on the official last day of summer, then people will stick around."

"And what about school?" Henry questioned.

"School? Hogwash, Henry, nobody learns anything on the first day back. This has to be big! Hillsbury has to appear on the map!" the mayor said, clearly unwilling to hear any more arguments. "I'll see to those permits. You see to getting the bay cleaned up." Before Henry could respond, the mayor exited the office, chest puffed with determination.

Henry rubbed his forehead. This was just what he needed. Three days left of summer, and he had to contend with a delusional mayor on one hand and a missing boy on the other.

There was a soft knock at the door. Ava poked her head in. "Ready for Mrs. Liman?" she asked.

He wasn't. He was far from ready. But he nodded anyway. "Ava," he said, "what do you think of the mayor?"

After considering this for a moment, Ava just smiled. "*I* didn't vote for him," she said. Then she ushered in Patty Liman. Henry jumped to his feet and pulled out a chair for her, ready to listen to whatever this woman had to say concerning the whereabouts of her only child.

Patty Liman, the town librarian, was told for years she would be unable to have a child. Her husband, Bill, a headhunter whose job required him to travel often and allowed them to live in a place as secluded as Hillsbury, tried for over ten years to have a child with her. While in her early twenties, Patty was diagnosed with ovarian cancer. For a short time, it didn't look like recovery was an option, but she persevered, overcame the chemotherapy, and eventually beat the disease. But the lasting effects of the treatment had left her virtually infertile, a fact the doctors had initially failed to mention. So throughout her late twenties and early thirties, Patty and Bill tried to start a family to no avail.

Bill died fourteen years ago in an apparent plane crash. The plane was never found. His job required him to travel often. A

good friend of his, Carl Reeves , worked in the travel indus-
try. Bill and Carl met at St. John's Secondary School—a small
Catholic school just outside of Hillsbury—and they had been
friends ever since. Carl was fascinated with aviation, which
resulted in him getting his piloting license. He flew both small
planes and helicopters, and he was known and trusted in the
community for it. He was given the key to the city at the age
of thirty-one for rescuing a group of amateur hikers who had
been making their way up the small mountain (many referred
to it as a hill) by Cape's Side Bay when one of them lost their
footing, breaking their leg in three places.

One fateful day in May, fourteen years ago, both Carl and
Bill were headed to the same town for business. Carl offered
to give Bill a ride in his plane. Naturally, Bill accepted. The
night before the trip, Patty took Bill out for a romantic picnic
at Cape's Side Bay. She packed wine, travel cups, fresh bread
from Thomas O'Leary's bakery, and cold cuts. They sat on the
blanket and looked up at the clouds and held each other in
their arms.

Day slowly turned to night. A mist began to cover Cape's
Side Bay. Despite the fact that the subject hadn't been breached
in quite a while, Bill found himself having the sudden urge to
try—just one more time—to have a child.

Patty rolled her eyes when he brought this up. "I'm too old
now. It's too late," she said.

But Bill insisted. "For old times' sake. Out here by the
bay, like when we were kids." He gave her a smile, which she
couldn't help returning. They locked into a passionate kiss.
Before long, Bill and Patty were madly undressing, and the two
made love by the misty bay.

As they were packing up for the night, they heard something coming from the cave just above Cape's Side Bay (not too
far from where Carl saved the injured hikers). Patty thought it

sounded kind of like growling. As the sun continued to sink, neither Patty nor Bill figured it was a good idea to investigate the sounds in darkness. But Bill suggested Patty make Henry aware of it in the morning. Night fell on the bay, and the couple headed home.

The following morning, Bill boarded Carl's plane and the two of them left Hillsbury for the last time, never to return.

Patty had brought Henry a coffee that morning and informed him of the sound she'd heard in the cave the night before. At the time, Henry did not entirely believe Patty but assured her he would look into it. As their meeting drew to an end, the phone call came through informing them that the plane had not yet made its destination. It had disappeared from radar and not a single person at any airport within a hundred-mile radius could get any kind of signal from it. It was simply gone.

Patty dropped to her knees. Henry rushed to console her, assuring her everything would be all right. But it wouldn't be. After a long investigation, the plane (along with Bill and Carl) was theorized to have fallen somewhere in the Atlantic Ocean. Investigators deduced that the plane had exceeded its weight capacity.

One month later, Patty woke up in the middle of the night with a feeling of nausea. The illness, which she shrugged off as a cold due to the changing season, continued for over a month. She noticed a slight weight gain as well, something uncommon when suffering from an illness. The doctor gave her antibiotics and sent her on her way. It wasn't until she paid a visit to her cousin, Esther, who was in her third trimester of pregnancy, that Patty began to understand. Esther had been describing (sometimes in uncomfortable detail) what being pregnant felt like: the constant urinating, weariness, fluctuating constipation, and—of course—the heartburn and nausea. Patty could feel every one of these symptoms. But how could such a thing be possible? She was unable to become pregnant! At least that's what she'd been told by doctors . . . the same doctors currently prescribing her antibiotics for a sickness she may or may not even have . . .

That very evening, Patty purchased a home pregnancy test. She *could* have gone back to the clinic and asked her doctor to specifically check for a pregnancy, but a part of her was worried that the answer was still going to be "no." How embarrassed would she feel, walking into that clinic with her head (and hopes) held high, expecting positive results, only to be told that she was still as barren as ever and just needed to be pre-scribed something for acid reflux? The looks of pity she would get, especially since everybody at the clinic knew about Bill's accident. If that happened, she didn't think she could ever face those same doctors again.

Patty decided it was best to visit a drug store outside of Hillsbury. The last thing she wanted was to be seen by some-body and kick off a strain of gossip. She ended up traveling fifty miles out. On her way back, she stopped in a dingy gas station bathroom and put the test to use.

Seven months later, Joel was born. And what a blessing he was. Patty had lost the love of her life, only to be granted a child. She named him after Bill's father, something the couple had agreed upon back when they'd first tried to start a fam-ily. For Joel's first birthday, Patty took him for a walk in his stroller to Cape's Side Bay, the place she believed he had been conceived. They sat in the grass overlooking the bay, watching the fisherman reel in their prizes. As she drank in the sights, smiling, her eyes caught the cave. The sound she'd heard a year earlier rang as vividly in her memory as ever.

When it started to get late, Patty strapped Joel back into the stroller and wheeled him away down the dirt path. She looked back one more time at the cave, inexplicably drawn to it.

The next day, Patty made a visit to Henry at the ranger office to follow up on the bear. Henry shook his head and told her that there was no bear, that all searches for bears in the area had turned up nothing. He assured her that he himself had checked the cave less than a year ago and found nothing but rocks and beer bottles. It was simply a place for teenagers to go and drink when they couldn't do it in front of their parents. Though she wasn't entirely sure why, Patty was disappointed by the news. Every year on this anniversary, Patty would visit Henry and ask about the bear. The final time was seven years ago. Henry insisted there were still no bears around Cape's Side Bay.

As Patty was leaving the office, Henry's phone rang: a call bearing the bad news that Henry's sister had gone missing.

◜◜◜

That was the last time Henry and Patty had spoken, until now.

Henry helped Patty into her seat before reclaiming his own. He leaned forward, interlocking his fingers atop the desk, and spoke.

"Your boy . . ."

Patty nodded, fighting off tears. As Henry was about to inquire further, she viciously spat, "It was the bear!"

Only five people had ever reported hearing a bear in Hillsbury. Patty was one. Two were boys just having a laugh and wanting to scare everybody. Bill Liman was the fourth (though he was mostly prompted by Patty), and the fifth was Henry's sister, Jill, who mentioned hearing a growl in the bay area three weeks before her fateful fishing trip.

"Patty, you know—"

"I know what I know, Henry! There's a bear in the park. It lives in that cave."

Henry leaned back in his chair. "I've told you, Patty, we checked the cave—*I've* checked the cave. There are no bears in Hillsbury Park, or Cape's Side Bay, or anywhere else around here."

"You're wrong; you haven't checked," she responded.

"We've sent drones; there's nothing there."

"Drones!" Patty brushed Henry off.

"Patty, listen . . . I'm gonna do everything I can to find Joel, all right? But I need you to cooperate. Okay?" Patty nodded, albeit reluctantly. Henry grabbed a pad of paper and a pen, sliding them across the desk to her. "Write down what he was wearing, who he was with, if anyone—"

She cut him off again. "He was with three other boys. I saw him. He thought he was sneaking out through the window, but I saw him. I should have stopped him, but . . ." She broke down, unable to say any more. Henry grabbed a tissue and walked it over to her. He sat on the chair next to Patty, rubbing her shoulder.

"Write down everything you can remember," he said gently. "We'll find your boy. I promise."

Fresh dew still coated the grass as Ava took her morning hike through the campgrounds. There were a total of fifty-seven campsites in Hillsbury Park, and all were occupied save for two. Every morning and every night, Ava did a walk-around. She made sure everyone was settled in and not disrupting the other campers. She made sure no one was having negative encounters with wildlife (there may not have been any bears in Hillsbury, but there were more than enough skunks and bees to cause trouble every now and then). She watched as kids played catch and Frisbee. She watched adults still trying to put out campfires from the night before, and others still trying to figure out how to light one to begin with.

The campgrounds were a jovial place, a place where people could get away from all their problems for a while. With campers becoming more and more numerous, many had wondered if the county would extend the campgrounds to accommodate more tourists. The issue for most people was that any sort of expansion would take up more of the park, which many folks believed should have been considered a nature preserve. There was talk, well before Ava's time, of turning a portion of Cape's Side Bay into a campground instead. Talks fell through after the water began to dry up.

"Excuse me, miss?"

A woman appeared at Ava's right, interrupting her train of thought. She had two small children at her side, both wearing the kind of apprehensive frown usually reserved for kids certain they were about to be in trouble. "My son found this earlier this morning, just outside our campsite."

Ava glanced down at what the woman was holding. Then she grabbed her walkie-talkie and called for Henry at once.

Within minutes, Henry pulled up in his Jeep to the campsite where Ava was waiting. She jogged over to the driver's side window. "What is it?" Henry asked.

Ava removed the object from her pocket. Henry looked down at it in a sort of wondrous shock. He held it up to his eyes to make absolute sure he was seeing what he was seeing.

A claw.

Five and a half inches of horrific claw from no animal he could identify.

"Where did you get this?"

"Some kid found it when he was playing in the woods this morning."

Henry couldn't take his eyes off the thing. It was ivory, curved and sharp at the end, but just next to the tip were sharp-looking quills.

"You ever see anything like this before?" Ava asked, frowning.

"I don't think so," Henry replied. He actually had to force himself to pry his gaze away from it. "Keep up with your rounds. I'll bring it in." Ava was about to turn away when he added, "And, Ava . . . let me know if anything else pops up."

"Of course."

"Some morning, huh?" Henry said after a moment.

Ava smiled. "Some morning, boss." She continued back on her rounds.

Henry remained parked for a while, peering down at the hideous claw. Even after he wrapped it up in a handkerchief, he sat and glared through the rearview mirror, which currently pointed in the direction of Cape's Side Bay.

Back at headquarters, Jeffrey and Morgan sat outside in the mud. Morgan removed a pack of cigarettes from his khakis. "Where'd you get that?" Jeffrey asked, unimpressed with his pseudo-friend.

"Claudia," Morgan answered, and suddenly Jeffrey was more interested in the cigarettes. "Want one?"

"No, my dad will be back any minute."

Morgan shrugged and lit a cigarette; he took a puff and immediately coughed. "You're a dweeb," Jeffrey mocked.

"Whatever, man." Jeffrey continued to smoke. "So, what do you think's going on? Y'know, with Mrs. Liman and all that?"

Jeffrey looked over his shoulder through the window of the office, where Patty was rocking back and forth restlessly in a chair. "I dunno," Jeffrey said. He grabbed Morgan's cigarette and took a drag.

They heard Henry's Jeep rumbling down the road. "Shit!" they said at once. Morgan stumbled about, flicking the cigarette away. Jeffrey ran up to it and hid it in the mud just as the Jeep pulled in. Henry jumped out and walked toward the front door before turning back to Jeffrey.

"I need you two boys to go out to the park. See if you can find the Liman boy. But don't go too far. Stay safe."

Jeffrey stepped closer to his father. "Everything good?" he asked.

Henry nodded. He was unsure but didn't want to let the boys on to anything just yet. "Yeah, think so." Jeffrey turned away, but suddenly Henry grabbed him and spun him around. "Bring a walkie. Keep me in the loop." Then he took a quick sniff and asked, "Why do you smell like an ashtray?"

Jeffrey just shrugged. "I'll keep you in the loop," he promised, eager to steer the conversation out of those dangerous waters. He rejoined Morgan and the two boys walked off.

Henry entered the rangers' headquarters, rushing past a still-panicked Patty. He went straight to his office, shutting the door behind him, and wasted no time picking up the phone. After a few short rings (during which Henry retrieved the claw and stared worriedly at it), someone on the other end answered.

"Bentley? It's Henry. I'm gonna need you to come to the park. We've got a problem."

Bentley Trundle was the deputy sheriff of Hillsbury. Henry preferred discussing matters with Bentley as opposed to Walden, the head sheriff. Walden was one of those people who always seemed to be inches away from retirement. He never really took matters too seriously either; with very little crime to worry about, he figured it was a safe bet that most calls to the sheriff's office were either accidents or pranks. For the most part, he'd be right. But not always. Henry was positive that this would be one of those rare times.

Bentley Trundle was two months shy of celebrating his fortieth birthday. His wife, Elise, was in the early stages of planning a grand surprise party for him. She had been arranging with Henry to hold it at the park rangers' headquarters. Most of the town would be invited, as most of the town liked Officer Trundle. Many folks whispered that Walden would use the party as an opportunity to step down as sheriff and appoint Bentley his successor. What a birthday present that would be!

Bentley had no children. He often said that he simply considered the people of Hillsbury, both the locals and the tourists, to be his family. At least, that's what Bentley's public side would say. In truth, he had *always* wanted a child. It was just something that never happened; neither he nor Elise could ever find the right time, and with biological clocks ticking away, "the right time" seemed more and more elusive every day. Bentley had made his peace, and he focused his energies on just being the best deputy sheriff the town could have.

Patty, trembling with worry, watched as Bentley pulled up in his squad car. As far as she was concerned, they needed a wildlife expert, not the police. Upon entering the ranger office, Bentley gave her a polite nod. An avid reader, he'd spent many winter days huddled up inside her library. He crossed the lobby to Henry's office and clicked the door shut behind him.

"What's Patty Liman doing here, Henry?"

Over the phone, Henry had given Bentley very little information, which was quite unlike the head ranger. "Something's going on, Bent," Henry started. "This morning on my way here, I found something troubling. And now my assistant ranger, Ava, found something else."

A barely perceptible twitch shook Bentley's body at the mention of Ava's name. Over three years ago, the two had been in a love affair that would have set the town afire if ever brought to light. Bentley figured it was the frustration of being number two to Walden all these years, working tirelessly to protect the town and the people in it. Elise never understood those frustrations. How could she? She didn't live his life. He needed someone to talk to, and Ava was there. She listened. She cared. Somehow, it all came crashing down around them, and before either of them knew it, they were sleeping together. After a year, an increasingly worried Bentley said that they should stop seeing one another. Ava agreed. A year was a long time for any kind of secret to be kept in Hillsbury; the longer they went on, the more they risked getting caught. Bentley didn't want to lose what he had with Elise, and Ava had no interest in being labeled a home wrecker. So the two had said their goodbyes and hadn't been in each other's company since.

Henry pulled out the plaid shirt he had found on the side of the road. He set the claw down next to it. Bentley examined them both.

"A tusk?" he asked.

"Claw, actually."

"A claw? Jesus, Henry, that thing's huge."

"Here's what I've got so far: a torn piece of shirt, with what appears to be blood and some sort of foam, I'm guessing electrical. A claw that looks like the fang of a saber-toothed tiger . . . and a missing boy, Joel Liman."

Bentley sank, dismayed, into his chair. "That's why Patty's here?"

Henry nodded. "Great way to end the summer."

Bentley gathered his thoughts. "Who else knows about this?" he asked, pointing to the shirt.

"You and me."

"Okay, good, good. So let's write that one off, from the public at least. No need to start a panic over a shirt that could have come from anywhere, right?" Henry nodded in agreement. "And the claw thingy?"

"You, me, Ava, my son, and I'm guessing a whole bunch of campers out there."

"How many?"

"Well over a hundred. We're booked, minus the two wheelchair-accessible sites. And I don't suspect those will stay empty much longer."

Bentley's eyes darted to the calendar hanging on the wall behind the desk, where a red Sharpie had been used to indicate the looming presence of Cape's Side Bay's busiest time of year. Henry was right: on Labor Day weekend, there was no such thing as an empty campground. "We need to find a way to nip it in the bud."

"Well, that's easy," Henry said. "I figure we just tell them it's not from around here, that someone brought it with them."

Bentley nodded. "Good, good."

"But we've still got a missing boy out there."

"I need a smoke," Bentley said after a moment. He stood up, beckoning for Henry to join him. They stepped outside into the muddy parking area. A gentle rain had begun to spray the park. Bentley glanced around as he lit his cigarette. "At least the weather's cooperating," he quipped sarcastically.

"Just a morning drizzle, won't last. Usually means we're in for a good day."

"You sure 'bout that?" Bentley puffed his cigarette. "We're gonna need to put out an Amber Alert."

"You don't think that'll start a panic?" Henry asked.

Bentley knew it would, but he also knew it would be their best bet at finding the Liman kid. "I'm gonna give Walden a call. Patty tell you anything else?"

"He wasn't alone last night. He was with some friends."

"Who?"

Henry shrugged, "I asked her to write it all down."

Bentley flicked away his half-spent cigarette. "Good. Get those names from her and find out what the kid was wearing. Meet me at the Wolf Trail in fifteen." Henry nodded and stepped back inside. Bentley activated the radio in his cruiser and spoke into the mouthpiece, calling for an Amber Alert and asking all the troopers to keep their eyes out for Joel Liman.

Patty Liman's hands shook as she sipped her tea. Henry approached, squatting in front of her. "Mrs. Liman, I'm gonna need the names of the boys Joel was with last night."

She pointed to Ava's desk, where the notepad sat. "Great." Henry walked over to the pad and read the names. "I'm also gonna need to know what Joel was wearing last night, if you could recall?"

For a brief moment, Patty couldn't remember. Then the memory of seeing her son sneaking through a window flooded her head. "I should have stopped him . . . it's all my fault." She broke down into tears once again.

"It's not your fault, Patty. There's no way you could have known. Now, please . . . tell me what Joel was wearing."

Patty looked up at Henry with half-vacant eyes. "Plaid," she whispered. "He was wearing plaid."

Henry's eyes filled with horror.

Hillsbury Park was made up of six trails and a campsite (as well as a fishing spot before the bay dried up). The trails were all named after animals that could be found in and around Hillsbury Park: wolf, turtle, snake, rabbit, ferret, and eagle. The Wolf Trail was the only trail you could get to by way of the rangers' headquarters, which was why Bentley decided to start there. While he waited for Henry to meet him, he opened a PowerBar and took a big bite. He hated the flavor and texture, but in his line of work, he rarely had the chance to sit down and enjoy a warm breakfast while on duty. He munched the chalky, flavorless bar with reluctant acceptance.

Henry came into view, walking over slowly. "What do you have for me?" Bentley asked, taking the paper with the names of the other boys. "Find out what he was wearing?" The expression on Henry's face was blank, the color gone; he looked as though he had just seen a ghost. "You all right?"

Henry spoke up. "Plaid. Blue-and-red plaid."

"No shit." Bentley was stunned. For a minute, neither of them said anything. Their thoughts strayed back to the blood-splattered plaid cloth.

"Well . . . let's get crackin'." Bentley tried to remain optimistic. "I called in for the alert, so all eyes and ears should be out on the kid. Why not get Ava to let the campers know about Joel?"

"What if they ask about the claw?" Henry worried.

"I thought we had an alibi for that? Someone, a hunter, had it with them and dropped it. Right?"

Henry nodded and called Ava on his walkie-talkie, informing her of what was going on. When she responded, Bentley turned away, trying hard to focus on the sound of birdsong rather than Ava's voice.

"Have you had a chance to look over where Joel was last seen?" Bentley asked as he stopped over a fallen tree trunk.

Henry shook his head. "I haven't had a chance to breathe so far. I was in there with Patty, filling out some paperwork when Ava called me about the claw. That's when I called you, and here we are."

Here we are, indeed, Bentley thought. *What a clusterfuck.* Typically, calls for this weekend were in regard to burns due to fireworks or the occasional cars bumping into one another in a parking lot. Missing children were not something Bentley Trundle or anyone in the Hillsbury Police Department was used to dealing with. In fact, until a few minutes ago, Bentley was hard-pressed to remember the last time he'd ever spoken the words *Amber Alert* out loud. "A missing boy. Christ. This has the potential to be the worst summer since—" Bentley stopped himself.

Henry finished the thought for him "Jill. Since Jill."

Bentley stopped walking and put his arm on Henry's shoulder. "I didn't mean to . . ."

Henry shook his head. "It's okay, Bent. If anything, you're right."

They continued their walk. As they got deeper into the Wolf Trail, an officer from the Hillsbury Police Department contacted Bentley through his walkie-talkie. "*Deputy Trundle, do you copy?*"

Bentley seized the walkie and looked at Henry curiously. "Go for Trundle."

"*We got some follow-up on those local boys.*" Henry stepped closer to Bentley to hear the conversation better.

"Okay, whatta ya got?"

There was a moment of pause on the other end. "*We're going to need you to come in.*"

"Copy," Bentley replied as he switched directions and headed for the mouth of Wolf Trail. "Sorry, Henry, sounds like I gotta deal with this first."

But Henry was already a few steps behind him. "I know. I'm coming with you."

Ava continued her patrol through the campgrounds. She noticed the campers shooting her a glare every once in a while. There was a feeling in the air that something was amiss. Somehow, word of the mysterious claw had already spread, and most campers weren't buying the rangers' explanation of its appearance.

Ava passed a campsite rented by a family that was huddled around their morning fire, listening to the AM radio. The Amber Alert broke through; they immediately looked over at Ava. She offered the family nothing but a confident look and continued walking, albeit at a bit more of a hurried pace. That was when Bruce Archer appeared, bumping into Ava and startling her.

"Ava! Hey!" He wore a wolfish grin and made no effort to hide the fact that he was checking her out from top to bottom.

"Yes? What?" she asked irritably, pushing him away from her.

Bruce stuck a cigarillo between his teeth and lit it. The smoke floated almost mockingly into Ava's face. She swatted it away. "I hear you got a missing boy."

"Yes. And we're hoping all campers and guests in the park will keep an eye out and help us look for him. Is that all?"

She'd already taken a few steps away when Bruce called out, "This have something to do with that claw the Wilson kid found?"

This comment caught Ava's attention. She turned back to Bruce. "Absolutely not," was her stern response. The last thing she wanted was this idiot spreading rumors about dangerous animals dragging off teenagers in the dead of night. That would do *wonders* for the mayor's Labor Day weekend turnout.

Bruce remained eerily calm, taking the cigarillo from his mouth. "I've seen *the bear.*"

"You've been drinking." She could smell the stench of alcohol on his breath. "You've probably seen a lot of things, Bruce."

"Drinking don't matter. I know what I saw. You got a bear problem."

"There's no bear, and there's no bear problem."

Bruce took another puff of the cigarillo. Then he nodded at Ava and let her on her way. Once she was gone, Bruce approached his buddies and pulled them into a huddled conversation.

As Ava continued through the campsites a brisk breeze surrounded her. It was refreshing to feel it on her back after such a warm summer. She took a moment to enjoy it. Soon enough, summer would transform into a gray autumn. The leaves, while looking gorgeous, would lose their luster, and eventually Hillsbury would be covered with snow. Over the years, Mayor Tremblay had tried to make the area more inviting for winter tourists, but he simply couldn't get enough travelers to bite. Travelers in winter generally wanted one of two things: warmth or a ski resort. Hillsbury had neither. The park itself shut down to the public on the twenty-ninth of October, and the next seven months were spent filling out annoying amounts of paperwork, trimming trees, and keeping up with maintenance. Not Ava's favorite time of the year, to be sure, but necessary.

She was on her way to the south-side restrooms when she noticed a pile of garbage sitting right next to a garbage can. *Raccoons*, she thought. She made her way to the pile, slid on her gloves, and began to clean up the mess.

The final piece of trash left on the ground was a pornographic magazine. She shook her head, smirking, and tossed it into the trash. Then she noticed something odd about the ground where the magazine had lain: footprints. Footprints unlike anything she had seen before.

The print had three toes, like a bird, one on the left and the right, and one in the middle. The outer toes each had a claw that extended forward, but the middle toe was vacant of a claw. She quickly took a picture of the print and dusted the dirt over it, removing the evidence. Ava followed the tracks into the bushes, removing each one as she went along. She moved branches and pushed stones out of her way, stepped over logs, until finally the tracks stopped.

Ava glanced around, surrounded by wilderness. The sun was beaming down on her, the cool breeze all but gone. Sweat started to trickle down her brow and arms. She gave the area one final look. Nothing but trees and a few playful squirrels. Two squirrels in particular caught Ava's attention. They were chasing each other (as squirrels do) but not in any sort of playful way. One was eating something and the other was trying to get it from him.

Having loved squirrels since she was little, Ava smiled and followed them with her camera out, taking pictures as they ran. The critters stopped in the branches of an oak and ran straight up it. Ava zoomed in her camera for the perfect shot . . . and snapped the photo.

The flash momentarily blinded the squirrels, forcing the one in front to drop its food. Feeling guilty for making the squirrel drop its lunch, Ava hastened over to pick it up.

But when she drew close enough to see what it was, it dawned on Ava that what the squirrels had been eating—what they'd been fighting over—was not food at all.

FRIDAY AFTERNOON

THE SUN WAS now directly overhead. Jeffrey and Morgan had been searching for Joel Liman for at least two hours, and both of them were feeling fatigued. Morgan collapsed underneath the nearest tree with a loud exhale.

"You have any water?" he asked. Jeffrey removed his canteen and tossed it over to Morgan. "I don't think we're gonna find anything, Jeffrey," Morgan said after a few gulps.

Jeffrey refused to believe this. He wanted Joel Liman to be okay. He *had* to be okay. "Don't say that."

"But it's true! The kid's been missing since last night, and we've searched the park. Ava's been all over the campsites, and your father—he's been everywhere else. The kid's gone." Jeffrey said nothing, snatching back his canteen, and proceeded to walk away. "Where you going?" Morgan called after him. Receiving no answer, he hurried to follow.

The boys made their way to the tip of Cape's Side Bay. They looked down at the swamp, neither of them able to remember a time when it had been a clean, sparkling bay bursting with tourist activity.

"I can't believe people used to fish here." Morgan sniffed as he scanned the bog. Jeffrey looked around the bay and up at the cave high above, lost in thought. Before he could speak, Morgan cut him off.

"No, no. HELL NO, Jeffrey. We are not going in that cave!"

Getting in the cave would be a long shot without proper rock climbing equipment, but what if they could just get close? Jeffrey knew Patty Liman well, and he knew that regardless of what she might say in public, Patty still believed there was a bear in Cape's Side Bay. She also believed this alleged bear lived in that hilltop cave. Which made no logical sense: How would a bear get in and out of a cave so high up on the side of a mountain? Unless, of course, the bear had massive claws . . .

An eerie feeling struck Jeffrey. He ran toward the cave side of the bay.

"Jeffrey, wait up!" Morgan stumbled after him, weaving among the stones that dotted the trail. He kept his eyes fixed on the back of Jeffrey's head, preventing him from seeing the vine hanging low in his path. It wrapped itself around his foot, practically yanking him off his feet. His knees skidded against the dirt and rocks as he jarringly met the ground. He rolled over, clutching his bloody kneecap.

Jeffrey could hear him squealing in pain and ran back for him. "Lemme see." Jeffrey observed the knee. It was just an abrasion, skin scraping across a rough surface and leaving a thin layer of blood, but nothing serious.

"You okay?"

Morgan was in a lot of pain, but to be fair, he'd never been much of an outdoorsman. Sure, he loved nature and animals. The thought of being a park ranger had intrigued him, but after one week on the job, that fantasy had extinguished. He was also entirely aware that Jeffrey had only gotten him the job because he was in love with Morgan's sister. Frankly, this never really bothered him. Who was he to stand in the way of that? He'd even told himself, on many occasions, had Jeffrey been the one with the cute sister, Morgan probably would have done the exact same thing.

Jeffrey wrapped Morgan's arms around his neck and heaved him to his feet. "Don't put too much pressure on your left leg, got it?" Morgan just nodded. They turned and walked back the way they had come. Jeffrey looked up, taking note of the sun's movement across the blue sky. He realized it was way past lunch, and they hadn't eaten anything since early morning.

"You want a piece of my granola bar?" Jeffrey asked his injured friend. Morgan nodded again. Jeffrey settled Morgan down on a log and went through his pack. He found two granola bars buried at the very bottom.

"My mom always makes me bring these, just in case. Brought two granola bars with me all summer; this is the first time I've eaten one." He handed one to Morgan, who immediately tore into it, chewing as though he had never tasted food before. He offered Morgan the canteen again to wash down the taste of oats and raisins.

As Morgan continued to gorge himself, Jeffrey sat and looked around at his surroundings. He took living in Hillsbury (and working in the park) for granted. He never truly realized the beauty of his surroundings before.

"I know you like Claudia."

Morgan's voice pulled Jeffrey out of his moment. "What?" Jeffrey said weakly, trying to recover and simultaneously keep his expression and voice casual. He wasn't sure he succeeded on either front.

"My sister. I know you like her," Morgan repeated. Jeffrey said nothing. His mind raced. "And I just want you to know, I'm okay with it." Morgan smiled. "I'll even put in a good word for you if you'd like!"

Once the shock wore off, Jeffrey somehow managed to chuckle, hoping he sounded at least a little bit unfazed. "It's all right. I'm sure she'd rather be with guys her own age."

Morgan finished his granola bar and placed the empty wrapper into his pocket. "I wouldn't be so sure about that. She usually gets annoyed when my other friends come over, but not you."

Jeffrey couldn't help but grin. He got back to his feet. "C'mon, let's get back to headquarters. Get some real food in us." He moved to help Morgan up, but Morgan gave him an uncharacteristic thumbs-up and assured him he was okay to stand on his own.

"Crap," Morgan said a moment later. "Forgot the canteen, though."

"I'll get it." Jeffrey quickly jogged back to the stump and picked up the water bottle. That was when he noticed something red streaked along the fallen tree.

"Jesus, Morgan, how much did you bleed?"

Morgan gave Jeffrey a quizzical look. "I'm not. It's mostly all dried."

Jeffrey took a step back. Behind the log he could see a trail of blood. And not far beyond that . . .

"What is it?" Morgan called from the trail.

"Nothing," Jeffrey lied. "Let's get back to headquarters. I'll tell you when we get there."

"No," Morgan said. "I don't want you babying me. What is it?"

Jeffrey took a breath, collected his thoughts. "A bloody trail. Dry blood running from the tree. It looks like it's leading toward the bay."

"Where Mrs. Liman figures there's a bear?" Morgan asked. Then he shocked Jeffrey by saying, "Let's go check it out, then. We should check it out."

"But . . . you're injured."

"If that Liman kid is out there like you think, shouldn't we at least try to look for him? A few scratches on my leg shouldn't stop us from that. Right?"

"Yeah." Jeffrey agreed. "You're right."

So the two junior rangers headed back in the direction of the cave. Though he was glad to have Morgan's willing assistance, Jeffrey couldn't bring himself to tell him about the bloody smear he'd spotted on a rock nearby—the smear that looked remarkably like a small hand print . . .

Henry Carter sat at his desk, flipping through old missing person cases.

He doubted he'd find answers in any of them. But he just couldn't stop his brain from drifting inevitably toward Jill and Marcia. Just like Joel Liman, they'd vanished. Just like Joel Liman, their loved ones were at an utter loss.

When word got out about Joel's disappearance (and it would), the town would have a panic on its hands. The mayor would not be happy with a crisis so close to the Labor Day festivities. Henry was rubbing his forehead in frustration and pondering what on earth he was going to do next, when Ava burst into his office. Henry had never seen Ava so distressed; he stood up at once.

She gasped as she gripped his desk with white knuckles. "I think I know what happened to Joel."

Ava didn't slow down until they'd approached the garbage can by the south bathrooms. Barely able to keep up, Henry skidded to a halt behind her. Ava glanced down, fearful.

"Here," she said. "Here's where I first saw it."

"Saw *what?*"

Ava seemed to have lost the capacity for articulation, so she showed Henry the picture she took of the footprint in the dirt. "This was here?" Henry questioned.

Ava nodded. "Not just here. They led all the way into the woods. Then they stopped, just randomly. I hid the tracks so they wouldn't start a panic."

"Good call. Where'd they lead?"

"About five hundred yards in that direction, but—" She stopped herself again. Henry leaned in closer. "There's something else you've got to see." She reached into her pocket and handed Henry a Ziploc bag. "I found this, right around where the prints ended. Couple of squirrels were playing with it and . . ."

Henry flipped the Ziploc bag over and examined its contents: a single human ear.

"My God," barely escaped his lips before Ava broke down into tears. "Hey, hey, we don't know whose this is yet . . ."

"What does it matter whose it was? It was still *someone's*, Henry!"

"Could have just been . . . a hunting accident or something." Henry could barely believe his own lame explanation. He ran a hand through his hair and took a few deep breaths to counter the sick feeling that was bubbling up from the pit of his stomach. "All right. Okay. You stay here with the campers, make sure they're safe. I'm gonna contact forensics. And, Ava," he added as an afterthought, "get ahold of my son. Make sure you guys never leave each other's sides. Got me?"

Ava nodded in complete understanding. Henry ran off, leaving her standing by the trash can, face covered in tears. Unbeknownst to her or Henry, Bruce Archer had been using the nearby restroom, and he emerged just in time to catch the end of their conversation.

Henry hung up the phone in disgust. Forensics had told him it would take as long as two business days to get any results. He decided to call Sheriff Walden to see if he could fast-track the situation, but his call went directly to voicemail. Here he was, on the busiest weekend of the year, with a missing boy, a piece of shirt, and an ear too small to belong to an adult. His mind was spinning. He had been on the go all morning, with barely a chance to breathe. In his tenure as a park ranger, he had dealt with people constantly getting lost in the woods, several annual drownings, and perhaps a handful of deaths caused by untrained rock climbers. But today . . . today had already outdone all those things combined, and he barely had a handle on what was happening. *What next?* he thought bleakly.

· The answer came sooner that he'd thought: his personal phone rang.

"Hello?" he answered in an uneasy tone.

"Henry? How is everything?"

It was Rachel. Obviously the Amber Alert hadn't reached everyone yet.

"Uh, you haven't heard?"

"Heard what?" she asked curiously.

"It's been rough today. Things have been . . ." He was tripping over his words, trying to determine the best way to explain the events to his wife. Rachel spoke again before he could continue.

"Well, you can tell me in a couple minutes. I'm bringing Sarah down to the park. I brought you and Jeff some lunch."

Henry was horrified at the thought of his wife and daughter being in the thick of all this mess. "Rachel, I don't—"

"Don't be ridiculous, we're already pulling up. Love you!" She ended the call. Henry dropped his phone onto his desk and rushed to the entrance. Through the front window, he saw Rachel and Sarah walking toward the main entrance. In a moment, he was through the station doors and standing in front of the minivan.

"You shouldn't be here."

Rachel helped Sarah out of her seat, blissfully unaware of anything. "What are you talking about?"

Henry didn't know how to even begin explaining things. As he was gathering his thoughts, the mayor pulled in. "Gimme a second. Don't leave Sarah alone!"

Mayor Tremblay exited his car and removed his hat as Henry approached him.

"Mayor Tremblay, I—" Henry began.

The mayor locked eyes with him and growled between his teeth. "We need to talk." Henry turned to Rachel to tell her to take Sarah home, but before he could, the mayor put his arm on his shoulder. "They're perfectly fine," the mayor assured a very confused Henry. "Let's go inside."

Mayor Tremblay shut the office door in a huff. Henry leaned against the wall, arms crossed.

"I'm hearing rumblings you want to shut the park down," the mayor stated.

Henry nodded. After all the discoveries he'd made that day, he was giving the thought *serious* consideration. Besides, an empty park would be easier for a search party to comb to locate Joel.

The mayor shook his head and straightened a framed picture of Henry and his family on the wall. "That won't be necessary."

Henry quickly jumped in. "Mr. Mayor, with all due respect, we have a missing kid out there. On top of that, we've discovered . . . things."

The mayor nodded. "I know, I'm aware of the 'claw.' And the ear."

"So you understand my concern, then?"

Mayor Tremblay walked around the office, looking over Henry's diplomas and awards. After a moment he responded. "I do."

Henry waited for the *But*. . . Sure enough, Tremblay turned to him.

"But . . ."

There it is.

"There is no need for concern."

Henry could not believe his ears. "Tremblay!"

"Henry, you listen to me. My answer is no. You will *not* be shutting Hillsbury Park down on the eve of the biggest weekend of the season. Your campgrounds are booked solid, and by tomorrow afternoon, your park will be at capacity. Vendors are on their way. Ferris wheels, whack-a-mole . . . it's all happening, Henry. We just have a little bear problem."

Henry had to shake his head. He was sure he'd heard wrong. "I'm sorry, did you say 'bear problem'?"

The mayor nodded. "Exactly. I've spoken with several authorities on the matter, and they've all assured me this is simply a bear problem. It's bizarre, for sure, but it is what it is. I'm sure Patty Liman will be happy to hear that."

"There's no bear in Hillsbury Park."

"You're wrong, Henry, there is. As I said, several experts have assured me this is nothing more than a bear. One bear."

The mayor was dead serious on this, forcing this so-called truth onto Henry. "Now, you're going to go outside and let your wife and daughter run around the park and play and have fun. You're going to show a good example to the rest of our guests. Understand?"

Henry was in utter shock. He had no idea what was out there, but he was confident it was no bear. "I think you're underestimating the gravity of this situation, sir."

"No, I'm not. Let the police do their job and conduct the search on the missing boy. All of whom, by the way, agree about the bear. Including your friend Trundle . . ." Henry stared at the mayor in disbelief as he continued. "And you focus on *your* job: keep the people in the park safe and, more importantly, happy."

Tremblay concluded by extending his hand to shake on it. "Agreed?"

Agreement was the furthest feeling from Henry's mind, but what choice did he have? When Mayor Tremblay made a decision (however ill-advised it may be), Henry could either cooperate or lose his job. Tremblay was right about one thing, though: it was the law's responsibility to search for Joel now. Henry could only do his part and keep the park as safe as possible.

He reluctantly shook the mayor's hand. Mid-shake, he felt Tremblay's grip tighten, and he was slowly—but firmly—pulled closer to the older man.

"And just so you're aware . . . I'll be putting a bounty on the bear later this afternoon." The mayor spoke in very hushed tones now. Henry's eyes widened. "So expect to see some of the loons from Hasaga over the next day or so, and be sure to keep your guests in line."

Tremblay broke the grip and exited the office, leaving Henry in silence.

Fifty miles east of Hillsbury, and 2,030 feet above sea level in the middle of the popular ski village, Mount Foggerty, lay the town of Hasaga. Boasting a population of thirteen hundred, Hasaga was known primarily for one thing: hunting. A trailer park, fitting seventy-five trailers and several tents, was a popular spot for hunting families to spend their nights and for non-hunters to while away their days.

In the middle of the park was a lawn bowling green, which (come Labor Day weekend) was the home of the annual Hasaga Trailer Park Lawn Bowling Championship and Cookout. The trailer park community would get together to enjoy a potluck and barbecue. The meat would be from a local animal, hunted that summer and judged by a panel of three with very discriminating taste. During the barbecue, folks could participate in a ten-hour-long lawn bowling tournament. It wasn't exactly a high-quality tournament; most of the participants only played the game on this day every year, and they were fueled less by their enthusiasm for the hobby and more by the copious amounts of beer and other spirits with which they washed down their barbecue. Like its neighboring town Hillsbury, Hasaga was a tight-knit community. It definitely drew a different kind of crowd, but the people who called Hasaga home loved what they loved and had their priorities straight.

Several hours before the break of dawn that Friday, a group of hunters set out for the day. They packed their trucks and Jeeps with rifles, bows, arrows, netting—whatever they felt would aid in the day's hunt. Typically, the Friday of Labor Day weekend was the day in which Hasaga's hunters caught whichever unfortunate creature was to be served up for the annual barbecue.

Tyson Marchman had just turned fourteen and his mother was finally allowing him to go out on a hunt with his father, Victor. He had dreamed of this day his entire life. Victor Marchman had won the barbecue contest the past three summers, and Tyson was ecstatic to be invited. Nothing would be better than standing side by side with his dad as they reeled in the gold medal for the fourth year in a row. Victor often told his son that the two keys to becoming a successful hunter were understanding and respect.

Respect not only for the sport but also for the animal. Victor would never hunt for game. He had no desire to line his house with bear rugs or hang antlers on the walls. Whatever he hunted, he did so for food, selling the meat to a local butcher. Last year's winning entry was a goat he took down with a bow and arrow. Bows and arrows made things more difficult than rifles, but Victor insisted that it resulted in a more tender piece of meat. The sound of a bullet firing out of a gun created a sense of fear in the animal, causing it to tense up. But a bow and arrow was silent . . . while remaining just as deadly.

There was something about the feeling of the arrow shooting from his fingertips that created a sense of power in Victor. It wasn't a higher power feeling. It was more of a realization. A realization that on this planet, we are one and meant to live as one. Death is a part of life. You cannot have one without the other. In Victor's eyes, the death of *any* species is meant to help the life of another. The death of an animal to be fed upon by another is the highest level of respect one could be given.

Victor had taught Tyson the basics of using a bow, but Tyson didn't think himself to be all that good at it. As they inched closer to their destination, butterflies filled his stomach and a feeling of nausea overcame him. He almost wanted to ask his father to pull over so he could be sick on the side of the road, but he wouldn't dare show weakness in front of Victor.

They pulled into the hunting grounds and exited the car. Victor carried the gear to where he and his son would set up a hunting blind.

"Want me to carry anything?" Tyson asked politely.

No response from his father. They quietly set up the blind and waited.

Victor scanned the woods through his binoculars but there was no sign of any deer. He tapped his son on the shoulder. "Okay. Let's try moving to another spot. Remember what I said. Stay slow. Got it?" Tyson nodded as the two exited the blind and made their way farther through the forest.

A strange feeling ran through Victor. This area was typically overpopulated with deer, especially at this hour in the morning. They stopped by a stand of trees and Victor surveyed the area. Tyson looked around, confused.

"Where are they all?"

"I don't know!" Victor hissed. The sun was beginning to rise. The window for hunting their prey was closing. Victor had wondered if the other hunters were having the same luck. Just yesterday he'd seen at least seven deer by this point. Today was the competition day; the deer you caught today was the deer you'd be judged on. He wondered if they would make an exception for him. But of course they wouldn't. Not if he was the only one without an animal.

But the sun rose, and the deer never came. Victor stood and accepted defeat. "C'mon," he said to his son.

"Where we going?"

"Home." Victor was clearly disappointed. This was Tyson's first outing, and he hadn't gotten the chance to hunt anything.

"Ah, man. Can't we go for a hike or something at least?" Tyson groaned.

Feeling bad for his son (and himself), Victor agreed, and together they hiked around the forest for a couple of hours. The entire time, Victor noticed the lack of wildlife. Hardly any birds were heard. No squirrels or chipmunks running around. Nothing. It was more eerily silent than he'd ever heard the forest before.

After the hike, Victor treated Tyson to lunch at a local tavern. Tyson ordered a bison burger and fries. Victor was happy to eat anything that wasn't deer. Despite their lack of success, at least he was getting to spend quality time with his boy. Victor looked into Tyson's eyes and recalled the day he was born. "You're growing up so fast," he said.

"Ah, Dad, don't get all gooey on me," Tyson laughed.

Victor gently tossed a fry at Tyson. "How's the burger? Good?"

Tyson nodded. Victor looked down at his watch. "What time is it?" Tyson asked.

"It's late. Your mother's gonna be pissed." Victor smiled. It was coming up on two in the afternoon, much later in the day than it would have been had they caught a deer. Victor and Tyson finished their lunch, paid the bill, and made their way back to the trailer park.

As they drove into the park, they passed a man smoking outside his Jeep. Tyson recognized the Hillsbury Park sticker on the jeep immediately. "What's the Hillsbury ranger doing here?" he asked his father. Victor parked the car and was considering approaching the ranger when he noticed Dean Scranton carrying a deer over his shoulders, followed by a big group of people.

"Well, I'll be damned!" Victor slammed the door shut and stomped over to Dean. "What the hell is that?"

Dean turned to Victor and dropped the deer on the ground. "A deer. My spoils of victory. Why?"

"My boy and I were out there all morning. We didn't see nothin'!" Victor was almost shouting.

"I know. Dean here's the only one to kill anything today." This came from Dean's half-brother, Flynn.

"What spot?" Victor asked Dean.

"Same as yesterday," he answered with a straight face "Now, if you'll excuse me, I have judges to visit." Dean slung the deer back over his shoulders and carried it off with a triumphant grin.

Victor stormed back to Tyson and the truck. "C'mon," he said to his son as they walked toward their trailer. Henry followed close behind. Victor stopped, remembering the Hillsbury park ranger. He looked his way and walked over.

"Can I help you? You look far from home."

"I hear you're a hunter," Henry said. His expression was unreadable.

"I am, yeah. Most here are."

"I also hear you're the best."

Victor jerked a thumb over his shoulder in the direction Dean had gone. "Not today, I'm not."

"You and I both know that deer wasn't caught today."

Victor narrowed his eyes. Without turning around, he said, "Tyson, go to the trailer. I'll be there in a minute." Tyson did as he was told. Victor stepped a foot closer to Henry. "You've got my attention, Mr. Ranger, sir."

"I've come from Hillsbury—"

Victor cut him off. "I know where you're from."

Henry flicked his cigarette aside. "My mayor's about to put a bounty on an animal. A bear."

Victor frowned. "There aren't any bears in Hillsbury."

Henry nodded. "I know. And you know. My mayor and the police force, on the other hand . . . look, this bounty is happening, I'm a couple hours away from having God knows how many hunters crawling all over my park. All of them with firearms." He took a breath and Victor noticed the sound of slight desperation in his voice. "I need to speak with you in confidence."

Victor nodded his head. "Sure."

Henry continued. "A boy has gone missing, and a body part has been found. I have no clue if one belongs to the other, but this is my situation. I don't think we're dealing with a bear. I think we're dealing with someone who wants us to *think* it was a bear."

"What do you want me to do?"

"I want you to call the mayor, tell him you'll take care of the bear personally. Tell him who you are, all of your credentials, so he knows and trusts you're doing this in good faith. Then I want you to hunt down and find the son of a bitch who's terrorizing my park."

Victor did not know what to make of this proposition, though he could understand why the ranger came to see him. A public bounty on an animal would draw out everybody, not just hunters. It would cause more problems than it would solve. Victor nodded.

"Get me the mayor's number."

Ava sat behind Henry's desk, staring absently into space.

Patty Liman had just left the office, driven home by Sheriff Walden. Ava finally had a moment to herself to catch her breath. When she became a park ranger, she'd never imagined having to deal with a day like today. She figured there might be days when people got injured, maybe even an accidental death or two, but nothing like this. A part of her *did* kind of enjoy it: the thrill of a mystery, the excitement of something new . . .

though the image of that ear being chewed by a squirrel was not one she'd be able to shake anytime soon.

Bentley Trundle had stayed behind to begin coordinating a proper search of the park and surrounding woods. Ava glanced up from her work when he knocked and entered the office.

"Oh." He was obviously startled to see Ava behind the desk. "Henry in?"

Ava shook her head.

"Any idea when he'll be back?" Bentley continued.

"He went to Hasaga. Not sure for what, wouldn't say."

"I think I know." Bentley lowered his head, ashamed of what he was about to say. "The mayor's about to issue a bounty for the bear."

"Bear? What bear?" Ava asked.

"The one in the park. The one that killed Joel."

Ava couldn't believe what she was hearing. "You're kidding me, right?"

Bentley shook his head. "Afraid not."

"How could you? Are you insane?" She rose from her chair now, fists shaking.

"Look, it's not as if I had much of a choice. Tremblay's crazy. He hired these guys to say it was a bear. They showed me proof and evidence that it *was* a bear. What was I supposed to do, Ava? Lose my job? Then what help would I be?"

"Well, what help are you now?"

She walked to the door and held it open, gesturing for him to leave. Bentley approached her, but not to leave. Tentatively, he reached out and took her by the arms. "I will get to the bottom of this, Ava."

"Get out. You've done enough." She pushed Bentley away. He took a few steps toward the door before stopping.

"Ava . . ." His voice was as calm as ever.

"What?" she snapped, furious.

Bentley marched over and embraced her with a kiss. It was a passionate kiss, one he had been waiting to give her for a long time now. She shoved him off.

"What in the hell are you doing? What about Elise?"

Bentley couldn't resist. There was just something about Ava, something he was madly attracted to. "I can't control myself around you."

"Maybe don't be around me, then. Goodbye, Bent." She stood silent, waiting, until he left headquarters, and then she slammed the door shut after him.

Bentley stepped outside, exhaling heavily, and went straight for his car. Jeffrey and Morgan were sitting on a curb, and when Jeffrey saw the deputy sheriff, he stood up and called out.

"Mr. Trundle? Officer? Sir?"

Bentley was not in a mood to speak with anyone. He turned and gave Jeffrey a vicious stare.

"Sorry, sir. It's just, Morgan and I have been . . . we've been looking for Patty Liman's boy. I haven't been able to get hold of my dad, and . . ."

"And what? Spit it out, for Christ's sake." Right now Bentley wanted nothing more than to leave the park.

"There's something you should see."

Bentley just sighed. "Okay. Fine."

The boys proceeded to lead Bentley into the woods. The deputy followed, trying (and failing) to keep his mind off the scene inside rangers' headquarters. Thinking about Ava was painful, yet he couldn't bring himself to think about anything else. To make matters worse, the afternoon was hot as hell. He longed to put as much distance between himself and the park as possible, yearning for the solitude of the air-conditioned sheriff's office.

As far as he was aware, there were no new men in Ava's life. She was a career-oriented woman who didn't have time to go looking for love. At least, that was what she'd told him.

For all he knew, though, she could have been lying. The worst part was, things were fine at home for Bentley. Better than they'd been in a long time. He had no reason to cheat on Elise again . . . save for the fact that he was completely obsessed with Ava. When she wasn't around, he could move on with his life as though she didn't exist; out of sight, out of mind. But seeing her again only refueled the fire burning within him. It wasn't quite love that he felt; he was sure of that. But it still burned: an obsession, a *lust*, that he could barely explain, let alone control. He felt like a recovering addict who was about to relapse.

"Are you planning on telling me where we're going at some point?" he snapped irritably at the teenagers.

"Cape's Side Bay," Jeffrey said.

Bentley stopped walking and looked at the boys. "Cape's Side Bay?"

Jeffrey nodded.

"There's nothing at Cape's Side but swamp."

"And blood." Morgan spoke up now. "We found a trail of dried blood. It leads to the bay."

"And you followed this trail all the way to the bay?" Bentley rubbed his forehead, and his palm came away slick with sweat.

"Almost, not quite," Jeffrey said. "But it's not hard to miss. You can see the trail and follow it. The only place it could go is the bay." Bentley could hear the trembling in Jeffrey's voice. It was clear that these boys were not joking or simply hungry for attention. They had seen something out there, something that had left them shaken. Bentley nodded and gestured for them to continue. As they drew closer to the bay, the trail of dried blood appeared, staining the grass a deep crimson. Bentley squatted down and stared at it.

"It's old. About a day."

"Think it might be Joel's?" Morgan asked.

Bentley stood back up. "I'm not sure."

They continued walking until the trail ended and they stood facing Cape's Side Bay itself. They looked around at the wilderness: the rocky cliff, the cave high above, the swamp below, and a bloody handprint two feet above the water on the rocks.

"That what you wanted me to see?" Bentley asked, receiving a nod from both boys.

Bentley took a deep breath. He removed his walkie-talkie from his belt and switched it on.

"This is Deputy Sheriff Trundle. I'm gonna need divers, and I'm gonna need them at Cape's Side Bay. Repeat, I need a diving team at Cape's Side Bay." He looked around at the murky swamp water, adding, "And tell them to bring powerful lights."

For the first time that day since sipping his morning coffee, Bentley Trundle managed to smile. "Why don't you two boys head on back to headquarters? You did well today. Thank you."

Jeffrey let out a smile of his own, proud of the work he had done. In fact, it was the first time all summer he'd felt useful. Morgan clapped him on the shoulder, and the pair raced back to headquarters.

Alone, Bentley stared out at the dark bay. *What in the hell is going on here?* he wondered.

Victor followed Henry down the rough dirt road of Highway 21, heading toward Hillsbury. Victor was uncomfortable with this entire situation. He knew where both the mayor and Henry were coming from, and he worried many innocent people would get hurt, or worse. Weapons were not to be taken lightly, especially not near campgrounds in Hillsbury Park, populated by mostly families with small children. He also was not entirely comfortable searching for a killer. He was no cop or detective, just a hick from the country who enjoyed hunting and the odd game of Yahtzee (as far as Victor was concerned, a night among friends that didn't end with a game or three of Yahtzee was a wasted night indeed). But then his thoughts strayed to Patty Liman and what she must be going through. This alone kept Victor from turning back. He had Tyson waiting for him back home; the thought of his boy suddenly going missing, the thought of him not being home to greet Victor upon his return, was enough to wrench his gut. No parent should have to go through that.

Henry stole a glance at his rearview mirror to make sure Victor was still behind him, but ended up seeing something that caught him off guard.

Behind Victor was a convoy of trucks, at least a dozen of them, all bearing logos of a traveling carnival company. Tremblay had gone through with it after all. The plan must have been to set up everything tonight and be ready for guests first thing Saturday morning. By Sunday (the busiest day of the year), the fair would already be established with the visitors and be deemed a huge success. Henry could only shake his head at what he was seeing.

Victor, though, had no idea what was going on, so he pulled over to the side of the road. Once Henry noticed this, he stopped as well, leaving his Jeep and approaching Victor.

"What's wrong?" he asked.

Victor watched as the dozen trucks drove passed them. "What is all this?"

"Hillsbury Labor Day carnival and fair or some bullshit, I dunno. The mayor's gone off his rocker."

"You got a missing boy and a bear and your mayor's first reaction is to have a carnival?"

"Well, in fairness, it was planned before all that happened." Henry decided to change his angle on the conversation and reassure Victor. "They'll be at an entirely different area of the park. It'll be fine, safe. I promise."

Victor looked on as the last of the trucks passed by. He thought for a moment and nodded. "All right, but if I get the feeling something ain't right, I'm done. Pulling the plug. Get me?"

Henry got him, all right. The two returned to their vehicles and headed to Hillsbury. Not long after, a call came through on Henry's Bluetooth.

"Yeah?"

"Henry, it's Trundle."

Hoping for some kind of positive development, Henry raised the volume. "I'm just on my way back from Hasaga."

"I know. I spoke with Ava. But, look, Henry, two things. One: I was just with your boy and the other kid. They led me toward something. When you get back, I'm gonna need you to meet me at Cape's Side Bay. I've got divers coming."

"Divers?" Henry trembled for a moment, dreading the answer to his follow-up question. "Divers for what, Bentley?"

"I'll clue you in when you get here. The other thing is, I spoke with the parents of the boys, the ones who were out with that Liman kid last night. They are all accounted for. According to the parents, two of the boys slept at the other's house, and the third kid, he's been in his room all day playing video games."

There was silence on the line. Henry thought for a moment. "So what're you thinking?"

"I'm thinking either Patty's lying or the boys snuck out. Most likely snuck out. That doesn't change the fact that they're all accounted for."

"Have you spoken with any of the kids yet?"

"Not yet, was waiting for you. But then I ran into Jeffrey, who led me to the bay . . . something's up, Henry. Just get here soon."

Bentley ended the call. Henry ruminated on all of this for a moment. Checking to make sure Victor was still close behind, he lowered his foot onto the gas pedal and pushed the Jeep past the speed limit.

Bentley stood at the edge of the bay, his foot on a rock, toes hovering over the swamp water beneath. *A handprint covered with blood, a claw, an ear, and a piece of clothing.* Things were beginning to unravel in Hillsbury, and Bentley was not enjoying it. As much as he was loath to admit, the handprint looked like it belonged to a child. But Bentley was no expert on things like that. He'd made some calls; the forensics department was on their way. *The experts will know more,* he'd told himself a hundred times over since then.

The divers were getting the last pieces of their equipment on as Bentley walked over to the leader of the diving team, a man by the name of Richard.

"Good luck in there."

The diver gave Bentley the "a-okay" gesture and jumped into the swampy water of Cape's Side Bay. Bentley looked out at the swamp that had once been a gorgeous bay. The thought of this area being packed with people seemed almost unrealistic to him now. He knew an older gentleman who'd passed away just over a year ago, who told him stories of the bay. All of them were horror stories with not a shred of positivity between them. Bentley always assumed they were urban myths, but looking out on the swamp on this day, under these grim conditions, the old man's tales suddenly took on an entirely new light.

Whatever aura surrounded Cape's Side Bay was mimicked in the bay's appearance. When the aura was good and fresh, it was a bubbling place, full of fish and wildlife. Nature flourished. When the aura turned, so would the vegetation. There had been undocumented occurrences of this over the past seventy-nine years. With the operative word being *undocumented*. All hearsay. Locals always told tales of the drought in Cape's Side Bay, but there were never any records to justify these fables as fact. And with the passing of the old man, whose name had escaped Bentley, there were no remaining citizens with this knowledge (if it could even be called knowledge). For all he knew, those people were all being fed the same fairy tale as children, stories to deter the kids from wandering into the waters of Cape's Side Bay. Generations of local myths about dark auras and strange happenings could've been chalked up to nothing more than a few cautionary tales for overexcited children.

Richard emerged from the water and removed the oxygen mask from his mouth. Bentley walked two steps over and waved to him, but the diver paid him no mind, instead calling out to another diver.

"Marcus, bring a lantern!"

A second diver grabbed a flashlight, jumped into the water, and swam toward the first. Both bodies vanished into the dark waters below. Bentley rushed over to the two divers who remained onshore.

"What'd he see?"

One of them simply shrugged. "How should I know, buddy? We just do what we're told."

Out-of-town jackass, Bentley thought. He'd actually been amazed with how quickly the divers had arrived and assumed

CAPE'S SIDE BAY   69

he had the Amber Alert to thank for that. Missing children reports were extremely serious and tended to much more quickly than other reports. Bentley just felt like the gravity of the situation was lost on these particular people.

The head diver rose from the water once again, this time swimming to the edge of the bay. Bentley helped him back onto land. Richard glanced up at him, squinting through a fringe of wet hair.

"We're gonna need more time down there. But it's interesting."

"Interesting? How?"

Richard walked over to his truck and turned on the CB radio. "Hi, we're gonna need a tow. A big one. Thank you."

"A tow for what?" Bentley asked in confusion.

"A tow for the pick-up truck you got down there."

Ava poured herself a cup of coffee. She hadn't started out as much of a coffee drinker. She was turned off by the idea of caffeine and the effects it could have on one's body. Becoming a park ranger, however, turned her into a sort of coffee connoisseur. Today she filled her cup under the impression that it was going to be a very long day. There was no way she would let herself go home and call it an evening until Joel Liman was safe. She upended a pack of sugar into her coffee and mixed it with a wooden stick as the front door swung open behind her.

She turned to see a woman in her late thirties standing there, tears pouring down her cheeks. Ava dropped her coffee mug, spilling the hot coffee all over the floor, and rushed over at once. The strange woman dropped to her knees.

"What is it?" Ava asked.

"My son!" the woman cried out. "My son!" And she screamed at the top of her lungs.

Ava helped the woman to her feet and lowered her into a chair. The woman wiped the tears from her cheeks as Ava handed her a glass of water. Ava sat on a chair across from her, stunned. "What's wrong with your son?"

The woman opened her mouth but was unable to speak. Something horrible had happened. Ava could feel it in her bones.

"Would you mind telling me your name?"

"Vera. Vera Curtis." The woman's hands shook so much it was a wonder she didn't spill all of her water.

Ava pulled a pen and notebook out and jotted down everything Vera told her.

"My boy was home last night. He stayed home and played video games. We just got him this new game he wanted . . ." Vera broke down into tears. Ava placed her hand on Vera's knee.

"It's all right. It's okay," Ava assured her. "Where's your son now?"

The woman turned her head and looked out the window at her beat-up old station wagon.

"In my car. The trunk of my car."

The words *the trunk of my car* circled Ava's brain like a bad dream. She stood up at once and ran out of the headquarters. A couple of futile tugs told her that the trunk was locked. She whirled back around to see Vera slowly following her outside, half in a daze, as if she were sleepwalking.

"Give me your keys!" Ava screamed. Vera went through her purse and fumbled about with a few objects before finally finding her keys and handing them to Ava. Ava frantically unlocked and opened the trunk.

Ava's eyes filled with tears. Shock. Pain. Agony. It filled every corner of her mind, body, and soul.

David Curtis lay asleep, still breathing, in the trunk of his mother's station wagon. He was curled up in the fetal position, his arms tucked between his legs.

His eyes had been sewn shut.

Both eyes were swollen and bruised. There was a gash on his left cheek that looked like a stab wound from a knife. Ava grabbed the side of the station wagon for support as a wave of nausea hit her. She promptly emptied the contents of her stomach onto the ground.

Moments later, Henry and Victor pulled up to the head-quarters. From where they parked, they could only see Vera and her station wagon.

"Who's that?" Victor asked. "The kid's mother?"

Henry shook his head, frowning. "No. That's Vera Curtis."

They approached, puzzled. "Vera?" Henry asked. "Is every-thing all right?"

Vera didn't move, didn't speak. Now Henry could hear Ava crying.

"Ava?"

He noticed her lying on the ground and rushed over. "What's wrong?"

"The boy!" she cried out. "That poor boy!"

"What boy?" Henry lifted Ava into a standing position, holding her lest she topple over again.

Victor, who was now staring directly into the trunk, answered the question for him. When he spoke, he sounded like he was about to be sick too. "This boy."

Henry peered into the trunk and covered his mouth, white with shock.

Victor turned away, glancing around at the surrounding park, hands on his hips. When he could find his voice again, he locked eyes with Henry.

"That's an interesting bear you've got here."

FRIDAY EVENING

Bruce Archer was born to a wealthy family. When he was five, however, that wealth was lost forever. It turned out his father had a rather large gambling problem. The issue with Reginald P. Archer's gambling problem was that he had no skill with any games of chance whatsoever. He would win the odd game here or there, but never enough to cover his staggering losses. So, while Bruce Archer was born into money, he'd never actually experienced wealth.

His grandfather owned two of the most beautiful cottages on the lake in Hillsbury. His father would eventually lose these properties as a result of his addiction; they now belonged to two wealthy families who preferred renting them out rather than enjoying them themselves.

Reginald's gambling problem also Reginald's a toll on Bruce's mother, Amber. She understood his addiction and had been a helpful, supportive rock throughout the early years of their marriage. But Reginald never fought it. He allowed the disease to consume him, until Amber reached her breaking point. The man she'd married was gone, drowned in a mire of losses and heavy drinking and even more losses. However, she could not bring herself to ever leave her husband. And so, she lived out the rest of her days depressed, lonely, and even abused—both emotionally and physically.

Bruce was only nine years old when his father's life was consumed; he had no pure understanding of the situation. All he understood for sure was that his parents fought. A lot.

He felt his luck start to turn, though, once school started that year. That was the year he'd met Peter Epsy, who would later become his best friend. Peter and Bruce had attended the same school for years, but that year was the first time their paths had crossed. Whether or not the meeting of these nine-year-olds was fate remained to be seen.

While Bruce's family was from money and owned property (once upon a time, at least), Peter's family had never known wealth at all. Their summer vacations consisted of staying in Mr. Epsy's brother's RV in the Hasaga trailer park. Peter looked forward to each summer in Hasaga the way other kids his age looked forward to Disneyland. Peter *loved* it there. The wave pool, the lawn bowling tournament . . . and each trip would end with a lovely bonfire. Since Peter's father worked twelve-hour days at a factory and wasn't allowed very much vacation time, the entire Epsy family learned to treasure every moment of their fleeting summer trips.

Peter was always a shy boy. Never spoke much to other children. He had a few friends, but they were just fellow classmates. Most of them lived on the other side of town and their parents would not allow their children to cross the highway that separated them. The trailer park offered an opportunity for Peter to be a child, to enjoy himself and have fun with other children for a longer period of time than a school day. Only one child was able to cross that highway, simply because his mother didn't bother checking up on where her son was going. Bruce would just tell his mother he was visiting a friend and leave it at that.

The highway was not all that dangerous to pass if done correctly. A tunnel underneath the highway with a fully paved walkway allowed pedestrians to travel to either side safely. Most parents were just paranoid. It would only take one child to decide to cross the road instead of taking the underpass, and the rest of them would follow suit. Crossing the road would save several minutes, and the impatience of youth found that both enticing and exciting.

Over the course of the school year, the two boys became the closest of friends. Once summer hit, Peter asked his parents if he could invite Bruce to Hasaga with them. Mr. and Mrs. Epsy agreed; they were quite fond of Bruce. He was quiet and polite. But first they wanted to clear things with his parents, so they asked Peter if they could meet Bruce's mother. Peter didn't see this as an obstacle, but Bruce felt otherwise. He knew that if his mother found out he'd been visiting Peter on the other side of the highway, things would get bad for him. Even if he lied and told her he'd used the underpass every time, she'd still find out he'd been breaking rules. And word seemed to spread fast among the parents of Hillsbury; if Peter's folks caught word that Bruce had been lying to his mother for months, what would they think? Would they stop liking him? Would they forbid Peter from playing with him, fearing the rebelliousness would become infectious? Bruce was torn. He would love to be away from his argumentative parents for two weeks. Doing this, however, would mean admitting to his mother where he had been going. It was a lose-lose situation. As crushing as it sounded, Bruce decided the best course of action would be to decline Peter's offer: make up some excuse and tell him he could not join his family in Hasaga. So Bruce resigned himself to a dull, dreary summer, just like all the others.

Until something downright miraculous happened.

That morning, as he was getting ready for school, his mother helped him tie up his shoes as usual. She was halfway through when she said, "Tell Peter Epsy I said you can go to Hasaga with him."

Bruce's stomach lurched. He was in shock, from both her permission and the sudden revelation that she'd known about the invitation in the first place. But how . . . ?

"His parents called me last night," she said as if reading his mind. Bruce had no idea what to even say. His mother didn't seem upset at all. In fact, she seemed fine. She was . . . smiling. He couldn't remember ever feeling more confused.

"I know things at home aren't great. But we love you, both of us," Amber told him. "Even if it seems we don't, or if it seems we're mad at you. We both love you unconditionally." She wrapped her son in a tight hug. "I just wish you would have told me where you were going. You know how I feel about that road." She spoke with a tone he couldn't recall hearing before: neither upset nor disappointed, but caring. He returned the hug as tightly as he could. Amber released Bruce, wiped away a tear, and smiled.

"I love you."

"I love you too, Mum." Bruce smiled back. He opened the door. "What's for dinner?"

Once again defying Bruce's wildest expectations, Amber grinned. "Wanna order a pizza?" Of course he did! He nodded frantically. "Pizza it is! Now, don't miss your bus."

"I won't." Bruce left the house, his insides as bright as the morning sun.

Hasaga was blistering hot that summer. Being high on the side of a mountain, the town usually enjoyed cooler climates during the summer months, but this year the heat seeped through with a vengeance. The wave pool was almost always full to capacity, much to the dismay of Peter and Bruce. The long lines meant less time in the pool, but the beach waiting for them at the end of the day was worth it, and the bay was a fantastic place to lounge and enjoy a picnic.

Hillsbury Park was also a great place to be if you were a child, specifically a child with a grand imagination. Peter fit that bill. Bruce? Not so much. With such a dreary home life, one would think Bruce spent *hours* escaping into his own imagination, but any time he tried, his fears would take over. Darkness lurked in the mind of Bruce Archer, and he did not—even for a second—enjoy being alone with this thoughts. What made his friendship with Peter so welcome was that Peter could open Bruce's mind to possibilities like never before. Peter's imagination lived in a happy realm, one he could skillfully invite Bruce into whenever he wished.

It was Saturday, August 7, and the Epsys were going to Hillsbury Park for the day. They only had three days left of their family vacation, and today would be the final day they spent in Hillsbury. They'd spend the final two days saying goodbye to their Hasaga friends and packing for the trip home. Due to its remote, mountaintop locale, it was often impossible to find a decent radio signal in Hasaga and the surrounding area. Mr. Epsy clashed with the radio knob for a while until finally settling on the only clear signal he could get: talk radio. The boys in the back seat would have obviously preferred to listen to music, but anything was better than awkward silence. After announcing last night's final baseball scores, the program shifted gears to current affairs. Apparently, word was spreading of dead fish popping up all over Cape's Side Bay earlier that morning. There was an interview with a local fisherman talking about how strange it was to see all the fish pop up from the water, dead. The reporter then announced that the bay would be closed for the remainder of the day while geologists inspected the area.

Mr. Epsy turned the volume down, noticing the boys' glum expressions in the rearview mirror. "That's okay, we can still enjoy the park!" he said with a smile.

When they arrived at the park, caution signs had already been erected to prevent tourists from going over to Cape's Side Bay. The bay closing was bad news for local business but turned out to be great news for the Epsys and Bruce. Tables at restaurants were now available, so Mr. and Mrs. Epsy decided to stay later than usual and enjoy a night out at a restaurant. Mrs. Epsy placed her blanket out on a beautiful patch of green grass in the park. Mr. Epsy unfolded his raggedy lawn chair and whipped out this Walkman.

Bruce was in awe; he had never seen a Walkman before. He was surprised to see Mr. Epsy with one, of all people. Peter's father worked hard for his money and usually spent it all on his wife and child. Mr. Epsy saw Bruce's awestruck expression and chuckled. "Neat, isn't it? This was an anniversary gift from Mrs. Epsy," he said proudly. "An anniversary I forgot all about, too. I had to work three hours overtime at the plant that day. Then I was stuck in some of the worst traffic I can remember. By the time I got home, all I wanted to do was sit in my recliner, watch the ball game, and fall asleep. Instead, I walked through the front door to find a candlelight dinner waiting for me. And in the middle of the table, wrapped up with a bow . . ." He gave the Walkman a little rattle. "This." He turned to smile at his wife. Mrs. Epsy smiled back, blowing him a kiss. "After that, I promised never to forget an anniversary again. Lucky for me, I'm married to a lady so amazing, she didn't even mind that I'd forgotten."

Bruce felt entirely out of his element. He'd never, not even once, heard his parents speak about each other the way Mr.

Epsy had just spoken of his wife. And he'd definitely never seen them display this kind of affection. A weight seemed to drop, quietly but firmly, in the pit of Bruce's stomach as he suddenly became quite aware of just what he was missing.

"Hey, Bruce! Look at this!"

Peter had come running over, excitedly waving a yellow flyer. The flyer touted that Hillsbury Park would be adding campgrounds the following summer. It had been printed to look like an old-timey treasure map, with the treasure being the location of the new campgrounds. Peter waved it in front of Bruce's face.

"Wanna go look for treasure?"

Bruce's lack of imagination couldn't see past the flyer's primary purpose. "That's for camping."

"Yeah, to everyone else! But to us . . . this map leads to a great big treasure chest! Full of gold coins and pearls and other stuff!"

It was incredible just how infectious Peter's imagination could be. Bruce decided to play along and join Peter on his quest. Mrs. Epsy was fine with the boys leaving, so long as they brought along a backpack filled with snacks and water, which Bruce volunteered to carry.

The flyer (or map, as Peter insisted on calling it) was inteded to lead people to the new campground area so they could look at the space and, hopefully, book grounds for the following summer. The boys decided to reverse the map and stated that the treasure was on the other side of Hillsbury Park.

Which meant that Peter's imaginary treasure had been buried right by the waters of Cape's Side Bay.

The two boys snuck under signs marked *BAY CLOSED* and *NO TRESPASSING*. Peter suddenly felt a force against his chest. Bruce looked up to see Peter's hand holding him back.

"What're you doing? The treasure's that way!" Peter pointed straight ahead, but when he looked up, all he could see were hundreds upon hundreds of dead fish in the bay. His jaw dropped. "Holy cow! That's a lot of fish!"

"What do you think happened?" Bruce asked.

Peter took a short step forward, eyes as wide as they'd ever been. "I dunno."

"Maybe we should go back." Bruce was starting to get an uneasy feeling. *Something* must have caused the death of all these fish, something that could still be lingering in the air . . .

"Don't be a scaredy pants!" Peter insisted. "We've got treasure to find!"

"What treasure? That's a map to a campground. We aren't going to find anything, Peter!" Bruce lost his grip on the fantasy and managed to pull Peter back to reality with him. Peter knew deep down that Bruce was right, that there was no treasure, and there would never be a treasure.

"Fine." Peter sighed, sounding considerably defeated. "We'll go back." He folded the map and shoved it in his pocket.

The boys headed back at a much slower pace than the frenzied one with which they'd arrived. They were trekking through the woods that separated the bay from the park when they noticed something. It was quiet. *Dead* quiet. Not a single bird could be heard. They realized this at the same time and looked up. Just as Peter was about to remark on the eeriness of it all, they heard leaves rustling to their left.

Bruce jumped. "What was that?"

"Probably a chipmunk or a squirrel or something," Peter said, though he didn't sound convinced. Cautiously, they tried to resume their journey, until they heard the sound again.

Peter graced Bruce with another playful expression and said, "C'mon!"

"C'mon what?"

But before Bruce could finish the sentence, Peter was rushing off to chase whatever was making the sound. Upset and nervous that his relaxing vacation was starting to feel an awful lot like *Lord of the Flies*, Bruce hurried to follow.

Peter was small and quick. He had been the fastest student in his class for the past three years. It took every ounce of energy Bruce had to keep up with him, especially in the heat. He closed his eyes and took deep breaths as he ran. When he opened them again, he saw that Peter had stopped and was staring at something. Bruce skidded to a halt, kicking up dirt and almost colliding with him.

"What is it? Why'd you stop?" Bruce asked, panting.

Peter raised his index finger to his lips for silence before pointing to a rock.

Bruce stared at the rock for several moments until he spotted what Peter had been watching: a large lizard had slowly crept out from behind the rock.

The lizard was about half a foot long with a long, skinny neck. The eyes were large and green with yellow circles at the center. Its flesh was green, and it had long quills protruding from its arm like whiskers. The creature's snout resembled more of a bird's than a lizard's. It was like nothing they'd ever seen before.

"What is it?" Bruce whispered.

"A lizard," Peter returned.

"Well, obviously, yeah. But . . . what kind?"

Peter shrugged. "A dinosaur?"

"It's not a dinosaur!" The volume of his voice went up, only slightly, but it was enough to make the lizard twitch. It blinked twice, glancing around.

Peter shushed him and said, "It's gotta be a dinosaur. Maybe a few of them survived the meteor shower?" Peter's imagination was starting to come off its leash.

"It's a gecko," Bruce assured him.

"A gecko? It's not a gecko."

"Well, why not?"

"Geckos are tiny. And they aren't indigenous to this region."

"So because it's not a gecko, your next guess is dinosaur?"
Peter nodded. "Pretty much, yeah."

Bruce was in utter disbelief. "But . . . but dinosaurs have
been extinct for millions of years." Bruce loved dinosaurs. He'd
read countless books and magazines about them. There was
just no possible way that he could be looking at one right now.

"Maybe some survived."

"None did. It's fact. We learned about it in school."

"School might be wrong."

"It's not a dinosaur!" Angry and impatient, Bruce's voice
culminated in a yell. The startled lizard (or whatever it was)
stared up at them, blinked again, and ran off into the woods.

"Great, now it's gone," Peter groaned. With a sigh, he
turned around. "Let's go back to Mum and Dad."

"We can still find that thing. It's still out here somewhere!"

"Probably not. It probably went back to its . . ." Peter struggled to think of the right word, settling on, "*house*, or whatever
it lives in."

"We found it in the first place, didn't we? No reason why
we couldn't find it again."

Peter stopped walking, intrigued. Bruce was right. He
turned back to Bruce with a smile, and the pair once again ventured off in search of the creature. The trek took them deeper
into the heart of the woods than Peter had ever been before.

After a few minutes, they saw it: the lizard was perfectly
visible, leaning forward, its chin resting on a twig. Bruce took
a cautious step forward.

"Don't scare it!" Peter hissed. Bruce held out a hand, signaling for Peter to stay put. Then he took three cautious steps
toward the lizard, whose eyes were almost entirely shut.

Each breath it took was heavy and slow, as if it were in pain. Bruce knelt down beside it, close enough to reach out and touch it. Somehow, the creature seemed a little bit bigger up close, like an optical illusion. As carefully as he could, Bruce slid the backpack from his shoulders and pet the lizard softly on the top of its head.

"What in the heck are you doing, Bruce?"

Bruce ignored Peter and poured some water into the lid of the water bottle. He placed it by the lizard's mouth, allowing it to take a sip.

"It's okay, it's okay," Bruce said softly to the animal. Then he turned to address Peter. "He's sick or injured or something. Just needs help."

Peter hesitantly took a couple steps toward Bruce, who was still petting the lizard. He squatted down next to him, hands trembling. "Wh-what do I do?"

"Be gentle, just rub the top of his head. He likes it." Bruce demonstrated. Peter reached in closer. The lizard's right eye opened to take him in before slowly closing back into a slit. Peter rubbed the top of the lizard's scalp.

"You like animals?" Peter asked, hoping Bruce couldn't hear the shaking in his voice.

"Love them. I want a dog, but my dad said no. And my mum's allergic to cats, so we can't have them either."

"What about a lizard?" Peter laughed.

Bruce noticed that the water bottle's lid was now empty. "All done? You want more water? Yeah, you do." He filled the lid with water once again.

"Can I do it?" Peter asked. Bruce nodded and handed him the lid. "What do I do?"

"Just slowly put it under his chin, just enough for his tongue to get into it and absorb the water."

Peter's hands shook, not enough to spill any water, but enough for Bruce to see that he was nervous.

"It's okay," Bruce assured Peter.

Peter took a deep breath and gently slid the water under the lizard. Then he watched with delight as its tongue flicked out and lapped up the water.

"It's so cool!" he said. Bruce nodded in agreement. "Should we name it?"

"I dunno. You want to?"

Peter thought for only a second. "Barnabas!"

"What kind of name is that?" Bruce asked.

"It's *his* name," Peter said, looking directly into the slits of the lizard's eyes. "Barnabas it is! How's he doing with the water?"

The lid was empty. "All done. Should we give him more?"

"I think it's good. That's enough."

"Oh, come on, just one more?" Peter begged. "It's fun!"

Bruce reluctantly agreed and filled the lid with more water before handing it over to Peter. This time Peter's confidence was booming. He held the lid to the lizard's mouth.

"Not too close," Bruce warned. Peter didn't listen; he reached out with his right hand and gently lifted the lizard's jaw off the ground.

"Peter, what're you doing?"

"I'm helping him," Peter said with a smile. The lizard's tongue entered the lid once more and he drank the water. "See? He likes it."

Then the lizard began making a gasping sound. "What's that?" Peter asked.

"He can't breathe. He's having trouble breathing. His neck's too high." Bruce was becoming a bit panicked. He hated seeing an animal in pain.

"What do I do?" Peter moaned, guilt filling his belly.

"Lower his head, rest it back down on the twig."

Peter cautiously placed his hand under the jaw of the lizard, swapping it for the twig the injured creature was resting on. As he continued to move the lizard's head, he needed to readjust his footing on the ground below. He shifted his back foot another few inches, unaware of a gopher hole in the earth. He tripped over it. As he stumbled, Peter dropped the lizard's head; it slammed against the ground and instantly began to fill the quiet forest air with squeals of pain.

Peter looked on in terror. Bruce tried to help Peter to his feet, but the lizard (using whatever energy it had left) lunged forward, brandishing a sickle-shaped claw at the end of its foot and stabbing Peter through the hand.

Peter screamed. Bruce had no idea what to do. The lizard's claw was stuck inside Peter's palm, and Bruce couldn't figure out a way to remove it without risking the creature attacking him as well.

"I'm . . . I'm gonna get your dad," Bruce said.

Peter's eyes filled with fear. "My dad? No! He's so far away! Help me!"

"I don't know what to do?"

"Get it off me! Get it off me!" It was clear from Peter's voice that the pain was agonizing.

Bruce glanced to his left and spotted a large rock. He picked it up and threw it at the lizard, just grazing the creatures face and landing to the left of the lizard. The lizard turned to face Bruce, hissing. Bruce wasted no time throwing a second rock, this time with enough force that it propelled the lizard off of Peter. It didn't go far, though, because its claw remained embedded in Peter's palm. Still sobbing and screaming, Peter scooped up a rock of his own and started beating his scaly attacker over the head, over and over, until the lizard finally broke loose and ran off.

"He's . . . he's gone," Bruce said, panting.

"Good!" Peter screamed. "That mother fucker!"

Bruce was startled. He had never, not even once, heard Peter use language like that before. Bruce helped him up. "You okay?"

Peter wasn't sure how to answer. His right hand was throbbing in pain; a purple and blue tinge had started to form around the spot where claw punctured skin.

"Help me get it out."

"We should get outta here first, before that thing comes back," Bruce said.

"What about my hand? If my parents see, it they'll never let us out here again. We need to think of something."

Bruce had to admit, Peter made a good point. He reached out and pulled with all of his might, removing the claw. Peter immediately put pressure on his hand to stem the flow of blood. Five smaller quills from the claw were still sticking out of him, but Peter was just relieved that the claw was gone.

"Thanks," he said between heavy breaths. A quick glance at the wound told him the purple and blue tinges were growing bigger. "What do we tell my parents?"

"Maybe a rock fell on it?" Bruce thought out loud.

"A rock? Are you kidding me? Look at this thing; looks like some Indian's spear stabbed me. No, how about . . . oh! A bee! A bee! I got stung! Simple!"

Bruce wasn't sure that this was the best choice of lies. "I dunno . . ."

"Well, why not? Look at that thing. Looks like a bee stinger, doesn't it?" Bruce looked closer. The wound was indeed starting to swell like a particularly nasty bee sting. In fact, the spot where the quills were stuck was quickly expanding into a painful, red lump.

"Bees only have one stinger. You've got a bunch in you," Bruce explained.

"Help me pull, then." Peter tried to pull at one of the quills. Pain exploded across his face. Sweat dripped from his forehead. Bruce helped as much as he could, and after a few agonizing moments, each quill had been removed. Peter gazed at one of them. It was just over an inch long, but the tips were curved. They were clearly meant to stay lodged for long periods of time in whatever prey the lizard stabbed.

"Let's go!" Peter marched off, clutching his wound, eyes bloodshot and full of tears.

Bruce took one last look at the fallen quills before hurrying to catch up.

They were halfway back to the park when Peter noticed something strange and stopped dead in his tracks. "Bruce . . . look." He held his hand up for Bruce to see.

The impossibility of what Bruce saw next (combined with the craziness he'd already witnessed that day) made him feel as though he were stuck in some damned dream. But this was real, all of it. The strange, oversized lizard had been real. It's menacing claw and sinister quills had been real. The discolored wound they'd left behind had been real.

And the fact that the wound was now miraculously healed . . . that was real too.

The bluish-purple tinge that had surrounded the stab wound was gone. Vanished. Not only had it disappeared, but it left no markings to indicate that it had ever been there at all.

Peter, of course, saw this as a blessing: it meant he wouldn't have to lie to his parents. But Bruce was a bit more skeptical. His mother was very religious and his father was a drunk. He heard a lot of tall tales in his house. This felt like one of those tall tales, too outlandish to be real and yet inarguably real at the same time.

"This is great!" Peter said with a wide smile.

Bruce tried to smile back. Peter turned his hand over and over to see if it really was gone. "Dude!" He couldn't help but laugh. "Can you believe this?"

The nervous feeling Bruce had was fading. Peter was so delighted and relieved that Bruce almost felt guilty not sharing the sentiment. Maybe, perhaps, the stab wasn't as bad as it initially seemed. Maybe the boys' fear had made them overreact. Bruce didn't have an answer. But the wound had healed. That was all that mattered.

They returned to Peter's parents shortly before sunset. Mr. and Mrs. Epsy treated them to dinner at a lovely Italian restaurant. The adults devoured cannelloni with stuffed peppers while the boys enjoyed pizza and Shirley Temples. It was—despite everything—a perfect end to a perfect day.

The following morning, they packed their bags and relaxed in the park with a few rounds of lawn bowling and Go Fish. That night, they sat side by side by the bonfire. Mr. Epsy wrapped his arm around his wife and planted a passionate kiss on her lips, which she was only too happy to return. Peter tried to catch Bruce's eye so he could make a gagging gesture with his finger, but Bruce was too busy smiling at the couple to notice.

At the crack of dawn the following day, the car was packed and Bruce and the Epsys left Hasaga. Bruce was taking many fond memories of the trip with him, and he was more than a little upset to go back to a house occupied by his argumentative parents.

Peter and Bruce rarely saw each other after that trip. Shortly after school began, Peter started to complain of bad headaches. One day in early October, his teacher sent him home after he was seen repeatedly bumping into doorways when leaving class. Less than a year after their Hasaga trip, Peter was diagnosed with a brain tumor and passed away.   Bruce was devastated. He spent hours in his room weeping at the loss of his best friend. He considered Peter a brother. They'd even made a pact to go to the same college and be roommates. Bruce had kept the events of that fateful day in Cape's Side Bay a secret from everyone. He knew the lizard, the one Peter named Barnabas, was what killed Peter. He also knew he had no way of proving it. Bruce returned to the park every summer once he became an adult, hoping (with increasing futility) to see that accursed animal again. He never did.

Until now.

Bruce stood against a tree trunk as storm clouds began to circle above him. Hillsbury had secrets, and he'd spent his entire life trying to expose them. Not for pleasure, but for closure. Whatever happened that day caused his friend's passing, of that he was sure. As far as the rest of the world was concerned, Peter Epsy died of a brain tumor. But as far as Bruce Archer was concerned . . . there was a lizard roaming Hillsbury that had a lot to answer for.

As he watched the police drain Cape's Side Bay, as he watched them tow an empty pickup truck out of the pit of swampy muck that had once been a beautiful bay full of fish, he had a feeling the time for those answers had finally come.

The mayor's fist slammed down against his desk. His eyes were filled with a rage neither Henry nor Ava had ever seen.

"I will not close down Hillsbury Park. Not this weekend!" He stood up from his chair and looked out his window. The sun was just beginning to set and clouds were moving in from the east.

Henry looked over at Ava then back at the mayor. "Mr. Mayor, with all due respect—" He was cut off immediately.

"No. With all due respect to *you* and your crew: this is a police matter now. So when the police come in here, or call me, or email me, or text me, or Snapchat me, or whatever goddamn else they can do to get my attention, I'll listen. You, Henry, are a park ranger. Your duty is to the park."

"And I'm telling you the park isn't safe!"

"Then *make* it safe." The mayor growled between his teeth. At that moment, his phone rang. He waved to Henry and Ava to leave his office so he could take the call.

Henry shut the door behind him and pulled out a pack of cigarettes.

"I can't believe that guy," Ava fumed, still unable to shake the image of that poor child in the trunk of his mother's car.

"Believe him. Tremblay worries about one thing this time of year and one thing only: reelection."

"And he thinks he'll get it with a missing boy and another kid's eyes sewn shut?"

Henry was about to answer when Tremblay opened the door. His face was pale white, almost ghostlike. He lowered his head, admitting defeat. He seemed to have a great deal of difficulty saying what he said next.

"Hillsbury Park . . . will be closed until further notice. No camper on the grounds will be allowed to leave or enter the park until further notice." He softly shut the door behind him.

Henry paused for a moment, flipping a cigarette between his fingers. "I'm gonna visit Trundle. You head over to the park. No one in or out. We're in lockdown." Ava nodded. Henry went on, "And, Ava . . . make sure my boy's okay." Ava nodded again and the two left city hall.

As Ava drove back to headquarters, she could hear and see the sirens from the police behind her. They were no doubt on their way to block any and all incoming traffic to Hillsbury Park. A park that was only an hour away from closing. A park that had reached capacity earlier that day. A park with hundreds of visitors still packing from their picnics and barbecues . . .

What a mess, she thought as the cop cars raced past her. Her thoughts drifted back to that poor boy, his eyes sewn shut, distracting her. When a deer suddenly jumped out in front of the car, Ava spun the steering wheel hard and swerved onto the shoulder. The tires screamed in protest.

After a few deep breaths, Ava exited her car and watched as the deer pranced back into the forest, completely oblivious to how close it had come to its own demise. Hillsbury didn't have many deer. In all the times she'd driven down this particular stretch of road, Ava had never seen a deer. It was more than a little unusual. *But today*, she thought, *today was the day for unusual.*

The sun beamed down on what little was left of the swamp water in Cape's Side Bay, its final push of light before the dark of night took over. A cloud was rolling in from the distance. Victor Marchman watched as trucks strolled in one by one with the equipment to drain the bay of its once luscious water. Just to his left, he saw the carnival workers setting up tents, placing tarps over their games, and preparing for the rain that the dark clouds promised to bring.

Bentley Trundle had been at the head of the draining of the bay, but he received a call on his radio and was forced to leave. Another officer took his stead, who was helping escort the divers out of the water to make way for the trucks. Huge lengths of tubing were being placed in the water. The truck that would be siphoning out the water was so monstrously loud that Victor felt bad for the campers nearby. The business of the police, the divers, or the campers were not his concern, however; he had been hired—asked—to hunt the bear responsible for this. After the discovery of the young boy, Henry Carter informed Victor that his aid would no longer be needed. The case had changed; the prime suspect went from a wild animal to a lunatic. No common citizen, hunter or not, need be involved in such a case. But Victor had a son—and morals. So if he could help find the person responsible for the gruesome mutilation of a young boy in Hillsbury, he would do so.

Rain began to slowly sprinkle down on Victor. He glanced up once at the cave before wandering off.

Bentley Trundle stood at his desk with the windows and night sky looking down on him over his shoulder. He was staring at two photographs, his eyes swelling. He tossed them down on his desk and took a seat. Then he slammed his head into the palms of his hands and began to weep.

Henry Carter entered at a frantic pace.

"Bentley!" he shouted as he made his way toward the deputy sheriff's desk. Bentley didn't move, didn't react. He simply slid the two photographs toward Henry. "Take them."

"What're these?" Henry asked.

"Take them!"

Henry slowly picked up the two pictures. When he looked at the first one, his mouth dropped open. He covered it with his free hand. The picture was of Chris Randall.

Both ears cut off. Clean cut. Henry flipped to the next picture: Mitchell Rooney. This picture was far more gruesome to look at. Two knife wounds to the cheeks, much like David Curtis, but his eyes were not sewn shut.

In Mitchell Rooney's case, it was his mouth.

"Were these the other two boys? The ones with Joel Liman and David Curtis?" Henry asked.

Bentley nodded, his face still hidden within the palms of his hands.

"I thought they were accounted for. Spent the night at the other one's house?" Bentley finally lifted his head from his palms. "The kids lied, Henry. Kids lie all the time. If you want to sneak out of your house, what do you do? You lie. Each kid told their parents they were going to the other one's house for the night. Neither parent was the wiser. It wasn't until we put two and two together that we realized what had happened. We sent one of our guys over to the Randall's—good guy with two kids of his own—and this is what he found." Bentley wiped away a tear. "No parent should have to endure this."

Henry took notice of the material used to close Mitchell's mouth and secure the wound around Chris's ears. He flipped back to Chris's picture. He looked closely at the ears. It was tough to tell, but it appeared that both ears were sewn shut as well.

"What's this?" Henry spun around the desk and shoved the pictures in front of Bentley's face. "Look. What is this?" He was pointing at the thread the assailant had used.

Bentley shook his head, "We're not entirely sure yet. We think it's some sort of copper or something."

"Copper?" Henry was in disbelief. "Copper? What sorta copper has that hue to it?"

Again, Bentley did not know what to say. "They're running tests as we speak. It's nothing I've ever seen." He was clearly devastated.

"So what happens now?" Henry asked.

"Park's closed. We begin our investigation."

"A manhunt in Hillsbury. Never thought I'd see the day."

The two sat across from each other, speechless, for what felt like an eternity before Bentley broke the ice and stood to his feet, still shaking from the pictures.

"Coffee?" he asked Henry, who nodded.

Both men knew they would be getting little to no sleep tonight. Bentley poured two cups and passed a mug over to Henry.

"I'm guessing you don't have any suspects?" Henry asked, relishing the warm feeling of the hot mug cradled in his shaking hands.

"As of now, I would say no. But, also, Henry . . . yes."

Henry looked up with renewed interest. "Not one single person—man, woman, or child—is not a suspect in this case," Bentley told him. "Not one, in all of Hillsbury, Hasaga, all surrounding counties. The problem," he sipped his coffee before continuing, "is if this was an isolated incident. If this all happened Thursday evening, well beyond the closing of the park, and the majority of campers were at their sites enjoying a late-night bonfire, the suspect could be long gone. Or, the suspect could be right here. Right now."

Henry looked at Bentley quizzically. "Bentley, if you're insinuating that I, or Ava, for that matter—"

Bentley cut him off. "No insinuating. The reality of the situation is it could be anyone. I'm hoping I can trust you."

"You can."

Bentley smiled grimly. "I was hoping you'd say that. And I hope you don't take this as an insult when I tell you that I can't. I can't trust you as much as you can't trust me."

Henry understood what Bentley was saying. But he still didn't like it. He got to his feet. "I'd better get back to the park."

Bentley stared into the depths of his black coffee. "Good luck, Henry."

Henry nodded. "You too." And he left the office.

As soon as Henry was out of sight, Bentley threw his coffee mug as hard as he could against the wall. His diploma wobbled on its nail, and a photo of him with his wife fell off the wall entirely, meeting a messy end on the coffee-stained floor.

Jeffrey and Morgan sat in the rangers' headquarters, waiting. Headlights seen through the window got Jeffrey's attention. He nudged Morgan and they both stood.

At Henry's behest, Morgan had phoned his family and asked them to pick up him and Jeffrey, to get them away from the park before things got messy. The boys ran up to the car; neither could wait to get home after the emotional day they'd had. As they approached, the passenger window rolled down slowly, revealing that Morgan's parents had not come at all. Instead, it was Claudia behind the wheel.

Jeffrey couldn't help but smile. There she was, the girl he'd been waiting all summer to see. The stress of the morning's events made him realize just how much he'd missed her.

"You want shotgun?" Morgan asked with a sly wink.

Jeffrey was too mesmerized to realize this was a rhetorical question. He blurted out, "Yes," a little faster and louder than he'd intended. Morgan just chuckled and took a seat in the back.

Claudia unlocked the passenger door. Jeffrey gripped the handle tight and opened it. He jumped in beside her. "You look taller," she observed.

His heart leaped into his throat. He could feel himself turning bright red.

"Yeah. Maybe. I dunno," he said in what he hoped was a suave and confident voice. Unnoticed by either of them, Morgan rolled his eyes in the back seat.

Claudia shifted the car into gear and drove off. She so rarely got the opportunity to take the reins of the family vehicle, so she was clearly determined to enjoy every second of it. She cranked the volume dial on the radio. A sugary pop song was playing, and she reacted to it with an excited squeak. "I hate to admit it, 'cause I don't like being a fangirl. But I. Just. Love. This. SONG. Is that bad?" She giggled.

"It's bad if *we* have to hear it," Morgan grunted.

Jeffrey didn't care. He could barely hear the music over the sound of his mind swirling with thoughts of Claudia: of their future together, of their life after the car ride, of how they would totally (probably) live happily ever after. He could eventually take over as park ranger from his father. It wasn't his ideal job, but frankly, that wouldn't matter if he got to marry Claudia. Then the grim, terrifying realization struck that, in order to make any of these fantasies a reality, he would probably have to get around to *speaking* to her at some point.

He turned his head to address Claudia and found himself staring at an exceptional number of police cruisers speeding down the road toward them.

Claudia pulled the car over to collect her thoughts. "What the hell is this?" she asked.

"You don't know?" said Morgan. "It's been a messed-up day. Joel Liman went missing."

"Joel Liman?" Claudia looked astounded. "Are you serious? He's missing?" Morgan nodded solemnly. Claudia bit down on her lower lip. "I remember babysitting him, like, three years ago. He . . . he was a good kid. Do you think all these cops are here because they found him?"

"Highly doubt it. There's been no sign of him anywhere."

"Just the other boy." Jeffrey spoke at last.

Claudia whirled to look at him, her voice somber and soft. "What other boy?"

"David Curtis."

"Holy shit, he went missing too?"

"Not sure," said Morgan. All we know is that his mother brought him in, and something was . . . wrong with him, I guess. That's when Jeffrey's dad told us to call for a ride. Which took you long enough, by the way."

"Yeah, well, I was out with Bobby."

"Bobby? Bobby who?"

"Bobby Rengard."

"Who the hell is Bobby Rengard?"

"My boyfriend."

"You don't have a boyfriend!"

She didn't. Morgan had said he was *sure* that she didn't. Unless of course it was someone she met at camp. Jeffrey was suddenly overcome with a very queasy feeling.

"We just started going out," Claudia snapped back at her brother.

Unknown to Claudia, a police officer pulled off the road behind her. The officer approached her car and knocked on the window. Claudia was reluctant to lower it because of the rain but ultimately did so.

"Yes?" she asked, still a bit perturbed at her brother.

"We have to ask you to turn around, miss."

"What for?" she asked.

The officer flashed his light around the interior of the car. He held it for a moment on each of the boy's faces.

"Who're these two?" he questioned.

"The one in the back's my annoying brother and this is his friend. They work at the park. I'm just driving them home."

"Not anymore, you're not," the officer stated.

"You serious?"

"'Fraid so. If you could turn around, please, Officer Brennan will escort you back to the ranger office." He turned off his flashlight and walked away.

Without saying a word, Claudia started her car and spun it around. She followed the police cruiser back to the ranger office. They came to a stop in the parking lot and sat there, in silence, wondering what on earth to expect next. Morgan was blinking rapidly, trying to figure out why the police wouldn't let them get to safety.

Officer Brennan eventually approached the car and asked them to step out. He escorted Claudia and the boys inside. Jeffrey noticed Ava entering to his left from the side door with three small children at her side. Behind her came a veritable procession of dozens: men, women, children, dogs, anyone who was visiting the park that day and had yet to leave was entering the rangers' headquarters.

Jeffrey approached Ava. "What's going on?"

Ava just shook her head. "Not now." She continued leading the visitors into headquarters.

Not now? Jeffrey thought. *Then when?*

Police cruisers pulled up onto the various trails in Hillsbury Park, blocking any and all entrances. The campers were all in a state of panic. Henry drove his Jeep right up to a cruiser. He slammed his door furiously and walked up to the officer on duty.

"Just what in the hell is going on here?" he demanded.

"Forming a blockade. No one in or out."

"But coming this close to the sites? You're gonna cause a panic!"

The officer had nothing to say after that. Henry marched into the campground and walked around the sites. Families approached, asking him what was going on. He explained the Amber Alert for the missing child and how Joel had yet to be found. He assured them that everything would be all right soon.

"Just stay in your sites, get some rest. Everything is going to be fine." He had to repeat the words so often that by the time he reached the end of the campsites, he had them committed to memory.

All lies, he thought. Or maybe not. He wasn't sure of most things anymore. But one thing he did know: all of these campers would be issued refunds. The mayor was not going to be happy with that little piece of information. Henry looked up at the sky. Darkness was setting in. He had a long night ahead of him. Better get back to headquarters. He could only imagine the chaos ensuing over there.

FRIDAY NIGHT

The rain let up as quickly as it had started. Clouds were moving rapidly, pulling back like wispy curtains to reveal the beauty of the stars behind them. The tarps covering the carnival stands were puddled with water. It had rained a large amount in a short period of time, a kind of storm much more at home in the tropics than in Hillsbury. The only water flowing in Cape's Side Bay now was runoff from the rain. A tow truck had loaded the dripping pickup and driven it off, and the last group of divers had returned to their desks to submit their reports.

Victor Marchman took this opportunity to walk down inside the bay and make his way over to the cave high above. Three inches of rainwater met his feet at the bay's bottom. Every few steps he heard a crackling sound. He stopped and reached down into the shallow water, feeling around for several seconds until his fingers touched something that was neither rock nor dirt. He lifted it up and stared at it.

It was a piece of an eggshell.

Unusual, he thought, though there *had* been a whole pickup truck down here. Maybe the egg had come from the truck? A local chicken farmer who took a wrong turn, perhaps? He dropped the eggshell back into the water and continued his hike in the bowels of Cape's Side Bay.

As Victor reached the edge of the bay where the cave loomed above, he removed his backpack. Initially he had not intended to bring his climbing gear, but after Henry described the layout of the area, he knew he would be foolish to not investigate the cave first. As he unpacked his gear, memories of when he first taught Tyson to climb raced through his head.

"You want to properly inspect each piece of equipment before you use it. Got it? Everything you bring with you is valuable to your safety. These aren't the walls in a gymnasium; this is nature. It's fierce and shows no mercy. Understand?"

Young Tyson looked up at his father and nodded.

"Yup, got it!"

"Good, let's get inspecting!"

"Yay!

Victor removed a rope from his pack.

"Can you tell me what type of rope this is?"

Tyson placed his finger against his lips and thought for a moment.

"Um, Kermit. It's Kermit."

Victor chuckled. "Not quite. We're not climbing a rope made of puppets. It's kernmantle."

Tyson nodded. "Kernmantle, yeah, yeah."

Tyson was only eleven. Victor knew he would soon want to join him on his hunts and climbs, but his mother would never allow it. Still, to whet the kid's appetite for such things, Victor figured he might as well teach him some of the ins and outs. He moved the rope over to the side.

"Rope looks good. What's next?"

"Hooks!" Tyson blurted out.

Victor smiled. "They're called carabiners."

He pulled the carabiner out. Tyson stared at it.

"But it looks just like a hook! Isn't it a hook?"

"Not quite. Well, sort of. Do you know how many types of hooks there are?"

Once again, Tyson rested his finger against his lips and thought. This one was trickier. Tyson could not think of the answer, so he shook his head.

"Two," Victor explained. "There are two types. You have your locking . . ." He displayed one to his son, then the other. "And you have your non-locking. Each one as important as the other, each with a specific purpose. You must understand the purpose to successfully use each tool. Make sense?"

It did. Tyson just didn't know when to use either.

"Now, what else? What are we missing?"

"The vest . . . Harnest!"

Victor laughed again. "HarneSS, not HarneST. But good, yeah, the harness for sure." Victor tousled his boy's hair and retrieved the item in question, holding it out to Tyson. "Wanna try it on?"

Tyson nodded. He grabbed the harness from his father and began wriggling into it.

"Okay, slow down, slow down." Victor crawled over and helped his son. "First, gotta get it around your pelvis like this." Victor secured the harness around his son's pelvis. "Then we get it up over your hips like so."

"I think it's too big." Tyson frowned.

"Well, of course it is! This is my harness; I'm bigger than you. One day when you come with me, we'll get you your own harness that'll fit proper. For now, I'm just showing you."

Tyson smiled. He couldn't wait for the day he'd get to go climbing with his father.

Victor was now halfway up the cliff. He had yet to take Tyson climbing; heck, it was only earlier that day he had taken his son out to hunt for the first time. He was a busy man. Maybe too busy lately. He worked in construction and made a good amount of money, but the hours were draining. He'd looked forward to his summer in Hasaga this year more than ever: to relaxing, to hunting, to enjoying the lawn bowling tournament. *Maybe this year, someone else might actually win besides Mrs. Wilson*, he thought with a smile. She was a nice lady, but he was getting really tired of seeing her take home the trophy every single year. He even looked forward to the barbecue, regardless of how he felt about Dean's cheating.

Deer would be a mighty fine treat right now, Victor thought.

He entered the cave, having no idea what to expect in there. No one (no one on record, at least) had ever ventured into that cave. Scaling that rock wall was not some prized adventure like a trek up the Himalayas. It was just a simple, everyday cliff face, a little over two hundred feet up. The park and surrounding woods had always provided more than enough mystery or adventure for Hillsbury thrill-seekers, leaving the cave—in the grand scheme of things—largely forgotten.

Victor removed a flashlight from his belt and pointed it into the blackness. It was dark, frigid, and dry. Dry for a cave, dry for a desert. There was not a trace of dampness about the place. As Victor touched the walls, sand and grit chipped off with as much ease as cracked stucco.

Unusual, he thought. He removed his harness and secured it between a rock and the wall until he'd need it for the descent. On his belt, he holstered an additional flashlight and a gun.

Can't be too cautious.

Victor plunged into the belly of the cave.

Henry shut the door of his office behind him. Ava was sitting in the chair reserved for guests, looking more than a little concerned. "What'd you find out at Trundle's?" she asked.

Henry walked over to his desk and took a seat. "More questions. The other boys have been accounted for. Mitchell and Chris." A sigh of relief escaped Ava's lips, but Henry shook his head. "It's bad, Ava. Real bad."

"What do you mean?"

"I mean, what you saw in Vera's trunk wasn't an isolated incident." Tears welled up in Ava's eyes; she covered her mouth in horror. Henry slid a box of tissues over to her. Henry tried to continue, startled at how much his own voice shook. "The, uh . . . the Mitchell kid had his mouth . . . sewn, and the other boy, Chris . . ." The word *Chris* came out weak and cracked. Henry cleared his throat and tried again, much more carefully. "They took his ears, Ava. Someone out there is doing this to local boys."

Ava was speechless. They sat there for a while, across from each other, neither saying a word until the phone rang.

"Excuse me." Henry reached to answer it but then turned back to Ava. "You can stay here if you'd like. You don't have to go out there with those people. But Ava, what I just told you is confidential." Ava nodded, understanding, and exited the office.

Henry put the receiver to his ear. "Hello?"

Ava closed the door quietly. She took a seat next to the water cooler, avoiding eye contact. Jeffrey noticed the distraught look on her face, so he made his way over to her, busying himself at the water cooler so that he too wouldn't have to look her in the eye.

"Everything all right?" Jeffrey asked. Ava looked uncomfortable, unable (or unwilling) to say much. She simply shrugged.

"Well, if you need to talk, I'll be over there getting my heart broken." Jeffrey sauntered off.

Ava watched as he walked over to Claudia and took a seat next to her, offering her his water. Without hesitation, she took it and drank the cup dry.

A second later, Henry burst out of his office and left the headquarters. Jeffrey and Ava finally locked eyes, exchanging quizzical expressions.

Henry's foot sank into the deep mud outside the headquarters. The rain had only let up an hour ago, and everything was still squishy and unpleasant. He made his way over to where a tow truck was parked. The driver was waiting for him, accompanied by a police officer.

"Mr. Carter?" the officer asked.

"That's me," Henry said.

"Follow me, sir."

The truck driver marched his way to the back of the truck, revealing what he'd towed. Henry's jaw dropped. He couldn't believe what he was seeing.

A blue pickup truck. But not just any blue pickup truck. The very same truck his sister and her girlfriend had gone missing in. The plates were a match. The interior was exactly as he'd remembered it.

"I assume you recognize the vehicle?" the officer asked.

"I do. I do." Henry was in tears.

"Any idea why we'd find it in the bay?"

Henry looked up at the officer. He could feel his knees shaking and was suddenly aware of just how much energy it was taking to keep himself upright. "What? What do you mean?"

"The bay, Mr. Carter. That's where we found it."

"What on earth was it doing there?" Henry asked.

"Well," the officer started, staring deep into Henry Carter's eyes, "we were kinda hoping you'd be able to tell us that, sir."

The moonlight shining down on Hillsbury was more vibrant than the fluorescent lights of Las Vegas. The town was silent; the lights in the homes were shut off. While Henry and Bentley tried to keep the news of the day quiet, word was beginning to spread around town. Festival or not, some families did not wish to be in Hillsbury during these dark times.

Most visiting families had opted to stay. They spent good money on their cottages and had alarm systems in place to keep them safe. They would show no fear to whoever was responsible for the terrible crimes. Most of them fell into the trap of believing that nothing so tragic as the fate of Joel Liman's friends could ever happen to *them*.

Bentley had locked up his office for the night and had just arrived at his house. The Trundle's home was a very old house that had been in the family for four generations. Bentley's father had started renovating it twenty years back, but he died before he could complete the work, which left Bentley and his family with a house that changed from bright and modern to positively archaic from one room to the next. Aside from building a small dock at the edge of the property, Bentley had never had time to finish the work his father started. He and his wife had had many long, late-night conversations regarding the fate of their mismatched house. Now, as he stepped out onto the driveway and stared up at its quiet façade, Bentley found himself wishing tonight could be just another regular night. He wished he could sit and chat with Elise about finally replacing the old windows in the guest bedroom, or changing the dining room's severely outdated floral wallpaper. As aimless as those conversations ended up being—and as few results as they tended to yield—Bentley would rather have a hundred more of those than have to sit down and recount to her what he'd seen in Hillsbury tonight.

Thankfully, Elise was already fast asleep when Bentley entered, lying on the couch with an open book spread across her stomach. Bentley had no intention of waking her; he turned the lights off and closed the door as quietly as he could. He was carrying a bag of wine bottles that he had bought earlier in the day, before all the craziness had started. The original plan had been to come home at a normal, decent hour and spend the evening enjoying the wine with his wife.

Life finds a way to ruin our plans. He thought of his father's words. Gerald Trundle was never much of a wordsmith, but he did spout a few dour gems every now and then.

Bentley set a wine bottle down on the dining room table. He walked into his kitchen and cracked open a beer, leaning against the counter as he drank. He needed this moment. A rest, a beat, something to take his mind off the horrid mutilations of those three boys. And what could possibly have happened to the Liman kid? He shuddered at the thought.

The kitchen was suddenly flooded with light, temporarily blinding Bentley. He jumped and spun around to see Elise, messy hair, half-awake, standing by the light switch.

"Welcome home." She smiled drowsily at her husband.

"Finally." He chugged his beer back.

He had kept Elise mostly in the loop throughout the day, but he had spared her the gory details about the way the boys were found.

"Anything turn up?" she asked. "About the boy?"

Bentley sipped his beer and shook his head. He understood her curiosity, but he just couldn't bring himself to recount it all out loud. "FBI should be in by sunrise. Then it'll be out of my hands." Elise walked over and rubbed his shoulders. "Frankly, I'll be glad. It's tough, Elise. It's real tough."

Elise glanced into the dining room and noticed a bottle of wine. "What"s that?" Without waiting for a response, Elise crossed into the dining room and picked it up.

Bentley placed his beer on the counter and walked over to her. "I bought it . . . for us to drink, but . . ."

"But everything that happened today kind of killed the mood, huh?" she finished for him.

He lowered his head in acknowledgment. He'd had every intention of drinking that wine with her on the couch, watching one of those horrible romantic comedies she liked, but how could he now? "It hasn't been easy."

"Wanna just go to bed?" she offered.

He nodded. Elise wrapped her arm around her husband and led him to the stairway, shutting off the lights behind her.

Not one individual locked up in the rangers' headquarters was happy about it, but nobody made a fuss. They all understood the severity of the situation and wanted to stay clear and allow the police to search Hillsbury Park high and low until Joel Liman was found. The truth, of course, was that they were all being questioned, and the police were searching for a kidnapper. Every camper crammed in that small building was a potential suspect.

Jeffrey, Morgan, and Claudia all sat close to the front entrance. They would be the last people interviewed by police. Not that it mattered; once interviewed, they were still expected to sit and wait.

"I gotta pee. Think they'll let us piss?" Morgan asked. Claudia rolled her eyes at her brother.

"I'd imagine so, yeah," Jeffrey answered.

Morgan jumped out of his seat and waddled toward the bathroom. Jeffry noticed a police officer stop Morgan halfway down the hall. He appeared to ask Morgan a couple of yes-or-no questions before allowing him to use the restroom. Jeffrey looked at Claudia, who was playing a game on her cell phone.

"I don't think you're supposed to be on that thing," he told her.

"Well, until they tell me to put it away, I'll do what I want."

Moments later, as if on cue, an officer sauntered over and told Claudia to put her phone away. She stuffed the phone into her purse and gave Jeffrey a devastatingly angry stare, as if getting caught was somehow his fault.

"Don't look at me." Jeffrey had no interest in taking the blame for her mistake.

"Whatever," she growled. "What do you think's going on?"

"You don't know?" he asked, surprised. "Joel Liman went missing last night. Remember?"

"Yeah, but you said you were looking for him all day. Why all this now? Why so late?"

She had a point. It didn't make sense that the police would show up just before closing, secure all the visitors in an isolated room, and question them. This should have been done during the day. There was more to this story, more than Jeffrey's father was willing to tell him. Jeffrey shrugged at Claudia. He didn't have an answer and didn't feel like making one up. Claudia glanced around the hallway, eagerness rushing through her blood. She looked down at Jeffrey, who was slouched in his chair, the tips of his fingers bridged together. He was visibly tired.

"You know this park better than these cops do, right?" she asked.

He blinked. "Why?"

"I'm thinking you'd probably have a better shot at finding that boy than the police."

She wasn't right because there was something more at play here, though he had no clue as to what. "Not necessarily. Ava over there"—he pointed to the assistant park ranger, who was helping a young girl purchase a bag of chips from the vending machine—"she and my dad, they know the park better than anyone. And if they couldn't find him . . ." He cut himself off.

"Then what?"

"Then he's not out there and the cops are looking for something else."

Claudia stared deep into Jeffrey's eyes. "But what is it?"

"More like who," Jeffrey said.

"Oh!"

Claudia finally understood. They sat in awkward silence for a bit. The thought of a kidnapper or murderer running around their neck of the woods was enough to make anyone's skin crawl. Her family had been living in Hillsbury their entire lives, and they'd rarely (if ever) been subjected to violence, let alone a kidnapping or a murder.

Jeffrey studied Claudia's face: the perfectly lush lips, the rosy red cheeks, the shine in her bright blue eyes. "So . . ." he started, but then stopped just as quickly.

She looked lost in her own worried thoughts but then came snapping back to reality. "So, *what?*"

"So, you have a boyfriend?"

She hummed and nodded in response. His stomach was uneasy.

"It's nothing serious. Maybe it is, I dunno. Who can tell? We're both so young." Not exactly what Jeffrey wanted to hear. "Why do you ask?" Her eyes pierced him, as if willing him to respond with, *I'm in love with you.*

Instead, he mustered up some courage and threw the girl of his dreams a curveball. "There's someone I like. I just—I just don't know how to ask her out. Or how to tell if she even likes me."

"She probably doesn't. If you can't tell whether or not she likes you, she probably doesn't. I'm not trying to be mean about it. It just is what it is. If she liked you, you'd know it."

Jeffrey sank lower in his chair. Morgan marched his way back and took his seat. "Lineup's huge! If you gotta go, I'd suggest going now."

Eager to get away from Claudia for a bit, Jeffrey got up and headed toward the restroom. He walked past Ava, who grabbed his arm. "Have you heard from your father?" she asked with a worried expression.

Jeffrey shook his head. "Not since earlier, when he rushed out."

"Me neither."

Ava bit her lip. "If you hear anything, let me know, okay?"

Jeffrey nodded. "Of course."

Bentley lay in bed, wide-awake, next to his wife. He watched over her as she lay sound asleep. Silent. Peaceful. He wished it could be that easy for him. He found himself tossing and turning, one minute too hot, the next too cold. Nothing felt quite right. His head was spinning with thoughts of those boys. And Joel Liman was still out there, still missing. He began questioning his job, his capabilities in being efficient within it. Maybe he was never meant to be a cop. Maybe Walden had never stepped aside and promoted Bentley because maybe Walden knew he wasn't the right man for the job? Maybe it was time he and Elise left Hillsbury and started life anew somewhere else, somewhere distant?

Visions of Ava entered his thoughts. He couldn't shake her beauty, her hair, her lips. Those big beautiful eyes of hers . . . his heart sank within the bowels of his stomach at the thought. He felt like a teenager, observing his crush walk by, unable to do anything but watch her pass.

She was bewitching.

He rolled over, facing away from his wife, too guilty to lay beside her while thoughts of another woman swam through his mind. He stared at the window. The curtains were open, letting the moonlight in.

The moonlight . . .

His thoughts shifted gears yet again. The moon was so bright and vibrant, like he had never seen it before. It was a beautiful sight. *Almost too beautiful,* he thought. But was it just him, or was the moonlight getting brighter by the minute?

The heavenly body hovered atop the lake behind their house. It was common for the light to shine down and cause a radiant reflection on the calm waters, but this was different. This grew at an abnormal rate. It appeared to an overtired Bentley that the moon was getting bigger.

Not possible, he convinced himself, rubbing his bloodshot eyes. *It can't be growing.* No, not growing. Upon further inspection by the deputy sheriff, he surmised that the moon was not in fact growing, but rather getting closer. His eyes squinted at the image bursting through the bedroom curtains. He looked at his wife, still asleep, still silent, still at peace.

The room was now covered in moonlight; Bentley threw on his slippers and made his way down the stairs. He scurried to the back door and opened it quickly. He burst outside and stared up, straight up at . . . a typical moon. A typical moon on a typical night, hovering above the typical lake. Nothing unusual about it.

Maybe it had just been an illusion, a trick of the light caused by the moon glistening over the lake water. Bentley stood there in the heat of the deep, quiet night, feeling like a fool.

A penance, he thought. A penance for thinking of another woman while lying in bed with his wife, the true love of his life. He quietly closed the door behind him; tiptoed up the stairs back into his bedroom, removed his slippers, lay in bed, and wrapped his arms around Elise.

The clouds had dissipated in Hillsbury by now. It was a beautiful clear night. The day's harrowing events notwithstanding, it was one of the most beautiful nights the town had seen that summer.

Henry could not see the night sky. He was sitting in a room he had never visited: an interrogation room. A middle-aged man entered the room with a briefcase in hand. He said nothing, only placed his briefcase on the table in front of Henry and opened it. He removed several photographs and spread them across the table. Five photographs, all of Jill's pickup truck, the one found at the bottom of the bay earlier that evening. Henry looked up at the man; he was a member of the Federal Bureau of Investigation.

They got here earlier than Bentley expected, Henry thought.

"Do you recognize these pictures?"

The man finally spoke, his voice raspy and deep. He punctuated the sentence with a yawn, a not-too-subtle indication that he did not enjoy having to question some small-town park ranger in the dead of night. Henry ignored his rudeness and looked at the pictures. They were of the truck's exterior, interior, rear, front, and a duffel bag.

"Sort of."

"Sort of?" The agent scoffed. "Either you do or you don't. It's simple, Mr. Carter."

It wasn't that simple, Henry thought. He knew the truck, obviously. He wasn't too sure about the bag, though. And he hadn't seen the pictures before at all. The truck looked new, not a dent on it, unusual for something found under ten feet of water.

"I recognize the truck. The bag, I haven't a clue."

"But you know the truck?"

"Looks like my sister's. Though I'm not entirely sure how it could possibly be hers. She's been missing for—"

The agent cut him off. "Seven years."

"Yes, that's right." Henry voice was soft.

"And you don't know how it ended up at the bottom of the bay? The bay you're the ranger for?"

Was Henry being accused of something? He already had this conversation with Bentley. He shook his head. "Doesn't make any sense to me."

The agent closed his briefcase with a quiet click. "Doesn't make any to me either." Then he exited the room without another word, leaving Henry alone with no answers and a table of photographs of his missing sister's truck.

After what felt like an eternity of waiting, it was time for Jeffrey, Morgan, and Claudia to be interrogated.

They were taken into Henry's office, the door locked behind them and guarded by one officer, and the blinds drawn shut. Officer Dingwell sat in Henry's chair and told the three

teenagers to take a seat across from him. Dingwell's hair was
thinning; the stubble on his chin, while thin, was from not
having shaved for an entire week. He stunk of salami and
olives. He was Trundle's most trusted officer, hence his presence. Trundle would have been there himself, but he was simply too tired. It was now nearly two in the morning; Dingwell
and the other officers wanted to get this night over with sooner
rather than later. The three teens were the last to be questioned.

"So. . ." Dingwell took a deep, phlegmy breath. "What
were y'all doing at the park?"

The three teens answered at the same time, each saying
something different. Dingwell raised his right hand to stop
them. "We'll start with the lady."

Claudia smiled at the mild compliment. "I just came to
pick up these two."

"So you haven't been in the park?" Claudia shook her head.
"Where have you been all day?" He leaned back in Henry's
chair as far as he could and crossed his arms. He meant to come
across as intimidating, but the teenagers thought he looked like
a goof.

"I . . ."

As Claudia began her alibi, Jeffrey's heart sank. He had
already heard of her adventures with Bobby Rengard, and he
had no interest in hearing them again.

"I was at home with my mother. We were baking. She was
teaching me to bake."

Jeffrey's eyes lit up. No Bobby Rengard. No date. Was it all
a lie? Or perhaps she was telling the officer a fib?

Dingwell gave the girl a stern look. "So if I call your mother,
she'll tell me the same?"

Claudia nodded. "The very."

Dingwell picked up his pen and scribbled something down
on his notepad, then his eyes shifted to Morgan.

Now, Morgan was a very easily intimidated person. Having to converse with a police officer (or a parent, or any member of authority or the opposite sex) made him uneasy and nervous. Dingwell immediately recognized Morgan as the weak link, and if he were ever to get any sort of information out of these three, Morgan would probably be the easiest one from which to extract it. The officer locked eyes with Morgan. A lump immediately grew in the teenager's throat, goose bumps forming on his arms, butterflies blossoming from the cocoon of his stomach. He could feel sweat coursing from his armpits.

"And what were you doing at the park today?" Dingwell said with an excruciating smile.

Morgan somehow gathered up the courage to speak to the officer. "Working, sir."

Working? Dingwell thought. He flipped through a pile of papers. "What's your name, son?" His tone had softened.

"Morgan Burton, sir."

Again with the sir, Jeffrey thought.

"And you?" Dingwell turned to Jeffrey.

Jeffrey had expected this to be intimidating for him as well. But now that Dingwell's eyes were on him, now that *he* was in the hot seat, Jeffrey realized he had nothing to fear. He was a junior ranger at Hillsbury. He had been all summer long. And he was completely, and utterly, innocent.

"Same, sir. Working."

Dingwell leaned back into his chair. "I meant your name, young man. I kinda had a feeling you were working, didn't think you'd dress like that for fun.'"

"Jeffrey Carter."

"Jeffrey Carter?" Dingwell nodded as he read their names off a piece of paper. The paper itself was a list of staff members working in the park that day. The two boys checked out, but Dingwell wasn't done yet. "So, we have here Morgan Burton and Jeffrey Carter?" he stated. When this elicited another nod, Dingwell fixed his attention on Claudia. "I'm going to ask you to leave. Go straight home, say nothing. You don't belong here. You may go."

Claudia was just as confused as the others, but she did as she was told and got up. Just before she opened the door, she turned to Morgan. "What should I tell Mum?"

"You can tell her he'll be home shortly, no worries," Dingwell promised. Claudia muttered a quick goodbye to the boys and left.

Dingwell stood from Henry's chair and walked over to the side of the desk closest to Jeffrey. Perching there, he wet his lips and fixed the boys with another demand.

"Tell me what you know about Bruce Archer."

A leaf, already teasing the sight of fall with a red hue upon it, escaped from a branch high above the grounds of Hillsbury Park and softly made its way fifty feet down to the dirt path below. Bruce Archer stepped over the leaf, leaving a muddy trail behind him.

Something evil lurked deep within this park. Whatever it was had lain low throughout the years but was now ready to reveal itself. Bruce regularly attended Hillsbury Park during the summer, always a camper—rarely for fun—to find the lizard he discovered as a child with his late friend Peter Epsy. He had always been weary of traveling to the park alone, for if he ever came in contact with the lizard again, he would most certainly need assistance killing it. And so, he would gather four or five of his biggest friends: nasty, confrontational folks whom he nevertheless trusted with his life. None of them, however, knew his secret. They only knew Bruce invited them camping once a year, typically at the end of summer for the long weekend. These trips always ended up being a good time, mostly by accident. At some points—some microscopic, fleeting points—Bruce would get so caught up in enjoying himself that he'd momentarily forget the true purpose of these getaways. Never once had they sighted anything even close to the lizard in Hillsbury Park. Until today. Until the claw.

That claw . . . the color, the texture, the shape, the quills. Those horribly unapologetic quills, the ones that hooked into your skin and wouldn't let go without a considerable amount of pain. Peter's agonizing cry haunted Bruce. Perhaps he should have spoken up and made his knowledge of the claw's origin known to Ava or Henry? No. Better not. At best, he would be branded a fool. At worst, a suspect.

A few hours ago, Bruce left his friends at the camp-site without even bothering to say where he was going. His friends became curious when he didn't return after a while and informed the rangers that Bruce was missing (a fact to which he was oblivious).

The park was eerily quiet: no birds, no wind brushing against the leaves, only silence. He held on to the grip of his boot knife tightly. The knife had belonged to his father, one of the few things he kept after his passing. The blade was approx-imately five inches long. The grip over the years had begun wearing thin, and so Bruce would wrap it almost annually with paracord. It wasn't a particularly sharp knife; mostly he kept it around as a deterrent to anyone who might give him any trou-ble. If Bruce ever had the opportunity to use it on the lizard, he was not even sure it would be able to pierce its scaly skin.

He sat under a large oak tree and waited. He was certain he was in the spot he visited all those years ago, and he was certain the creature would return. With all of the commotion from earlier the park was quiet and still. He knew if he went in alone, he himself could find the beast and end its reign of terror once and for all. He looked up at the night sky. Beautiful, clear, the complete opposite of the night before . . .

Last night, he thought, spitting the words out like poison. If only he'd gone out, perhaps that boy wouldn't be missing. Perhaps Bruce could have stopped the beast before it struck. A chill of guilt flooded his veins. He continued to sit under the shelter of a carnival tarp he'd stolen. A man and his knife, in the dead of night, waiting.

Bruce's eyes grew heavy, the lids opening and shutting; the speed at which they would do so grew increasingly slower until his mind shifted from thoughts to fantasy, and he fell asleep.

His rest would last only a moment before he was awoken by a rustling coming from the west of the park, in the direction of Cape's Side Bay. He sat up and gripped the knife in his right hand. The sound got increasingly louder. His eyes focused. Years of anticipation came to a boil. He'd dreamed out it for decades: him, saving Hillsbury and Cape's Side Bay from the lizard. He always imaged it would take a team of many, but now he'd be doing it alone. Whether he thought he could or not.

Suddenly, he heaerd another sound, this time from the opposite direction. He turned his head, then turned back to look where the original sound had come from. What was this trickery? He braced himself, squatting, ready to pounce, knife firmly wrapped in his hand, eyes fixated on the trees to his right and left. The noises grew louder and louder, then they abruptly stopped.

He braced himself but found himself unprepared as a barrage of police officers swarmed him. He was tackled from behind and flung to the ground.

The next thing Bruce Archer knew, he was being read his rights, handcuffed, and herded into the back of a police cruiser.

SATURDAY MORNING

EXACTLY ONE HUNDRED and eleven miles northeast of Hillsbury was a town called Tuncton. Population: sixty-two hundred. Few—if any—tourists visited this small town. Tuncton was sort of an empty space that gradually morphed into a town over the ages. Once a place to bury the dead during some long-forgotten war, tombstones were staggered throughout Tuncton in no specific manner.

It had two fascinating landmarks. The first was Rainbow Bridge Road; an old wooden drawbridge that rested high above churning waters, waters that made their way to Hillsbury Park and (at one point) Cape's Side Bay. The bridge was painted in bright vibrant colors by an unknown graffiti artist with considerable talent. The paint brought some much-needed life to the town, but no one admitted to being the artist. Rumors circulated that the work was indeed that of professionals hired by the mayor in an effort to draw tourism, a fact the mayor regularly denied. The road for one mile on each side of the bridge was subsequently painted to raise money for charity. Thus, Rainbow Bridge Road was born.

The second landmark was the gas station, owned and operated by the McKelvie family since the dawn of the twentieth century. The gas station itself began as a corner store, before Donovan McKelvie renovated and upgraded it to a gas station in the sixties. The station was handed to each first-born male in the McKelvie line . . . until the late seventies, when Archie McKelvie and his wife had three daughters: Monica, Sandra, and Estelle. Monica was given the gas station, much to the chagrin of the other McKelvie family members, most notably Warren Hudson.

Warren's mother was Archie's younger sister, which meant that even though he was the next male heir in line to acquire the gas station, Warren had been robbed of his inheritance. He surmised that since Archie did not bear a male child, the gas station should have been left to him (and, subsequently, his new son, Warren Jr.). Archie refused. The courts backed his decision, despite Warren's legal protests.

Monica was a whole other story. While respecting the gas station and what it meant to her family, she wasn't in love with the idea of living and working in Tuncton for the rest of her life. Estelle, on the other hand, had developed a fondness for it after spending the majority of her childhood there. Monica posed the idea to her father about giving the gas station to Estelle instead. After some brief hesitation, Archie allowed Estelle to take possession.

This act sent waves throughout the Hudson household. Warren took it as a direct insult and a slap to the face. This led to a fateful evening when Warren Hudson left his wife and kids in the middle of the night, visited the closed gas station, and filled two jerry cans to the brim with gasoline. If he couldn't have the place, nobody could. Anger clouding his vision, Warren set the station ablaze.

The next morning, a devastated Archie and Estelle sat on the gravel and watched as firefighters quenched the final bit of flame from their beloved family business. The most precious place in Estelle's life was literally up in smoke.

After a swift investigation, crime scene data led them to the truth behind the matter. The tire tracks used to gain access to the gas station matched those on Warren's car. His footprints were also found at the scene. Warren was given prison time and a hefty fine, along with a restraining order that forbade him from being any closer than two hundred miles from the gas station. Once Warren was eventually released, the humiliated Hudsons left Tuncton and never returned.

Over time, the gas station was rebuilt with a fresh, new design. Thanks to Estelle, it also served fresh coffee and baked pastries every morning. It became a favorite stop for passing truckers and campers. Estelle had done a fine job of breathing new life into an old business, and Archie, on his deathbed, told her how immensely proud he was of the work she'd put into it.

That was all she'd ever wanted.

Estelle didn't marry until she was in her forties and never had kids of her own. Her sister, Sandra, though, had three boys; her middle child, Steve, was very enthusiastic to learn the ropes of McKelvie Gas and Corner Store. So Estelle spent weekends teaching him, until he was good enough to be left on his own for entire shifts. The two of them rotated days, taking it in turns to uphold a family business they were immensely proud of.

It was during one of Steve's shifts when a most curious thing happened.

Saturday morning of the long Labor Day weekend was always slow for the gas station. Since tourists rarely came in either direction over the weekend (and Tuncton was far from civilization) their Saturday clientele was limited mostly to truckers. Steve leaned against the counter in the gas station just before sunrise, prepared for a slow, quiet day. The roads were empty. The odd car or two had passed Friday morning, but none stopped for gas. Probably people who had taken a wrong turn somewhere and had no idea where they were.

Steve sat, half-asleep, filling up on Estelle's hot brewed coffee to keep at least one eye open. Which might explain why, at first, he couldn't be sure of what he saw out the front window. An illusion, perhaps? A mirage? He rubbed his eyes and focused on the strange sight across the street: a woman, blond, stumbling across the dirt road, walking toward him, dazed. She was completely nude.

What on earth? Steve thought. He rushed to the entrance, assuming she needed help. Then he screeched to a halt, second-guessing himself. What if she was dangerous? What if this was some kind of trick? Suddenly, halfway across the road, the woman outside crumpled to the asphalt.

Abandoning all misgivings, Steve opened the door and ran toward her. She lay on the street, still breathing but not moving. He slapped her on the cheek.

"Hey! Hey, wake up!"

Nothing.

He looked around frantically for help, but of course their surroundings were deserted. Steve grabbed the stranger by her arms and tried to lift her up. She didn't weigh much, but Steve's scrawny frame wasn't built for heavy lifting. He had to settle for grabbing her from behind and pulling her back toward the gas station. Her bare feet were dragging on the dirt, and when Steve looked down at them, he saw that they were bleeding. When he finally got her inside, he rested her against a shelf of chocolate bars, hopped over the counter, and frantically dialed 9-1-1.

Henry's head was resting against his crossed arms on the interrogation room table. Save for one restroom break, he had not been allowed to leave. He had not been granted a phone call, not even to his wife, though he had been assured she was notified and informed that everything was fine. He was neither asleep nor awake, but in a state somewhere between the two. His racing mind had not allowed his exhausted body to sleep.

He was abruptly removed from this state of limbo by the sound of the heavy metallic door creaking open. He looked up, his eyes dewy from the quasi-rest, and saw only a blur. He rubbed his eyes with his fists until his vision was clear. The man from the night before had entered, still in the same clothes, sipping a coffee. In his free hand, the man was holding a folder, which he placed onto the table before taking a seat across from Henry.

"Your park," the man said, glaring at the folder and the photos from the night before, "is giving me a headache."

"Well, I—"

"I don't care what you have to say. I don't. I care about those three boys. I care about finding out who did that to them. And I care about the fourth boy, the missing one. That's what I care about. But," he leaned forward and glared into Henry Carter's eyes before finishing his sentence, "you can't help with that. Can you?"

Henry had no idea what to say, but the man kept going. "Four boys go missing one night, three show up mutilated the following evening, and on the same day, your sister's vehicle appears buried under the water of the bay, in mint condition. Untouched, as if someone had just placed it there. But the interior of the vehicle was dry. That bag," he pointed to the bag Henry knew nothing of, "filled with your sister's belongings. Her ID was inside. So . . . you can go, Mr. Carter."

Henry blinked. The agent was clearly venting his frustration over the puzzling events of Hillsbury Park. But letting Henry go? Why keep him all night if he was just going to let him go now?

The metal door creaked open once again, and two officers came in and escorted Henry from the interrogation room. On his way out of the station, he saw someone sitting at an officer's desk, handcuffed, arguing with the officer who was taking his statement. It was Bruce Archer.

What in the world is Bruce Archer doing here? Henry wondered.

It was an unusually chilly morning, considering the time of year, though the sun was still just barely beginning to show signs of life. Henry had never been so happy to see his Jeep. He slumped into the driver's seat and gunned the ignition. He shifted into reverse, but before he could release his foot from the brake pedal, a 1965 black Cadillac parked directly behind him, blocking his exit.

Frustrated and tired, Henry slammed the Jeep back into park and swore under his breath. "You gotta be kidding me."

The Cadillac's engine went silent. Henry exited the Jeep and moved toward the Cadillac. "You mind getting out of my damn way?"

The passenger window on the Cadillac lowered with a smooth mechanical *whirr*. A dark skinned American man who looked like he was in his early twenties smiled at Henry. "Get in," he said.

The man had a thick English accent. He was dressed in a blue denim jacket with a black T-shirt underneath. Dark, thick-framed glasses covered his eyes.

"Get in? Are you out of your mind?"

"Henry Carter, my name's Corbin Mench. Please, come in and have a seat." Corbin reached across the controls and opened the passenger door for Henry.

"Why should I?"

Corbin merely pointed to the seat. "Please."

This stranger was not going to budge. While Henry didn't agree with what he was about to do, he knew he had little choice. He gripped the door handle, took a breath, and entered the Cadillac. Corbin graced him with a grateful smile. Henry shut the door, praying he wouldn't regret it.

Corbin drove through Hillsbury in silence. Henry was not sure where they were headed, and Corbin wasn't telling. At least Henry didn't have to worry about driving; at least he could just lean his head against the window, take in the beautiful sights of cottage country, and allow his weary eyes to shut if they wanted to. But as the drive continued, Henry grew increasingly more curious as to what this man wanted with him.

"You have a lovely town, Henry." Corbin smiled as they passed the last of the cottages. It was the first thing either of them had said in a while. The sound of Corbin's voice made Henry jump.

"Thank you . . . ?" Henry had a hundred questions and decided to settle on the most relevant one. "Would you mind telling me where we're going now?"

"Not at all. In Hillsbury, you have these cottages, these famous cottages, these most coveted cottages. Then you have the park, *your* park. The bay—or what *was* the bay, I suppose. And then you have the farmlands. Those are often mistaken for the town of Caserta, but in actuality, the farms are part of Hillsbury. Correct?" He was. Henry nodded. Corbin pulled over to the side of the road and placed the car in park.

"Henry, I wanted to speak to you in that room, but the agent in charge felt it would be best to do it off-site. I have jurisdiction, but what I study is not always taken . . . all that seriously."

"What do you study?"

"I work for the government. But before I get into any sort of detail with you, I need you to sign a confidentiality agreement."

Henry was quite confused. "Confidentiality? For what?" Corbin started the car and began to drive.

"Caserta is a farming town. Despite its Italian name, it's home to many Dutch immigrants. I haven't studied Caserta much, just what I looked up this morning on my way in. Seems like a nice place; I thought it was the target at first. But it wasn't at all, Hillsbury was. The outskirts of Hillsbury, just before the county of Caserta begins."

Henry could only hope Corbin would inform him as to what in the world he was talking about. The Cadillac pulled over again on a dirt road, parallel to a cornfield.

"Cornfield to the right, pumpkin patch to the left," Corbin said as he exited the car. Henry followed. Corbin leaned against the car. "The Van Tassels own the property here. Are you at all familiar with them?" Henry shook his head. He knew many people in Hillsbury, mostly the cottagers and campers; he didn't spend much time on the outskirts. "They're just your typical farming family. For generations, most of the corn sold in local stores has come from here, as have pumpkins and other vegetables. Anyway, Mr. Carter, you asked me who I was and I told you my name, Corbin Mench, but I have yet to tell you what I do."

Finally, Henry thought.

"I am an astrobiologist." Before Henry could comprehend what this could possibly mean, Corbin added (looking a tad embarrassed as he did so), "Well . . . more accurately, I'm an exobiologist, but my business card says astrobiologist. So, there you go."

"There I go?" a frustrated Henry said after a moment. "What the hell is . . . what does that even mean?"

"I study life. Specifically, *outer* life."

"Outer life?"

"Outer life." Corbin pointed to the sky, spinning his finger around. "Like extraterrestrial beings and whatnot."

Henry scoffed at the man, unimpressed. "Right. Can you take me back to my car now?"

Corbin kept a straight face and reached into his pocket. He removed his government ID card and handed it to Henry. "I assure you, I'm serious. I work for the government."

Henry read over the card twice. Either Corbin knew a *very* good forgery artist, or he was telling the truth.

"What I'm about to tell you is classified information, but what I'm about to *show* you is public spectacle. Though I figure few people will catch it." He had Henry's attention now. "Last night, a UFO was spotted over Hillsbury."

Henry stared at Corbin for a good, long while. Corbin clearly expected him to verbally react, but Henry couldn't seem to find the words. Skepticism must have been written all over his face. When it became clear Henry was not going to dignify this with a response, Corbin continued. "So . . . that's the classified information. And now you're thinking I'm some kind of crazy person. But I assure you, I am not."

"Well, what's the public spectacle?" Henry asked, half-curious, half-humoring. Corbin walked back around the car and opened the door. "We must drive a little farther for that." Henry groaned and shook his head. All he wanted to do was go home. Taking Corbin's car was a better option than walking, though not by much.

Banners remained hung with pride throughout Hillsbury, touting the big Labor Day fireworks celebration. Even though every camper had packed up and left, the rest of the town (most notably Mayor Tremblay) would not let their spirits dampen. The festival would continue, even if on a smaller scale. While Tremblay had dreamed up and spent a fortune on the carnival, he knew that it might be in the people's best interest to see a muted version of it. Keep it operational, but keep it realistic, keep it safe, and most of all, keep it fun. He would be remembered as the mayor who brought great joy to Hillsbury during dark times. This was a legacy he could live with.

It was just past seven in the morning when Ava arrived at Hillsbury Park. She still hadn't heard from Henry and was unsure what state the park would be in after the police force had vacated the premises. She was certain she would be cleaning piles of garbage and fixing pathways ruined by police cruisers. And she was unsure whether she would get any help.

She parked her car at the side of the headquarters and made her way in. The muddy parking lot had completely dried up, and at first glance, you'd suspect the night before was like any other: a calm, peaceful, warm summer's night. She threw on her ranger jacket and entered the building. As cold as it was outside, it would most likely be colder inside. The police shut off the power overnight and she had forgotten to turn it back on when she locked up. Which was understandable: she'd just wanted to leave after that long, miserable day.

I was right, she thought upon entering. *It's like a freezer in here.* Ava rushed to the coffee maker and immediately began brewing herself a morning libation. At this point, she was more interested in just *holding* the warm cup than she was actually drinking anything.

As the water boiled, Ava made her way into Henry's office. Dingwell had left it in shambles: notes strewn all over the place, pictures dropped on the ground. Several of the family photos Henry kept on his desk had been placed facedown. Figuring Henry most likely had a worse night than her, Ava took it upon herself to tidy his office for him. One of the picture frames was cracked: it was home to a picture of Rachel with Sarah and Jeffrey, three years earlier, on vacation at an amusement park. The sun was in full bloom. The smiles on the children's faces told the story of how fun that day must have been. Ava smiled at the picture and stood it back up. *I'll run out and get him a new frame once I'm done here*, she promised herself. She stacked the loose papers into a pile and opened the desk drawer to store them, and that's when she saw it.

The mysterious claw was nestled snugly in a handkerchief in the drawer. Henry was able to keep it out of police evidence. Ava gently picked it up to observe it again. She'd forgotten just how eerie it was. That cream-like sheen, those quills protruding from its tip . . . could this very claw have been responsible for the severed ear found in the park?

Suddenly the room filled with a deep baritone buzz, like an angry hornet. Ava was so startled that she nearly jumped out of her skin, and one of the quills nicked her fingers. Blood quickly welled from beneath the wound; it stung like a paper cut.

The buzz continued, and a very embarrassed Ava realized it was nothing more than the cell phone in her pocket. Hurrying, she grabbed a tissue from the desk, applying pressure on the small but painful wound. With her other hand, she dug angrily into her pocket, fished out the phone, and answered it.

"Hello?"

Silence, followed by a click. Ava slammed the phone down and rushed to the bathroom. After sucking out some of the blood to ease the pain and gradually stop the bleeding, Ava ran her finger under a jet of cool water. She also administered antibiotic cream from a first aid kit, and blanketed it all with an adhesive bandage. She returned to Henry's office and (very carefully) placed the claw back into the top drawer of his desk. Finally, Ava cast a dark glance at the phone, wondering who on earth had called without bothering to speak.

She had grown tired of games and surprises after the past twenty-four hours. She remembered the banners and signs she passed on her way to work that morning, thinking about how much fun this weekend used to be, how much fun it should have been. Ava fixed the stack of papers, keeping it straight and perfectly aligned, then placed them atop the claw in the desk drawer. She sat at Henry's chair and broke down into tears.

The '65 Cadillac pulled over to a lookout point in Caserta. Corbin shut the door ever so gently as he exited the car. He looked down just above the tire, where a few inches of dust and dirt had collected. He pulled a napkin out of the inside pocket of his denim jacket and wiped the vehicle clean.

Henry looked around. Despite Caserta's close proximity, he had never had a reason to visit it before. "This is Caserta?" he asked, knowing full well it was but wanting to make sure they weren't on the outskirts of Hillsbury anymore.

Corbin nodded, wiping his glasses on his shirt. "Yes, just barely outside your hometown."

"So, you gonna tell me what we're doing here?" Henry was growing more irritated by the minute; he still hadn't spoken to his family since the night before. He tried calling from his cell phone during the ride but there was no answer. Henry figured they must have still been sleeping.

"You ever see a crop circle, Henry?" Corbin grinned in excitement, though Henry couldn't be sure why—nor could he be sure if this stranger was being serious.

"Crop circle? Like aliens?" Henry asked blankly.

Corbin shrugged and moved his head as if to say *yes and no*, but with a definite inclination toward the former. "They're a phenomenon, or so the public—the general audience of their artists—believes. Most are just the work of bored farmers. We have determined which are real and which are fake: Twenty or thirty years ago, that wasn't the case. We weren't as educated in this matter as we are now."

"You were in this business twenty years ago?" Henry asked, acknowledging Corbin's youthful appearance.

"Not quite. Colleagues of mine. Predecessors. We didn't have certain technology that we have nowadays to determine what is from Earth and what was brought down from the heavens above."

"Look, I don't mean to seem—"

Henry was quickly cut off by Corbin. "You're anxious to return to your wife and kids, I understand. My apologies. I get excited. I asked you about crop circles. Mr. Carter . . . Henry, can I call you Henry? Hillsbury has been a hub for Radioactic Sputs for many years, longer than you've even lived here. What caused these Sputs," Corbin shrugged, "we may never discover."

"I'm sorry, *Radioactic Sputs*? Are those even words?"

"Defined by Webster's or any reputable dictionary? No. Defined by the government in this country or any other? Indeed."

"Okay, I'll bite. What are they?" Henry hated himself for asking the question, but he was certain Corbin was going to tell him one way or another.

"It's rather simple in its terminology. You know the term *radioactive*, naturally. Well, Radioactic is radioactivity caused by foreign beings. Unknown creatures. A Sput is a reading on a chart. Simple."

"Let me guess: It's an alien chart?" Henry replied sarcastically.

Corbin nodded. "Precisely. And the Radioactic Sput reading has been increasing astronomically in Hillsbury over the past few years. The problem with our technology versus Radioactic Sputs is that we are not quite there yet. We're merely guessing. Educated guesses to be sure, but guesses nonetheless. And in the case of Hillsbury . . . well, we guessed wrong."

"How can you be sure?"

"You don't believe in extraterrestrials, I take it?"

Henry shook his head. He most certainly did not. Corbin rested his right arm on Henry's shoulder and turned him ever so slightly to face the township below. They looked down at the cornfield they had parked next to moments before. "Do you believe in your eyes?"

Henry was stunned. In the distant cornfield (the very same cornfield he'd been standing next to minutes ago), was a crop circle. Or rather, a crop *shape*. It was rectangular, stretching at least fifty feet in length. Inside this rectangle were two smaller rectangles. The first of these was made of tiny triangular shapes flowing in an *S* formation, each strand weaving in and out of each other. Each *S* shape appeared to be created by smaller rectangles. The second smaller rectangle had lines—dash marks—both thick and thin, flowing in various directions.

"What is it?" Henry could barely get the words out of his mouth; shock and awe had paralyzed his tongue.

"A type of crop circle. More specifically, it's a message."

"From whom?" Henry's eyes never strayed from the cornfield as Corbin pulled a sheet of paper and a pen out of his jacket pocket.

"For me to divulge that information, Henry, you'll have to fill out the confidentiality agreement."

A town as small as Tuncton lacked a large enough population to warrant a hospital, and so those living there had to travel for medical attention. Tuncton, Leafsview, Martindale, and Collingwood townships all shared the same hospital: St. Joseph's. The good news was (thanks to the low population of the area) traffic was at a minimum, and getting to St. Joseph's was rarely ever a hassle.

A woman known only as Jane Doe lay in room 249. Discovered completely naked at the McKelvie Gas and Corner Store, she was now clothed in a medical gown, her hair tattered, a large scar running down her throat. Though her left hand was untouched, the nails on her *right* hand had been ripped off. One eye was swollen, lost in a fleshy sea of black and blue, though the doctor had found no evidence of physical trauma. A more logical explanation was that the bruise stemmed internally. The right side of her head had been shaved and a large wound, which had been wired shut, lived there. Her legs were under a warm blanket being used to keep up her body heat (when Steve had brought her in, she'd been terribly cold). Her lips had shifted from a luscious pink to a pale blue during the half-hour drive from the gas station to the hospital. All in all, the mystery woman was in dire straits.

Steve sat with the stranger, worried sick as to what was happening with her. She had no one, as far as he knew. He was dozing on the chair across from Jane Doe's bed, slipping in and out of sleep, when the woman's eyes opened.

Jane Doe gazed around the room without a trace of recognition. A single strand of sunlight snuck through the half-closed venetian blinds and beamed onto her face, causing her to squint. She turned her head, her vision blurry, watching blue and white blotches scurry about. On her left sat a suture tray consisting of forceps holding lacerated tissues, sterile towels, a bowl of gelatin for eating, a cup of water, smaller bowls, a pair of scissors, a needle, and two medical knives. Her eyes became fixated on the scissors and needle, which were clearly making her uncomfortable. Her eyes bulged and her mouth dropped open, but where there should have been a scream, a scratching, clawing shriek left her throat in a blip, just enough for Steve to jolt from his slumber.

He rushed over at once to see if she was all right. In her terror, her arms flailed, removing the pulse monitor from her finger. A nurse hustled into the room. "What's wrong? What happened?" she asked.

Steve had no clue. Before he could say a word, the nurse was holding Jane Doe down, calming her, and injecting her with a sedative. Steve took a few deep, panicked breaths. The nurse tried to give him a reassuring smile.

"If you don't mind," she calmly started, "the police would like a few words with you."

Ava's foot sank into a hole in the grass, making her stumble. *Damn weasels!* They'd had a weasel problem a couple years prior and set up traps to catch them, but it appeared they had returned to Hillsbury Park with a vengeance.

Ava slowly removed the bandage that was wrapped around her hand, checking to see how bad it looked now. To her astonishment, the wound had vanished entirely. She felt no pain; it was as though the incident never took place. Confused but grateful, she tossed the bandage into a trash bin as she completed scouting the campgrounds. When the campers were driven from the park in the chaotic mess of the previous night, Ava expected the event to be a disaster, but thankfully, the campers had all departed in a sensible manner. No questions,

no fusses; just refunds and goodbyes. Ava figured the missing boy was on all of their minds, and if they could assist the
authorities in finding the boy, they would do so, even if that
meant losing their weekend camping excursion.

Picnic tables and charcoal barbecues scattered about the
park area. The smell of hot charcoal still lingered from before
the evacuation. She snatched up some fragments of litter with
her trash picker and filled the large black garbage bags. Garbage
cans were located all over Hillsbury, yet potato chips, soda cans,
and wrappers of all sorts occupied the green grass below. When
her job was done, she tossed the full garbage bags into the back
of her ranger vehicle and returned to headquarters.

She saw it before she even pulled in and rolled her eyes. A
vehicle with the license plate *Mayor1* was parked—crookedly—
out front. She had no patience for Mayor Tremblay this morning. As she was about to turn the knob and let herself into
headquarters, she felt the gentle caress of fingers on her shoulders. She turned to see Bentley standing behind her. Startled
for a moment, she took a breath.

"Jeez, you crept up on me." She removed a strand of hair
from in front of her eyes.

"Sorry." He withdrew his hand. His tone was soft, soothing. "I needed to see you."

"Okay, 'bout what?"

"Us."

Us? This was another discussion she was definitely not in
the mood for. "Bentley, there's no us. We've talked about this,
and talked and talked and talked. It was fun. But it was stupid.
And now it's over. End of story."

But to Bentley it wasn't that simple. He had barely slept the
night before; visions of Ava had danced across his mind. He
was certain that what began as an affair brought on purely by

physical attraction had manifested itself into something else. Something he could no longer live without.

"I think I'm in love with you."

Ava released all the tension from her shoulders. Frustration exhaled from her body and she caught her grip. "You're not. Go home to your wife." She turned her back to him and prepared to enter the headquarters and deal with the mayor, but Bentley pulled her back again.

"I don't want to go. Can't we go somewhere and talk about this?"

She whirled around, growing more frustrated by the second. "I've got work to do."

"How about coffee, during your break? Can we talk about it then?"

She took a deep breath, squinting at the sky as if praying for aid. She *did* have feelings for Bentley; whether those feelings amounted to love or not, though, was another matter entirely. She forced herself to look into his eyes, and she could see the need there, the desperate desire to speak to her. He reminded her of a puppy staring out the front window, waiting for its master to come home.

It took a great deal of effort, but Ava finally said, "Fine. Meet me at O'Leary's for lunch."

Bentley's face lit up like the sun. He moved to kiss her on the cheek but she turned away. "Lunch," she stated before entering the headquarters.

Mayor Tremblay was sipping a fresh cup of coffee as Ava entered. The pot was mostly empty. Her incident with the claw had robbed her of her morning brew, and now the mayor was gulping down her second chance. Ava felt her dislike for the man reach new heights. She composed herself with what she hoped was a polite smile.

"Mr. Mayor, welcome. What brings you here this morning?"

He swirled some coffee around his mouth; she could hear it splash from cheek to cheek, and she winced. *Vile.*

Tremblay grinned. "The campgrounds are vacant, are they not?"

"Yes, sir."

"Good. Good." He downed the rest of his coffee with a mighty gulp and placed the empty mug down on her desk. "I'm reopening the park as of this afternoon."

Ava's eyes opened in shock. "What?"

"The park is perfectly safe, dear. Last night's events have been isolated. I spoke with Sheriff Walden, and he assures me all is good. The festival, the fireworks, the party . . . all of it will go forward as planned. We may not draw as big a crowd as we usually do, but people will come." A condescending grin slithered across his face, and he chuckled merrily as if at some humorous joke. "They always do!"

"What about the boy? The Liman kid? He's still missing!"

"That's true, he is. He'll be found, or his remains will be, at least."

"Mr. M—"

"It's over, Miss Trillium. The police have made an arrest in conjunction with these crimes. Didn't you see? Didn't you hear? Bruce Archer was arrested last night." He placed his fedora atop his head. "The park opens at noon." Tremblay would neither say nor hear another word. He sauntered outside, started his car, and was gone.

Ava watched him drive off, feeling helpless. She wasn't ready for this.

Corbin pulled his car up in front of Henry's house. They exchanged a handshake. "I'll see you this afternoon," Corbin said. Henry nodded absentmindedly, gazing up at his house. He couldn't wait to see his family. The Cadillac sped away, and Henry rushed up the front entrance, bursting through the front door.

Rachel was putting the finishing touches on a pancake. Sarah was perched at the table, playing with the remnants of her breakfast. When Rachel saw Henry appear, she dropped the final pancake (and the spatula) onto the floor.

"Henry!"

Rachel rushed toward him and wrapped his body in a giant hug. Sarah bounced up from her chair, her smile almost too big for her little face, and joined in. Jeffrey had just been walking down the stairs when he spotted his father.

"Welcome home, Dad." He grinned.

Henry released himself from the girls and walked over to Jeffrey, pulling him into another hug.

When the overwhelming feeling of relief finally faded, Henry turned and grinned at his wife through watery eyes. "So, what's for breakfast?"

"It's on the ground!" Rachel said before she burst out laughing.

Henry retrieved the spatula from the floor and said, "Let me take it from here," and gave Rachel the biggest kiss he'd ever given her in his life.

He was home.

Inside the small prison in Hillsbury lay two cellblocks. One was vacant, as usual. The other was the current home of Bruce

Archer. Archer, whose family was once full of riches and owned the most luxurious, sought-after cottage spaces in Hillsbury, was now a prisoner. He sat on the rock-hard, cold mattress, not looking at anything in particular, simply waiting, waiting for his turn to speak.

SATURDAY AFTERNOON

THE PARK WAS OPEN.

Ava sat at her desk, alone in the station. Henry had not checked in, which meant no Jeffrey, and she was sure that yesterday had scared Morgan away for good. She was unsure who would arrive first, if anyone arrived at all. On any typical year, today would be the final full day for the park, the night before the fireworks and festivities. But, of course, this was not a typical year. Even before all the chaos and sadness, Mayor Tremblay postponed the fireworks until Monday in hopes it would drive more business and tourism in Hillsbury for one extra day. Today was an anomaly.

Ava begrudgingly raised the main gates. Admission was free on the Labor Day weekend, another aspect of the park Mayor Tremblay had vied for changing (or, as he put it, *correcting*). They'd explained to him that free admission would drive the numbers up, which in turn would cause the tourists to spend their money on local businesses and the festivities within, where the profit margin was two hundred percent.

When Ava told Henry she didn't vote for Tremblay, she was not lying. Her interest in politics was slim to none, but her interest in Hillsbury, in her home, was enormous. She never once thought that Tremblay was right for the town. She felt he needed to get away to some other city, where he could charge his people a fee just to gaze upon the stars. Even still, Tremblay was the mayor, and if there was something that he wanted done and he got the vote of confidence from the other elected officials (whom Ava was certain had been bribed more often than not), then Ava had no choice but to do as she was told.

So Hillsbury park, after being closed for nearly seventeen hours, was now reopened.

Henry stood in front of the mirror brushing his teeth. He felt dirty. He had not showered, brushed his teeth, or changed his clothes in over twenty-four hours. The showering and clothing he could live with, but his teeth longed for a good scrubbing. He spat out his toothpaste and looked at himself in the mirror. The events of the previous day had taken a toll on the park ranger. He noticed yet another gray hair. He shook his head and picked up the tweezers.

"Another gray," he mumbled to himself before plucking it out.

He combed his fingers through his hair. Several strands came out with his hands. Henry stared down at them, as if their absence was somehow mutinous. He had no interest in going bald. "Great." Henry tossed the strands of hair into the toilet and furiously flushed them.

Henry made his way into the kitchen. Rachel sat at the table with a coffee in her hand, the phone resting in front of her. "Where're the kids?" Henry asked. Rachel looked around.

"Playing downstairs. I think Jeffrey's in his room."

"What's wrong?" Henry asked as he sat down next to his wife, noticing something off in her expression.

"What happened last night, Henry?" Rachel was visibly shaken.

Henry held his wife's hands to try and calm her. "People went missing the other night. Kids. Boys. It happened at the park."

Rachel's eyes glistened. "I thought it was just Patty Liman's boy."

Henry shook his head. "At the time of the Amber Alert, we had only known of the one—of Joel Liman. It wasn't until later—"

"Are they all right?"

Henry shook his head. He couldn't lie. He couldn't pretend this was going to have a happy ending, not after what he had seen, or the strange new developments brought upon him by Corbin Mench. "Liman's still out there, somewhere. Look, Rachel, I have to go to work—"

"No!"

"I *have* to go to work." Henry tried to be as calm as possible. Rachel was a mess, furious and sad and scared.

"No! Why? Why do you *have* to?" She stood with jolting suddenness and stomped over to the counter, turning her back to Henry. Henry slowly followed. He placed his hands on her shoulders. She nudged him off. He tried again.

"I have to go to work. Make sure you and the kids don't leave the house." Henry kissed his wife on the cheek and left her sobbing in the kitchen. Jeffrey walked down the stairs a few moments later and noticed the state his mother was in.

"Mum? What's wrong?"

Henry paused at the Jeep and glanced back at his house, hoping today wouldn't be as long or strenuous as the day before.

Then Jeffrey burst through the front door and ran up to Henry. "What're you doing?!"

"Jeffrey—"

"Don't you see Mum? Don't you know what this will do to her? What last night did to her? She was up all night worried about you—putting on a brave face for Sarah and me!"

"Jeffrey . . ." Henry stopped himself, gained his composure, and refocused his words. "I have to go in. There are people . . . it's my job. Do me a favor, look after your mother and sister for me. Okay?"

"You're not even listening!"

For the first time that morning, Henry raised his voice. "I have a RESPONSIBILITY, son!"

They stood there for what felt like a long while, glaring at each other. To Henry's shock, Jeffrey broke the silence first. The boy now wore the same expression Henry often did when asked by Mayor Tremblay to do something nonsensical; Jeffrey was letting his father have his way, but making it very clear that he didn't like it. "Just promise me you'll be home before dark," he muttered.

When did he grow up? Henry thought. "I will."

The gates were up when Henry got to the park. That was odd. Perhaps with all the commotion the previous day, Ava had forgotten to close them? Then he spotted Ava's vehicle in the parking lot and wondered if she'd been allowed to leave at all?

Inside, the headquarters smelled of rich coffee. A smile, if only for a moment, was visible on his face. He looked around. No sign of anyone.

"Ava?"

The blinds in his office were open, so the entire headquarters was visible. No one was there. But the coffee pot was full and warm, which meant somebody had to have been there recently. Henry picked up a walkie-talkie and switched it on.

"Ava, come in. This is Henry, over." He waited for a response. "Ava, this is Henry, do you copy?" He tried one more time; this time the static sounds at the other end of the walkie-talkie could be heard. Then . . .

"Hi, Henry."

Henry smiled, relieved. "It's good to hear your voice. Where are you?"

"Rabbit Trail. Just filling in some weasel holes. You?"

"Headquarters."

"Be right there."

She was back within minutes, greeting Henry with a giant hug. "You okay?" he asked her.

She nodded. "As okay as I can be."

"So what's going on here? The gates were open."

Ava's shoulders sagged. "Tremblay paid me a visit this morning. As of twelve noon he reopened the park."

"Is he nuts? How could he do that? Does he even know—"

"He says everything's fine, and they found their man."

"What man?"

"Bruce Archer."

Henry needed to take a seat. It all made sense now, why he saw Bruce at the police station earlier that morning. *They think it's him.* His thoughts flitted to Corbin. Surely Corbin would have told them what was really going on? "That's not right. They can't open the park. They . . . they can't."

"Sorry, Henry, I had no choice."

He nodded, understanding. "Anyone come in yet?"

"Just some of the carnival people."

"Jesus, that's still happening too?" Henry couldn't believe it. "Fireworks still on for tomorrow night?"

"That's the plan, according to His Honorable Sir," Ava said mockingly.

Even though Henry signed the confidentiality agreement, he had not been told exactly what was going on. As far as he knew, some strange patterns formed in a cornfield on the outskirts of Hillsbury, he had one missing boy, three boys retrieved but brutally mutilated, and his sister's pickup truck was found without a scratch on it. None of it made sense, but Corbin assured him they were somehow all connected and Hillsbury was ground zero for everything to come crashing down. He noticed that Ava was waiting for him to say something, anything.

"Well then," Henry spoke, "I guess we'll treat this like any other day."

He got up, clapped his hands together, and poured himself a hot cup of coffee.

Corbin had spent a considerable amount of time in police stations, some of which were so small they had offices affectionately referred to as "broom closets" by their occupants. But here in Hillsbury PD, Corbin had been ushered to an office so tiny, he was convinced he'd been mistakenly led to an *actual* broom closet. At least there was a (small) desk, and all the files he needed were close at hand. But offices like these reminded Corbin that (despite the beauty of the country) places like Hillsbury made much better way stations than they did homes. He carefully studied the photos of the three boys. The material used to sew the eyes, ears, and mouth shut was not one he had seen before. Ever. And he had seen plenty of extraordinary materials. The next photo was the crop circle. He still needed to crack the binary code in the bottom half of the triangular shape. Perhaps in doing so, he could find out why this happened to these boys?

Corbin had seen this type of mutilation in the past, but mostly on men and woman, all over the age of twenty-five. His first report of such a sighting was on his second investigation, when he was still new to the field of astrobiology. The man with sewn-shut eyes was addicted to child pornography. The mouth belonged to a forty-year-old prostitute. The ears were taken from a crooked sheriff: all adults, all indulging in some sort of criminal activity.

But these were boys, boys too young to commit any crime so foul. Corbin needed an answer. *What could it all mean?*

The summer heat was back full-force this afternoon. As Ava made her way to O'Leary's to meet with Bentley, she watched several city workers raise banners on lampposts around the main hub of Hillsbury. This downtown core consisted of a hardware store, a convenience store (the only place in town to buy bags of ice), the ice cream parlor, O'Leary's, and Jett's Fishing tackle shop, which was now simply "Fish & Tackle Shoppe." The banners were three feet long with two different designs. One design featured fireworks exploding with the catch phrase: *An Explosive Night. An Explosive Town.* The other had a beautiful picture of what Cape's Side Bay once was, with the same tagline. Ava shook her head, but then gradually started to understand the situation. Maybe this was what the town needed after their horrific Friday? Maybe a fun time in the park with a carnival and fireworks would get everyone's mentalities back together? *Maybe*, she hoped.

She could see Bentley waiting for her inside O'Leary's when she parked. A waitress came to take his order, but he smiled through the window at Ava, most likely telling the waitress that he was waiting for someone. Ava smiled; he always treated her well. *Why did he have to be married?*

She locked her car and entered O'Leary's. Bentley stood to greet her and pulled out a chair. "What would you like to drink?" he asked.

"Just a coffee. One milk."

Bentley nodded and waved the waitress back to the table. They sat across from each other in silence as the waitress served them their coffees. A strand of hair slid from behind Ava's ear and placed itself in front of her left eye. Bentley reached in to remove the strand, but Ava pulled back and did it herself.

"Are you crazy? People will see you," she whispered through her teeth.

They were in a public place together, but it wasn't very busy. Most people were still in their cottages for the day, and with the campers all gone, there weren't many customers at O'Leary's. Even still, a few folks would pop their heads in for a latte or cappuccino, and word simply traveled too fast in this town for Ava's liking.

"I don't care," Bentley fired back. "I'm leaving Elise."

Ava sighed. She'd heard this before. When their affair first began, he'd told her the same thing, many times. As strong as their connection was, Bentley Trundle still loved his wife.

"I mean it." He softened up and leaned forward, arms resting on the table. "Every night I lie next to Elise is a lie. I can't do it anymore. I'm . . ." He lowered his voice to the faintest of whispers. "I love you, Ava."

Her eyes couldn't help but well up. As much as she pushed him away, as much as she knew how wrong it was, her heart wouldn't lie. Would it? Perhaps what she felt for the deputy sheriff was more than just the lust she assumed it was. Perhaps their connection was real, and perhaps he was not meant to be with Elise after all. Maybe Ava was the one destined to be with him. After all, she deserved it . . . didn't she? Her heart had been broken numerous times; love had tricked her in the past. Why couldn't this be her shot at love? She didn't owe Elise anything. Heck, she hardly *knew* Elise. Gazing into Bentley's eyes, she could tell he was serious. This was for real. This time, he really would leave his wife for her.

"I don't know," she muttered. As much as she wanted to say, *Yes, leave your wife and be with me!* she could not bring herself to. She told herself she was not and would not be that person, even if it meant breaking her own heart. Bentley slammed his fists down on the table, upsetting some of his coffee.

"Ava, please. I can't—" He fought to lower his voice again. "I can't stop thinking about you. That's why I called you this morning—"

"*You* called?"

He nodded. "Yes, but Elise was in the other room and I . . . I need you." He wiped the spilled coffee with a napkin.

"You'll leave your wife?"

"Yes. Yes. A hundred times yes." His eyes filled with sincerity, never straying. Not once did Ava feel he was putting her on. She leaned back in her chair, cautiously optimistic.

"I'll need to think about it," she said, just before sipping her coffee. She almost blurted out, *Yes*, but a rash decision in this situation would not be wise. She needed to make sure of her feelings.

"Yeah?" Bentley was smiling. Her answer was better than a no.

Ava nodded. He reached over and cupped his hand over hers with a smile. She rubbed her hand, where the claw wound had been. While visibly there was no sign of it, she felt a slight burn from the infected spot.

"Hurt your hand?" he queried, noticing the bandage.

"Cut myself. Paper cut. Nothing big. Should probably rinse it off. I'll be right back." She got up and left the table.

Alone in the restroom, Ava turned on the tap and ran her hand under the cold water. She looked up at herself in the mirror and noticed she was trembling. *Ava,* she thought angrily. *What are you doing?*

Henry stood at the front entrance of the rangers, headquarters and watched as carnival folk drove in. The park had attracted a few visitors, but with the heat picking up, he was sure more would come as the day went on. He promised Rachel he would be home for dinner, but it looked like that was all he would be home for. He received a call from Mayor Tremblay soon after arriving at the park, informing him of a ribbon-cutting ceremony that evening. Thus, the carnival would officially begin. Tremblay would cut the ribbon, and he requested Henry be there for a photo op. Henry flicked the ash from his cigarette and took a drag as a truck full of carnival workers drove past, waving happily, oblivious to the goings-on of Hillsbury.

The black '65 Cadillac was the next vehicle to enter the park. It slowly made its way through the dirt parking lot and parked on the far side of the headquarters. Corbin stepped out, a rag already in his hand, and began wiping the dirt from above the tires. Henry took one final drag from his cigarette and placed it in the ashtray. He smiled and shook his head at

Corbin. "Y'know you're never gonna keep that thing clean in Hillsbury, right?"

Corbin looked up, waved, and gave his vehicle one final wipe. He approached Henry, shaking his hand. "How are you?"

Henry shrugged. He had no idea how he was. He opened his office door for Corbin, who was holding an easel and paper. The astrobiologist looked around the office, much larger than the one he was given at the police station, and shut the blinds. Henry had offered Corbin the office to use any way he liked. The easel was set up in the back corner, behind Henry's desk.

"I hear your mayor has reopened the park."

"Yeah. I'm not sure that's a good thing," Henry responded.

Corbin finished setting the easel up and looked at Henry. "I'm sure it is." He pulled a pack of bubble gum from his denim jacket and placed a stick in his mouth, offering a piece to Henry (who respectfully declined). Corbin chewed the gum thoughtfully for a moment, then said, "I need you to take me to Cape's Side Bay."

The bay was dry as a bone this afternoon. Water left from the rain the night before had completely dried up. All was quiet, with the exception of the carnival workers in the distance. Henry's Jeep pulled up as close to the bay as it could get before he and Corbin walked through the woods. Corbin's first thought of the bay was, *It's a dump*. His second thought, *It makes sense*.

He paced back and forth slowly, looking out at the crater that stood before him. "So this is Cape's Side Bay. Very interesting." Smiling, Corbin carefully entered the crater that had once been filled with pristine blue water. He squatted down and began scooping dirt into a canister. He noticed eggshells (the same ones Victor had stepped on the night before) and plucked one up, examining it in the sunlight before gingerly slipping it into an airtight bag.

"This is where they found that truck, right? Your sister's truck?" Corbin asked. "And this was the last place those boys were seen?"

"Well, no, it's the last place they *assumed* the boys were seen," Henry explained. "One of their mothers saw them sneak out, heading in the park's direction. The boys have no recollection of the night, aside from hanging out together."

Next, Corbin noticed the bloodstained handprint on a rock to the opposite side. "Any idea whose that is?"

Truth be told, Henry hadn't been given much information about the handprint. "Not really. I just figured it belonged to one of the boys."

Corbin nodded, though he appeared skeptical. He peered at the cave high above. "Bear cave?"

"A cave, yes."

"The infamous cave, though, right?" Corbin stared at it. "Do you believe in God, Henry?"

Henry was startled by the abruptness of the question. "Yeah, I suppose I do."

"But not aliens or extraterrestrial life?"

"I'm not sure what I believe anymore." And that was true. The events of the past few days had really toyed with Henry's head.

"It always fascinates me that a person can believe in one and not the other," Corbin said, wearing a sad smile. "Why can there be God but no aliens? And why can there be aliens but no God? Why can't the two coexist?" Henry wasn't sure if he was being asked the question or if it was rhetorical. He hoped it was the latter, because this was something he *definitely* didn't have the current mental strength to try and answer.

"Do you know how you get into my line of work, Henry?" Corbin queried, cleaning his glasses with his T-shirt.

"I don't, no."

"You have to be smart. Very smart. When people hear *UFO, alien, extraterrestrial*—whatever, they scoff. It all sounds absurd. When people believe in sightings of the unexplained, they typically come to the conclusion that these foreign beings are looking to cause our extinction. But no one ever stops to wonder: Why? *Why* would someone travel the galaxy with the mere goal of bringing extinction to an unsuspecting planet? The idea, frankly, is a laughable one." Corbin began climbing out from the interior of the crater. Henry offered his hand in assistance. "You get into my line of work by being smart. There are seven levels of intelligence: smart, intelligent, super-smart, super-intelligent, genius, me, and godlike."

Well, at least he has his humility, Henry thought.

"When you've surpassed genius, the government takes you away. Out of school, away from friends, and they offer you any number of jobs within the standard government. Now, when you've even surpassed that—which I can tell you right now, Henry, is not common—then you're in my boat. And it's a rocky boat. When you meet my level of smart, you don't get a cozy government job. They don't even give you a choice. Your brain is too powerful for them to control, so they give you a position. And if you fail to comply with the position they've assigned for you, that's when *you* become extinct." Corbin dusted off his pants. "I've been doing this job for a lot longer than you'd think, and if you asked me what I feared more: Them . . . (he pointed up to the sky) or us? I'm answering *us* every time."

The police had taken Steve's statement regarding how he had discovered the Jane Doe and the state she'd been in. The officer on duty was an old classmate of Steve's, typical for a county this size. The woman had been asleep for hours, ever since her episode that morning. Nurses checked in on her every half hour. Her vitals were good, but still, Steve had been given no answers and did not want to leave her alone. He sat up in his chair, assuming it was about time for another check-in, and this time he wouldn't let the nurse leave without getting some kind of answer out of her. His foot tapped an unsteady rhythm against the floor; he was growing impatient. Just as he was about to stand up and start pacing, the doors of room 249 swung open and several nurses entered at once.

None of them paid any attention to Steve. They unlocked the wheels of the bed and proceeded to roll the woman away. Steve held the last nurse back. "Wait! Where are they taking her?"

The nurse consulted her chart. "You are?" Steve knew she wouldn't tell him if he was honest, so he kept his mouth shut and gave the nurse a stern look. She sighed and caved to his question.

"She has a pharyngeal abrasion. We're taking her in for some x-rays to make sure she doesn't have anything caught in her esophagus." The nurse then exited the room and closed the door behind her, leaving Steve by himself and even more confused.

Bruce Archer waited in the interrogation room. He, unlike Henry, was offered a phone call. He promptly turned it down. He had done nothing wrong, and he knew that, and he had no reason to worry unless he was presented with some shred of evidence, something that could link him to the missing boy (Bruce was unaware of the other three mutilated boys).

The metal door swung open and Bentley Trundle entered. He took a deep breath, filled with disappointment and uncertainty. Bentley took a seat across from Bruce. He glanced down at the handcuffs, which kept Bruce bound to the chair. Bentley rubbed his forehead. "Mind telling me what you were doing at the park, Bruce?"

Bruce rolled his eyes. "Camping. Just like I do every year."

Bentley opened his file and read. "Every year. That's what it says here, yeah. Why'd you leave after dark?" Bentley leaned in to intimidate Bruce. Unfortunately, Bruce was almost twice his size and difficult to intimidate.

"I wanna speak to my lawyer," Bruce said, the words slithering out from between his teeth like the hiss from a snake.

"You're gonna play that game, Bruce?"

"No game. You're gonna accuse me because you need a swift answer—someone to take the fall—so you can have your Labor Day fireworks. I ain't your fall guy, Officer Trundle. And I want my lawyer."

"You declined your phone call."

Bruce made a motion of zipping his mouth shut. He leaned back in his chair and crossed his arms. Bentley grew furious, leaving and slamming the door behind him. He knew getting a lawyer involved would see Bruce free by the end of the day. They had no evidence to suggest he was the kidnapper, aside from his odd presence in Hillsbury Park after hours. That kind of trespassing charge would amount to nothing but a small fine. Barely a slap on the wrist.

Determined not to let that happen, Bentley stormed back to his office.

Rachel was preparing lunch for Sarah when Jeffrey walked into the kitchen. "Hey, I'm making your sister a grilled cheese, want one?" she asked.

"I'm not hungry." Jeffrey sat next to his sister, who was once again blowing bubbles in her milk. "What're you doing?" he asked playfully.

Sarah giggled as the bubbles began spilling over the rim of her cup. "I'm making bubbles."

Rachel placed the finished sandwich in front of Sarah. "That's enough. Drink your milk. Ketchup?" Sarah nodded. A second later, the doorbell rang. "Would you mind getting that for me, Jeffrey?"

Jeffrey rose from his seat and opened the front door. To his amazement, standing on the opposite side, mere feet away from him, was Claudia. She was wearing a tight T-shirt (which he noticed first) and a wide smile (which he noticed second).

"Hey!" she said.

Jeffrey felt a smile of his own growing as if of its own accord. "What are you doing here?" Last night seemed like just a fluke, an extraordinary circumstance. Jeffrey didn't think he would have seen Claudia again so soon.

"I was just walking around. Started getting hungry," Claudia said. "Wanna get lunch with me?"

"Uh, I, that's . . . yeah! Sure! Where?"

Claudia shrugged. "I dunno. Somewhere?"

"'Kay, I'm just gonna tell my mum. Just so she doesn't worry that I've been, y'know . . . killed, or . . . stuffed in a trunk or something."

Claudia frowned. "That's not funny, Jeffrey."

"Yeah. You're right. Of course it isn't." Jeffrey silently fumed at himself, cursing his tongue for operating on a separate wavelength from his brain. Swallowing hard, Jeffrey called over his shoulder. "Mom, I'm gonna go get lunch!"

After a moment's pause, Rachel's voice carried from the kitchen. "But I thought you weren't hungry!" Claudia reacted with an amused expression.

Still smiling at Claudia, still trying to act nonchalant, Jeffrey called back, "Yeah, okay, I'll be back by five, bye!" in a single breath before exiting the house.

Rachel peered through the blinds in the kitchen and spotted Jeffrey walking down their driveway with Claudia Burton. She immediately understood.

Already interested in girls. He's growing so fast.

The two teenagers walked along the streets. The eerie silence was broken only by the occasional passing car. As much as it would have made sense for cottagers to leave a day or two early, it was mainly locals that left town.

They walked in silence, both a little nervous, both a little anxious. Jeffrey in particular was anxious to know whether that whole Bobby Rengard thing was real or just a fib to piss off her brother.

"I guess you want to know about Bobby Rengard, huh?" Claudia suddenly asked, as if reading his thoughts. It was so startling it almost made him jump. He fumbled over his words again, struggling to play things cool.

"No, it—"

"We *did* go out. That wasn't a lie. But it was during the day, and it wasn't a date. I was helping him with something."

"Helping him with what?"

"I was helping him with . . ." Claudia took a deep breath and collected her thoughts before continuing. "I had a crush on Bobby in ninth grade, but we never really hit it off." (Jeffrey couldn't help but smile and tried to pass it off as squinting into the sun.) "We remained friends and it turned out the reason we never hit it off was because he was gay, and he had a crush on Larry Kaswack. So anyway, Bobby made a pass at Larry, and turns out Kaswack doesn't like guys. Bobby was devastated, so I had to be there for him."

Jeffrey nodded, trying as hard as possible not to appear exuberant. "Oh. Okay."

"It was a rough day. He was really heartbroken. Then when I got home, Mum asked me to pick you guys up at the park, and clearly I didn't want to, not after all that—and Morgan rubbed me the wrong way and that's why I went with the date. It was stupid, I dunno. Anyway, I just wanted to get that off my chest."

Jeffrey smiled at her. She had no idea how much of a weight this was off *his* chest too. Still, he kept things close to the vest. "It's all good."

"So I heard they reopened the park?" Claudia asked curiously.

"Yeah, I . . . heard that too." Jeffrey knew the truth, thanks to his father. He also knew the park should never have been allowed to reopen at all.

"Surprised you aren't working."

"Nah, my dad said it wouldn't get too busy. Besides, I figure I earned the day off after everything that happened yesterday."

He shared a knowing smile with Claudia, who had, after all, experienced the same stressful night he had. She returned the smile, and—ever so gently—her fingers met his, curling around them.

Jeffrey felt as if a warm explosion had been set off some-where in the vicinity of his stomach. His face turned a fiery red. *Was this really happening?*

Henry's Jeep rolled in beside Ava's parked car in an empty spot at the rangers' headquarters.

"Who's that?" Corbin asked when he saw Ava walk toward the building.

"My assistant park ranger. Her name's Ava. Anything you say to me you can say to her."

"Henry, I don't think you quite grasp what I do. I can't just go about talking astrobiology to people. Heck, most have no clue as to what that even means. Matter of fact, when I first told you, you asked me what it meant. I had you sign that confidentiality agreement for a reason."

"She can sign it." Henry gave Corbin a firm glance, making him aware that this was not negotiable.

Corbin reluctantly agreed. "Very well. But no others."

"No others," Henry echoed as they exited the Jeep. "I don't know anybody else who'd believe you, anyway."

Even though it was close to three in the afternoon, not very many visitors had made their way to the park. The ones who did mostly just walked the paths and made their way back to their cars after only an hour or so.

Ava poured herself a hot cup of coffee. This was already her third cup today, but she was running on fumes and needed to keep at it. If she and Henry were the only employees in the park, she had to stay alert. This third cup would be different: no milk and two packets of sugar. *Variety is the spice of life*, she thought. Then the front door opened and Henry entered, followed by a fellow she had never seen before.

Henry hastened to make introductions. "Ava this is Corbin Mench: astrobiologist. Corbin, this is Ava Trillium, my assistant." Corbin stopped to shake Ava's hand; he hesitated at first, taken by her beauty. He could not believe a small town such as Hillsbury could harbor such an angelic creature. "Very nice to meet you," he said with a grin.

She smiled back and shook his hand. "British, wow."

"It surprises you?"

"Don't get too many around here. That's all. You sound so smart."

He laughed off her compliment. Henry kept the mood serious by adding, "He is," and opened his office door. "Ava, I need you to understand that what we're about to speak of is confidential. We'll need you to either sign a confidentiality agreement, which Mr. Mench will give you, or I'll have to ask you to leave the headquarters until further notice." Henry held the door open as he spoke.

Ava blinked, unsure what to make of Henry's statement. At first she thought it was a joke, until Corbin produced a stack of papers covered in legalese. "Okay, I'll bite. Why am I signing it?" She took the paper from Corbin and read it over. "Is . . . is this for real?" An expressionless Henry gave her a slight nod, barely even noticeable. She signed the paper, and before she knew it, she was seated in Henry's office with the door shut and the blinds closed.

Henry tried to get Ava up to speed while Corbin filled in the blanks. Ava's head swirled. This was clearly overwhelming her. Henry assured her he'd felt the exact same way.

Corbin finished his explanation with, "Any questions?"

"Aside from, *Are you serious?* No. I'd say I'm good."

"Very well." Corbin withdrew three photos from his brief-case and pinned them to the wall. Each photo showed one of the local boys after their mutilations. "Here we have three of the four missing boys. Found. Why were they found?" He looked first at Henry, then at Ava. Neither had an answer. "Do you notice anything unusual about them?"

Henry crossed his arms. "Just the obvious."

"Well, what's the obvious?" Corbin retorted.

Henry tried to keep his impatience in check. "Their wounds are sewn shut with an unfamiliar material. Trundle said he believed it to be some sort of copper, but I've never seen copper that looked like that."

"Not quite. They each possess a certain material, an uncommon material that is being analyzed as we speak. But the mystery here is: sewing requires a needle, and needles leave puncture wounds. So where are those puncture wounds? The mouth and eyes look clean and wound-free. No insertion marks. No bleeding. Just the sewing job."

"Who cares?" Ava blurted out. "Forget insertion wounds, or whatever! Why the hell did someone need to do this to these kids anyway? What would the purpose be?" She took a deep breath to calm herself and then muttered an apology.

"No, no. No need to be sorry," Corbin said. "What happened to these boys is interesting, but it's also terrifying. None of us want it to happen again. Now, to answer your question, Miss Trillium . . . *is* it *miss?*"

Ava hesitated for only a second before answering, "Yes."

"To answer your question, Miss Trillium, there could be any number of reasons for this. For starters, are either of you familiar with the three wise monkeys?"

Henry answered. "Japanese lore. Hear no evil, see no evil, and speak no evil, right?" The words were barely out of his mouth when a sick feeling twisted through his stomach.

"And that's exactly what we have here. David Curtis, see no evil. Chris Randall, hear no evil. Mitchell Rooney, speak no evil." Corbin let this sink in before asking, "Why?"

He looked at both Henry and Ava, knowing he would not receive an answer, but trying to gauge what was going through their minds at that moment, studying them to see if they were focused on his presentation or just horrified at the circumstances behind it.

"There's no answer," Corbin stated before making a retraction. "Well, there *is*. But at this point, I don't have it."

"When will you have it?" Henry asked gravely.

Corbin shook his head. "Statistically, findings pertaining to the wise monkeys are quite common." He paused to collect himself. "But . . . not with children. *Never* with children. There's more to this. We're missing something."

"What about the crop circle?" Henry asked. Corbin pointed to him as if to say, *Glad you asked*. He flipped over a paper on the easel, revealing several drawings of the crop circle he had shown Henry earlier in the day.

"My apologies. I'm no artist and this is not exactly to scale—I had to rush it—but the important aspects of the message are clear." Ava stared, mesmerized, at the shapes. *Uncanny*, she thought.

"The top portion here," Corbin pointed his marker to the two *S*-shape formations, "are common in messages. These are DNA strands, similar to ours here on Earth, but with several discrepancies. These discrepancies are what tell us who is sending the message."

"Well, who is it?" Henry pressed, but Corbin was not about to let that slip just yet.

"The bottom portion here," he pointed to the dashes, "is the message. These messages we receive are typically written in reverse. In reverse of what we would read here on Earth. The DNA strand is the signature, essentially. This DNA strand is quite common in these sorts of findings, and it's how we determine whether what we are looking at is legitimate or not."

"Okay, Corbin, this may be common for you, but we have no idea what's going on here." Henry was growing frustrated.

"I know, it makes no sense to the naked eye." Corbin rubbed a hand across his mouth in thought. "I'm not quite sure of the message as of yet. It's small, smaller than any I have seen. At first glance, it appears convoluted, but in reality, it's very brief. It's also important. That much I know, as they've gone to great lengths to make it appear very large." He pointed to the dash marks next. "If you look here, the dashes are numbers, each one consisting of ones and zeroes. Not exactly as *we* know them, of course, but after several complex math equations, we can correlate these dashes to ones and zeroes and thus see the decipher as . . ." He flipped another page on the easel. "Binary code. International language—intergalactic language."

"Intergalactic? Oh God." Ava rolled her eyes. This was all starting to sound pretty hokey to her.

"It sounds far-fetched, I know. I was once sitting in your shoes. But I assure you, you want to find out what happened to those kids, and why? This is a piece of that answer."

"A piece?" Henry was hoping for more.

"Yes, a piece. If and when we translate this message, it still may only be a portion." He switched gears briefly. "Hillsbury, particularly the park and even more so Cape's Side Bay, has been a hub for Radioactic Sputs, but why? And why reveal it now? We're overlooking something. A piece of this puzzle is still at play, and I am very sorry, but as of right now, I am as befuddled as you both are. This puzzle may remain unfinished until we find . . . well, until *they return* the missing link." With that, Corbin pressed his marker firmly against the piece of paper on the easel and wrote in large, ominous letters: *JOEL LIMAN*.

"'*They return*'?" Ava echoed. She didn't like the sound of that at all. "What's that supposed to mean, Corbin?"

"The million-dollar question. It could mean he was a victim of a higher power, a lesson for us to learn from. We will get to the bottom of this. I don't believe this means anything more than what it is indicating, however. You see, when multiple crop circles are discovered, a bigger message of power is being displayed. Usually catastrophic. In fact, multiple crop circles discovered within a close radius of each other have not been reported since, well—" Corbin stopped short of what he was saying. He could see in the eyes of both Henry and Ava the knowledge he was bestowing on them was difficult to swallow, without indulging them further. "Well," he continued, "a long time. My thoughts as of now is this could be a play in hand by a higher power. What and how it relates to Hillsbury and Cape's Side Bay, as of now, I cannot say."

"So, something bad is happening?" Ava's voice trembled.

"You just said . . ." Henry clapped back.

"I know what I said, and like I said, this crop message could be isolated to the Liman boy. Could be related to his family bloodline. It will take more investigating. We'll get to the bottom of it. We always do. You can trust me."

Outside, the sky was a beautiful, rich shade of blue, with not a cloud to be seen. Corbin inhaled the fresh air as he exited the headquarters.

"It's not every day I get to breathe in air like this. Typically it's gas fumes and sewage." He took another deep breath, his smile lingering just a moment longer than usual on Ava. "I could get used to this. Anyway, much work still to do. I should be heading back." He held Ava's hand and gave it a gentle kiss. "Thank you for your time. And if anything unusual arises, please let me know. Any information is crucial information. Remember that. Take care." He waved to Henry and began to walk toward his car.

"Corbin!" Henry called out to him. "If you're not busy tonight, why don't you swing by? The mayor's having a ribbon-cutting ceremony to officially open the carnival for the weekend. Could be fun."

Corbin smiled. "Sounds like a good time."

"Something the town needs," Henry returned, not sure if that was how he truly felt or if he was simply echoing the mayor's sentiments.

"Sure, why not?" Corbin said before waving one more time to the park rangers. He entered his car and drove off. Ava took a step toward Henry, her eyes never straying from the car. "Well, this is all . . . strange."

"What do you make of it?" Henry asked.

Ava shrugged. "I don't even know how to start answering that, Henry."

"Yeah. Me neither." Henry turned back to enter headquarters, holding the door open for Ava. "You two seemed friendly."

"What does that mean?" she said defensively.

"Just means—I don't know. It just means what it means. Should be a fun night tonight." Henry couldn't keep from smiling.

"You wipe away that grin, Henry Carter," Ava told him, though by the time she returned to her lukewarm coffee, she was smiling too.

Evening was quickly approaching. If this town was going to rebound from last night's lockdown fiasco, the mayor's ribbon-cutting ceremony was going to have to do the trick. If the night was a failure, the future of Hillsbury could potentially be in jeopardy. None of this was of any concern to the sixteen-year-old boy who'd just walked his crush to her front doorstep.

Claudia smiled at Jeffrey. "Thanks for having lunch with me."

Jeffrey nodded. "No problem."

"So I'll see you tonight? Ribbon cutting?"

"I'll be there."

Claudia stepped forward and planted a kiss on his cheek.

"See you tonight," she said with a nervous smile before disappearing into her house.

Jeffrey was elated. Never in his life had so many feelings coursed through him like this. Was it a date? What should he wear? Should he have offered to walk her to the park? So many questions, and he possessed the answers to none of them. Regardless, he didn't stop smiling for the entire walk home.

He was halfway there when a Jeep pulled up next to him, honking. It was his father. "Need a ride?"

"What're you doing here?" Jeffrey thought for sure his father would still be at work.

"Promised your mother I'd be home for supper. So here I am. Hop in."

Jeffrey got into the Jeep, staring out the window and reminiscing about the wonderful afternoon he'd just had. "So you heard the park will be open tonight?" Henry asked him.

"Yeah." Jeffrey didn't want to let his father know he would be going with Claudia. He didn't much feel like dealing with the embarrassing array of verbal abuse his father would undoubtedly thrust upon him.

Then Henry threw a wrench into the equation by saying, "I'm gonna need you to suit up tonight."

"Suit up?"

"Work, yeah."

Jeffrey could not believe his ears. "I can't. I have plans."

"You're a junior ranger. You're gonna suit up."

"What about Morgan?" Jeffrey pleaded.

"Morgan can suit up too, but if his parents say no, they say no. I know for a fact your parents will agree to this."

"Serious, Dad, I have plans."

"Change them."

Once the Jeep parked in the driveway, Jeffrey stormed out and into the house, refusing to speak a word to his father. Henry entered the kitchen and greeted his wife with a hug. "Told you I'd be home," he said, stroking her hair.

Rachel beamed at him. "I know you did. What's wrong with Jeffrey?"

"Told him I needed him to work tonight. He got upset 'cause he said he had other plans. But I need him."

"Other plans?"

Henry shrugged. "Yeah. Who knows?"

"Well," Rachel started, "he was out all day . . ."

Henry began setting the table for dinner.

"With Claudia Burton," Rachel finished.

Henry stopped what he was doing and looked up at Rachel. "Claudia Burton?"

Jeffrey placed the headphones securely over his ears, submerging him in the repetitive sounds of *Shooter of Honor 3: Heroes of Gun-Town*. He had the audio cranked as loud as it could get, so he didn't hear his father knock three times before entering.

He glanced over, fuming. "Haven't you ever heard of knocking?" Jeffrey shouted before throwing off his headphones and lying on his bed.

"I did. Three times. How loud were you listening to that?"

"Not loud enough." Jeffrey opened a gaming magazine and pretended to read.

Henry perched himself on the edge of the bed. "Look, I wanted to talk to you about tonight."

"Talk about what? About how you're gonna make me work?"

Henry was too full of empathy to be angry. He remembered when he was sixteen all too well. "I'm sorry, son. I shouldn't have just told you like that. I should have asked." Jeffrey stopped pretending to read and looked over at his father; he'd rarely heard the old man apologize. "Truth is, Jeffrey, I really need you, and life isn't always fair."

"Trust me, I'm figuring that out the hard way."

Henry pulled the magazine away from him. "You got it good. Real good. You have any idea how many kids out there in this world would kill to have it like you do?"

"Then they can have it."

Henry rolled his eyes.

"Your mother told me you spent the day with Claudia Burton."

For the first time since Henry entered the room, Jeffrey locked eyes with him. "So?" he growled.

"So . . . is that who you had plans with tonight?"

Jeffrey didn't answer. He didn't need to. Henry understood.

"All right. Look . . . I need you tonight, but I don't want to take you away from whatever it is you have going on. Tell you what, why don't you and your friend hang out at the park. You can still be on duty, but no uniform."

Jeffrey was shocked. "Wait . . . serious?"

"Serious."

Jeffrey thought for a moment. What would it matter? They were going to go to the park anyway. All he'd have to do is make sure no one polluted, which would have probably been the case whether he was on duty or not.

"Sure. Okay."

Henry smiled at him and opened the door. "C'mon, then. Your mother's got dinner ready."

A cloud rolled in front of the sun, alone but dominant. This single cloud was enough to cover the sunshine from Hillsbury, if only for a few minutes. It was during this period of semidarkness that Bruce Archer was released from police custody.

He walked down the police station's front steps and took a deep breath. The rancid smell of his cell and the interrogation room was now a thing of the past. No evidence had been found connecting him with the missing boy, or any of the other recent strangeness. As of now, Bruce was a free man . . . but a free man being watched. He knew that as long he stayed in Hillsbury, all eyes would be on him.

There was only one place for him to go.

SATURDAY EVENING

CORBIN SAT IN his tiny office pondering the message left in the cornfield. He had been studying it for hours; it was one of the most difficult messages he had ever had to decode. The construction of the code had several red herrings placed sporadically throughout. Every time Corbin thought he was close, a new problem arose. Thus far, he was able to calculate that it was a message containing at least two numbers and an uncertain amount of letters.

Corbin removed his glasses and rubbed his eyes. The tiny digital alarm clock (which was at least as old as he was and had seen better days) displayed its bright red digital lights into his eyes. It was nearly seven o'clock.

Seven.

Seven Deadly Sins. Corbin didn't know why, but that popped into his head.

Hillsbury was guilty of all seven.

Lust: The number of affairs he'd noticed while in Hillsbury was disquieting. It seemed part of the town's very identity at this point. For decades, men had been known to bring women who weren't their wives to the bay, using the water's tranquil seclusion to seal many a rendezvous.

Gluttony: Overpriced, over-served restaurants and bakeries, welcoming the men and women sneaking around town with their secret paramours, and happily using that knowledge as an excuse to increase their prices.

Greed: The sin of desire. It could have been printed on Hillsbury's coat of arms. Each new cottage erected was larger and grander than the one before . . . until the one before would undergo renovations. Rinse and repeat.

Envy: To know Mayor Tremblay was to know envy. The two went together like white on rice. In fact, when Hasaga first opened for tourists, residents of Hillsbury, led by a then much younger, much more rambunctious Tremblay, sent threats to the town and the park. Ever since the opening of the trailer park in Hasaga, Hillsbury had focused its resources on always being a notch or two "better" in every way.

Wrath: It was true that the town was safe from violence, but that didn't mean the hometowns of the seasonal residents were safe. Background checks indicated domestic abuse performed by both men and women (covered up, of course). Wealth was used to cover up the ugly to assert power over others. The town as a whole was more or less aware of these cases. Corbin could not find evidence that Bentley or Henry were aware, but one simply had to look close enough to uncover these truths. Besides, Henry was a park ranger; there was no reason for him to investigate domestic affairs.

Pride: The father of all sins. Hillsbury was prideful. It was the best summer spot in the country, but that was not enough. Now Mayor Tremblay had plans to one-up his end-of-season celebrations. The town reeked of pride. *And the pride goeth before the fall* . . .

Sloth . . .

Corbin's train of thought screeched to a halt. This sin was harder to uncover. Sure, the town basically neglected God and his teachings, but his findings couldn't bring up anything drastic enough to fit the bill. Sighing, Corbin rubbed his brow.

Something wasn't adding up. But whatever the sum of all these parts was, it was not going to be good. He needed to uncover the truth. He needed to know if this connection was genuine or just in his head.

But right now, more than anything else, he needed a break.

Henry fastened the final button on his ranger shirt and kissed Rachel goodnight. "I won't be too late," he promised.

Rachel did her best not to show how nervous she really was. Even though the mayor and police had informed her that everything was safe in Hillsbury, she still had her concerns. Something just felt *wrong* about tonight.

"Be careful," she told him in a soft, somber tone.

He nodded, then turned to face the stairs. "Jeffrey, need a lift?"

"No, it's okay," came Jeffrey's voice.

"Well, that's it, then," Henry said, trying to shake off the unpleasant, ominous feeling creeping up his spine. "I'll see you tonight."

Henry left a few moments before Jeffrey made his way downstairs. Rachel grabbed her son by the arm and gave him the kind of stare only a truly concerned mother was capable of giving. "You be careful tonight. Promise me."

"Of course. Bye, Mom." Then he was gone.

Rachel turned back to Sarah, who was busy playing with a vast assortment of dolls in the hallway. "Just you and me tonight, kiddo," Rachel said, sitting down next to Sarah. She reached out and picked up one of the dolls. It happened to be completely nude. "Where are her clothes?"

Sarah shrugged nonchalantly. "I was playing 'laundy' so I flushed her clothes down the toilet. I thought it would work like a washing machine."

Rachel set the doll back down, rolling her eyes. "Of course you did."

Mayor Tremblay gallivanted around the park with a large pair of scissors in his hands, scouring for photo ops like a vulture on the prowl for fresh carrion.

It was a particularly beautiful night. The stars were in full view. The carnival was set up and the lights were just beginning to hum to life. One side of the park featured games: whack-a-mole, bucket toss, break-a-bottle (a game in which you threw a softball at a pyramid of three beer bottles in the hopes to shatter them all and win a fairly small prize), and several different basketball games (all with the same end goal: get the ball in the basket). The middle section featured a plethora of food vendors, from pretzels to pizzas to corn dogs to funnel cakes to cotton candy, with a giant beer tent at its center. The far side of the park consisted of two haunted houses, a children's boat ride that twirled three times, and a fortune teller, palm reader. When Henry had first seen the fortune teller he thought she was a customer, or at the very least an assistant. She looked to be only twenty years old and wasn't wearing a single gaudy piece of clothing.

Nobody's gonna be hungry or bored here tonight, Henry thought, staring at the expanse of colored tents and stands.

"Henry Carter!"

Tremblay was shouting at him from across the fairgrounds. He'd clearly had one too many beers and hadn't even cut the ribbon yet.

"Beautiful night! Gorgeous night!" he said, waving his large scissors precariously.

Henry leaned back into an awkward, quasi-limbo stance to avoid them. "It certainly is. Looks like you lucked out."

Tremblay didn't let the slight insult go by unnoticed. "Why, Henry," he said, slurring each word, "luck had nothing to do with it. God knew Hillsbury needed to see some light, and he said, as he did way back in the Bible, Chapter One: 'Let there be light.' And voila, here we are!"

"Here we are," Henry retorted.

"Have you had a corn dog?" Tremblay shouted.

"I have not."

"Then, by all means, come, come, let's get you a corn dog!" The mayor wrapped his arm around Henry and shepherded him toward the corn dog stand. Henry watched as the mayor ordered two corn dogs, wincing. He hoped the man would be in good enough shape to cut that ribbon when the time came.

"How are you enjoying the evening so far?" the mayor said with a mouth full of food.

"Good. I mean, I only just got here, but it looks good."

This was exactly what Tremblay had hoped to hear. He smacked Henry proudly on the back, a little too hard. Henry (who'd been mid-bite with his corn dog) gave a start and almost choked.

"I must be off. My assistant is waving me down. Must be getting close to snippy snippy!" He snipped the large scissors twice, and then departed.

Henry was very happy to see him leave. After that first bite of corn dog, he found the flavor and texture revolting and tossed it into the nearest trash can.

"Tremblay get you that?" someone asked.

Henry turned and smiled. The young woman was dressed in freshly pressed ranger attire. "Hey, Ava. How'd you guess?"

"He made me have one too. They're atrocious. I think that's his nephew working the stand."

Henry glanced up at the corn dog vender. "Wouldn't surprise me."

"Like I always say." Ava sighed. "*I* didn't vote for him. We're closing at ten tonight, right?"

"Yeah, I'm hoping we can get everyone out of here by nine or so." A quick look around told him that the crowd was growing. The heat was drawing people out of their houses. "I doubt it'll happen, but you never know."

Just then, Ava spotted Bentley at the beer tent. "Excuse me a second," she said, and made her way over to the deputy sheriff. When she was close enough for him to see her, she smiled. "Hey, stranger."

Bentley's face was deep in his red Solo cup. He chugged his beer and slammed it down, never making eye contact with Ava, his eyes fixated on the bartender. "Another," he demanded.

"Everything all right?" She leaned into him. He chugged this next beer back and didn't look at Ava until he'd downed every last drop.

"No." He tossed his cup into the trash can and stormed off. Ava followed after him.

"You wanna talk about it?"

"Not particularly," Bentley said.

"Something's bothering you, Bent."

"No kidding. Are you a detective? How'd you figure that one out?" His tone was rude and obnoxious.

"I'm only trying to help."

"Yeah. That's all I wanted to do too. But sometimes shit happens and it's out of your control." Bentley stormed away from Ava, leaving her hurt and confused.

Henry lit his cigarette as he sat on the wooden deck at the side of the rangers' headquarters. He didn't like to be seen smoking in front of park visitors; he was afraid it would seem unprofessional. He looked up at the dark blue sky with the cigarette hanging from his lips and the sun setting in the distance and wondered about the universe and its workings. Of all his years looking up at those stars, he never truly wondered if they were alone in the universe. Not until now. Not until he met Corbin. Now he knew there was much more at play and he was just a small piece of some sort of giant puzzle. He wasn't sure how he felt about that, but he didn't have a say in the matter. As he was about to flick his cigarette away, headlights appeared in the distance. Someone was coming to the rangers' headquarters. He took one final drag of his cigarette and stuffed it into the ashtray. The car rolled to a stop, and out of the passenger side walked Patty Liman. She was dressed all in black and had her hair in a bun. She looked at Ranger Carter.

"Mrs. Liman." Henry approached her, offered his hand for a shake. She refused.

"A carnival?" Disgust dripped from her voice.

A sense of guilt overcame Henry. He lowered his head. "Now, Mrs. Liman—"

"You listen to me. I have a son. My son! And he's missing somewhere in your park!" Henry pulled out another cigarette; Patty swatted it out of his hand and burst into tears. Her brother, Neil, exited the car and grabbed her, looking apologetically at Henry.

"Sorry, she just told me she wanted to speak to you." He focused his attention back on his sister. "It's okay. It's okay."

"My boy!" Patty cried out at the top of her lungs. Though no one had given up hope in finding Joel, the gravity of the situation (and the fact that everyone's worst fears were growing likelier by the minute) was setting in. Neil helped Patty back into the car. He turned to Henry. "Mind if I have one?"

Henry offered Neil his last cigarette. Neil took several long drags. His hands trembled. "We're having a vigil tomorrow night, outside of the house. We know it's the big firework night, but it was also Joel's favorite night. He looked forward to it every year. It'd mean a lot to Patty and myself if you could come." He returned the cigarette to the park ranger, who said very little at first and just stared at the pain and suffering in the man's eyes. He thought about his own children, about how he would feel if this sort of thing ever happened to them.

"I'll do my best," Henry said, his voice just above a whisper. Neil gave a slight smile and thanked the ranger. Then he got back in his car and drove off.

The night sky hovered over Hillsbury Park with the stars shinning down on the tall treetops. Mayor Tremblay lifted high his oversize scissors and waved at the multitude of cameras. Then, with a mighty *snip*, he cut the banner.

"The Hillsbuy Park Labor Day Festival has officially begun!" he declared amid a sea of flashbulbs. He beamed at the hundreds of people staring up at him. What had begun as a disastrous weekend was now turning into a massive success.

He thought of the families who'd left after the park lockdown, and the campers who were forced to evacuate. *Those fools. They don't know what they're missing.* Tremblay smiled at another photographer. *But they'll find out. And next year, they'll be HERE.* He stepped down from the stage, doing so slowly, in case anyone wanted to take an action shot of him. When his foot hit the grass it sank from beneath him. His ankle twisted and he fell, howling in pain and dropping the scissors.

Henry and a paramedic rushed over to him. "Mayor Tremblay, you all right?" the paramedic asked.

The pain was visible on Tremblay's beet-red face. "Does it look like I'm all right? Help me up!" Henry helped the paramedic walk Tremblay over to a picnic table and let him sit. Tremblay smacked the hands of the paramedic away whenever they tried to touch his ankle.

"What happened to him?" asked a familiar accented voice; Corbin had appeared from the shadows.

"Not sure." Henry hastily shook Corbin's hand. "Didn't think I'd see you here."

"Didn't think I'd see myself here. But there's such a thing as being *too* involved with your work. Sometimes overworking causes us to overlook certain things. A night out in the park may help me in the long run."

Henry gave the man a friendly slap on the back. "Come on, what do you say we get you a beer?"

"I'd say make it two." The two men laughed and walked off, leaving the paramedic with the unenviable task of tending to the humiliated mayor alone.

The typical evening hush had fallen over St. Joseph's Hospital. Steve knew it would soon be time for him to leave, and he hadn't decided yet whether he'd return again tomorrow.

Jane Doe still had not woken up. He'd heard she had a minor episode as they wheeled her for x-rays earlier, but aside from that, she just lay there, peaceful and still. The nurse quietly opened the door and took a peek at the woman, asking Steve if she'd woken or stirred at all. "Not yet," Steve said, half-disappointedly.

Not wishing to be rude, the nurse gestured to her watch and gently said, "I'm afraid visiting hours are over for today."

Steve nodded and stood up. His legs wobbled slightly; he hadn't realized how long he'd been sitting there. He was about to follow the nurse out when he decided he needed to know (and felt he deserved to know) what the x-rays showed. The nurse replied that she wasn't entirely sure herself, clearly hesitant to discuss it with him.

"Well, can you check the chart? Please?" Steve asked. "I found her this morning outside my shop. I've been with her all day. She has nobody, nobody but me."

The nurse caved. She walked briskly to the foot of the bed and retrieved the anonymous woman's chart.

"Well?" Steve asked. The nurse looked up at him.

"In a nutshell . . . her pharynx, esophagus, and stomach are all scratched."

"Scratched? How?"

"Unfortunately, we don't know yet. For now, she needs rest." The nurse put the chart down.

"That's it?" Steve was frustrated, tired, and hungry for answers.

"You can come back tomorrow. Perhaps we will have more by then." Then the nurse walked away to resume her rounds.

Jane Doe's heart monitor suddenly began beeping at a quicker pace, then quicker, and even quicker still. Her eyes flung open, her mouth opening to its full extent. She gasped for air. Steve was stunned; he had no idea what to do. He was already halfway out the door.

"Hey! Hey, nurse! Something's wrong!"

The nurse ran back down the hall and entered the room. By the time she'd put her stethoscope in her ears, Jane Doe had settled down.

"Heartbeat's normal," the nurse said. "It's okay. Everything's fine."

"Do you know what that was?" Steve asked.

But before the nurse could answer, Jane Doe reached out and seized her wrist. The nurse nearly screamed. Most of what came out of Jane's open mouth was just air, but a word had begun to claw its way to the surface, a painfully hoarse word that started with an *R*. "Re—" Each syllable would drain Jane Doe of her energy. "Re-k-k . . ."

The nurse removed herself from the woman's clutch and tried to calm her. "Easy, easy."

"What's she saying?" Steve asked.

The nurse shrugged. "Maybe her name?"

"Reckon . . ." Jane Doe tried one more time. "Reck . . . on . . ." And with that, exhausted, the mysterious woman fell asleep.

The nurse glanced at Steve, puzzled. "Has she ever said that before?"

"She's never said *anything* before."

SATURDAY NIGHT

THE CARNIVAL WAS electric. Everyone was having a grand time, everyone—that is—except the mayor.

Even though he'd merely twisted his ankle, Tremblay had been taken to the hospital for further testing. His injury wasn't serious at all, but the way he'd treated the paramedic was incredibly rude, so the medical team opted to transfer him to the hospital on grounds of a "technicality," just to cause him to miss his own party. Tremblay would have been proud if he could have seen the numbers his carnival was bringing in; the crowd only grew more and more dense after the ribbon cutting.

Claudia sank her teeth deep into a cloud of cotton candy. She handed it to Jeffrey, who seemed rather repulsed by it, but he indulged just the same. The sugary treat stuck to the interior of his mouth. He tried to break it free with his tongue, rolling his eyes in whichever direction his tongue would swat.

Claudia giggled. "Having trouble?"

"No, no," Jeffrey said, his words hardly understandable with his tongue pressed firmly against the inside of his cheeks. Claudia took another large bite and noticed one of the many basketball games. The main prize was a stuffed banana with googly eyes—bizarre, to be sure, but cute enough that it attracted Claudia's attention. She wandered over to it. "Wanna win me a prize?" she asked Jeffrey, who had just now removed the final piece of cotton candy from his cheek.

"Yeah, sure," he said, though Jeffrey was far from sure. He loved sports, but basketball was not his strong suit. Give him a batting cage and he could hit the ball for hours. But try to toss a ball through a hoop? Not his bag.

"It's five dollars for three balls," the operator informed him, and Jeffrey foraged through his wallet for whatever change he could find. He slid the array of bills and coins toward the worker, who handed him a black basketball. He bounced it twice on the counter and then spun it around in his hands. The object of this particular basketball game was to get the ball in the basket a minimum of two out of three attempts. If you made all three shots, you would win the large prize (a larger version of the googly-eyed banana). His first attempt missed widely. The ball *did* make contact with the backboard, which Jeffrey still considered a minor victory, but he needed to sink the next two baskets to win Claudia a prize. And something told him winning that hideous banana would score him some major points.

As if reading his mind, Claudia leaned in and gave Jeffrey a soft, slow kiss on the cheek. "For luck," she whispered.

His heart pulsated at a rapid pace. *For luck?* If anything, he was more nervous than he'd been before. He gripped the ball tightly, shut his eyes, and released it toward the basket.

Swoosh! Nothing but net.

"That's one! One more and you win the pretty lady a prize," the worker explained as he handed Jeffrey his third and final ball. Claudia clapped her hands frantically, less excited about the prize itself than she was that someone was actually willing to win it for her. While only seventeen, Claudia had seen her fair share of boyfriends in the past. The embarrassing

Bobby Rengard incident notwithstanding, her track record hadn't been great. Just before going away to camp that summer, Claudia had found herself in a two-month-long relationship. To a teenager—whose days stretch much longer than those of an adult, and whose feelings are much more fragile—two months is almost a lifetime. This boy introduced Claudia to two things she was not accustomed to: love and heartbreak.

She found out she was being cheated on. And after the boy apologized, Claudia opted to return to his arms. Soon after, he cheated on her again with her best friend, Sandra (who was now, of course, her *ex*-best friend). These events drove Claudia to leave Hillsbury and become a camp counselor for the summer. She'd needed to escape, to go somewhere that didn't remind her of how badly she was hurting.

During her time away at camp, she met another boy: Ash. Ash spent hours at the gym working on his physique. His lifelong goal was to join the military and save humanity. From what, Claudia wasn't sure, but he showed an interest in her and she couldn't resist those biceps. So they hung out frequently at camp, enjoying meals together and teaming up whenever possible.

Then things took a turn: Ash had started to get aggressive with Claudia. He wanted to have sex; she wanted to wait. So he pushed and pushed. It got so bad that at one point, he drank himself silly and proceeded to touch Claudia inappropriately. He even did this in the mess hall, in front of other counselors. Claudia tried to remove herself from his clutches, but he was too strong, too powerful, and he forced himself on her. She squirmed and squirmed until he struck her, a backhand straight to her face. A swarm of counselors rushed in and grabbed Ash, pulling him off of her; but the damage had already been done. Ash was sent home that night. Claudia's face was red for days.

The other counselors assumed it was from where he'd struck her. Claudia let them go on believing that.

How could she have let it get that far? Was it her fault? Should she have spoken up sooner? She was wracked with guilt, with humiliation, with self-pity, and she found herself feeling like she would just as soon die alone than fall victim to something like this again.

And now . . . Jeff. Jeffrey Carter, a year her junior, a boy from a good home, with a good family. She'd been uncharacteristically rude to him the day before, both because she was frustrated with being on lockdown, and also because she was afraid. She was afraid because Morgan had told her Jeffrey had feelings for her, and she—if being honest with herself—had no interest in a boy a year younger than she was.

That night, however, she'd had a conversation with Morgan, who informed her that her actions toward him had nearly crushed the boy's heart. Claudia knew that feeling of hopelessness all too well. So she'd lain awake and pondered.

The decision wasn't easy. Her relationship with Ash had ended less than two weeks ago, hardly enough time for her (or *anyone*) to move on and feel comfortable with another person. But her initial attraction to Ash had been based on biceps and a thrill. There would be no thrill with Jeffrey, and—she concluded—perhaps no thrill could, in actuality, be the biggest thrill of all.

The ball smacked the side of the rim and lunged out directly at Jeffrey, whose reflexes were quick enough to catch the ball before smashing him in the nose.

Dammit! he thought. Jeffrey glanced at Claudia with a look of disappointment. An apology for failing was halfway out of his mouth when he noticed she was smiling at him. Claudia wrapped her arm around her date (which, she decided now, was exactly what he was) and said, "You tried! At least you sunk one, right?"

Jeffrey considered playing again until he remembered that his wallet was now empty; cotton candy and corn dogs didn't come free. As the young couple turned to leave, the game operator called them back. He reached up with a stick and pulled a googly-eyed banana off the rack.

"For the lady," he said, handing the stuffed fruit to Jeffrey with a wink.

Jeffrey couldn't believe his luck. He handed the banana to Claudia, who—although she hugged the prize tightly to her chest—never took her eyes off her date.

"See, Jeffrey Carter?" she said quietly. "You *are* a winner."

Corbin was busying himself at the whack-a-mole stand. It was a good way to vent some of his work-related aggression. Not many people believed in what he did, or respected him, or had even heard of his line of work. Though Corbin was loath to admit it out loud, this sometimes got very, very lonely.

In the deepest, darkest corners of his thoughts, Corbin Mench sometimes found himself yearning for something simpler, something more . . . normal, for lack of a better word. A life where he could have normal hours, normal relationships, normal friends. A life where the things he said wouldn't go way over everybody's heads and leave them staring at him, as nonplussed and googly-eyed as the hideous stuffed bananas these carnival vendors were shelling out as prizes. A life where he wasn't chasing aliens or deciphering crop circles but simply *living*. He loved his job, but sometimes . . . *sometimes* . . . he looked at someone like Henry Carter and thought, *God, how did I miss out on THAT life?*

Another plastic mole popped its head out of its hiding place, and Corbin let out a soft growl of frustration as he introduced the business end of the foam mallet to that mole's stupid, smiling face.

"Looks like you're having way too much fun."

Corbin looked to his left. Ava had approached holding two paper cups, one of which she offered to him. "Coffee?"

He lowered the mallet and accepted the cup. "How did you know? I've had more beer tonight than I've had in the last couple of years."

"How many is that?" she asked.

"Two pints," he laughed. "My head is spinning. I'm afraid I don't have much of a tolerance for alcohol."

As he collected himself, Ava asked a follow-up question. "How are you enjoying Hillsbury so far?" She was always curious how foreigners viewed her town.

"To be completely honest," Corbin said over the rim of his cup, "I haven't been able to enjoy it all that much. Work has bogged me down a great deal." He looked at his surroundings: the colorful fair, the beautiful night sky, Ava . . . "But it does seem like a lovely place."

"And what about you? Where are you from?" she asked him.

"England. Marylebone, to be exact."

"Is that near London?"

Corbin nodded. "In fact, it is. You ever been?"

Ava laughed. "Nope, 'fraid not! How long have you been living abroad?"

He thought about it momentarily before answering. "I've been living here about five years. I go wherever work takes me, unfortunately, not the other way around. I have lived in a total of seventeen countries. Aside from England, this one has been my longest tenure. I don't think I've been home in . . ." He did some quick mental math. "Three years, this winter, I believe."

"You like that? Moving around all the time?" Ava inquired.

Corbin absolutely hated it, despised it, even. But it was one of the many necessary evils of being an astrobiologist. "Not in the slightest. But it is what it is and here we both are."

Ava could feel her own cheeks getting warm when he smiled at her. "Here we both are," she echoed.

Henry finished up in the restroom in the rangers' headquarters. He looked at his hair in the mirror, grinning. Not a single gray to be seen.

Outside the stars were in full view, and Henry continued to be amazed at how infrequently he admired them. He walked over to the bench outside, sat down, and called Rachel on his cell phone. He missed her, and he missed his daughter. More than anything, he wanted to make sure they were both doing fine and to let them know he was okay and that there would be no more horrific incidents like the night before. As the conversation with his wife drew to a close, he told her that he loved her and would see her soon.

"Must be nice!"

The voice came from around the headquarters, the speech slurred; clearly someone who had visited the beer tent one too many times. Henry turned to see Bentley sitting on the steps, a red cup in his hand. "Having someone who loves you."

"Bentley?" Henry sauntered over to the deputy sheriff. "You're drunk."

"I am," Bentley said in a rather satisfied tone.

"You're on duty tonight." Henry peered into the half-full cup of beer in Bentley's hand.

"Yeah, well, the other officers can handle it. We got bigger problems, Mr. Ranger," Bentley said.

"Problems? What problems?"

"Problems like Bruce Archer. Problems like he mutilated those boys and stashed the Liman kid somewhere and won't tell anyone where." He paused as he swallowed a belch. "Oh, and we had to let him free! You know why? 'Cause the law sucks, Henry! The law sucks!" Bentley raised his cup high above his gaping mouth and poured the remaining beer down his front. The majority of it missed his mouth and splashed all over his shirt.

"Maybe you should go home, Bentley. Elise can take care of you."

"Elise can't take care of shit!" Bentley shouted. "I don't want Elise; I want Ava! I want it to be like it was."

Henry fought to keep his expression neutral, but on the inside, his mind was racing. *So it IS true*, he thought. *Bentley and Ava . . . Jesus.*

The deputy's yelling began to slowly convert into a whimper. He was near tears. "I miss her, Henry. I love her. And now she's off with that government dipshit! What does he got that I don't, huh? What?" He threw his beer cup as far as he could and passed out.

The lights were dimmed for the night at St. Joseph's Hospital. The visitors had all gone home, and the night nurses and doctors were scattered throughout. Special supervision was being given to Jane Doe in room 249. The hospital had contacted several local news outlets, which would visit the next morning to spread word and help ID the woman.

The letters Jane Doe had spoken were *R-E-K*. The night nurses, who were none too busy that evening, spent their time hoping to figure out what name she was trying to blurt out, like some grim logic puzzle. One nurse brought up the idea that perhaps she was not saying her name at all, but instead giving the name or location of her abuser. The only thing anyone knew for sure was the case of this Jane Doe was shrouded in mystery.

The alarm sounded. Jane Doe's heart rate was spiking again. The nurses stormed in to see Jane Doe sitting perfectly upright in her bed, eyes wide open, seeming almost possessed. She looked over at them.

The head nurse slowly approached the bed. "Everything's okay, dear." She reached out and held the woman's hand, soothing her, calming her down. Her heat rate began to subside back to its normal rate. Then Jane Doe opened her mouth, and a thick yellow liquid came sliding out and landed in her lap.

"We're gonna need a cleanup!" the head nurse called out. Mops and paper towels were immediately brought in. The nurse studied the liquid, confused. "What is this?" she whispered to herself before looking at the woman's food tray. None of it had been touched. Jane Doe had not eaten in over eighteen hours; nothing in her system would cause her to discharge something so viscous. As the head nurse turned to leave the room, Jane Doe seized her wrist. The nurse spun around in shock.

"*Reckoning.*"

Jane Doe's voice was a whisper ladened with horror. "*Reckoning,*" she said again, eyes bulging.

Then, exhausted, wincing with pain, Jane Doe lowered her head back onto the pillow and fell unconscious, leaving the poor nurses even more confused than they'd already been.

Henry helped Bentley into the back seat of a cab and gave the driver some extra cash for his trouble. The cab drove several feet before coming to a stop again. The rear window lowered and Bentley's hand crept out, beckoning Henry forward.

Quizzical, Henry approached. Bentley chugged the water Henry had given him as he waited for the cab.

"The DNA matched," Bentley said, out of breath, his slur fading.

Henry leaned in closer. "What?"

"The ear. It was the kid's. No surprise there. Kind of a relief, eh? The blood print, the one found at the bay . . . it belonged to Joel Liman." Bentley took another long, slow sip of water. "Bruce Archer is out there, Henry. He's out there and he's guilty of these crimes. Believe me."

That was all. He rolled the window back up and the cab drove off.

Henry watched as it left the property. A guilty feeling hit him like a punch to the gut. He knew Elise Trundle well and considered her a lovely, kind woman. He'd had his suspicions about Ava and Bentley, but they'd been nothing more than that: suspicions. A lingering gaze here, a strangely playful smile there . . . Did Elise already know? If not, should he say something? Should he confront Ava?

Henry felt the familiar claustrophobic sensation of being caught between a rock and a hard place, and he silently wished Bentley had never opened his stupid, drunk mouth. Ignorance had been bliss.

As if he didn't have enough problems.

The park was closing up, and it just so happened that Corbin and Ava were the last two people playing a game of bucket toss.

"Okay, here we go. Last attempt at winning the lovely lady a prize," Corbin laughed. He got a firm grip on the ball and tossed it ever so gently with a backspin. Much like the basketball game, each player was given three attempts to sink a ball into a bucket. The bucket itself was pinned up at a ninety-degree angle, and on the back of each bucket was a spring, giving the game a certain level of difficulty. Three balls in scored you a large prize, two balls would win you a medium prize, and one ball would win you a free ball or small prize. His first ball missed and both Corbin and Ava laughed. He hit the bucket dead center and the ball furiously bounced back out.

"Well, that was no good, was it?" he said. He grabbed the second ball, gave it a kiss for luck, and softly tossed it—this time without the backspin. He sunk it, and the ball stayed in. Corbin threw his arms up in victory. "Yes! At the very least, I can go home a *pseudo*-winner tonight!" And his delight only grew when, a moment later, he managed to sink the third ball into the bucket and keep it there.

He chose a strange-looking stuffed purple monster prize and offered it to Ava, who gratefully accepted it. "My hero," she teased. "The evening would have been horrible if I couldn't go home with . . . whatever the hell this thing is supposed to be."

Corbin laughed heartily, harder than he'd laughed in a long time. Then the carnival lights shut off. "And that's that, then, isn't it? Closing time?"

Ava nodded. "I better get back to headquarters. Meet up with Henry for the final walk-through."

Corbin gestured with one hand. "I've got nowhere to be. Please, allow me to join you."

As the young astrobiologist and assistant park ranger made their way toward the rangers' headquarters, there wasn't a moment of silence between the two. They chatted about pretty much everything, each divulging more than either figured they ever would to each other. First Corbin told Ava about his childhood and being bumped up in school and eventually being the youngest in his university. Then Ava told her story about becoming a park ranger and how a series of fateful—though disappointing—events caused her to assist Henry at Hillsbury Park. The conversation continued until a flash of movement up ahead caught their attention. Ava froze, holding her arm across Corbin's body to halt him. He blinked, confused. "What is it?"

Ava pulled the flashlight from her pocket. "Not sure."

They stepped slowly and cautiously forward. The woods ahead were quiet once more, and utterly dark.

"A deer, perhaps?" Corbin queried.

Ava frowned. Since the eerie events of the day before, local wildlife in Hillsbury and the surrounding counties had seemed to thin out or fade away altogether. Obviously no one had told Corbin this yet. The sound of a twig breaking made them both jump. Ava clicked on her flashlight.

"Hello?" she called out in a very tentative voice, as if she did not want an answer. Corbin adjusted his glasses, peering into the gloom. Ava panned her flashlight from left to right. She did this several times, and just as she was about to give up, the light caught something shining in the distance: an eyeball.

During her years roaming the park, Ava had learned that there was a certain eeriness to the way light reflects off an eyeball. It created a distorted and disturbing image that could make even the sweetest, most innocent creatures appear frightening. At first glance, neither Ava nor Corbin could determine the nature of the eye. But then the body that eye was attached to rose from its knees and stood to its full height. A *person* lurked there in the darkness. But not just any person.

"Bruce Archer!" Ava was startled. "I thought you were in prison?"

"They let me go." He stood in the thick of the woods, several feet away from the beaten path, unmoving, as if he had taken root and grown there.

"Why?" Ava kept the light fixed on Bruce's face.

"I'm innocent."

Ava knew the police had verified this, but she still could not trust a man who skulked in the woods in the deep of night. He finally took a step forward. Ava stiffened; her hand moved to her walkie-talkie. Bruce raised his palm in peace.

"We spoke earlier. Yesterday," he said as he continued to step closer.

"Yeah. And?" Ava's heart raced.

"I told you I seen the bear."

"What about it?" Ava's voice was ragged. Nerves were getting the best of her.

"I seen that claw before." He stood only a foot away now, his hulking silhouette blocking out the forest behind him.

"A claw? A bear?" Corbin couldn't keep his questions silent any longer. "Would one of you mind explaining, please?"

Henry turned off the final light in the headquarters. He removed a pack of cigarettes from his chest pocket and was walking toward the front door when he saw Ava, Corbin, and (for some reason) Bruce Archer.

He stuffed the old half cigarette back into its pack and hastened to let them in. "What's going on?"

"You have a claw!" Corbin exclaimed, sweeping right past Henry toward the office.

"What about it?" Henry unlocked the office door for him, but Corbin did not respond. He burst straight in, glancing around fervently for any sign of the item. Henry opened the top drawer of his desk and removed some papers, revealing the claw beneath. Corbin's eyes widened. Ava bristled, clutching the finger where that claw had pricked her. Bruce turned white, his jaw set hard as stone.

Henry moved as if to pick up the claw, but Corbin stopped him yelling, "Wait!"

Withdrawing the rag from his pocket, Corbin used it to gingerly pick up the claw and hold it up to the light for a closer look. "This was found in your park?" Corbin asked in a whisper.

"Yesterday," answered Ava. "It was in the campgrounds."

Corbin shifted his eyes to Ava, then to Bruce. "And you claim to have seen this before, sir?"

Slowly, Bruce nodded. His eyes seemed glued to the mysterious object. "Years ago," he said hoarsely.

"Why wasn't I informed of this?" Corbin asked.

Henry shrugged. "Truth be told, I forgot all about it. It's just a claw."

"This is no claw," Corbin remarked. "It's a talon."

Henry and Ava exchanged suspicious glances, thinking the same thing: there were no birds in Hillsbury that possessed talons like this.

Corbin fixed his attention back to Bruce. "In what state did you first see this? Was it abandoned, like so?"

"No. It was on the lizard."

"Lizard?" Fear struck Corbin.

"Yeah, lizard. Looked like one, at least. I was a kid." Bruce walked up to the talon and stared down at the quills. "I'd recognize those quills anywhere. We were kids, just playing around in the park when we heard something. And there it was."

"Did it notice you?" Corbin asked, intrigued.

Then Henry cut in. "Hold on, Corbin. You can't trust everything this guy says. He's a drunk."

Corbin raised his hand in front of Henry's face to silence him. "Let him finish, please."

"He saw us, yeah," Bruce went on. "We even named him and everything."

Corbin's mouth was a thin line. As soon as he'd heard the word *lizard*, he suspected he knew the identity of the creature in question. But if it was indeed what Corbin believed it to be, then Bruce should not be alive to tell the tale. Thankfully, Corbin had a good sense for the truth, and right now Bruce Archer gave off no telltale signs of falsehood. Corbin set the talon down on Henry's desk, still resting atop the rag.

"No one touch this," he commanded. Then he walked over to the easel and flipped to a blank page.

"What's going on?" Ava was perplexed. The talon had been an unusual find, sure, but Ava had started to accept the flimsy explanation that it had been brought into the park by a hunter. Corbin, apparently, thought otherwise.

"This changes everything," he said. "Do any of you understand the gravity of this find?" No one answered. Corbin understood; this was a tough pill to swallow. The only person to ever see the talon's owner in the flesh was Bruce Archer, and even though Henry and Ava respected Corbin, this was still going to be a hard sell. His excited mind buzzed, simultaneously processing this new information while trying to ascertain the most easily digestible way to explain it to the rangers.

Because this talon—or more specifically, the thing it had belonged to—was key to unraveling the mysterious happenings in Hillsbury Park and Cape's Side Bay.

"Am I correct in assuming you discovered this lizard some-where along the shores of Cape's Side Bay? Before the water turned?" he asked Bruce, who nodded.

Bruce, for his part, still did not quite understand who this man was, but he could see he was far more educated than any-one else in the room.

"Are any of you familiar with Pliny the Elder?" Corbin's eyes gazed about the room, receiving no affirmative replies. "Right. Gaius Plinius Secundus, born sometime around 23 AD, and died by the volcano Vesuvius in Pompeii. A Roman author and philosopher, specifically a *nature* philosopher. His time was spent in the study of phenomena found within nature. In fact, many people are unfamiliar with this, but Pliny the Elder—or Gaius, as he was better known—was the very first person in my particular field of expertise."

Both Henry and Ava looked at each other, baffled.

"Pliny discovered various creatures unknown to this Earth. Henry, I asked you if you believed in God, and you said you did. I asked if you believed in extraterrestrials, and you hesi-tated. You never quite gave me a yes or a no, but I could tell you were a nonbeliever. Would that be correct?"

"Yeah," Henry answered after a brief pause. Corbin was right on the money. There was no point in lying about it.

"Ava, do you share these beliefs?" asked the astrobiologist.

Ava simply nodded.

"Pliny," Corbin continued, almost as if he forgot the God question entirely, "wrote many books, the last of which was known as *Naturalis Historia*, or *Natural History*. The first ency-clopedia. Pliny was as legitimate a human as you will ever find. So his words and his findings were taken for what they were: the truth. Now, of course, as with all things, time has a way of interrupting life and changing our course of thought. And as such, his findings and writings have been largely forgotten . . . but not all."

Henry rubbed the bridge of his nose impatiently. He wanted Corbin to get to the point. He'd missed spending the previous evening with his wife and had no interest in missing a second.

Corbin began to write on the easel at a frantic rate. *Catoblepas. Basilisk. Calydonian boar. Griffin. Ladon.* He stopped writing and looked around the room again, like a teacher ensuring his students were on the same page. "These all have one thing in common."

"Pliny," Bruce spoke up. Ava and Henry turned and stared at him. Bruce, not used to being the center of attention, suddenly felt his cheeks grow hot.

"Exactly!" Corbin snapped his fingers. "Pliny the Elder encountered each of these mythological creatures. Creatures believed to only exist in fables."

"What does any of this have to do with the claw . . . or talon, or whatever?" Henry asked.

"Well, Henry, another common denominator these creatures share," said Corbin, "is *that.*" And he jabbed a finger almost accusatorily at the talon on the desk.

Ava could hardly believe what she was hearing. Before she could voice her skepticism, Henry asked the million-dollar question: "Okay, so we've got crop circles and a mythological talon some ancient Roman guy knew about. So what, Corbin, does *any* of this have to do with Joel Liman and those other poor kids?"

Corbin stayed silent for a moment, scratching his head. "Until we figure out exactly which creature this talon belonged to, I'd rather not say."

"*Until* we find the creature, *until* we find Joel Liman . . . you're throwing a lot of *until*s at us, Corbin," Henry said, crossing his arms.

"I know, and I'm sorry. But you don't put a puzzle together before you get a good look at each and every piece. Every factor in this mystery could greatly impact another. There is no sense in jumping to conclusions until we have all the facts."

"How about jumping to one anyway?" Ava finally spoke up. "Just to give us some sort of satisfaction, regardless of how far-fetched it could be?" She couldn't keep the anger out of her voice.

Corbin sighed and sat on the edge of Henry's desk. He could see the need in their eyes, the need to understand what was going on. They were not satisfied, and perhaps there was no reason for them to be. He composed himself, choosing his words with great care, being sure not to say anything that might lead them down a path of unwarranted fear or—worse—false hope. But he had to start *somewhere*, and the most ideal place to start was also one of the heaviest. It was now or never. Taking a breath, Corbin cleared his throat and dived right into the deep end.

"God exists."

This elicited the kind of looks he expected, so he plowed on before anyone had a chance to raise a whole new slew of questions.

"God exists. And He exists among the stars. And furthermore, He is not a He. He is a *Them*. They exist in the stars above: The Heavens. One cannot exist without the other because there is no other without the one. The Bible, those stories, they're all true. Every one of them. But the chronology of it all is much more spread out than that book will lead you to believe. The lords are ruthless beings, you see. We are all loved, as a parent loves their child. But as is the case with parenthood, discipline is needed every now and then. To learn. To grow. I fear Hillsbury is in grave danger. The crop circle is a message from them."

"But didn't you say multiple crop circles would mean travesty? One was isolated to Liman?" Henry inquired.

"I did, yes. But in combining that crop circle with everything else." Corbin took a breath and pointed to the sky. "The three mutilated boys are all messages. As I said before, those types of messages typically find themselves on criminals, usually adults. Joel Liman and those boys are messages; what they mean, I am not certain. But I'm fairly sure they are warnings. We are all being warned of something great." He stopped and let what he'd said sink in.

"This talon belonged to a creature that was most certainly sent by the lords to Hillsbury Park."

"Why?" Ava asked breathlessly.

"Possibly to guard it," Corbin hypothesized.

"Guard it from what, exactly?" Henry pushed further.

"Evil, perhaps."

The room fell silent.

Henry—who'd been staring at the carpet—slowly looked up until he was meeting Corbin's gaze. His eyes were wet. He had the unmistakable air of resignation about him, like a soldier charging headlong into a battle they knew they were doomed to lose.

"So what next, Corbin?"

"We find out the truth," Corbin concluded, "by going into the cave above Cape's Side Bay."

Henry was the first to exit the headquarters, his old cigarette already tucked between his lips. Ava followed close behind. "You sure?" she asked her boss. Henry nodded, telling her to drive safe, and Ava walked somberly toward her car. Bruce came out into the parking lot next, with Corbin not far behind.

Bruce's gaze found Henry's cigarette, and he asked, "Mind if I bum one off ya?" Henry reached into his pocket and handed the pack to Bruce. "I just grabbed the pack from my desk."

"You good for a ride?" Bruce was clearly not sober enough to drive, and Henry didn't want to see the man locked up in a cell again so soon after his release.

"I'm good. Think I'm gonna walk it."

"Where you staying?" Henry asked.

Bruce had been a camper, but the campsites were still closed for the weekend, and Bruce's group had all departed Hillsbury. Bruce shrugged. "I'll find something."

Henry rolled a chunk of gravel beneath his boot. "Go to the Hillsbury High Set Inn and tell them I sent you. They'll treat you good." Henry had assisted the owner, Karen Spensen, by being her cosigner on the lease. He figured she wouldn't mind doing him a favor just this once.

Bruce lit his cigarette, thanked Henry with a jerk of his chin, acknowledged Corbin, and went on his way. Corbin gave Henry a pat on the shoulder.

"We'll need to leave at dawn."

"I know." The park ranger took a puff from his cigarette. There was no wiggling out of this. He had to accompany Corbin to the cave. He had to make the park safe: safe for the tourists, safe for his staff, and—most of all—safe for his family.

Corbin wished Henry a good night and made his way toward his Cadillac. He removed his rag and began to clean the hood.

"How long have you had it?" Henry asked.

Corbin glanced up. "The Cadillac? Almost five years. She's my baby." He spoke through a giant, toothy grin. "Always wanted one. The minute I saw it come up, I had to bid on it."

"Did your dad have one?" Henry asked.

Corbin tucked the rag back into his pocket. "Not even in the slightest. My father could never have afforded a luxury such as this. He was a bus driver, a common man."

"Couldn't be too common to have a son like you."

Corbin accepted the compliment with a smile and a nod. "My parents' DNA contributed to my smarts. I thank them for that every day. I don't see them often, unfortunately, not anymore. Comes with the territory. But as I told you: I don't have much of a choice in the matter."

"You face extinction." The park ranger smirked.

Corbin's smile faded. Henry had been speaking in jest; it was the truth. He was a slave to his mind and the government, the government of not just one country, but the world.

"Let me ask you something, Henry." Corbin removed the keys from his pocket. "Do you fear death?"

An odd question, Henry thought, but given the circumstances, he understood where it was coming from. "I suppose."

"And yet you believe in God. Aren't Christians brought up to not *fear* death but anticipate it, appreciate it? Look forward to the gates of Heaven and spending an eternity with God?"

As Henry thought about the question, an eerie feeling entered his soul. Heaven had always been easy to believe in. However, the way Corbin had stated it, the idea of Heaven seemed almost impossible. A place in the clouds full of those who came before? The gates always empty? No conflicts, only reward?

"Are you going to tell me there's no Heaven?" Henry asked.

Corbin unlocked his car door. "I most certainly am not. In fact, I myself am not privy to such information."

"You said God was an alien."

"No, I said they exist, and they exist among the stars. God . . . Henry, the idea of God and what God actually is are oftentimes confused. The presentation of what God means is what matters." Corbin unlocked his car door. "I'll see you in a few short hours. Get some rest, Henry."

With that, Corbin entered his car and drove off. With all the late nights and early mornings he'd had lately, Henry was thinking he should just set up a cot at headquarters. The good news was that tonight he might actually get around to having something resembling a good night's sleep.

Henry entered his house just past eleven. As he removed his shoes, he could hear the TV in the other room. Rachel was asleep in front of the TV. He sat on the ground, resting his back to the couch, and kissed his wife on the forehead. Henry closed his eyes and dreamed of morning.

SUNDAY MORNING

THE SUN STILL had yet to rise in Hillsbury, but Henry had been up for well over an hour. He had showered, brushed his teeth, and exterminated two newly discovered gray hairs from his head.

The coffee had finely finished brewing and Henry poured it into his travel mug. "I had no idea you even knew how to work the kettle." Rachel stood at the entrance to the kitchen, her hair a mess, still half-asleep. She grinned at her husband.

"What're you doing up?" Henry asked, even though he was happy to see her and have a chance to say goodbye before departing.

Rachel rubbed her neck. "Guess I passed out on the couch."

Henry nodded. "Waiting for me?" he asked.

She had been, but she knew he was busy and had no interest in making him feel guilty about it. "TV was boring."

"What were you watching?"

"Can't remember. That's how boring it was."

Henry laughed. "I'm sorry I have to leave so early."

"What adventure awaits you at this hour?" she asked.

Henry wanted to tell her he was climbing the cave at Cape's Side Bay but knew it would only worry her. So, he resorted to a white lie.

"Just getting the park ready for tomorrow night's fireworks."

"Lot of people show up last night?" She either bought his fib or was too tired to think too much about what he had said.

"Actually," his tone was one of surprise, "there were." He tightly sealed his travel mug.

"Maybe," Rachel yawned, "I'll bring Sarah to the park this afternoon. She can see the carnival. If it's, you know, a good idea."

Henry knew she was asking him if the park was safe now, if he was comfortable bringing his little girl there again. He hesitated, then nodded. "Sure." He kissed his wife goodbye; his lips lingered on hers longer than usual. Henry wasn't sure why he was suddenly so afraid, why his mind had suddenly turned the prospect of searching the cave into a macabre, one-way trip. All he knew was that if this *was* going to be his last time kissing Rachel, he wanted to make it count.

All his anxiety was lost on Rachel, who was too busy happily reciprocating. Henry wouldn't have had it any other way.

It was four thirty in the morning and the streets were quiet and calm. The carnival banners were raised, and the new banners were displayed to indicate that the fireworks would be moved from Sunday to Monday. No stores were open, not even O'Leary's. Henry found himself driving down a dirt road on his way to work. Never in all his years working at the park had he gone in so early. Though, never in all his years had he encountered a weekend such as this.

The air was warm, but a cool breeze brushed through the streets. Henry rolled the windows down and enjoyed the fresh air. Fall would be here soon, and summer would depart for another year.

Corbin was already waiting at the park when Henry arrived, sipping on a concoction that was half coffee, half hot chocolate, topped with a dash of cinnamon. He greeted Henry with a wave, wiping his glasses clean of smudges.

"All set?" Corbin asked.

"I guess."

Corbin entered Henry's Jeep and they made their way toward Cape's Side Bay.

Henry parked as close to the cliff as he ever had. With the water having been drained, there was no concern of the vehicle sinking or being swept away by the tide. He looked out at the crater, thinking of his sister's truck. *How did it get there? How was it in such good condition? WHY was it submerged to begin with?* His agitated thoughts were cut short by the sound of Corbin unpacking the climbing gear.

"So, no one's ever been in that cave?" Corbin asked as he strapped a harness around his legs and waist.

Henry shook his head. "No, not since the drought, at least. Not to my knowledge." Corbin gave him an uneasy glance before tightening the harness. "What?" Henry asked.

"Nothing. It's just all very unsettling. The creature, the message, the boys, the drought, the truck: a lot of unanswered questions have been raised around here over the past thirty years or so."

Henry didn't like the sound of that. There had always been stories around Hillsbury, but Henry had never attempted connecting any of them. He always saw them as individual urban legends, never pieces to something larger, or even fact, for that matter.

They began their way up the cliff. Henry was amazed that Corbin—a seemingly very *indoor* kind of guy—could be so adept at rock climbing. He presumed such a profession required one to be a jack-of-all-trades.

As their climb progressed, Corbin told Henry of one of his first cases, nine years earlier, which found him studying Stonehenge.

"A lot of discrepancies and misinformation regarding that *wonder* of the world," Corbin explained. "Do you know much about it? Stonehenge?" he asked the park ranger.

"Bunch of heavy rocks? Not much else."

"A bunch of heavy rocks, indeed, and then some. Some believe it was a place of healing, others a place of peace and love and positive vibrations. But Stonehenge's actual purpose is a burial ground. The question is, for whom? Warriors? Women? Children, perhaps? Some questions are destined to be unanswered. Some questions are destined to take us down various paths so that we veer away from the real answer. Unanswerable questions." They continued scaling the wall, slowly and carefully.

"My time studying Stonehenge taught me very much. It taught me to be one with nature and my surroundings. It also taught me that seeing is not always believing. There is far more at work in this world than we believe. So many 'random' actions are in fact very calculated. Bodies were buried at Stonehenge, that much is true. But the area is so much more. You see, Stonehenge is a calendar. It marks both the summer and winter solstices. The way the sun shines through it keeps mankind aware of the beginnings of both summer and winter. But, again, this is an illusion, a trick to keep us from seeing what it truly is." Corbin stopped speaking and continued upward.

"What is it?" Henry's curiosity peaked.

Corbin smiled and took a deep breath. "Atlantis. Stonehenge was directly related to the sinking of the great city of Atlantis. How? When? Why? I cannot say. This is just my theory. It's unproven, but I do stand by it. I've been biding my time collecting facts and documenting accounts. Stonehenge was a calendar, a calendar that saw the end of a city as large as Asia and Europe."

Henry was not sure what to make of all this. It sounded like the delusions of someone completely crazy. Yet still, here he was, traveling upward toward the cave in Cape's Side Bay because of a slideshow involving mythical beasts and cosmic gods. Suddenly, *crazy* seemed like such a relative thing.

Then they reached the cave.

Henry looked down at the park below, seeing it from above for the first time in his life. The carnival tents, the trees, the trails, the campgrounds . . . all of it looked spectacular from this height.

Corbin took a breath. "It's truly amazing, how the change of view can allow you to see something again for the first time."

They took a moment to stare out over Hillsbury. The sun was just rising, and the yellow glow was shimmering off the tree leaves, glistening. The sounds of the wildlife never felt so refreshing to Henry.

Corbin removed his harness and was setting it down by a rock when something caught his eye. "I don't think we're alone."

Henry glanced over and saw Corbin remove a third, unfamiliar harness from behind that same rock.

Henry clicked on his flashlight. Corbin did the same a heartbeat later. Both of them were thinking the same thing: this cave was uncannily dry. Caves were, by design, almost always damp. Something was very, very *off* about this place.

Corbin gently rested his palm against the cave wall. He removed it quickly, sucking in breath. "What is it?" Henry asked.

"Hot. Almost to a boil."

Henry tried it for himself and nearly burned his palm. The walls in the cave felt like the insides of an oven, yet there was no heat in the air itself. The two men stuck to the center, as far from the walls as possible, and proceeded onward.

"Keep a keen eye out for mildew, sludge, any sort of bacteria. We do not yet know what we are searching for, and I would much rather discover some type of clue before we stumble upon the creature itself."

"Maybe we should come back when we're more prepared," Henry said, unsure if he was nervous, scared, or serious.

Corbin pressed on. The cave grew darker and colder, yet the walls remained hot. The heat was causing the walls of the cave to glisten with a red glow. As they ventured deeper into the cave, it grew both darker and narrower. One moment they'd be shivering, and a few steps later, they'd sweat profusely. Corbin had experienced plenty of bizarre things, but even he admitted this was a new one for him.

Henry was just about to suggest that they turn back when Corbin saw it: a blue glow coming from behind a rock. Corbin rushed toward it and gently slid the rock to its side. Behind the stone lay icicles.

"Icicles?" Henry frowned. "I don't understand."

"This, Henry, is what's known as a hydrothermal vent. I've never seen one near a Sput before." He pondered this for a moment. "Some believe life itself was created by a hydrothermal vent. Fascinating." He almost smiled.

The beauty of the vent was lost on Henry, who fidgeted nervously. "So, what does it do?"

"It basically creates your hot springs. It's a pathway in the earth leading to two tectonic plates moving away or toward one another. In other words, Henry, it's a passageway. Cape's Side Bay is home to more than just Radioactic Sputs. It is a home to a passageway. The first I've seen located on a land mass reach-able by man. This is incredible."

Henry felt the icy rocks with his hands. The chill of ice beneath an incredibly warm surface was perplexing. Corbin was loving every second of it. He waved Henry over to another spot. "Come feel this!"

Henry took a couple of steps forward and tripped on some-thing. He collected himself and looked around quizzically. Something was on the ground beneath him. He lowered his flashlight for a closer look, and then his jaw dropped. His heart beating within him stuttered and sank into his stomach. He was speechless.

There below him lay the body of Victor Marchman.

Corbin spotted the body as well and rushed over. Victor was very cold, his skin blue and his eyes wide open with fully dilated pupils. Henry had only just met this man and asked him for assistance. Now here he lay, dead. A man who'd tried to do the right thing. A man, Henry realized with a chill, who had nothing to do with the cave, who had a family waiting for him back home.

"That's Victor Marchman!" Henry cried out in shock and fear.

"You know him?" Corbin sked.

"He was a hunter on vacation with his family in Hasaga." Henry's voice was trembling.

"Why would we find him here?"

Henry shut his eyes. "Because of me."

Slowly, Corbin stood up. His gaze implored Henry to explain.

"The mayor said we had a bear problem. Victor's the best hunter around. I . . . I asked him to come and hunt the bear."

"You asked him?"

"Yes but . . . I told him to leave. I had no idea he would come up here."

Corbin stared at the body, lost in thought. The state in which Victor lay, combined with the heat from the rocky walls and the dryness surrounding them, began to make sense.

"We must leave. Help me with the body." Corbin grabbed Victor's arms. Henry rushed to the legs and they picked him up and carried him to the cave entrance.

It took them well over an hour to bring Victor's body down from the cave. They did it as carefully as possible but still hit a few bumps along the way. When they finally got to the bottom, the two men sat and caught their breath.

"Any idea what's going on here?" Henry said in between breaths.

Corbin looked at Victor, then removed his glasses and cleaned them with his shirt.

"When I first came here, to Hillsbury and the bay, my feelings were simple: this was nothing more than the study of our life. We evolve; the beings overseeing us know that and pluck one or two of us out every once in a while for experimenting. Alien abductions, as you know but don't believe. The notion sounds crazy, and it's passed off as such, and no one is the wiser. This was my guess. Then I saw the talon and combined that with stories of a bear, and my next assumption was a catoblepas. Now, catoblepas don't typically possess talons, which made it strange. Of course, when you study the unexplained for a living, anything is possible."

"I'm sorry, but I'm not quite sure what a cato—whatever is?"

"Catoblepas. It has the body of a buffalo and the head of a boar. They originated in Ethiopia. The breath or stare of this creature would turn a man or woman into stone, or kill them instantaneously. My belief that the cave's inhabitant was a catoblepas faded as we delved deeper within it. See, during the times of both Pliny the Elder and the times of Leonardo da Vinci, there were far less humans on the planet, and more spaces for so-called 'mythical' beasts to roam unseen. The nesting grounds for such creatures are almost always near hydrothermal vents. But I am still not sure as to what we're dealing with here."

Henry stared at him. "But it's definitely not the bull thingy?"

"I can promise you that this cave houses no catoblepas. If we were in the presence of one, we would both certainly be dead."

"If you thought that's what we were dealing with, why'd we even go up there?"

Corbin rose to his feet. "I'm going to examine the body. You should inform this man's family," he said to Henry, ignoring his question.

The exhausted men stood, seized Victor's body once again, and carried him out of the crater that was Cape's Side Bay.

The church bells rang throughout Hillsbury. The sun shined brightly between the cross high above St. Ambrose, splashing a mural of shadows across the grass below. A beautiful formation of clouds hovered above the church.

St. Ambrose was built in the late 1800s. It was the first church built in Hillsbury, and for a time, it served the county of Hasaga as well. Hasaga would eventually erect their own church, leaving mass at St. Ambrose an exclusively Hillsburian experience. Each Sunday morning, Mayor Tremblay would take his seat in the front row to the left of the altar. He prided himself on being a churchgoer, a believer and follower in the

Lord (though anyone who knew him would use the term "follower of the Lord" loosely).

Elise Trundle sat just two rows behind the mayor, typically with her husband. But on this particular Sunday, Bentley was not to be found. Seated at the back was the Carter family: Rachel and her two children. Henry would make it out to mass when he could, but during the summer months, it was quite difficult for him with so many park duties to take care of.

As Father Donald began his homily, he glanced at his unusually small congregation. This weekend had been a horrific time for the small town, he was quite aware of that, and many people had chosen to leave. Those who hadn't were visibly apprehensive. A certain negativity seemed to permeate the air like fog, casting shadows over Hillsbury and its people. Donald spoke of God and his plan, how everything happened for a reason, and hoped it would be enough to soothe everyone. Yet the story told on the faces of the congregation was a story of waning faith. Four boys go out one night, three are found mutilated, one still missing, and no one has a recollection of anything occuring to them. Donald looked back at the statue of Jesus Christ behind him and took a breath.

"This is St. Ambrose's church. But who was St. Ambrose? He was, like many of you, wealthy. Hillsbury is a special town because those within it enjoy a blessed wealth. It operates under those of you who did not come from much, and those who still don't have much. The full-time residents of Hillsbury are hardworking. You know them on a first-name basis: Ed, Jett, Henry. The list goes on. St. Ambrose was elected bishop by his peers, and in being appointed bishop, he gave away his property and belongings, and he learned the scripture. He was not a man of the Lord when appointed, but still he died a saint. How can that be? Because we all have a choice in life. We live the way of the Lord, the way He intended us to, in the words that Jesus Christ taught us: 'Do unto others as you would have them do unto you.' Never lose sight of that choice." Donald inclined his head and concluded the sermon. "Tonight, we will be holding a silent vigil for Joel Liman. We pray he is found in good health." With that, his homily ended. He allowed the congregation to sit and ponder over what he had said before finishing the Sunday service.

As the church emptied and the parishioners thanked Father Donald for a wonderful mass, he told them to not take such a beautiful day for granted, but to go out and enjoy the weather while it was upon them.

Bentley Trundle waited in his car. He watched as his wife left the church and began walking home. Bentley quietly exited the car, avoided eye contact with members of the congregation, and approached the priest.

"Father Donald," Bentley said.

Donald smiled. "I didn't think I saw you in there today."

Bentley shook his head. "I need a confession." He sounded deathly serious.

Father Donald's smile faltered. "Allow me to finish up here. You can meet me inside." He was tempted to remind Bentley that there were scheduled times for confessions, but he could see there was something deeply troubling the deputy sheriff. Bentley entered the church as Father Donald said goodbye to the last remaining parishioners.

Bentley sat in the confessional. The room was no larger than his office at the police station. Unlike the stereotypical setup from TV shows or movies, *this* confessional was essentially an office. Two chairs facing each other, with incense burning in the back. Bentley tapped his feet nervously; thoughts of Ava filled his mind. He was not a religious man by any means, though he often attended Sunday service with his wife. His beliefs were fledging, and as the love he felt for Ava grew, his beliefs conversely faded. Bentley was not there so much to ask for forgiveness but to speak the truth. He had accidently told Henry about his love for Ava the night before, but he knew Henry was not someone he could confide in. The weight of this secret was crushing him, suffocating him. Bentley needed it off his chest. Now.

Father Donald entered the opposing side of the confessional. At once, Bentley's eyes swelled up. "Bless me, Father, for I have sinned."

"When was your last confession?" the priest asked habitually.

"It's been three years. Or . . . maybe longer. Probably longer."

"Definitely not since I've been at this parish." Father Donald had been in Hillsbury for three years.

"I have had adulterous thoughts of another woman. Other than my wife, I mean. Truth be told, Father, I don't think I even love my wife anymore."

Father Donald sat and listened, not saying a word, urging the deputy to go on.

"More so than just impure thoughts, Father. I acted upon these thoughts."

"How many times did you act on these thoughts?" Father Donald looked deeply into the eyes of Bentley.

Bentley was clearly unsettled. He squirmed in his seat, trying to recount the many times he and Ava made love in his mind. "Too many times. Too many to count."

Silence filled the tiny room. The expression on Father Donald's face never shaped into anything. No look of disappointment or anger. Just a still, silent expression.

"Why?" The father spoke, his eyes still fixated on Bentley's.

"At first? Lust. But now love. Actual love."

"Love?" Donald blurted out. "Love does not give cause to sin! You have broken a commandment. You married out of love; you had an affair out of lust. Cardinal sins: lust, gluttony, greed, sloth, wrath, envy, pride. The list begins with lust and ends with pride. Lust is the most slippery of slopes, Bentley. The devil tempted Adam and Eve with an apple. One single apple. An apple in metaphor only. A metaphor for lust, the lust Adam had for Eve and Eve had for Adam. And so they bit into this metaphorical apple and were banished from the garden for eternity."

Bentley fidgeted in his seat again. The look on his face told Donald this was not the reaction he'd hoped for.

"It ends with pride," Donald went on. "Pride is the belief that your accomplishments, your worth upon God's green Earth, are better than another's. Better than your wife's."

Bentley's eyes filled with tears now. Guilt flowed through his body like the blood in his veins.

"For every action there is a reaction, for every vice there is a virtue. The virtue for lust is chastity; the virtue for pride is humility. You asked to speak with me, which tells me you are looking to these virtues, looking to make peace with what you have done."

"No, Father." Bentley surprised the priest. If Bentley was not here to seek forgiveness for his sins, why was he here? "I wish to leave my wife. What once began as lust has transformed itself into love. I . . . I know it."

"Do you?"

"Of course I do! I—" Bentley stopped himself. The little voices of doubt that had been gnawing at him for days were suddenly speaking much louder than before. *Did* he love Ava? Or did he just not love Elise anymore? If not, why? Above all, if he couldn't answer any of those questions with certainty . . . then what kind of man was he? Bentley broke down. Every part of his body trembled.

Father Donald gently leaned toward the deputy sheriff. "If you are not here in reconciliation for the purpose in which it is intended, and you are here to just 'get it off your chest,' I would say that I cannot help you. Perhaps neither can God."

Bentley looked up at the priest through tear-soaked eyes. "Then what should I do?" He was astounded at how much like a sobbing child he sounded.

"Speak to your wife. Tell her how you're feeling. If anyone has a right to know, it's her. You owe her that, Bentley. If nothing else, you owe her that." Father Donald had only said what Bentley and had already known. He was hoping the priest would offer him a penance of prayer or something easier to swallow. Confessing to the Lord and to a parish priest was one thing; confessing to the woman he took a vow to love in sickness and in health so long as he lived was another.

The blue tinge on Victor Marchman's lifeless body was gradually returning to a pale white as his body temperature ascended. Corbin laid him upon a table in the police station's interrogation room. He offered Henry a mask and latex gloves.

"All the years I've lived in Hillsbury, I've never seen this room once. Now I'm inside it twice in two days," Henry muttered, taking the gloves. "What are these for?"

"Precaution."

"Precaution for what?"

Corbin retrieved a small knife and a bottle of what appeared to be iodine, ignoring Henry's question.

"What're you gonna do with that? Shouldn't we inform his family first? Is this even legal?" Henry pressed.

"We'll tell the family. But first we need to find out what caused his death."

"We know what caused his death: he got trapped in the cave."

Corbin was frustrated. "I'm trying to understand the circumstances surrounding your park, Henry! The next two days are its busiest, correct?"

Henry admitted defeat. "Yes."

That was all Corbin needed to hear from Henry before he inserted the knife into Victor Marchman's temple.

The sight was almost too much for Henry to take; he turned and covered his mouth with an arm. Corbin placed three drops of the bottle's contents on the wound. Blood rushed out as he did so. Corbin then poked a needle into the cadaver's left arm and took a blood sample.

"What're you looking for?" Henry disgust couldn't win out over his curiosity. He also knew Corbin was a scientist, not a doctor.

"A creature in that cave did this. A combination of his blood and the findings from his temporal lobe with the chemical I mixed into it should tell us *which* creature."

"Maybe we should just close the park?"

"Still a chance this is exactly as you suspected: a man who was in over his head in that cave."

Henry didn't appreciate the sarcasm. "Didn't you tell me there was some sort of plan from the creatures or God or whatever up there?" He jabbed a finger toward the heavens.

"No," Corbin calmly remarked. "Sort of. It's complicated. There is more to this. It's a detour from the plan. Something I have never seen before. Something that reminds me of . . ." Corbin trailed off.

"Reminds you of what?"

"Tell me about the people of Hillsbury. Not the year-rounders, but the visitors—the ones with the large cottages located all around your park. What type of people do you think they are?"

Henry shrugged. He had never really thought about them before. Aside from the odd wave here and there, a few chats, and pictures with the kids, he never really got too close with the guests.

"Wealthy people, right?" Corbin asked. "Nice people, seemingly. At least nice to you and your family."

Henry nodded.

"A façade by many, perhaps." Corbin rubbed his chin. "There is more at play here. The creature, the boys, the Sputs, the hydrothermal vent, the crop circle—all connected. All mapping something out."

"Mapping what out?" Henry leaned against a wall, already exhausted.

Corbin could only shrug. "Of that, I am not sure. Joel Liman, perhaps?"

Corbin placed a blood sample onto a glass tray. "Of course," he continued, "I could be wrong. It could in fact have nothing to do with the boy. And to be honest with you, Henry, that's what I suspect. My feeling as of this moment is that something very bad is on its way to Hillsbury."

Henry shifted uneasily. He felt a cold shiver tickle his spine.

"Whatever these messages mean, whatever we are being told or warned of, they will succeed in the act. There is no stopping it. The will of the beyond is unavoidable. So, I will find out the identity of the creature in the cave, and I will decipher the cornfield message, and I will figure out the mystery of the missing boy. I promise you I will come up with answers to all of the above. But in doing so, I cannot promise that any future the answers point to can be avoided."

"Couldn't there have been a mistake? A misstep?" Henry was looking for something positive to come from this, a glimmer of hope at the very least.

"Not likely. Let's hope that all these events are leading us to Joel Liman."

Henry thought for a moment. "And if it isn't regarding Joel?"

Corbin did not say a word. He stared at Henry, then returned to his work on Victor Marchman.

Henry stood up straight. "I should get my family out of here."

"Mr. Carter, what is to be done will be done. We are all sent out on specific paths. There is no escaping destiny."

"So, I'm just supposed to sit back and wait?"

"Precisely. After all, Henry, life is just us waiting for death."

Heaps of police officers stood in front of room 249 in St. Joseph's Hospital. Jane Doe had not spoken since the night before, but the event was rather cryptic and no one could truly understand why a woman hardly capable of speaking would utter something like *reckoning*.

Steve entered that morning with a warm coffee. At first the sight of all the police officers made him freeze; he feared the worst had happened to the woman overnight. After all, the x-rays hadn't looked good. Steve opted to come back and see her again rather than spend time with friends or family; if Jane Doe had survived the night, perhaps it would help her to see a friendly face.

He was just outside the door to 249 when an officer appeared, blocking his way.

"Can I help you, sir?"

Steve looked around for the officer he spoke with the previous day, someone who would remember him so he didn't have to explain himself, but these were all fresh faces. "I'm here to see the woman. The Jane Doe."

"Friend or family?" the officer asked.

"Neither, I guess. I found her."

"You're the guy?" the officer stood straight up as Steve nodded. The officer reached for his walkie-talkie clipped to his collar, never taking his eyes off Steve. "He's here," he said, speaking into the mic.

Steve fidgeted uncomfortably. "Can I see her now?" The officer remained silent. Suddenly, two other officers approached from behind and seized Steve by the arm. His coffee tumbled to the floor with a hollow splash.

The room was just like any other: a bed, monitors, medical carts, chairs for visitors, everything you would expect to see in a hospital room. The lights were off and there were no windows, making it unnervingly dark until the door swung open and a hand flicked on the light switch. An officer, balding with silver hair and deep wrinkles on his cheeks and forehead, followed Steve into this room. He motioned for Steve to sit on one of the visitor seats. Steve obeyed, his heart racing.

"Um . . ." He started to speak but really didn't know what to say other than, *What am I doing here?* He let the words die in his throat, gauging it unwise to question an officer of the law.

"You found the girl?" the officer asked, nose buried in his notepad.

"Yes. That's correct."

The officer wrote something down that Steve couldn't see. "And have you had any previous relations with this person?" The officer had gone from paying no attention to Steve to now almost paying too much. He watched the young man like an eagle watched a mouse. Steve shook his head.

"No, never. I already—"

"Already answered these questions. Things have changed."

"How?" Steve blurted out. As a panicked afterthought, he added, "Officer?"

"Your *girlfriend* spoke last night."

"Really?" Steve came very close to smiling. Any verbal response from the woman had to be good news, right? "She actually talked?"

"Just a word. We were hoping she would say more, but nothing else."

"Well, what did she say?" Steve had to know. What was so important that Jane Doe, whose throat had been slashed from the inside, had to say it out loud?

"She said *reckoning* twice." The officer looked back down at his notepad. Steve's expression shifted from optimism to quizzical. "We were hoping you might be able to enlighten us as to what she meant by that?"

"Uh . . ." Steve had no idea whatsoever what *reckoning* was supposed to mean.

"No? Didn't think so. Look, son, we'd like you to stay with the girl again, like you did yesterday. But today we'd like you to see if you can get her to speak again. See if you can find out what *reckoning* means. Make sense?" For the first time, the officer inflected in a way that indicated the two of them were on the same side.

"Uh, yeah, sure. Anything to help." And Steve did want to help, so long as he wasn't going to prison as a result. "Am I in any sort of trouble?"

The officer shook his head. "Not today, son." He snapped his notebook shut, placed it into his pocket, turned off the light, and left the room. Steve remained alone in the dark.

Steve made his way back to room 249. His plan that day had been to stay with the girl until at least noon. Now he had a reason to stay longer.

There was something about this girl that intrigued him, yet he had no idea what it was. He was drawn to her. It wasn't that he found her particularly attractive, though she certainty wasn't ugly. Perhaps it was the situation in which they had met that made him feel obligated to be with her. All he knew was she was a person with a past and a life just like he was, and from one human being to another, he felt obligated to help her reclaim them . . . whatever they were.

Only two officers remained outside her room, including the one who had questioned Steve. As Steve opened the door to room 249, he looked over at the officer, who gave him a subtle nod and let him on his way.

Inside, the room was silent, aside from the steady rhythm of a heart monitor. Jane Doe lay peacefully in her bed. She looked happy; Steve could have almost sworn he saw a smile on her face.

He sank into the visitor chair across from her. A nurse entered soon after, offering him a cup of hospital coffee, which—mild and bland though it may have been—he was very grateful to accept.

Alone again, Steve fixed his gaze on the unknown woman. "Who are you?" he whispered to her.

She lay still, her heart beating, her chest rising and falling peacefully.

"Who *are* you?"

Steve took Jane Doe's hand in his own and kept her company while she slept.

SUNDAY AFTERNOON

A CLOUD OF dust hovered above Highway 21, the main road, which lead from Hillsbury to Hasaga. Henry Carter had traveled this road more times than he could remember, but he had never dreaded arriving in Hasaga the way he did this afternoon.

Victor Marchman was dead, and even though he had told him to leave Hillsbury, it was Henry's fault. He was the one who brought him in. He was the one who asked for his assistance in killing what they both knew was definitely not a bear.

Henry pulled his car over to the side of the road and vomited. The whole of it finally hit him. The events of the weekend, the pressure and responsibility for people's lives . . . it was all too much for him. He leaned against his car for a moment and took several deep breaths. His cell phone rang: it was Rachel. He was relieved to see her name on the screen and not Corbin's or Tremblay's; he needed to hear a friendly, caring voice right now.

He held the phone up to his ear and answered the call. "Hey, honey."

"How are you?" His wife's voice was soft and calm on the other end.

Henry actually smiled. "I've been better."

"Where are you?" She hadn't heard from Henry since he'd left before the sunrise. He had promised to check in with her, but after finding Victor's body and his subsequent conversation with Corbin, he hadn't had the chance.

"Sorry I didn't call. Things got a bit . . ." He stopped himself; he did not want his wife to panic. He had half a mind to tell her to take the kids, get in her car, and drive. Drive into the sunset and never look back.

But he didn't.

Corbin was yet to come up with a conclusion to the events in Hillsbury, and he decided he'd rather stay positive until then. *The message was about finding Joel*, he told himself.

Henry settled for saying, "I love you."

"I love you too," Rachel responded.

"I'll give you a call later. Love you." And with that, he ended the call. He did not wait to hear his wife's voice on the other end. He needed to get to Hasaga and tell another loving wife that her husband was gone. It was not going to be easy. It was not going to be ideal. But it was something he had to do. Henry got back into his car and fired up the engine.

Corbin's eye stared directly into the microscope. He was studying the blood found in the temporal lobe of Victor Marchman. At first glance, the blood appeared normal, but soon a matter with a green tinge swam into view and killed the surrounding cells. Corbin focused the microscope to make sure his eyes weren'tplaying tricks on him.

He had studied various things through various microscopes on little sleep more times than he could count, and he had learned the hard way to double- and triple-check his work. This, however, was something he had read about but never seen in person.

It was in the readings of Pliny the Elder he first heard of this phenomenon. Much like the catoblepas, whatever killed Victor had the power to kill with a stare. Yet the green tinge implied that Victor Marchman was not killed by a stare alone. There were no markings on the man, no wounds of any kind. Corbin sat back in his chair and pondered. *If not killed by sight, then what?* He glared at the cadaver hoping an answer would simply appear. As if the man would turn his head to him and say, "*Hiss.*"

Hiss?

Hiss!

Corbin wheeled his chair toward the head of the cadaver and rotated its head to the left, with the ear tilted upward. He grabbed an otoscope and plunged his focus into Victor Marchman's ear.

Elise stood in her kitchen, juggling several tasks at once. Scrambled eggs, home fries, and bacon were all being cooked on separate elements. All the while, Elise was waiting for Bentley to return. He had missed church because he'd had something to deal with at work. On a weekend as eventful as this, it was easy to believe that. Aside from the food, she had home-brewed coffee and freshly squeezed orange juice ready and waiting for Bentley when he finally arrived.

Needless to say, it came as quite a shock when Bentley's first words upon entering the kitchen were an admission that he no longer loved her.

Elise's eyes filled with tears. She listened to Bentley's confession as if hearing it from outside her own body, as if she weren't standing in front of the stove but floating above the whole scene, spirit-like, separated from it all.

Bentley went on to say that his heart yearned for another, and that he had not been faithful. Elise threw the hot frying pan at him, just missing the side of his head. He tried to explain that he was lost and confused, but the pain spreading across Elise's face was so visible and powerful that he was reduced to stuttering incoherently through wracked sobs.

Plates, mugs, glasses . . . all were hurled at him. Elise had never been so upset or hurt in her life. She had spent years being the best wife she could, years that suddenly seemed to fly back at her and slap her in the face, like something angrily hurled into oncoming wind. It brought out a rage in her she had not realized she possessed.

Before long, Elise had a bag packed and was leaving to stay with her sister in the city, far from Hillsbury. As she headed to the door, she turned back to the man she once loved more than anything else in the world and spoke calmly. She told him just how disappointed she was, and how disappointing it was to discover that the past few years she had essentially been alone in the relationship, as if married to a ghost. She'd been more alone when they were together than she would be now that they weren't; and *that*—she told him before shutting the door and leaving him in their empty house—was the most bitter pill to swallow.

The old Jeep pulled up into the visitor parking of the Hasaga trailer park. On the grounds, the weekend festivities were in full swing. With the lawn bowling and cookout the following day, many had taken the time to practice their bowling skills (or lack thereof).

Only one deer had been hunted and killed for the cookout, so the winner by default was Dean. All *real* hunters knew the deer had been killed prior to the official day of the hunt, but with the lack of prizes from Friday, all were willing to accept it. All except for Victor. Victor would have argued the point and not backed down. Victor, however, no longer had a voice among the living.

Henry glanced around at the smiling faces of the campers. The weather was perfect for the festivities. He noticed Victor's son, Tyson, in the distance, the one whom he had taken out that morning for his first hunting trip. The boy was standing by a popcorn machine that one of the campers had brought from home, a large replica of an old movie theater popcorn maker. Henry watched the boy's eyes light up as each kernel exploded into a fluffy treat. Henry looked around the trailer park for Victor's wife. He was hoping to go unseen by most, to just speak his piece and then be on his way. The less time he spent in Hasaga, the better.

"Well, if it isn't the Hillsbury Park head ranger."

The voice was uneven, feminine, and one belonging to a person who had spent a good portion of her life behind a cigarette. Henry turned to see Hasaga's mayor, Belinda Thomas, standing behind him, cigarette in her mouth and all.

"Madam Mayor," Henry said as he shook her hand, her fingertips yellowed from tobacco.

Belinda had been mayor in Hasaga for the past twenty-one years; she herself was going on eighty-seven. She was mayor during the big drought they'd endured, and she was the mayor who single-handedly declined the paving of Highway 21. The people of Hasaga—the few people—loved Mayor Thomas. She was an aggressive woman who never faltered once she'd made up her mind about something. She would do all it took to see things through, regardless of whether anyone agreed with her or not. Still, she had her principles, which was more than Henry could say of most politicians.

"Find your bear?" she growled through her cigarette.

Henry actually chuckled, startling himself. "No. Not quite."

Prompted by the mayor, Henry pulled a cigarette of his own from a pocket. Belinda reached in with her lighter and lit it for him. "So, what can I do you for?" The old woman was no-nonsense; if the park ranger of a "rival" community was in town, something must have been afoot.

"Just came to check out the activities. Y'know we're having our own little festival down in Hillsbury."

"I'm aware," she hissed. "I'm also aware that you were here Friday looking for someone to track down and kill that bear of yours."

"There's no bear, ma'am, I assure you." Henry took a puff of his cigarette, hoping Belinda would not see through him.

"Well, bear or no bear, I hope whatever business you have here in Hasaga is of a positive note. This weekend means a lot to our visitors. I'd hate to lose them over something as stupid as a fictional bear." Belinda took one long drag of her cigarette and exhaled just to the side of Henry's face. Henry waved the smoke away as the mayor skulked back toward the lawn bowling tournament.

Henry looked around and saw Tanya Marchman exit her trailer. A nervous stir rustled throughout his innards. What he was about to do was necessary and respectful. He just wished somebody else could be the one to do it.

"Mrs. Marchman!" he called out, raising his arm skyward so she would have a body to match the voice with. Tanya was carrying out a bowl of punch she had made for the lawn bowling potluck. "May I have a word with you?" Henry was partially out of breath from the brief jog he took from the Jeep to the Marchman trailer.

"Sure?" Tanya wasn't entirely sure who this man was, but thankfully the badge on his shirt served as enough of an identifier.

"Maybe we should sit down." Henry's tone softened as he wiped sweat from his forehead. It was blisteringly hot out here.

The trailer was larger on the inside than Henry had imagined. There was a kitchenette, a bathroom, a separate room for the master bedroom, and although Henry could not see it, there was a bed somewhere in there for Tyson. Tanya placed the punch bowl down on the table in the kitchenette. She took a seat and invited Henry to sit next to her. "Coffee or anything?" she offered, though with her seating herself first, she clearly had no desire to make it. Henry shook his head and had a seat. He'd opened his mouth, about to speak, when Tanya began the conversation.

"Where's Victor?" Fire lived within her eyes. She knew something had happened to her husband, yet she did not look saddened. In fact, she looked furious.

"He, uh . . ." Henry could not bring himself to say it. But Tanya was smart enough that he almost needn't say anything at all.

Twin tears spilled down Tanya's cheeks. She covered her face with a hand. Henry rushed over to her to try and console her, but she shrugged him off.

"What happened?" her tone was calm.

"We're not sure." Henry silently cursed himself for not having more information before coming. "I hired him, then . . ." He played back the events in his mind. "He was on his way back. We think it was a heart attack." A lie. A good lie, he hoped.

"Heart attack? He was healthy." She grabbed a tissue; Tanya's anger was finally fading into sorrow.

"He was, but—he was on his way home. We found him in his car, on the side of a road." Another lie, this one possibly harder for Henry to cover. Corbin told Henry to inform the family it was a heart attack; he didn't give much other direction. So Henry was doing the best he could. He never considered himself a great liar. Victor's wife stared at the floor and covered her face with the palms of her hands. There was nothing left for Henry to say, nothing more for him to do. He had never met this woman before and only knew her husband through circumstance. As far as Henry was concerned, he himself was to blame for Victor's death. Tanya didn't need to know that. Knowing it himself was bad enough.

Henry stood up and gave Tanya one final glance. "I'm so sorry, Mrs. Marchman." He left the trailer, leaving the new widow alone with her tears and her memories.

Corbin sat at his computer. The small office was dimly lit for this early in the day. The blinds were shut, the door was locked; the only light came from the glow of the screen and a very small desk lamp. His glasses resting off to one side, Corbin rubbed the bridge of his nose.

His findings in Hillsbury were intensifying. On the white-board behind him, he had written *BASILISK* in large capital letters and underlined it several times. After studying the cadaver of Victor Marchman, Corbin was able to determine that this was the creature dwelling in the cave high above Cape's

Side Bay. Which made perfect sense to him after speaking with Bruce Archer.

A basilisk is serpentlike in appearance with the head of a bird. Its gaze (as well as its breath) could both paralyze or kill any man, woman, or child. At first, Corbin was perplexed because Bruce had told him he encountered the creature as a child face-to-face. If this were the case, how could the boy have lived? Corbin hastily studied up on the creature and learned that its stare wouldn't have been lethal if it had not yet grown to its full size or potential. The beast's only means of defense would have been the quills upon its talons, which is exactly what Bruce Archer had described.

According to Pliny the Elder, the only way to kill a basilisk is with the effluvium of a weasel. This course of action made even more sense to Corbin, as weasels had long been a problem in Hillsbury. Henry himself had had them trapped and shipped away, yet they always returned. The weasel preyed on the basilisk. However, with the basilisk making its home so high up in the cave, the only chance it had of encountering a weasel would be if it was drawn out into the woods.

As Corbin shuffled through his notes, he began to realize that the basilisk was not his only problem. The boys, each of whom were human portrayals of three wise monkeys, had most certainly not encountered the basilisk. Except for Mitchell, who was found with his mouth sewn shut and an unidentified substance on his left foot. A substance that had paralyzed the use of that foot. A substance that the basilisk could disgorge.

Pieces of the puzzle were taking shape. The boys were alone in the park that evening, the eve of a weekend that signaled the end of summer. The end of fun. It was the eve of the weekend where the wealthy enjoyed their summerhouses at the expense of the sins of their winters. The boys were a warning sign, a warning that the people of Hillsbury were unjust, that they were undeserving of what they possessed, that they prided themselves on materials things to an extent greater than their purpose. It was a town run by a mayor who, in a time of sadness and mourning, focused all his efforts on staging an ostentatious carnival. All in the name of money.

Of greed. Of power.

On the surface, Hillsbury was the ideal cottage town. Quaint, with small shops, where local business flourished. But wade in a little deeper, and you'd find yourself in a pool of sinners.

Corbin stared down at the cornfield photograph. He had dissected and deciphered the majority of it. He placed his glasses back onto his head and took a breath. He peered down at his notes to make changes and double-check the message. The notes read: *Fire. Blood. Animals. Darkness. 4.* The words were all plagues. Corbin had never seen anything like it but knew of it. Mostly what he knew of plagues came from history books. But if the world was millions of years old, and man had only been on it for thousands of years, then these plagues would be spread out over time. When condensed into a book, these plagues would seem to have happened almost simultaneously, but that was not the case. Time would pass and stories would be told and the book would be written as such.

The only message Corbin could make any sort of guess about was *Animals*, as they had mostly all disappeared from Hillsbury and its surrounding townships. But the disappearance of animals was not a plague, not one that he knew of. In ancient Egypt, animals attacked livestock as one of the fourth of seven plagues. The fifth plague was the extermination of that same livestock. The disappearance of animals in Hillsbury was odd. Sure, it would affect the hunters, but they were mainly in Hasaga (hunting was mostly off limits in Hillsbury). Corbin tapped his pen against the table, deep in thought.

What if they weren't plagues? What if they were warnings? What if he was being warned of things to come? What if it was up to him to save everyone? A noble thought for sure, but far from realistic. Corbin was no martyr, just a man with a large brain.

An alarm sounded on his computer. It rattled him so much, he knocked over his notes on the cornfield message. His papers scattered. "Dammit all!"

Corbin picked up the papers and slid them on his desk. He slammed off the alarm with a furious click. It was lunchtime. Corbin's mind worked a mile a minute, and he often neglected meals, leaving him hungry and irritable. He locked his computer, just in case some petty police officer decided to come in and snoop through his findings. That's when he noticed it.

One of the tabs on his web browser (one of seven that were open) had crop circles on it. Another tab had seven Bible verses. Seven. Seven deadly sins. One crop circle . . . One crop circle?

He grabbed his glasses from the edge of the desk and shoved them on his face. He squinted, then looked down at the hand-written notes he had just knocked over.

"It can't be."

The room was brighter than it had been in the two days Jane Doe had been lying there. The beeping from the heart monitor continued, incessant, and Steve looked on with hopeful eyes as he sipped away at yet another coffee. He had been tasked with finding out who this woman was. How he was going to do that, he had no clue. She only stayed awake for a moment or two before having some sort of fit, shaking and squirming, and then ultimately drifting back into slumber. Still, the police had asked him for help. He was (somehow) viewed as a person this woman trusted. He agreed to help her because she could not help herself. So he sat there, hoping—wishing—she would reveal herself to him. *Anytime now*, he thought. *Any time now would be great . . .*

Jane Doe's right index finger began to twitch. Steve leaned in, ever so slightly; he rested his coffee mug on the ground next to his leg. Her finger twitched at a quicker rate. He stood up and approached her bedside. Her eyes opened.

She stared directly at him. He held her hand. She gripped it back with all her might. Her eyes raced to the back of her head. Foam began to dribble from her mouth. Steve shouted for a nurse.

The woman was having a seizure.

"Help! Someone help!"

The woman's grip on his hand remained firm. A nurse rushed in with a tray and pried their hands apart. Steve stood back and watched as the nurse got to work.

Breathless, Steve began to wonder if he was the right person for this job. Maybe, just maybe, this stranger wasn't getting any better because she was just that: a stranger. Maybe, Steve mused, the key to curing Jane Doe was to find somebody who knew her as someone *other* than Jane Doe.

The carnival was now home to hundreds of tourists. It was becoming the epic festival Tremblay had promised.

The turnout was bigger than expected, and Mayor Tremblay could not have been more thrilled. He placed his arm around Ava as she made her rounds and growled under his breath to her.

"Henry had no faith. Always have faith. People want a good time." He sauntered away then, leaving her feeling more than a little uncomfortable.

Considering the amount of people in the park, things were going smoothly. A few stray pieces of litter here and there, but no arguments, no fights; everyone had a smile on their face. Jeffrey and Morgan were both working with her that afternoon. Jeffery did not come as a shock, but to see Morgan again was quite the surprise. She figured he needed the last couple of days' pay to help him with whatever nerdy hobby he was invested in at that time. Regardless, he was there and pulling his weight.

Corbin approached her from behind and tapped her on the shoulder, momentarily startling her before she broke out into a laugh and pushed him off.

"You scared me," she giggled.

"My apologies."

"What're you doing here?"

"Well, I was just in my office and my stomach informed me that it was coming on lunchtime. I figured why not enjoy my lunch with some company?"

Ava smiled at the astrobiologist and nodded. "I'd love to."

Jeffrey was emptying an overflowing trash can. The park was not equipped with cans large enough for this amount of people, so the trash cans were frequently overflowing. He had sent Morgan on a run to collect a few other cans from the trails and campsites that were no longer being used, but in the meantime, he had to empty them out and reinsert fresh bags.

Ava and Corbin approached him as they were making their way out of the park for lunch.

"Everything all right?" she asked.

Jeffrey shot her a look as if to say, *Yeah, right*, and continued with the trash.

"I'm gonna go get lunch. Be back in an hour or so."

Jeffrey tossed the full bag of garbage into the back of his turf vehicle. He hopped in and drove to the dump.

On Highway 21, just a few miles outside of Hasaga yet far enough from Hillsbury that people from town rarely ventured to it, lay a bar. It was meant to be a place for truck drivers to stop and get a quick bite to eat. It had a six-room motel attached to it, but it was old and rundown—not the most inviting of places. Most drivers opted for a quick meal before hitting the road to spend the night in a nicer town, like Hillsbury. Henry's thoughts were consuming him on his lonesome drive back. Informing a woman that her husband—the father of her child—had passed away suddenly was not something he ever expected when becoming head ranger. But it was what it was, and he dealt with it the best he could. A drink was something he felt he not only needed but deserved.

Unbeknownst to Henry, the bar was, in fact, the very tavern in which Victor took his son for lunch that Friday. It had been the last meal Victor Marchman would ever have.

Henry took a seat at a booth. Save for a bartender, a waitress, and a couple of drunks at the counter, the place was empty, which was to be expected; not many truck drivers passed by on Sundays of a long weekend. By week's end, though, business would be booming and all would be right.

A waitress with raggedy hair, a missing tooth, and dirty fingernails took Henry's order. A beer was all he wanted. Not too strong, but something for him to sip and take his mind off the events that had been plaguing his life over the past few days. She returned after a minute with his pint of beer. An inch

of white foam topped it off, and sweat trickled down the glass.
It was the most welcome sight Henry had seen in a while. He
picked it up and took a sip.

Steve chugged his water. He had been parched, and after the
nurses brought him a glass of tap water, he opted to head to the
vending machine and purchase a bottle instead. He finished it
quickly and sat with Jane Doe. She had not woken since her
seizure earlier that afternoon, but he felt oddly optimistic that
something would soon change.

Aside from a few freak-outs, the woman slept. The seizure
had been her first, and he saw that as a blessing in disguise.
Perhaps her body was forcing out whatever was ailing her system. He was not sure, but he knew she couldn't recieve proper
help until they uncovered her identity. Given the issues with
her throat, he knew the chances of her really speaking were
unlikely. Steve decided that when the woman woke next, he
would calm her down and try to distract her enough to keep
her from having another episode. He had a pen and notepad,
as well as an eight-by-ten paper with the alphabet listed on it.
He would ask her for her name, and then point to each letter
until she helped him spell it out.

It would take time, but he was certain it would work.

Jane Doe's eyes slowly slid open. Her right eye was clear
and bright blue; her left was bloodshot and painful to look at.
Around the iris was a yellow circle, which appeared to connect
with her natural blue eye coloring. Steve rested his arms upon
hers and gently leaned into her field of vision, making sure
his face—his *smiling* face—was the first thing she'd see when
coming to.

"Hi," he whispered, hoping she'd understand that he was a friend and could be trusted.

At first her eyes twitched, and for a moment she appeared as if she was going to have another frantic episode. Steve remained calm.

"Hi. It's okay." He began to comb her hair back gently and watched as her eager eyes relaxed themselves. She lay back, her head resting against the pillow, her eyes fixated on the young man. This was the longest she had been awake without an episode. Steve would take it as a victory. He smiled at her; a look of uncertainty crossed her face.

"I'm . . . I'm Steve." For some reason, he was nervous. Maybe because, after two days, he felt like he knew her—yet he knew nothing about her, and she had never seen him before (regardless of what the officers thought). He pointed to himself. "Steve."

She looked nervous, squirming with discomfort. From what Steve could tell, perhaps her vision was not what it should be—or once was? Her left eye looked tormented. He rubbed her arm gently, keeping his voice softly hushed.

"Hey, hey, it's okay. I'm a friend. A friend."

She looked Steve up and down. He was wearing jeans, a navy-blue T-shirt, and a hat with mesh backing. She calmed herself, and—at least for a moment—she appeared to trust him.

"Do you know where you are?" Steve asked. She shook her head. The movement was almost imperceptible. "You're at St. Joseph's Hospital, in Leafsview. I found you in Tuncton. Do you know where that is?"

Her eyes as wide as could be, Jane Doe shook her head.

"Do you know who you are?" He went right for the jugular with that one. He needed answers. If she didn't know where she was, what were the odds she knew *who* she was? He figured he better get that question out of the way instead of wasting any more time.

The woman paused for a moment before nodding, ever so cautiously.

Steve exhaled with relief. "Good, good." He leaned back in his chair and grabbed the paper. Fear took over her eyes once more, and Steve had to calm her and assure her that things would be all right, that she was safe. He held up the alphabet.

"Okay, I'm going to point to a letter. You nod when I'm at the right one. We'll keep doing that till we spell out your name. Understand?"

She nodded once again. The thought had crossed Steve's mind that perhaps her vision was so bad, she could not see the letters he was pointing to. Or perhaps she might even lie and give him a fake name. *Either way*, he thought, *only one way to find out*. He raised his pen and held it up against the letter *A*. No reaction. He slid over to *B*. Again no reaction.

This was going to take some time.

Corbin sat across from Ava at O'Leary's. Today's lunch special was a club sandwich and fries with a free pop and dessert. Which worked out perfectly because Corbin was a sucker for both club sandwiches *and* dessert. As he swallowed a bite of his sandwich, he couldn't help but stare across the table at Ava. There was a mutual attraction, for sure, though he had been hesitant to explore it.

Corbin sipped his drink through a straw, then cleared his throat. "So, Ava, what is it exactly you want to do?" He silently prayed his tone sounded as light as he'd hoped.

The query threw Ava off since they had already spoken on the matter. She had told him about her past and how she ended up in Hillsbury with this job. He noticed she was unsure of where he was going with the conversation, so he reworded his question for her. "I mean, I know biologist and whatnot, but have you ever thought of life after Hillsbury? Or is this where you settle? And I mean that with respect." He took another sip of his drink; he was—for the first time Ava had known him—nervous.

She had to delve deep into her mind to even think of an answer. She was settling in Hillsbury, of that she was sure. This was not her future. It was *somebody's*, but not Ava Trillium's. She was happy, most of the time, and being assistant park ranger paid her way through life. Whether she wanted to admit it or not, Hillsbury was where she belonged.

"Um, if I'm being completely honest, I'm not sure. I mean, yeah, I've always dreamed of being something great—doing something greater. But I'm not sure that's who I am anymore. Yeah. I dunno." She took a bite of her sandwich.

When their food was first delivered, she'd taken her knife and removed the crust, much like a mother would do for her child. Corbin found this strange, but to each their own.

"And what about you? You were chosen for this life; you didn't choose it. What would you prefer to be doing?" she asked the astrobiologist.

"Hmm." He grinned. Now there was a loaded question. There were hundreds of occupations he would love to try, if only for a day. Heck, he'd love to be a department store cashier just to experience what that would be like. He had never, in all his life, had a normal job.

"I'd love to say athlete, but I don't have those skills."

"What sport?" Ava asked quickly.

"Track," he answered, just as fast.

Ava seemed to like this response. "Ooh, interesting."

"I used to love running in grade school. Even to this day, I enjoy a short run of six kilometers every morning."

"Six kilometers! That's a marathon!" Ava had never run six kilometers in her life.

"Hardly, but I try when I can." He bit down into his sandwich, finding the honey mustard particularly enjoyable. He made a mental note to come back to this restaurant one more time before leaving Hillsbury.

"So, where do you go from here?" Ava asked, almost as if reading his mind. She knew his stay here was temporary. And she would miss him when he left. He had an idea of when he would be leaving, but his plans often changed at a moment's notice.

"Typically, as my research concludes, head office informs me where I am needed next. However . . . I think after this job, a vacation might be in order." He smiled and punctuated this by sipping his drink.

Ava couldn't help but ask about the investigation. "Find out anything new about the boys?" She was worried about them, as was everybody in Hillsbury. Corbin was hesitant to answer. His findings were beginning to add up, and he was certain the outcome was not a positive one. Not positive for the kids. Not positive for Ava. Not positive for the whole town. Maybe that, Corbin thought, was the real reason he had asked Ava out to lunch. Sure, he was attracted to her. But perhaps deep down, in his bones, Corbin knew that Hillsbury was a place he would soon *need* to leave, out of necessity. Perhaps he'd just wanted to spend some one-on-one time with the beautiful ranger while he still had the chance.

"No," he lied. "Nothing yet. Let's just enjoy lunch."

Ava gave Corbin a small smile and took a sip of her diet soda. He couldn't help but notice she was rubbing her finger as if it pained her.

"Everything all right with your finger?"

Ava nodded. "Allergic reaction to something."

Since accidentally pricking herself with the talon, the wound had healed, but every few hours, Ava felt a burning, itching sensation where the wound had been. It was extremely disquieting, like a phantom wound. As the itching and burning escalated, Ava excused herself and made her way to the restroom.

Corbin watched, concerned, before returning to his club sandwich.

Henry drove down the dirt road, cigarette dangling from his lips. Sunglasses were perched at the tip of his nose. He was driving slowly, not because of the pint of beer, but because he was distracted. Victor's lifeless body haunted his thoughts. As his foot grew heavy on the gas, his mind would shift, and he'd ease down on the brake, slowing him to below the speed limit. He had no recollection of the drive up until this point; it was as if he were driving in his sleep. Luckily, save for a pickup truck zooming past in the opposite direction, the road was empty.

Henry was consumed with his thoughts until a sound jarred him back to the present.

His phone was ringing.

It rang several times before he realized what it was. Henry retrieved it from his pocket and answered, still a little dazed. "Hello?"

The Jeep steered to the side of the road and came to an abrupt stop. Dirt flew into the sky, covering the vehicle.

Steve held the pen up to the *R* on his makeshift chart and received a positive response. As he wrote the letter down on his notepad, Jane Doe's head slipped down onto her pillow, and she once again made the trek away from lucidity. Steve wasn't aware that they were done spelling the name until he glanced at his notebook and read what he had written.

Jane Doe had revealed her identity, then laid her head down to rest.

The nurses were convened at their station when Steve came rushing toward them. They paused mid-laughter, noticing that the young man was panting and excited about something. One nurse—whose pink scrubs set her apart from her blue-clothed comrades—asked Steve what they could help him with.

Still out of breath, he answered. "I have a name."

At first the nurses were not sure what the young man was talking about, then something clicked with the nurse in the pink and she walked around from behind the desk to stand next to Steve.

"What name?" she asked.

"Hers. I think."

Steve held up the notebook, displaying a single name scrawled across the page in thick black ink.

Jill Carter.

Henry gripped the phone to his ear. He could not believe what he was hearing. His sister had been missing for over seven years. Now, all of a sudden, she wasn't.

The hospital asked him a few basic questions. At first he was too stunned by the revelation to answer coherently, and a nagging in the back of his mind had him doubting the call's validity. But the nurses assured Henry that the woman they had been watching over for the past twenty-four hours was his sister, Jill Carter, and they requested his presence at St. Joseph's immediately. The call ended, leaving Henry alone. Silent. Shocked. Near tears.

Minutes passed in the blink of an eye. Henry shook himself from a daze that somehow made him sluggish and filled him with adrenaline all at once. He started the Jeep and made his way back down Highway 21. The fastest way to Leafsview was to return to Hillsbury and take Highway 73; there was no easy route out of Hasaga, and this way he could pick up Rachel and the kids.

The sky was as clear as ever in Hillsbury. There wasn't a trace of rain or clouds in the forecast for the rest of the day. Mayor Tremblay had planned a small display of fireworks for that night, in preparation for the grand finale Monday night.

But Corbin Mench was at the local police station, his black 1965 Cadillac parked out back. He had a few more documents to look over before retiring for the night. Waiting for him on the front steps was Bruce Archer.

Corbin noticed Bruce as he left the station and wondered if he had stayed at the inn Henry recommended but did not feel like asking or engaging in a conversation with the strange man.

Corbin settled on giving Bruce a friendly nod as he passed. To his dismay, Bruce stood and followed him.

"Mr. Mench, I was wondering if I might have a word?"

Mr. Mench? Bruce was old enough to be his father, Corbin thought. He sighed and nodded to the man.

"I want to know what you found in the cave."

Corbin knew this question would come up; this was why these matters were kept strictly confidential. Still, Bruce had seen the beast before, even if it was in its infantile stages. Corbin felt a small tug of pity for the man and brought him into the office for an explanation.

Most of Corbin's research had been removed from the office. A few small boxes of paperwork remained, as did some pictures of objects Bruce had never seen before, and the photographs of the boys. A sticky note was attached to the bottom of the computer monitor; Corbin quickly removed it and shoved it beneath a pile of paperwork. As Bruce made his way inside, Corbin piled all of the loose pictures on top of each other and placed them facedown. He offered Bruce a seat before finally taking his own.

"It's quite remarkable, if I'm being honest. The creature you discovered that day is very dangerous. And I say 'discovered' because not many have come face-to-face with such a being in thousands of years. And yet here you are, a survivor of the basilisk."

"Basilisk?" The word felt foreign and cumbersome on Bruce's tongue. He couldn't remember ever hearing it before.

"Yes. A basilisk, King of the Serpents."

The name sounded exciting to Bruce, but it didn't explain much. "So . . . what is it, exactly?"

"Essentially a cockatrice, but smaller."

"And what's that? A cocka-thing?"

Corbin cleared his throat. "Where a cockatrice has the body of a dragon and the head of a rooster, the basilisk has the head of a rooster, the legs of a large bird—explaining the talon—and the body of a serpent. The basilisk can kill you with a stare."

"Then why am I still here?" A shred of fear fluttered through the man's body, thinking back to that fateful day in the woods.

"I pondered the very same question. My conclusion was that the basilisk was an infant still, not yet at its full potential. Its only means of defense were the quills on the talon, as you witnessed. Which also means that these events in Hillsbury are no coincidence. They've been part of a plan in the making since you were a boy. Perhaps longer."

"What plan?"

Corbin had no intention of revealing the plan to Bruce. He had deciphered the crop circle, but only Henry would be privy to that information, and only if he requested it.

Bruce grudgingly accepted Corbin's silence and moved on to the most crucial question. "How do we kill it?" he growled.

Corbin's eyes widened. "Kill it? You don't. You leave it be."

"That thing killed my friend and who knows who else, I ain't 'leaving it be,' Corbin." Bruce's tone was frightfully serious.

"Whoever kills the demon will die along with it. And even then, it is no guarantee. The only known substance that can weaken a basilisk enough for a spear to puncture it is the effluvium of a weasel."

"Efflu . . . what's that?"

"Effluvium is odor. The odor of a weasel." Corbin was starting to pack his remaining belongings while he spoke.

Bruce let out a howl of a laugh. "You're kidding me, right? The stench of a rodent will kill that thing?"

"I'm afraid I'm one hundred percent serious, Bruce." Corbin's face was the picture of sincerity.

"So how do I get the effluvium and how do I kill it?"

"You kill it like you would anything, I assume. A spear is the only weapon I've heard of being effective, though that was over two thousand years ago. I suppose you could try a gun, but . . ." Corbin rubbed the bridge of his nose and took a breath. "Killing a basilisk is a suicide mission. Its blood is lethal, and whatever you smite it with, the blood or venom of the basilisk will flow upward and into your body, killing you instantaneously."

"But the bastard wouldn't be able to hurt anymore innocent people, right?" Bruce wanted to make sure that if he did this, he was doing it for a purpose.

Corbin nodded. "Yes, but . . ." He stopped himself from speaking any further; he could see the hurt and determination in the eyes of the man who sat before him.

"Bruce, if you do this, I will not be party to it. You're on your own." Corbin made sure Bruce verbally acknowledged what he was saying, and then proceeded to tell the man he would need to trap a weasel before scaling the cliff at Cape's Side Bay and entering the cave. The weasel would need to be set free where and when it would come face-to-face with the basilisk. The creature would grow weak and the weasel would herd it toward the edge of the cliff, where Bruce, with his eyes shut, would stab the basilisk in the heart, killing it. At which time, Bruce himself would fall dead, instantly. Painlessly. Maybe.

"I can only *guess* it will be painless, there's no real proof of that, I'm afraid. To me, though, an instant death is a painless death."

Bruce nodded. He stood, shook the astrobiologist's hand, and left the office.

Corbin followed him out with his eyes. After waiting a beat, he flipped over the facedown pictures on his desk and studied every detail. Each one raised a question and an answer in his mind. His fist slammed against the desk. He retrieved the sticky note he had hidden and placed it atop the first photograph. It read: *GENESIS 19.*

Corbin enjoyed his occupation for all of its ups and downs. He found Earth, its history, and the future of the universe fascinating. But the one aspect that he could never come to terms with were the scenarios in which he was helpless to the cause. The events in Hillsbury were such a scenario.

Jeffrey tossed one final bag into the dump for the day. He was about to clock out; his father had given him the night off. He was hoping to talk to Claudia on the ride home and ask her out for a soda or something, but he wasn't sure if that was a good idea anymore. The two had seen quite a lot of each other over the past couple of days, and he didn't want to come across as needy or clingy.

As he was returning to rangers' headquarters, he saw Claudia's car already waiting there. *Early*, he thought. Claudia sat in her car, speaking to someone on the phone. She gave him a wave and a smile. He returned them both before heading for the station doors so that he could punch out for the night.

"Jeffrey!" her voice called after him. He turned back and saw that she'd left the car and was now jogging in his direction.

"Yeah?" He cleared his throat, hoping to sound more manly and adult, but, to his horror, his vocal cords betrayed him and the word came out as a prepubescent screech. Claudia grinned but mercifully did not dwell on this.

"I wanted to ask you . . . Patty Liman is having a vigil for her son tonight. I was thinking maybe we could go. Would be nice to pay our respects. Then we can come back here for the fireworks." Claudia blushed. Jeffrey could hardly believe what he was hearing. Only two days ago, he'd believed that this older girl was out of his league and already spoken for. Now, she was blushing and asking him to spend the evening with her. Jeffrey discreetly pinched himself to ensure that this was real.

"Yeah! Sounds good." He tried to flex his cheeks to decrease his own blushing, but instead it just made him look like he was picking his teeth with his tongue.

"'Kay, I'll pick you up at eight. Oh, don't tell Morgan." Then Claudia waved goodbye and jogged back to her car.

Don't tell Morgan? Jeffrey almost fainted at the thought. She wanted Morgan kept out of this because she wanted tonight to be just the two of them. Nothing could remove the smile from Jeffrey's face now. Nothing. He was as giddy as he ever remembered feeling.

Jeffrey made his way inside and punched out. He was officially off work for the day. One more shift to go before the end of summer.

SUNDAY EVENING

THE SKY WAS bright red, a beautiful sunset on the final Sunday before the tourists and residents of Hillsbury retreated back to real life. For Henry Carter, real life had taken a rather bizarre detour. His sister, Jill, had been found after being missing for seven years. He raced home as quickly as he could. The drive from Hasaga was possibly the most emotional ride of his life. It began with depression and guilt, then quickly veered to shock, excitement, and nervousness. The hospital had said Jill had been there since Saturday morning, discovered by a local gas station attendant. Not much else was revealed to him, other than that she'd spent most of the time sleeping.

Henry couldn't be bothered pulling into the driveway; he parked the Jeep on the side of the road and rushed up to the front door. Inside, Rachel and Sarah were ready to go. They had a bag packed and Sarah had her favorite stuffed animal dangling from her hand.

"Where's Jeffrey?" Henry asked.

"He's not coming," Rachel responded, her words laced with slight veins of guilt.

"Not coming? What do you mean, *not coming?* Where is he?"

"He's out with a friend."

"Friend? What friend?" Henry was not only upset, but he was also anxious to leave.

"Claudia Burton," Rachel calmly informed her husband. "I haven't even told him about Jill yet. I couldn't ruin this evening for him, Henry."

Henry took a deep breath and assured himself that he was overreacting, that Rachel was right. Jill was safe now, safe and alive, and if Henry had anything to say about it, she was going to stay that way. She'd have plenty of time to see her nephew. The world wasn't going anywhere. "All right. All right, that's fine. Let's get going." He squeezed Sarah's shoulder playfully. "Into the car, little soldier."

Sarah grinned, gripped her stuffed animal tightly, and skipped off down the driveway. Rachel pulled her husband back for a moment and stared into his eyes.

"You okay?" she asked, her eyes traced with lines of concern.

He looked back down at her and felt himself smile. "I am, yeah. I actually am." Rachel kissed Henry, and they followed their daughter to the Jeep.

As the final blast of sunlight graced Hillsbury, Bruce Archer knew he had only a small window to get to Jett's on the other side of town and hope to find something there with which to trap a weasel. He was not very knowledgeable about the hunting and trapping of weasels; it was not the most luxurious prize for hunters. Other than calling the wildlife authority once to help remove some raccoons that had taken up lodgings in his attic, Bruce had very little experience with small mammals or rodents.

He was waiting for his cab at the entrance to Hillsbury Park. He didn't have to wait long. Not many cabs were in business in Hillsbury.

He entered Jett's a mere ten minutes before they closed. Jett was getting older by the minute; even at forty-three, he gave off the impression of a man with many more years of experience under his belt. At some point, Jett had lost all his cheerful warmness. He was tired of his occupation and had flirted with the idea of moving somewhere else, somewhere warmer. But alas, the bait shop was a family heirloom, one he knew he would sorely miss if he ever left.

Jett asked Bruce what he was looking for, his tone tired and annoyed. He wanted to get Bruce out so he could close up shop.

"I'm looking to trap a weasel," Bruce replied.

Jett's shoulders dropped. He looked even more frustrated. "This is a bait shop for fishing. Does it look like we have weasel traps?"

"I know you have mouse traps and ant traps. I can see those. Wondering if maybe you had weasel traps."

"Why you looking to trap a weasel?" Jett fixated one eye on the man, the other half-shut.

"I got a weasel problem."

Seemed like a reasonable explanation to Bruce. If one needed a weasel trap, logic would most certainly dictate that one had a weasel problem.

Jett sized the man up and down. Weasel traps weren't dangerous. Still, Jett suspected something afoot from this malodorous stranger. Was he a stranger, though? He seemed familiar somehow . . .

Jett's squinty eye popped open, and he snapped his fingers. "Aren't you the fella that got arrested the other day?"

Bruce lowered his head in embarrassment. This was something he would have to live with, at least until the truth of what happened to those boys became public knowledge. "Unrightfully so. I was released. Charges dropped."

Jett wasn't sure if he believed the big oaf or not. He walked to the back of his counter, reached for something under it (which made Bruce a tad bit nervous), and pulled out a package of chewing tobacco. He grabbed a slab and shoved it into his mouth. He offered some to Bruce, who graciously declined.

"That sounds like the work of Trundle. Most people like that boy, but I dunno . . . he sorta rubs me the wrong way," Jett said. "Always looking for the easy answer to things. That ain't life." He knelt down behind the counter, disappearing from sight for a minute. Bruce glanced around the shop, paying special attention to the pictures on the walls of customers who came in and shared their prizes with the store. All the fish caught in Cape's Side Bay, before the drought.

Jett stood back up. "I don't have any weasel traps."

Bruce was dismayed by the news. He'd have to think of something else.

"But," the shop owner continued, "we've got rat traps. They may do the trick."

Rat traps? Bruce thought. Rats and weasels couldn't be much different, could they? After all, did it matter? Wasn't like he had a choice. It was either rat traps or no traps at this point.

"Sure, I'll take one." Jett smiled at Bruce and made his way to the back of the shop to find the rat trap and make the oddest sale of the day.

The only light in the small office was coming from Corbin's desk lamp. The tiny forty-watt light bulb flickered every once in a while, signaling its need for a change. Corbin was also signaling a change. His time in Hillsbury had come to an end, and now he would be off to write his final report and submit it for official government purposes. After his lunch with Ava, he told her that he would call her the next day, and perhaps he would make his way to the park for the grand fireworks display. He had lied to the girl. He felt uncomfortable doing so, but at least he would never have to explain himself. He wouldn't be seeing Ava Trillium again.

Hillsbury was about to receive a message in a big way. It was none of Corbin's business to be present for said message.

As he shut off the desk lamp and exited his office, Corbin saw Bentley Trundle in the distance, only just entering the station. Bentley stared at Corbin for a moment, then swallowed.

"What're you doing?" the deputy sheriff asked.

"Leaving. My work here is done."

"Done?" Bentley asked angrily. "What about Ava?"

"She's quite lovely. I only wish to have known her more."

Bentley marched toward the astrobiologist and punched him square in the jaw. "Fuck you," Bentley spat in his face. "You come to my town, make me let a killer go free, and steal my girl?" He was yelling now, and Corbin was lying on the ground, dropped by the unseen punch. A small trickle of blood graced his lip.

"Get off my floor and get out of my town." Bentley made one final disgusted sound before he turned and walked away.

Jeffrey stood at the front door of Claudia's house. When her father opened it, Jeffrey felt every nerve in his body tense up. Her father did not say a word. He just stared at Jeffrey intensely. He was wearing an unbuttoned plaid top with corduroy pants, and his chin was sporting gray stubble.

Jeffrey cleared his throat again. "I'm here to see—" Before he could finish speaking, Morgan appeared behind his father.

"It's for me, Dad." Mr. Burton looked at his son, then back down at Jeffrey. Now he could not be sure, but Jeffrey could have sworn the old man gave him a wink. Morgan closed the door behind him.

"I'm actually here for Claudia," Jeffrey clarified, though he had no need to. Morgan was doing them a favor.

"I know that, dummy. But if my *dad* knew that, he'd kill you."

The front door opened again and Claudia ran out. "Ready to go?" she asked. Before Jeffrey could answer, Morgan said, "Yup."

Why would Morgan be ready? Claudia unlocked the car doors and Morgan jumped in the back. Jeffrey looked at Claudia. "He's coming?"

She didn't look happy about it either. "He has to. Otherwise my dad wouldn't let me out so late. Don't worry," Claudia added with a wink. "We'll lose him at the fireworks."

The carnival was once again going full steam ahead. The visitors had gathered in droves, and nothing could possibly wipe the smile from Mayor Tremblay's face. Nothing except a group of about eight or nine visitors who were trying to leave.

He rushed toward a group as they were walking toward their car. "Folks! Folks! What's your hurry? The festivities are only just beginning! We have a firework appetizer later tonight! A small taste of what's to come for the big finale tomorrow!" The smile he wore was toothy and disingenuous, like a crocodile's smile.

"We're going to the vigil for Joel Liman," one of the visitors said. His wife added, "We'll be back. Don't you worry."

The mayor looked around and saw that many visitors were leaving the park for the vigil. He lit a cigar, muttering under his breath, as a new car made its way into the park. The car zigged and zagged throughout the parking lot before taking a space at the far end of the lot. Bentley Trundle exited the car. Tremblay glanced up from his cigar.

"Deputy Sheriff Trundle! Welcome to Hillsbury Park!" Tremblay shouted, arms wide open.

Bentley pushed past the mayor, legs wobbly, smelling of alcohol, and walked down the path toward the carnival.

Ava was leaning against a big oak tree, sipping on her freshly brewed coffee. She was not too fond of the coffee the vendors were selling, so she opted to make her own back at headquarters. She watched as a young boy, no older than seven, played Skee-Ball with his older brother. They put their tokens into the machine and watched with joy as the balls rolled toward them. The older boy bowled first, frustrated at his meager ten-point result. His younger brother tossed the ball down the lane with all his might. There was not enough power behind the throw, and upon reaching the lip, the ball began to roll back toward the boy. He tried one more time, producing the same result.

He tugged on his brother's shirt, hoping for some assistance, but his brother was far too concentrated on his own game. The small boy tried again, but still the ball rolled back. His brother was already on his second game but the younger boy had yet to score a single point. Ava could not watch these events play out again. She set her coffee down and approached them.

"Need some help?"

The boy stared up at her quizzically, then back at the lane. "No."

That wasn't the answer Ava was expecting. "You sure about that?"

"Yeah, I'm sure," he said, shoving the ball down the lane with all his might. It rolled back to him a few seconds later. He tossed it to the ground in frustration.

"Hey, hey, it's okay. Here." Ava picked up the ball and dusted it off. "Let me help."

She handed it back to the boy. Then Ava wrapped her hands around his, and gently swung the arm back and forth. "On the count of three, release. Got it?" The boy nodded, and with one final swing, she called for him to release. They watched as the ball rolled down the lane, floated over the lip, and bounced around the forty-point slot before falling into twenty points. The boy looked up at Ava with a bright smile. She returned the smile.

"Good luck," Ava told him, before returning to her coffee. She leaned back against the oak tree and watched as the boy tried and failed once more before his brother finally took notice and offered his help. A hand reached down and landed on her shoulder. She turned to see Bentley standing in the trees, partially hidden in shadow.

"What're you doing here?" she asked, startled by his sudden appearance. His eyes were glistening, but not from the moonlight. "Are you drunk?"

Bentley flailed his hand in a lazy, dismissive wave. "Drunk is a strong word." His breath reeked of booze.

"Let's get you a coffee." Ava wrapped her arm around Bentley and walked him back to rangers' headquarters. Before long, she'd forced him into a chair and pushed a cup of hot coffee into his hands.

"My head hurts," he muttered.

"Yeah, it'll do that." She pulled up a chair next to him. "So, you wanna tell me what's going on?"

Bentley took a long, deliberate sip of his coffee and tried to slow the room's spinning. It was a losing battle. "I did it. I did it, Ava."

"Did what?" Ava asked, though she had a gut feeling she already knew the answer.

"I told Elise everything. How I felt . . . how I feel. You and me. Everything."

A sick feeling boiled within Ava's stomach. She had told him a day earlier that she was willing to make it work, but now her feelings were uneasy. She was unsure if Bentley was the man she wished to have a future with because now she'd been given another possible option in the form of Corbin Mench. However, Ava was also unsure about Corbin himself. His enigmatic nature made him attractive, without question . . . but with such little information, it also made it difficult for her to make an educated choice. Of course, this was not the moment to bring any of this up with Bentley; he was both too heartbroken and too drunk. As much as ending things with Elise was what he had wanted to do, it could not have been easy to leave behind all their years together.

"Now we can be together." Bentley's voice broke the silence. The smile he gave her was lopsided but achingly genuine.

Ava tried to smile back, though she wasn't sure the expression on her face was all that convincing. He placed the mug down on the desk and reached over to hug her. She leaned in and hugged him back. Guilt washed over her. She was now officially the home wrecker she had never wanted to become. And from where she was standing, it didn't look like it was worth it in the end.

SUNDAY NIGHT

THE STARS WERE lighting up the night sky like candles in a church. Henry's old Jeep pulled up to the visitor parking lot at St. Joseph's Hospital in Leafsview. A nervous energy possessed his body and mind; he had not seen his sister in seven years. His daughter was only six and had never even *met* her Aunt Jill, knowing her only from photos and the stories Henry would share if he was in a good enough mood to do so without grieving. He was excited for the two of them to meet but nervous to see what kind of condition Jill would be in.

Normally quite frugal, Henry would have been disgusted with the cost of parking at St. Joseph's. Today, though, none of that mattered. No price was too high if it meant he got to see Jill again. It was amazing how something like this could put so much into perspective.

The interior of the hospital was dim and cold. The aroma of iodoform lingered in the air. Henry found himself wondering why they didn't try to drive the stench out with air fresheners or something. The building relied heavily on natural illumination from its vast collection of skylights, so when the sun set, St. Joseph's was quite dark. Only a few paltry fluorescent lights broke the shadows, dangling from chains attached to the ceiling. It was quiet too; St. Joseph's was almost never busy. A traffic accident two decades back had injured fifty people who'd all ended up here, but the hospital hadn't seen activity like that since.

Henry was unsure where his sister was being kept. He knew she was in critical care, but that was about it. He gripped Rachel's and Sarah's hands tightly and led them to the nearest information desk. Thankfully, the desolation of the place meant he didn't have to wait in line to speak to someone.

"Can I help you?" asked the woman behind the desk. Her eyes never strayed from her computer monitor.

"I'm looking for Jill Carter." Henry was out of breath as he spoke, from both nerves and the quick pace in which he and the family had entered the hospital.

That name caught the woman's attention. She finally looked up. "And you are?"

"Her brother. Henry Carter." He tapped his fingers along the counter impatiently, waiting for her to type something into her computer. Every second he wasn't seeing Jill felt like a wasted one. His feet shook as if he were dancing madly to an inaudible tune.

The woman finished typing. "ID, please?" she asked.

Henry wrestled with the pocket of his khakis and fished out his wallet. He slid his driver's license across the counter and waited for a response, his feet tapping even harder. On his right, Sarah took notice and looked up at her father, concerned. The gravity of this whole situation hadn't really sunk in for her until right now; she had never seen her father agitated like this.

Finally, the woman handed the license back to Henry. "Room 249, through those doors. Take the elevator to the second floor and it'll be on your left."

Henry hastily thanked her and pulled his wife and daughter in the proper direction with such abruptness that Sarah was nearly yanked right off her feet.

The second floor was more well-lit than the first. Henry led them out to the left, his pace and his pulse quickening. He was in such a hurry that Rachel gently told him he could go on ahead and they would catch up. As much as she missed Jill, Rachel understood that this was Henry's moment; she was more than willing to let the Carters have a private family reunion if they needed one. She took hold of Sarah (who looked very grateful she didn't have to keep pace with her anxious father anymore) and let Henry carry on ahead without them.

A nurse in pink scrubs was there to greet Henry just outside room 249. "Mr. Carter?" she asked. "Right through here, please."

Henry's entire body felt like it was going numb with adrenaline. He followed the nurse through the door of room 249 and—for the first time in seven long years—saw his sister.

Jill lay asleep beneath the covers in the hospital bed, her expression peaceful.

Tears flooded Henry's eyes. He couldn't help it. He couldn't help but notice the bruises, the wounds. He couldn't help but think of the pain she must have gone through, and of the strength it must have taken to endure it for all this time.

He took notice of a young man who sat, upright but asleep, in a chair at the far end of the room. "That's the man who found her," the nurse explained. Henry wanted to ask him so many questions, but instead he walked straight to his sister. He rested his hand on her shoulder and—with a shaking finger—gently grazed her cheek. The nurse noticed tears spilling down Henry's cheeks and kindly offered him a tissue.

After giving him a few moments, she spoke quietly. "Mr. Carter, there's an officer here who'd like a word with you."

Henry nodded. "Sure." He tore his eyes away from Jill and followed the nurse out of the room.

Henry was escorted to an office. A police officer sat on a comfortable-looking blue chair against the wall. He gestured to a second empty chair and motioned for Henry to have a seat. Henry had no idea who the office belonged to, but they were not present. The officer was consulting some papers and did not speak right away. For every second of silence, Henry's mind filled with worries regarding his sister's condition . . . and what had brought her to such a state in the first place. Henry finally broke the silence, unable to bear it any longer. "What happened to my sister?"

The officer cleared his throat slowly, methodically, as if he were prolonging the moment to better conjure up the right way to say something he wasn't looking forward to saying. "Well . . . to be perfectly honest with you, Mr. Carter, we're not quite sure. We know it wasn't good. Have you seen her?"

"Only briefly."

"We'll get you back to her room as soon as we can, I just . . . your sister has sustained some serious injuries. Her medical chart shows severe physical trauma inflicted to her vocal cords. We're not sure how it happened, but she's been struggling to communicate. The kid who found her had her spell her name using a graph he drew up. Other than that, she's only said one word."

Henry looked up at the officer. "One?"

"Yes, one word." The officer paused for a moment. He almost looked *embarrassed*. "Reckoning."

Henry was taken aback. Not exactly what he'd expected. But then again, what *had* he expected?

"Any idea why she might say something like that?" the officer asked. He was holding a pen to a notepad now. "Something so cryptic? Does it mean anything to you?"

Henry shook his head. "No."

"Nothing at all? Nothing from your past? Childhood? Something that maybe she just blurted out?"

"No. Nothing." Henry couldn't tell if this made the officer skeptical or disappointed or a combination of both. But he could tell the other man was not pleased. Obviously, this was their only clue regarding Jill's whereabouts; if it turned out to be a dead end, then they had nothing else to go on.

The officer leaned back, shoulders sagging, and closed his notepad. "All right. Thank you, Mr. Carter. If anything else comes up, if you remember anything at all or think of something, please let us know."

"Sure," said Henry. "Can I see my sister now? Please?"

The officer nodded and allowed him to leave. Henry passed Rachel and Sarah in the waiting room, giving them a brief smile and wave before reentering room 249.

The young man who'd found Jill was no longer present. This disappointed Henry; he'd wanted to thank the stranger and question him profusely. He cursed under his breath, agitated that his pointless detour with the officer had robbed him of this opportunity.

Jill's heart monitor was the only sound in the room, a steady beeping that was almost (but not quite) comforting. Henry approached the bedside, watching as Jill slept, eyes shut and motionless, lips gently closed. She looked at peace, which was good; at least she did not appear to be in any kind of pain. Perhaps the hospital had given her something to combat it. But he hoped not. He hoped Jill needed nothing but rest.

Henry took notice of bruises, of her fingernails, of all the mutilations performed on her body, and his eyes welled up once more. He bit down on his fist, hoping not to break down any further, but it was like trying to plug a breaking dam with a finger. The emotional weekend had reached its peak with Jill's discovery; it was all more than he'd ever had to bear. He was sad, happy, angry, reluctant, and it all came crashing down in one fell swoop.

He dropped to his knees, his head resting on the rail of the bed, tears flowing from squeezed eyes, strangled sobs squeaking forth from a dry throat. He could no longer control it. Henry Carter had finally succumbed to his emotions.

The lights on McMurray Street were all off, even though the sun had just set. The mayor had (reluctantly) agreed to allow the lights to be turned off for forty-five minutes in honor of the vigil for Joel Liman. Every second people spent at the vigil was a second they *weren't* spending at the carnival, and that frustrated Tremblay to no end. But not many shared his skewed priorities: hundreds of people flocked to McMurray Street in honor of Joel Liman.

Patty and her neighbors distributed candles to those making donations. It was a lovely sight, all of those concerned people littering the darkened street, holding flames that flickered gently in the hot breeze. Patty was overwhelmed and humbled by the outcome.

Jeffrey, Claudia, and Morgan all made small donations and were handed candles of their own. Patty beamed at them and thanked them for coming. Jeffrey and Morgan felt obligated to attend, as they were both present during the Friday morning search for Joel, finding pieces of the puzzle that was his disappearance, and in turn, answering questions about the prime suspect in the investigation. That all felt like a lifetime ago for the two teenage boys.

Patty spoke a few words to the crowd, thanking them and then praying her son would be found safe and sound. This was followed by Father Donald's prayer and then a church hymn. All those in attendance joined in. The sound reminded Patty of angels singing, and she smiled again, something she'd been unable to do since her son's disappearance.

The dusty road was dark, not a single light could be seen for miles. The possibility of deer hopping out in front of traffic would normally by quite high. Corbin drove slowly along the road, never looking back. At times during the drive, his thoughts strayed to Ava.

He was quite fond of the assistant park ranger; but he knew the two of them could never have anything substantial together. His profession—and the knowledge he possessed—kept him constantly on the move. A life settling down with someone was never in the cards for Corbin Mench. It was something he would never experience, a slice of someone else's life that he could only observe from afar. At times this did make Corbin sad; there had been several weekends when he would find himself alone in his room, drinking a glass of expensive scotch while wistfully dreaming of a life he *could* have had, had he not been born so intelligent. After coming across universal wave function and the many-worlds interpretation in his studies, he often found himself wondering if there was a parallel version of Corbin Mench somewhere out there in the multiverse, a version with a normal nine-to-five job who was happily married and deeply in love. Sometimes the thought gave him a quiet comfort; other times it drove him mad with envy.

He shook his head clear and focused on the road. The sooner Corbin got to a hotel, the sooner he could sleep, and the earlier he could rise and depart.

He had quite a lot of findings to report. Corbin hadn't dwelled on the whereabouts of the Liman boy; after seeing the fate of Joel's friends, Corbin grimly accepted the fact that Joel Liman would show up sooner or later, and when he did, the town would weep. They would never know what had really happened to the boy. No one ever would. He had been taken for a purpose. For a greater good.

A sign for a small motel thirty miles ahead was visible through the darkness. It was not a classy-looking place, but it would do. As long as it had a bed and shower, Corbin would be just fine.

His thoughts shifted once more to Ava. Perhaps she was worth turning back for? Perhaps he could include her in his life? Perhaps life was too short to turn away a good thing out of fear? Perhaps . . .

His phone buzzed. He glanced down and almost gasped: Ava's name graced his call display. A smile briefly crossed over his face before fading into the frown he had grown accustomed to whenever he felt an emotional connection to a woman. As much as he wanted to answer this call, as much as he wanted to hear her voice and turn around to be with Ava, he had to keep driving. He had to ignore the ringing and stay on course. When the phone finally stopped ringing, Corbin felt a powerful and conflicting blow of relief and immense regret.

A beep chimed, informing him that he had a voicemail, and he smiled again in spite of himself. Ava was special. But not special enough to change things. Suddenly, in front of him in the dark of night, a deer popped into view. Corbin swerved to avoid the creature. He stopped his car and watched as the deer hopped back into the field next to the road. Corbin gathered his thoughts, and his courage—the deer had startled him—and took a breath. He reached into the back seat for a bottle of water. As he looked back out the window, he could still see the deer running. *Unusual,* he thought.

Corbin got out of the car and walked into the long grass, in the same direction as the deer.

Corn.

Corbin rushed back to his car. He popped open the trunk and removed a drone. He sent it high in the sky above the field.

As he looked over the black-and-white night-vision footage taken from the drone, his worst fears became reality.

Another crop circle.

One crop circle was an isolated incident; when there are several, it can only mean one thing.

He hopped back into his car and drove off. Corbin drove around Hillsbury, to each town boarding it. Each town with a field. Each one with its own unique crop circle.

Seven in total. The seven deadly sins isolating the town. Hillsbury park was doomed. Corbin wanted nothing more than to contact everyone. Mass chaos would ensue, and there was no escaping this. The fate of Cape's Side Bay was put into motion long before Corbin even knew the town existed.

He needed a drink.

He made his way to a motel, far from the outskirts of Hillsbury, checked in, and ordered a whiskey from the hotel pub.

Disappointed, Ava slid the cell phone back into her pocket. She wanted to speak with Corbin, to see where their relationship (if it even was one) was headed. Bentley was asleep in Henry's office, and her feelings for both men left her feeling torn. How could she feel such a strong connection with Corbin if she was almost certainly falling in love with Bentley? Bentley loved her, that much was true. He loved her enough to leave his own wife for her. As much as Ava tried to push him and her feelings for him aside, she could not.

Bentley actually looked peaceful sleeping in Henry's chair. So at ease. So handsome. She reached for her phone and considered trying Corbin one more time, but she felt she had said all she needed to say in the voicemail she'd left for him. This had been her fourth attempt to get ahold of the astrobiologist.

Perhaps this was a sign that her destiny *did* lie with Bentley. She knew she could be happy with him. She always felt loved and welcomed and needed when she was with him. Elise had always been the X factor. Elise was Bentley's wife, a woman he had vowed to love forever and always. If Bentley could forego those vows and fall in love with someone else, who was to say that the same thing would not happen again somewhere down the road? Perhaps Ava would find herself being ditched by Bentley Trundle one day, in favor of the next pretty young thing he struck up a conversation with. Then again, perhaps they were kindred spirits destined to be together, and they needed to face this obstacle to be happy for the rest of their lives. There were so many avenues, and the mind never picked the logical one . . . it picked the one that sounded the most appealing.

Ava was brewing a pot of coffee when her finger began to sting. She looked down to where she had pricked herself with the claw and saw that it was turning red, almost like a rash. She made her way to the restroom and rinsed off her hand. As the water splashed over the reddened area, an odd new sensation sent chills down her spine. Ava sucked her finger, silently cursing herself for touching that damn talon in the first place.

The park was almost empty. Mayor Tremblay lingered in the shadows, waiting for the people to return from Joel Liman's vigil.

If anyone asked, Tremblay would say that he had gone to the vigil. He'd say he had stood among the crowd, holding a candle and chanting "kumbaya" or whatever it was they were doing. That—he assured himself—would earn him their respect.

Tremblay was optimistic that most folks would return to the park once the vigil was over, despite the hour growing late. He had, after all, promised them a tantalizing appetizer, a fireworks "warm-up" leading to the gigantic main event tomorrow night. Tremblay had teased the event to campers the way one teased dogs with raw meat. There was no way anyone would want to miss it. The mayor was certain that people would be talking about his Labor Day Fireworks Spectacular for years to come. And then every voice that had told him it would be foolish to pour all of his resources into the final day of the long weekend would be silenced!

So, he waited in the shadows of the park's large trees until a parade of headlights told him that the vigil had ended and the party was about to begin.

Tremblay was there to greet them, ready and waiting to drive thoughts of missing boys from their minds and fill the empty space with even emptier promises. Those few who knew Tremblay personally would have been sickened by his fake smile. But for the most part, the guests of Hillsbury Park were in the dark regarding his true intentions; if he told them he'd been at the vigil, they'd believe it. The thought made his crocodile-like grin grow even wider.

Henry made his way to the vending machine. In all the excitement regarding Jill, he had forgotten to eat dinner. Chips and BBQ-flavored peanuts would have to do. As the candy slid out of the machine, he looked over to see the young man who'd found his sister sleeping on a chair in the corner, alone. Henry approached and gently tapped his shoulder.

"Hey. Hey. Excuse me." Groggy, the young man opened his eyes. "Sorry to wake you, I just . . . I wanted to thank you. For all you've done for my sister over the past couple of days."

It took Steve a moment to realize that Henry was referring to Jill. "Oh yeah, man. No problem. Least I could do."

Henry pulled up a chair for himself. "I was wondering if you wouldn't mind me asking you a few questions? I'm Henry, by the way."

Steve sat up in his chair. "Steve." They shook hands. "What do you want to know?"

"When you found her, did she say anything about where she'd been?"

Steve shook his head. "No, nothing. Doctors say her vocal cords have been scratched. Honestly, I know it's kind of messed up, but . . . the morning I found her, she was walking by my gas station fully naked. And she just collapsed. I assumed drugs, but now . . . I dunno."

"And you brought her right here?"

"Right here. Right away."

"She was wearing nothing? Stark naked?"

"Stark, sir."

"Call me Henry, please."

"It was the strangest thing. I didn't know what to say when I got here. To be completely honest, I'm not sure the cops believed me at first. I hope you know I'm being honest, si . . . Henry."

"Yeah, I believe you." Henry thought for a moment. "All right. Go back to sleep. I'll see you around."

Steve nodded and slid back into a more comfortable position. Henry opened his bag of chips and walked back to room 249.

While the majority of Hillsbury Park was lit up with festival lights and smiling faces, something else lingered in the park's deep, dark corners.

Vengeance.

Bruce Archer stood alone, silent, concealed in the gloom of the forest while he set up his rat/weasel trap. He only had the one trap; he would have preferred several, but as this was a last-minute situation on a long weekend, his options were minimal. One would have to do. He felt the earth below, searching for weaknesses in the dirt where weasel holes could be found.

Bruce was not very knowledgeable regarding weasels. On his way to the park, he'd stopped to watch several videos of some outdoor-savvy teenagers teaching people how to catch them. So Bruce was not going in *totally* blind.

After the trap was all set, Bruce removed an apple from his pocket, took a bite, and sat behind a tree about a dozen yards away. Nothing left to do now but wait . . .

Time rolled on. Bruce checked his watch and saw that it was just past ten o'clock. Tremblay's fireworks would be starting soon.

Bruce's mind wandered to the thought of the basilisk. The creature that had brought him so much pain and trauma. The creature that had killed his best friend. The creature that had become his lifelong nightmare.

It was going to feel so good to finally watch it die.

A weasel popped its head out from behind a nearby tree. Bruce was startled but remained still and quiet. The scent of the trap must have finally caught the critter's attention. After taking a few cautious sniffs, the weasel entered the cage.

Bruce stood up, victorious. *Hard part's over*, he thought.

Mayor Tremblay continued to mingle with his guests. Those with small children pressed the mayor for information regarding the fireworks, as the kids were beginning to grow tired and cranky.

"Soon, soon," Tremblay hissed through his teeth. He couldn't understand why these parents were so ungrateful: the fireworks display was free, after all! Still, he decided to investigate the matter (not for the sake of the patrons, but simply to satisfy his own blossoming impatience). He made his way to the gated area where the fireworks technicians prepared to release their art to the public.

"How much longer? Some of these idiots are growing unpleasant," Tremblay growled.

"We're good to go, sir."

The mayor smiled. "Good. I'll give my speech, and when you hear me say, 'in all of Hillsbury!' you let out the first firework. And it has to be big. Got me? Big!" And before the head of the department could respond, Tremblay was gone.

Tremblay seized the podium and tapped the microphone to ensure it was on (he wasn't keen on repeating a mistake he'd made two years earlier). A pair of loud thumps issuing from a nearby speaker told him that the mic was working fine. So he raised his arms into the night sky.

"Welcome, welcome, one and all, to the first night of the great Hillsbury fireworks!"

A sea of voters erupted into applause before him, and Tremblay beamed.

Bruce made his way to the entrance of the cave high above the bay. This was the last place he ever thought he would end up. Decades of anger and hatred had all led to this moment. This was the most alive Bruce had felt in years.

The weasel in the cage was staring back at him, as if it knew what was about to happen. As if it knew its life was coming to a triumphant end.

"It's all right, little buddy." Normally, he would think speaking to such a creature was ridiculous. But now, in the heat of the given situation, it actually gave him comfort.

The interior of the cave was uncannily hot and dry. Nothing about the place felt right to Bruce. It felt dangerous and unholy. He could feel the presence of the beast all around him. The weasel began to frantically pace from side to side in its tiny prison, making a bigger racket than Bruce would have liked. He'd hoped to surprise the basilisk and had no interest in making such a dangerous monster aware of his presence.

After about fifteen meters, Bruce came to a stop. He knelt down and opened the cage door. The weasel immediately leaped out and rushed straight into the belly of the cave, as if it knew exactly what it had been brought to do.

Claudia grabbed Jeffrey's hand, and he immediately decided that whatever dream he was having was one he had no interest in waking up from. They had missed the opening of the mayor's speech from where they sat, tucked beneath a large tree, their lips meeting then parting then meeting again. Back at summer's start, when Henry had forced him to wear that embarrassing ranger uniform, Jeffrey never thought in a million years that he'd be making out with Claudia Burton before the season ended.

Now Claudia led them into the thick of the carnival to see whatever spectacle Tremblay was cooking up. Jeffrey didn't like the mayor much (he'd heard enough about him from his father), but even he had to admit that Tremblay knew how to dazzle a crowd. The man may not have been a great mayor, but when it came to pure spectacle, he was king. Except that one time, two summers ago, when Tremblay had made it five minutes into an impassioned speech before realizing that his microphone was off. That had been hilarious.

"As many of you know," the mayor was proclaiming, his voice echoing thunderously through the park, "our famous Labor Day festivities used to wrap up on this very night. But I say, why rob the people . . . *YOU* fine people . . . of an extra day of fun? We have decided to prolong the events and give our visitors, our community, the best weekend we can. Summer should end with a bang!" More cheers and applause. "Hillsbury is my home . . ."

A few dozen feet away from Claudia and Jeffrey, Ava groaned. She had left Bentley in the office to get a better view of the fireworks, but instead she found herself subjected to this moronic speech. Thankfully, her thoughts were too preoccupied to pay much attention to it. *I'm a home wrecker.* The thought came seemingly out of nowhere, striking her like a punch to the gut. *I never wanted to be one, but that's exactly what I am. And I'm getting away with it for some reason. God, poor Elise Trundle . . . I ruined her life, and nobody even knows.*

The truth would emerge eventually. It would have to, especially if she decided to start a new life with Bentley. *A life with Bentley . . .*

A slow grin crept across her face. A life with Bentley sounded wonderful. It sounded like the kind of thing that would make her happy for many, many years. Sure, maybe that happiness had to come at the expense of someone else's. But . . . didn't Ava deserve it? Didn't she deserve happiness? Hadn't she earned that right?

Leaving the crowd at the mercy of the mayor and his pointless words, Ava turned and inched her way back to headquarters.

Bruce removed a flask from his back pocket. He took a swig. Waiting was not his strong suit, never had been. Though when he stopped to break it down, he had waited all these years for this moment, so what was another few minutes? He sat back against a rock and made himself comfortable, or as comfortable as one could be in a hot cave that was supposedly home to a murderous mythological beast. The comfort lasted only a moment before the weasel let out a frightened squeal.

Bruce rushed to his feet, sliding his father's dagger out of the holster he wore at his ankle. A tremendous roar echoed through the cave. It sounded angry, which could only mean one thing: the effluvium was working its magic, and the basilisk would soon make its way to the cave entrance. Bruce's fist squeezed tighter around the hilt of the dagger, ready to strike.

Then . . . silence.

Bruce looked left, then right, seeing nothing but the cavern's gloom. Perhaps the weasel had killed the basilisk itself? Or perhaps it was the other way around? Before any more thoughts could trickle though his fragile mind, Bruce heard a whimper and looked down to see the weasel limping toward him. Its leg had been severed, almost torn right off. Up ahead, he could hear the basilisk breathing, deep and sonorous with an almost asthmatic scratchiness. His eyes closed to slits; one glance at the mythological beast would stop his heart. The sound of the creature's steps grew increasingly louder and louder. Panicking, Bruce shut his eyes completely. The footsteps stopped, and he could feel hot breath roll across his neck.

With his eyes closed, he was unable to determine the distance between the beast and himself, so he couldn't tell if he was within arm's reach. The breath trickled along his neck once again, this time stopping at his left shoulder. The basilisk was circling him, most likely sizing him up and determining whether Bruce was a threat or not. Bruce slowly turned with the creature, his firm grip still possessing the blade in his hand. When Bruce felt he had positioned the basilisk between himself and the cave entrance, he plunged forward with his dagger.

Steel pierced the beast and dug deep. Within seconds, Bruce began to feel cold. Corbin was correct: the blood within the veins of the beast was poisonous to man. His own blood chilled and thinned as the venom began to take over. Pain lurched into existence behind his eyes.

His eyes!

Bruce opened them as wide as he could. For the first time since he was a child, Bruce Archer stood face-to-face with the lizard from the park, the murderer of his best friend, the nightmare that haunted his dreams in the years that followed. With his final breath, he pushed through the basilisk's chest and drew the dagger directly into its heart. The two of them toppled out of the cave together. The life had left Bruce Archer's body before he could taste open air.

In his hotel room, Corbin held a bottle of single-barrel whiskey. He brought this whiskey with him on all of his cases but only drank it when the answers to the current dilemmas far surpassed human comprehension. He poured the liquor into a small glass, swirled it about, and stared down into it. A tear fell from his eyes. Hillsbury was lost to him. He took a sip.

In room 249 of St. Joseph's Hospital, Henry sat by his sister, head and arms leaning over to rest on the bed. He was half-asleep, but that changed abruptly when Jill's eyes shot open and she flung herself upright.

Henry jumped up and tried to calm her. "Jill! Jill!"

No response. She screamed. Her injured throat made it raspy and painful to listen to. Nurses rushed in through the door. "What happened?" the head nurse asked.

"I don't . . . I don't know! I was just sleeping and . . ."

With as much suddenness as she'd sat up, Jill fainted. The nurse took Jill's chart and scribbled something down. They didn't seem as fazed as he was. Perhaps this was nothing new. Perhaps Jill had been doing this since she'd arrived. But whatever could have—

Henry's thoughts were cut short as Jill lurched upright once again and let out another scream. This time, she didn't stop. Henry backed fearfully into a wall as nurses called out codes and doctors ran in. Jill's eyes rolled back into her head. She was clearly in a lot of pain. After several long, agonizing minutes, the screams finally stopped. The doctor checked her pulse and assured everyone in the room that it was steadily dropping back to a normal rate.

Henry turned away and saw, to his horror, that Sarah stood in the open doorway, looking frightened and confused. He rushed over and pulled her into a protective hug. "Everything's all right. Go back and sit with your mother."

Bentley Trundle slowly gained consciousness. He looked up and noticed Ava standing over him with a fresh coffee cupped in her palms. She knelt down and placed it on the table in front of him.

"All rested?"

He nodded and sat up, rubbing sleep dust from his eyes. "How long was I out?"

"Long enough. Here. I made you a coffee." Ava slid the cup closer to him. When he reached for it, their hands briefly touched. A chill of excitement flowed through her body. Bentley was the man she was meant to be with. Now, more than ever, Ava was sure of it.

Bentley took a sip and pulled back, wincing. "Careful, it's hot," she said, chuckling.

Why is she so happy? Bentley thought as he found himself returning the smile. Ava sat next to him on the couch and gazed into his eyes. An uneasy feeling crept up within him. He had no time to speak or think before Ava embraced Bentley Trundle with a kiss. While the two had had their share of kisses and passionate moments in the past, there was something different about this one. This one carried weight, carried substance. Bentley felt like he was not just *kissing* Ava, but like he was enveloping himself, *shrouding* himself, in the comfort he took from her very existence. There was something so utterly, profoundly *right* about this kiss. With a little reluctance, Bentley eventually retracted.

"Ava—"

She pressed her finger against his lips. Not another word was needed. She was all in. The next move was his. And it was the most important move. Would he truly choose to be with her? Or did he regret leaving Elise? If there had ever been a moment of truth in Bentley Trundle's life, it was this moment, on this horrible old couch, with his tongue still scalded from the hot coffee. Bentley looked into Ava's eyes, then shifted his gaze.

A moment of hesitation.

He had spent so much time with Elise, invested so much in their relationship. He looked back at Ava.

Those eyes.

They slayed him every time he stared at them.

His decision was made.

Bentley leaned in and initiated what would be their first last kiss. The kiss that would end their affair and begin their romance.

His life was going to change now. But for Ava, the change—he was certain—was more than worth it.

Claudia and Jeffrey watched, half-listening, half-lampooning, as the mayor gave his arrogant speech. Claudia looked down at her watch and saw that he had been blabbering for almost fifteen minutes. *Unbelievable*, she thought. She tugged on Jeffrey's shirt and whispered something into his ear. A moment later, they were racing off into the woods.

Forget the dangers. Forget the missing boy and his deformed friends. Claudia Burton was dragging Jeffrey Carter out to Cape's Side Bay and he was allowing it. His father would be so disappointed, and he did not care; nothing could stop him from enjoying this moment.

Claudia stopped as they reached the edge of the bay, just before the grass transformed into what used to be swampy water but was now dry dirt. Jeffrey wondered how the bay could possibly dry up so fast, but the thought vanished quickly when Claudia's lips brushed against his. She began to remove her shirt.

"What're you doing?" he blurted, then silently berated himself for asking such a dumb question.

"What do you think?" She responded by grabbing his belt and unbuckling it. Jeffrey's heart began to beat fast, faster, the fastest it ever had. "Take my bra off," she whispered seductively.

He steadied his shaking hands so that he could wrap them around her and reach for the bra strap. The moment he spent grasping for it felt like an eternity. When he found it, he struggled, twisted, turned . . . but the bra remained firmly in place.

Claudia rolled her eyes. "Figure it out yet?"

"I think so," he lied. He had never thought that such a small piece of plastic could pose such a challenge. He twisted and turned some more until he felt the latch release, and her bra loosened. *Finally!* Grinning, he looked back at Claudia's face. Her attention had shifted. He must have taken too long to undo the bra. "Claudia?"

"What is that?" she asked. She was staring up at the cave above the bay. Jeffrey followed her pointing finger and saw something unbelievable enough to actually make him forget all about breasts.

Bruce Archer and some kind of large lizard were plunging out of the cave's mouth. Jeffrey and Claudia watched, transfixed, as Bruce and the lizard separated in midair before the lizard's body erupted in flames and vanished. An instant later, Bruce was impaled on a high metal stake.

Claudia screamed. The metal stake was a grounding device for the power generator the carnival crew had installed. Bruce's body came to a stop in this grisly position, the pole protruding through his chest, arms spread wide, eyes wide open. Blood dripped from the puncture wound and slid down the metal rod, producing sparks.

The sparks continued to fizz and pop with increasing vigor until Bruce's body went up in flames. The two teenagers could do nothing but stare, agape, as a bolt of electricity sizzled through the man's body.

The crowd continued to cheer politely for the mayor. Tremblay looked at the fireworks crew and gave a slight nod. His speech was coming to an end. It was time for the big finish.

"And so I conclude by simply saying: Welcome! Welcome one and all to the very first ni—"

All the lights around Tremblay went dark. His microphone turned off. The carnival fell silent.

Stunned and confused, the mayor knew something had to be done before the crowds dispersed, or the local paper would have a field day crowning the entire evening a disaster.

Tremblay rushed over to the fireworks crew, hissing, "Light 'em up! Light them all! Now!"

They obeyed. The first howling firecracker exploded into the night sky, and the temporarily stunned crowd clapped with amusement. One by one, the visitors assumed that the lights had been doused for the fireworks show.

And if any had asked, Tremblay would have told them exactly that, wearing the most assuring smile he could muster.

Ava and Bentley were deeply immersed in kissing, oblivious to the world around them. His shirt lay on the floor, hers unbuttoned. Bentley slid his hand up Ava's thigh and was about to continue upward to remove her shirt when—with a sudden crackle—all the lights and computers in the headquarters shut off, plunging them into darkness.

Ava sat up. "That's strange."

"Power outage?"

"Maybe. What would have set that off?"

Bentley stood and peered out the window. The familiar orange glow of nearby lampposts was gone too. Everything was black out there. "Looks like power's out all over the park."

Ava began to button up her shirt when the thunderous roar of a firework shook the building, startling her. Bentley noticed her jump and he chuckled. "Just firecrackers, park ranger. This isn't a code blue or anything." He laughed. Then he ducked when Ava playfully tossed his shirt at him. "I'm not putting this back on! We were just getting started!"

"Gotta find out what happened to the power."

"What happened was Trundle set it to shut off so nothing would distract anyone from the glorious barrage of fireworks he probably bankrupted the town by purchasing." Bentley slithered toward Ava and tapped the tip of her nose before kissing her once again. She gave in to his embrace, but they were interrupted again by the sound of forceful banging.

"That was no firecracker," she mumbled. Ignoring Bentley's disappointed groan, Ava poked her head out into the hallway and saw Jeffrey and Claudia slamming their fists against the main door. After ensuring that her shirt was buttoned properly, Ava let them in. "What are you two doing here?"

The teenagers did not say a word, but they were gasping and sporting expressions of pure terror.

A cavalcade of colors lit up the night sky. Jeffrey and Claudia brought Ava and Bentley to the bay. They stood staring at the charred body of what used to be Bruce Archer, fallen from the cave and speared to death by the generator stake. The bursts of Tremblay's fireworks bathed the grisly scene with intermittent illumination, first in green, then in purple, then in stark red. Ava turned away from the sight, wincing.

So THIS caused the power outage, Bentley thought. He shifted his attention to the two teenagers. "And you guys saw this happen?" Both Jeffrey and Claudia could only nod. "All right. I'm gonna get Walden on the line. This park isn't safe anymore."

"Anymore?" The word charged out of Jeffrey's mouth before he could help himself. "It hasn't been safe since Joel Liman went missing!"

"Take him home, please," Bentley told Claudia, who agreed. She grabbed Jeffrey's hand and pulled him away from the bay.

Ava stared at Bruce's body one more time. "What in the world was Bruce Archer doing in that cave?" she pondered.

Bentley frowned. "I don't know. But I'm willing to bet that your friend Mench does."

Henry sat in darkness on a chair in his sister's room, fast asleep. The term *long weekend* had taken on a whole new meaning for Henry and his family. His wife and daughter were given an unused bed in a room adjacent to Jill Carter's.

Henry's cell phone vibrated and he sat up at once. He rubbed the rheum from his eyes and noticed Ava's name on his call display. He answered, his voice groggy from misuse. "Yeah?"

"Bruce Archer's dead." It was evident from her tone that she had been crying and was trying to hold each word steady.

Henry exited the room, whispering so as not to disturb his sister's sleep. "What do you mean, *he's dead?* What happened?" He heard the phone switching hands, followed by an answer from Bentley Trundle.

"Found him at the bottom of the cave. Looks like he was up there trying to do something and fell."

Henry backed into a wall and slid to the floor, his feet giving way beneath him. He had a pretty good idea why Bruce was up there.

"We tried to get ahold of Mench," Bentley went on, "but no such luck. Figured *he'd* know what Bruce was doing in the bay so late at night." Henry nodded. Tears began to flood his eyes. "Also figured you'd be our best shot at getting ahold of him."

Henry regained his composure. "Do me a favor. Keep this quiet. Inform his family tomorrow. Tremblay won't want the publicity until after the festivities."

"Yeah," Bentley agreed. "How's your sister?"

"She's—we don't know yet."

"Keep us updated. I'll try and make my way to Leafsview as soon as the chaos around here winds down."

"Thanks." Henry ended the conversation with the deputy sheriff and immediately dialed Corbin Mench.

Corbin sat on the bed, laptop resting on his knees, typing away at his dissertation. While working amid the paranormal and unexplained, Corbin had never quite witnessed a case such as Hillsbury's (at least not firsthand). As he fleshed out a thesis and mused over what could possibly have led to the events in the sleepy bayside town, his phone rang. His first thought was to dismiss the call; it was most likely Ava Trillium, and if there was one person he needed to remove from his memory, it was her. But perhaps she was deserving of a proper farewell? Maybe he owed her that much? He caved to his emotions and glanced down at his phone. The call was coming from Henry Carter.

Corbin closed his computer and answered, but before he spoke, he took a moment to mentally prepare himself for the conversation he was about to have with the park ranger. Because he had a feeling he knew exactly what the unexpected phone call would involve. "Hello, Henry."

The ranger's voice was almost accusatory. "I'm going to assume you know about the death of Bruce Archer?"

Corbin's heart sank. This particular death was inevitable, but still the news of a person's passing was hard to take. "I do."

"He was going after the beast in the cave, wasn't he?"

Corbin poured himself another glass of single malt whiskey. "Can I ask you something, Henry?"

"What?"

"When your sister first went missing, what did you tell yourself? What did your mother tell you? Your wife? Father Donald? What was the one consistent phrase you heard from everybody, that you believed?" Henry hesitated, so Corbin spoke for him. "'God has a plan.' Am I right?"

Henry didn't need to answer. Corbin was right.

"And you believed it, didn't you?"

"Yes."

"Well, perhaps it will uplift your spirits to know that your Lord and savior does, in fact, have a plan. Though I cannot in good faith allow you for a second longer to believe that the plan is strictly for you. Or Jill. Or me, for that matter. The plan is far superior to that, far greater than anything we could ever comprehend." Corbin let that settle in for a second before continuing. "The death of Bruce Archer was all part of the plan. The same plan involving your sister. The same plan involving Bruce meeting the basilisk when he was just a boy."

"What *is* the plan?"

"Well, that's the mystery, isn't it? Asking me the plan is like asking me the meaning of life. Who knows?"

"Cut it with your bullshit." Henry was growing frustrated; he wanted answers.

"We've known each other for two days Henry, and frankly, I've been extremely honest with you. Perhaps too honest. You've asked questions and I've done my best to answer them."

"You were supposed to find Joel Liman. Now, instead of recovering a missing boy, we have a dead man!"

"I was not there to find a boy. I was there to gather information so we could grasp a better understanding of *the plan*. It's all part of *God's* plan."

"You said you didn't know what it all meant!"

"True. And at the time I didn't, but as the facts and information began to present themselves to me, I started to see what we were dealing with." Corbin took a sip of his whiskey. "There isn't much crime in Hillsbury, is there, Henry?"

"What does that have to do with anything?"

"Just because a township sees very little in terms of the illegal doesn't mean it lacks indecency. The people in Hillsbury are far from pure. Sure, you have the locals who spend their days in honest business. But their honest businesses feed off the unjust careers of those staying in the cottages. Judges who can be paid off. Vice presidents who have no issue laying a family man off just to save a couple bucks. Bookkeepers with women on the side. Henry, Hillsbury's law enforcement itself is as corrupt as any. A sheriff who should have stepped down years ago. His deputy, engaged in a romantic affair with your assistant for over a year. A courtroom judge can be paid off, but the *real* judge—the cosmic judge—cannot. And God's plan, at this juncture, is to set an example after over two thousand years of mankind disregarding his very existence. Earth is his experiment, and he isn't liking what he's seeing."

It was a lot to take in. Henry took a deep breath. "What's to become of Hillsbury?" he asked.

"Genesis 19." Corbin finished his whiskey. "At first I believed the message in the cornfield was regarding plagues, specifically the plagues of Egypt. Unfortunately I overlooked several binary numbers and was misled. I was *meant* to be misled. I figured it out, of course, but by that time, there was little I could do. The message in the cornfield was a reference to

Genesis 19." Corbin sipped his whiskey. "Stay with your sister, Henry. You'll be safer there."

"My son is in Hillsbury."

It was these five words, more than anything else the ranger had said, that finally made Corbin pause. He struggled for what seemed like a long, long while to come up with an answer. He'd grown to like and respect Henry Carter during his short stay in Hillsbury, and it pained him to have to be the one to say this. But therein lay the dilemma: Corbin had allowed himself to get too personally attached to this case. It was unprofessional. And it brought nothing but complications.

His feelings for Ava were a complication.

His friendship with Henry was a complication.

And, *My son is in Hillsbury* . . . that was the kind of complication that could make you lose sleep. Those kinds of complications had driven people into early graves.

My son is in Hillsbury . . .

"Then may God have mercy on his soul. I'm so sorry, Henry." Corbin hung up the phone, took a deep breath, and disappeared back into the safety and numbing comfort of his dissertation.

Henry immediately dialed his son's number. When Jeffrey's voice came through the speaker it was like being hit with a tidal wave of relief. "Dad?"

"Are you all right?"

"Yeah, why?"

"Did you hear about Bruce Archer?"

"Yeah. We saw him."

"Jeffrey, I need you to listen to me very carefully, okay? I need you to leave Hillsbury. Right now."

"What? Dad—"

"Something bad is about to happen. I need you to leave, you hear me?"

"Yeah, but I'm at the Burtons' house. How am I even going to leave? I don't have a car or anything."

Henry swore under his breath; that was actually a very good question. "All right, listen to me, okay, just listen. When Mr. and Mrs. Burton go to sleep, you take their keys . . . you take their keys and their car and you keep driving until you get here. You hear me? No stopping."

"Jesus, Dad! I'm not gonna just steal—"

"Don't argue with me."

Jeffrey didn't like the idea of leaving Claudia behind. But something must have gone horribly wrong to get his father so worked up. "Where am I even supposed to go?"

"St. Joseph's Hospital."

"St. Joseph's? That's Leafsview. Why Leafsview?"

"It's where your Aunt Jill is."

Jeffrey entered the kitchen in the Burtons' house. Claudia was seated at the table with Morgan, regaling him with the grisly tale of Bruce Archer's demise.

"You look like you've seen a ghost," Claudia remarked when he walked in. "What's wrong?"

"We have to go."

"Where?"

"Leafsview."

"For what?" Morgan chimed in.

"My—" Before he could finish, Jeffrey rushed to the sink and vomited. Claudia hurried to his side, rubbing his back.

"Jeff? What's wrong?"

Jeffrey rinsed his mouth and splashed some water on his face. "We have to go to Leafsview."

"I don't understand. Why Leafsview?"

But Morgan didn't need any explanation. Excited and eager to help out, he got to his feet and said, "I'll distract Mum and Dad."

"I want to know what's going on first!" Claudia demanded.

Jeffrey's voice shook when he spoke, and he feared he might be sick again. "My aunt's alive, and she's in Leafsview. At St. Joseph's."

"What in the hell is she doing there?" Morgan blurted out.

"I don't know. But my dad told me I had to go. Hillsbury isn't safe."

"Isn't safe like how?"

"Your dad is probably a mess right now," Claudia said. "He doesn't know what he's saying."

"Maybe. Or maybe he's right. Either way, I gotta leave."

"Then I'm coming with you," Claudia stated firmly, her hand still rubbing Jeffrey's back.

"Yeah, me too," Morgan said with a grin. "We'll wait till Mum and Dad are sleeping. I'll grab their car keys and meet you both out back."

Jeffrey forced a weak smile and stood up straight. "You have no idea how glad I am that you volunteered to do that before I brought it up."

"What?"

"Nothing. Sounds like a plan."

Bentley pushed open the front door, ushering Ava into his house. He felt an undeniable emptiness. Elise had packed up and left, though she'd only packed what she could; the majority of her belongings remained in the house.

"Welcome to my humble abode." Bentley locked the door behind them. "Want a drink or anything?"

"Do you have any wine?"

"Coming right up."

Ava walked slowly through Bentley's home, staring at every picture that adorned the walls, every trinket decorating the shelves. Elise's influence was all over this place. Ava felt sick to her stomach, but what was the point? There was no turning back now. It was done. She had a life to live, so she might as well enjoy it. Her observations came to a close when Bentley held a glass of red wine out in front of her.

"A toast." He grinned. "To new beginnings." Ava smiled and toasted her glass.

As if on cue, the moment was ruined by a knock at the front door.

"Who the hell could that be?" Bentley wondered. "I'll be right back."

He left Ava alone in the living room. She took a hesitant sip from her wine glass and wondered if she should try to duck out of sight, just in case Bentley didn't want her to be seen in there so soon after Elise's departure. A conversation had begun in the front hall, and Ava perked up her ears, curious.

"Mayor Tremblay."

"Deputy Sheriff."

"To what do I owe the pleasure?"

"It's about the power outage at the park tonight. I haven't the foggiest clue as to where Henry or his assistant are, so I came to you."

"Uh . . . sure."

"Tomorrow is our biggest day of the year. Our most important. Everything hinges on it, Trundle."

"I'm aware, Mr. Mayor."

"We can't afford any more unexpected power outages. And furthermore, the power is still not back at the park. I've made a few calls, and an electrician will take a look first thing in the morning, before installing backup generators. *Several* of them. Tonight's fiasco was easy to cover up, but we might not get so lucky again. Now, I am up for reelection soon, and you're up for sheriff. So it would be in both of our best interests for tomorrow night to go off without a hitch. Understood?"

Ava did not dare show her face in front of Tremblay. She assumed Bentley nodded because the mayor continued with, "Excellent. Have a good night. Oh, and . . . say good night to the assistant ranger for me as well." Tremblay gave Bentley a wink before leaving.

Bentley gulped, returning to the living room to find Ava white as a sheet. "He . . . he knows."

But Ava was more concerned with the other matters Tremblay had brought up. "The park can't be open tomorrow. Not after tonight."

"What choice do we have? Tremblay calls the shots. Whether he's right or wrong, we have to do what he says."

"Like hell we do. All I need to do is not go to work."

"If you don't go in, he'll just get some of my people to do your job."

"Bent—"

"You know he will. Best we can do is show up and watch after everyone, especially at Cape's Side Bay. Prevent another Bruce Archer from happening."

As much as Ava hated to admit it, Bentley's reasoning made sense. They were among the few who knew what had happened tonight at the bay. It was their responsibility to keep such a thing from happening again.

"Now," Bentley said, his tone reverting to its old playful self, "can we go back to enjoying our evening?"

Jeffrey waited in the Burtons' backyard, tucked between the shed and the fence. He waited for Claudia to give him the signal that all was clear, meaning Morgan had the keys and was waiting in his parents' car. It was coming up on midnight, and Leafsview was not exactly close; they would have to leave soon if Claudia and Morgan expected to make it home before their parents woke up.

A soft creaking noise came from the side of the house. Jeffrey looked up and saw Claudia with a finger pressed over her mouth. She gestured for him to follow, and together they made for the driveway.

Morgan was behind the wheel of the car, key in the ignition. Claudia and Jeffrey gently opened the back doors and slid in. "All set?" Morgan asked. Jeffrey nodded.

"Okay. Next stop: Leafsview." Morgan started the car and pulled out into the street.

The drive was long and layered in awkward silence. As they made their way farther past the borders of town, streetlights became more and more scarce. "Never realized how dark it was out here," Morgan commented.

"You want me to drive?" Claudia said. "I should probably drive since I'm the only one with a license."

At first, Morgan was insulted. Then he realized his sister was right. If they were to get pulled over for any reason, they'd have a lot of explaining to do. "Yeah, all right. I'll pull over in a bit and we'll switch."

Jeffrey was too dazed to really contribute to the conversation. The thought of his long-lost aunt returning had never occurred to him. What state was she in? Where was she? How was she found? Where had she been all this time? So many questions. *Too* many questions. They made his head hurt.

"You okay?" Claudia rested her palm over his. He looked up at her.

"Yeah, just—" The words died in his throat when a large burst of light appeared ahead of them. Morgan squinted and raised an arm to shield his eyes. Claudia yelped and grabbed hold of the dashboard.

As quickly as it came, the light vanished. Everything was dark again. Jeffrey and Claudia turned their heads to look out the back window. Morgan followed suit.

"What was that?" Morgan asked. Nobody had an answer. He faced front again, ready to pull over so that his sister could take the wheel . . . and saw a naked boy standing in the middle of the road, arms crossed, hands covering his genitals.

Morgan gasped and swerved out of the way, sending his parents' Toyota rolling into a ditch at the side of the road.

The back door swung open and Jeffrey wobbled out of the car before turning back to help Claudia. From what he could tell, there was no serious damage to the vehicle, aside from a few scratches and a small dent to the bumper. The worst part of the whole scenario was that they were nose-first in a ditch with no visible means of escape.

"Morgan? Morgan, you okay?" Jeffrey called out.

Morgan's face was squished against the steering wheel. He didn't answer. He didn't even move.

Claudia was struck by a wave of fear. "Morgan?" She rushed to the driver's side door and swung it open with all her might.

"It's all right. I'm all right." Morgan's voice gurgled from bleeding lips. He opened his eyes and unbuckled himself. Claudia helped him exit the car and then pulled him into a fierce hug.

"You scared the shit out of me."

"What happened?" he asked, releasing himself from Claudia's grip.

"I don't know, you're the one who swerved!"

"Shit! The kid!" Morgan rushed up the incline to the road. Darkness surrounded him; nothing more. No bright lights. No boy.

Claudia and Jeffrey clambered up beside him. "What kid?" they asked in unison.

"You didn't see him? A boy was standing right in the middle of the road! Right here!"

Claudia and Jeffrey exchanged confused glances. "I didn't see a boy, Morgan," Jeffrey said.

"But . . . he was there! That's why I swerved, so I wouldn't hit him!"

Jeffrey looked around and took a breath. "There's no one here."

Disappointed, Morgan turned back to assess the damage on his parents' vehicle. "So what're we gonna do about this?"

Jeffrey was already sliding the phone from his pocket. "Only thing we *can* do at this point. I'm calling my dad."

Henry was quick to answer. He'd obviously been waiting expectantly for news from his son. "Jeffrey?"

"Dad."

"What happened? Are you all right?"

"Yeah, I'm fine, we just . . . we had an accident. Nobody's hurt. I'm with Claudia and Morgan. Morgan saw something—"

"Don't tell him that!" Morgan snapped, suddenly embarrassed. Jeffrey ignored him.

"Morgan thought he saw something on the road. A boy. And now the car's in a ditch."

"Is everybody okay?"

"Yeah, like I said, nobody's hurt. Car's not even in super bad shape. It's just stuck. We're stranded here."

"All right, text me your coordinates and I'll see what I can do. And Jeffrey, you three stay off the road. Hear me?"

"Yeah, for sure, Dad." Jeffrey ended the call and looked back at his friends. "He's gonna get us help."

"How long will that take?" Morgan asked with a shiver, glancing around nervously at the blackness that surrounded them.

Jeffrey shrugged. "I don't know. For now, let's just get back to the car. It's safer."

Henry stood up. He searched his contacts for a tow truck company; he needed them from time to time in the park. Something moved in his peripheral vision, and he noticed Steve lurking near the door. Henry raised his eyebrows as if to ask, *Yes?*

Steve walked in, hands in pockets, looking out of place. "Everything okay?"

"Yeah it's . . . my son was on his way, but he got into a bit of an accident. Just gonna call a tow truck, if I can find a damn number."

"He's in Hillsbury?"

"Just outside of town." Henry said.

"I got a cousin. Just a tow driver, he's stationed in Hillsbury this weekend for some festival. I dunno if you know about it."

"Oh, I know about the festival. Believe me."

"Well, I could give him a call if you'd like? He'd probably do it pro bono too."

Henry wasn't enthusiastic about putting his son's safety in Steve's hands. Then again, Steve had found and rescued Jill, and the offer came without a price tag. Right now, Henry would take all the gift horses he could get. "Yeah, sure. You wouldn't mind?"

Steve shook his head. "Not at all. I'll call him now."

"Thanks."

Steve left to make the call. Henry sat back next to the hospital bed and took his sister's hand. "Little Jeffrey's coming." Tears welled up in his eyes. "He's not so little anymore. He missed you . . . I can't wait for you to see him. He's . . . he's so big now, Jill. He's so grown up, y'know?"

Henry's voice cracked and failed him. He rested his head in Jill's lap and continued to weep.

Darkness resided over Hillsbury Park. No wind, no clouds. It was as though life itself had been removed from the equation. The dried-up swamp of Cape's Side Bay housed lifeless generators—and drops of Bruce Archer's blood. The basilisk that once made its home in the cave high above was no more, neither was the weasel who had been digging up holes throughout the park.

A boy walked to the bay and stepped into it. A naked boy, with crossed arms, hands covering his genitals. The boy the entire town had been searching for. The boy named Joel Liman.

Softly, Joel puckered his lips and began to whistle.

MONDAY MORNING

AVA STOOD BY a burned-out generator in Cape's Side Bay, waiting for the new ones the mayor had promised the night before. The sun was only just beginning to creep its weary head through a slew of clouds high above. Ava checked her watch. It was half past six.

Bentley approached from behind a tree. "Any sign of anything?"

Ava shook her head. "No mayor. No generators. No nothing."

"Well, knowing Tremblay, they'll be here any minute now. He's not one to let these things dwell."

"It is a holiday, though. Maybe he doesn't want to pay people for overtime work."

"Won't make a difference. He thinks tonight's gonna contribute to him being reelected."

Ava looked at Bentley, frowning. After overhearing his conversation with Tremblay, she'd been preoccupied with the fact that Bentley was up for the position of sheriff. After knowing him so long, Ava was sure Bentley would do everything within his power to obtain the job if he truly wanted it enough. But exactly how far would those ambitions take him? Would they outpace his morals? "And what about you?" she asked him.

"What about me?"

"You're up for sheriff. Tremblay believes *you* have as much riding on today as he does."

Bentley scoffed at the notion. "Today's just another day. A damn busy one, sure, but just another day. My job is my job, and I do it better than anybody. That's why I'm up for Walden's position." His tone was stern, serious, and the point hit home. Ava's suspicions slowly trickled away. By the time Bentley placed his thumb and index finger against Ava's chin a moment later and pulled her in for a kiss (a kiss she embraced wholeheartedly), those suspicions had all but vanished.

Rumblings sounded nearby. Ava and Bentley unlocked their lips and watched as two trucks carrying two massive generators apiece rolled their way toward the bay.

"Four of them?" Ava questioned.

"Backups for the backups. Can never count out Tremblay for the absurd."

"This weekend must be costing the town a fortune."

"And then some. I'm sure he's worked out a way where no one will feel that burden until his time in office is long gone." Bentley put his arm around Ava as the trucks rolled to a stop. "Just sit back and enjoy the show. 'Cause if one thing's for sure: it's gonna be a great one."

Henry lay asleep with his wife's head on his shoulder and his daughter in his lap. He was awoken by the hum of his cell phone. Gently, to not wake his family, he pulled it out of his pocket and read a text message from Jeffrey: *Just parked.*

He lifted Sarah's head from his lap and removed his wife's head from his shoulder, subtly waking her.

"What's wrong?" she asked.

"Jeffrey just got here," Henry whispered. "I'm gonna go get him. Go back to sleep." He gave both girls a kiss on the cheek and left.

The tow truck was just leaving when Henry exited the hospital. He ran to his son, grabbing him with both arms and giving him his first hug in as long as Jeffrey could remember.

"Dad?"

"I'm just glad you're all right," Henry responded after finally releasing him.

Morgan looked around almost in a panic. "Um, where'd the tow truck guy take our car?"

"His garage. He told you the address, genius," Claudia responded with a snippy tone. She was clearly tired from the long night.

"How am I supposed to know where that is? I can count the amount of times I've been to Leafsview on one hand."

Henry stepped in before Morgan's panic could spread. "It's okay; his cousin's in the hospital. I'll call your parents and we'll get the car back."

"No." Morgan's voice trembled with fear. "They can't know."

"They can and they will." Henry turned his back to the teenagers and began to walk toward the hospital.

Claudia rushed to match his stride. "Mr. Carter, my brother's right. If my parents find out, they're gonna kill us."

Henry turned back. "They're not going to kill you. You saved my son's life, and possibly more than you know."

"What's that supposed to mean?" Jeffrey asked, concerned.

Henry ignored the question, staring intently and seriously at Claudia and Morgan. "Thank you. Both of you. From the bottom of my heart. I owe you. But I have to call your parents." He turned back to the hospital, marching toward the doors while the others fell in step behind him. "Now come on. You're probably all exhausted. There are spare beds inside."

Jeffrey exchanged confused glances with the Burtons. They didn't know how to respond to that, so they simply followed Henry.

Morgan gulped. "He's gonna tell Mom and Dad," he whispered to his sister. "What do we do?"

"Sit back and face the music, I guess," mumbled Claudia. "All good deeds go punished."

Mayor Tremblay arrived at the park. His cigar was already lit and dangling from his lips. All the games and rides and food trucks were being powered by the brand-new generators he'd rolled in. He'd saved the day. And voters would remember that. He stomped over to Ava, who was standing amid the fairground looking lost and a little overwhelmed.

"Where's Henry this morning?" Tremblay sounded tired; his voice was raspy and hollow.

Ava shrugged. She had not seen Henry since the day before and hadn't heard from him since they spoke about Bruce Archer's passing. She imagined he was still at the hospital with his sister, but Ava new better than to offer any unnecessary details to the mayor.

"Y'know, young lady . . . I believe you're in for a promotion. Don't you?" Tremblay took a puff of his cigar, the smoke narrowly missing Ava's face. "I mean, I think you've paid your dues. Maybe it's time you start thinking of what your life would be like as head ranger of Hillsbury Park."

"Sir?"

"Just think about it."

"What about Henry?"

The mayor took a long puff and exhaled straight up into the sky. He lowered his head and gave Ava a sly smile before walking away to speak to the electrical crew.

"What say you, boys? These gennies won't blow as easily as the last ones, will they?" Ava tried to listen in, but Tremblay's voice vanished in the distance.

Bentley snuck up behind Ava and surprised her with a kiss. She pushed him off of her. "Jesus! You scared me."

"Sorry. My intentions were noble. Honest."

"You can't just creep up on someone like that. Especially not after everything that's been going on."

"Even if I have . . . these?" And he held up a dozen roses.

Ava couldn't help but smile. "I guess I'll forgive you this time."

"I figured as much." He offered her the flowers before looking around. "You seen Tremblay?"

"Unfortunately. Hey, let me ask you something."

"Go for it."

Ava collected her thoughts. "He offered me a promotion."

Bentley was stunned but visibly excited. "A promotion? That's great!" He leaned in to kiss her once again, and once again Ava pushed away. "What is it?"

"A promotion that would involve the removal of Henry as head ranger."

Bentley failed to see the issue before realizing Ava didn't like the idea of someone losing their job for her sake. "Look, Tremblay isn't fond of Henry. You know that. Heck, *everyone* knows that. So if he gets reelected, he's gonna put in motion plans to remove Henry and replace him with someone he likes. And . . . well, you've seen the way Tremblay leers at you. *You*, he likes. Even if it's for uncomfortable reasons."

Ava was shocked. "You knew about this? Henry's your friend."

"What else can I do? I back Henry, and Tremblay'll get someone else to take over for Walden whenever the old man retires. And what are you complaining about? This is good news for you! When the promotion comes, Henry won't suspect you had anything to do with it."

"Because I don't!" Ava fought back.

"Okay, okay, relax. Look, whether you get the promotion or someone else does, it's happening. Might as well accept it for what it is."

Ava looked closely at Bentley and began to think she'd made a horrible mistake.

Henry opened the door to room 249. Light was creeping its way through the blinds. Jeffrey followed nervously behind his father; he had not seen his aunt since he was nine years old. He was a different person back then, a young boy who still played with action figures and watched Saturday-morning cartoons. He was a teenager now. His interests had changed. A *lot* had changed. He pictured what his aunt might look like after all this time. Gray hair. Wrinkles. All the telltale signs of time's ruthlessness

Henry led him toward the bed, and Jeffrey gasped. Aunt Jill miraculously looked the exact same as she had when he was nine. It was as if all those years had never taken place.

"She looks . . ." he began.

"The same," said Henry. "I know. Uncanny, isn't it?"

Henry pulled up a chair for Jeffrey, but he remained standing. He rested his hand on Jill's. Tears flooded his eyes. He had been nervous during the entire drive here, but to see Jill like this—unconscious and plugged into machines—was a bit too much for him. He dropped to his knees in tears, Henry's comforting arm holding him steady as he wept.

MONDAY AFTERNOON

MORGAN AND CLAUDIA were offered a pair of beds in room 251, where Rachel and Sarah had stayed the previous evening. Neither thought they would fall asleep, but the long night took its toll on the teenagers, and before long, they found themselves fast asleep. They slept for so long that even when their parents arrived, confused and worried, they opted not to wake them until they'd had their rest.

Mr. Burton was quite upset with Henry for allowing his kids to pull their clandestine late-night road trip. Henry insisted he'd had no clue that the Burton kids would be with Jeffrey until it was too late. A lie, of course, but a necessary one.

The Burtons informed Henry of the power outage at the park and how the mayor had ordered more generators for the night's festivities. Henry couldn't help but chuckle. A man is killed, a boy is missing, three other boys mutilated, yet Tremblay insists the party continue. He had never met a human being with such skewed priorities.

Henry excused himself from the Burtons' company after realizing he had yet to speak with Ava. He was the head ranger of the park, and whether he was there or not, it was his duty to make sure the park was operating smoothly and—knowing how Tremblay was running things—*safely*.

Ava watched the last few drops of coffee plummet into the pot. Staying at Bentley's last night had been great, but very little actual sleep had been had, and right now, she felt like she needed the caffeine more than ever. She cupped her hands around the mug and embraced the rich scent of the Colombian coffee. The heat pushed through the ceramic mug, stinging her infected finger. She flinched and sucked on the finger to relieve the pain. This wound was like nothing she'd ever felt before. Most times she forgot it was even there. Other times she wished someone would just chop the damn finger off. Ava made a mental note to go see a doctor about it when all the craziness of Labor Day weekend was over and done with.

Her phone rang before she could take a single sip.

"Henry! How is everything?"

Henry's voice came through the speaker, hesitant and distant, as if he were incredibly distracted. "To be totally honest with you, I'm not sure. Jill's here, but . . . I just don't know at this point." There was a pause and a brief change in volume as Henry presumably left a busy room for someplace quieter. "How's everything at the park?"

"Interesting. Tremblay's got backup generators for the backup generators. He doesn't want to have another incident like last night."

"He may not have a choice." This was a confusing response; Ava frowned. "Ava, I'm gonna need you to watch over that bay very carefully. Any strange activity, any unusual behavior, anything . . . and we shut it down."

"Shut it down? That sounds a bit extreme, doesn't it?"

"Tell that to Bruce Archer."

Ava shuddered at the thought.

"Keep everyone inside that park safe today, okay?" he concluded.

"When do you think you'll be back?"

"I'm not sure. I don't think anytime soon. I'll let you know."

"Okay. Take care of yourself, Henry."

"You too, Ava."

He hung up rather abruptly. Ava sighed and raised the coffee mug to her lips.

"Was that Henry?" Bentley's voice said from somewhere behind her.

"Yeah, it was. He wanted to make sure everything was okay."

Bentley nodded. "How is he? With his sister and everything?"

"He sounds fine. But . . . I don't know what's going on with Jill. He didn't sound too sure about it himself."

Bentley stared at the coffee pot as if considering pouring a cup for himself, then changed his mind and leaned against the wall. "Do they know where she's been all these years?"

"I just told you everything I know, Bentley."

Ava's harsh tone took Bentley by surprise. He took a step closer to her. "Are you all right?"

"It's been a long weekend," Ava said, turning from Bentley and heading toward the front entrance.

Bentley followed after her. "Something you want to tell me?"

Ava didn't bother to answer. She left the headquarters and continued walking. But Bentley continued to follow, grabbing her arm. "Ava . . ." She spun to face him, scowling. "I love you," he said.

She could see the sincerity in his eyes. "I know you do. And I love you too."

"Then do you mind telling me what's going on?"

For a long while, Ava stared at him, choosing her next words carefully. She was still upset that Bentley was so willing to suck up to the mayor's demands just so he could secure a spot as sheriff once Walden was out of the picture. She wanted to scold him for that, to lash out at him for that. But . . . how could she when she was doing the exact same thing?

She'd worked extra hard this weekend to keep the park running smoothly. At first she assumed it was all because of the tragedy surrounding Joel Liman and his friends. But the more Ava thought about it, the more she realized that she was subconsciously trying to prove to everyone around her (including herself) that she was fit to step into Henry's position, a position that was tenuous at best, considering how much Henry and Tremblay disliked one another. Even though she didn't want Henry to lose his job, Ava felt like she'd earned something bigger. Like she *deserved* it. And she did . . . didn't she?

Her mind was flooded with so many thoughts that at first she didn't hear the sound. The soft gentle noise that she always associated with her mother.

Whistling.

"Do . . . do you hear that?" she asked Bentley.

"Hear what?"

"Whistling."

Bentley looked around, as if he could see the sound. He shrugged. "Nope."

"It's coming from . . ." She listened more intently to get a sense of its direction. Before long she was sure of the noise's source. "Cape's Side Bay."

"You sure of that?"

"Positive."

Bentley looked like he was on the verge of laughing at her. "Probably just a worker whistling while he sets up a generator.

You know, people do that sometimes while they're working. They whistle tunes. It's a thing."

Ava ignored him. "It doesn't sound like an adult. It sounds like . . ."

And without another word, she raced off, leaving a stunned Bentley in her wake.

Ava rushed through the forest. She leaped over tree roots, pushing branches out of her way, until she got to the bay. She bent over to catch her breath. A panting Bentley caught up to her, looking terribly confused. But Ava only had eyes for the bay.

And the bay was empty.

The new generators were all in place, the workers already gone. And yet Ava could have sworn this was where the whistling had come from.

Bentley looked at her with an inquisitive expression and received no response (either verbal or otherwise) in return. So eventually, he cleared his throat, breaking the silence. "What do you say we get some lunch?"

Ava stood up straight, shaking her head as if waking from a daze. "Yeah. Food would be good right now."

Henry, Sarah, and Rachel sat across from the Burtons at a local diner in Leafsview. The parents of Claudia and Morgan were in disbelief that their children would do something as crazy as steal their car. They both had their suspicions that Henry had put them up to it.

"I think the events of the weekend, with my sister showing up, I think it really has taken a toll on everybody. Especially the kids," Henry began.

"Particularly Jeffrey," Sarah chimed in. "He hasn't seen his aunt in over seven years. For her to just appear like this, out of the blue . . ."

"It's obvious nobody's head was in the right place last night. But their hearts were in the right place. I asked my son to come to St. Joseph's immediately. So I have to apologize: I had no idea he'd drag your kids into this, nor did I think he'd take your car."

"No one is saying your boy is the reason . . ." Mr. Burton began.

Henry held a palm up to stop him. It was obvious to everyone that Jeffery was the instigator, though he was only doing what his father had demanded of him. A fact Henry was consciously omitting. "If you wouldn't mind, Sarah and I would like to make this up to both of you, *and* your kids. How about dinner tonight? On us. And a hotel room."

"Hotel room?" Mr. Burton was confused.

"It was a long night and an even longer day. I don't think it'd be safe for any of us to drive back home at night. I'll most likely stay at the hospital, but Sarah, Rachel, and Jeffrey will be—"

Mr. Burton cut him off. "We intend to return home once the children wake up, Henry. We had no desire to leave the house today, period. We fully expect to make it home in time for Tremblay's grand fireworks display."

"The fireworks. Of course." Henry forced a grin. "Well," he began, "the offer stands. At least allow us to take you and the family out to dinner?"

The Burtons exchanged glances, neither wanting to commit to an answer. Henry hoped, for their sake and for the sake of Claudia and Morgan, that they would agree.

Mayor Tremblay's car pulled up to Cape's Side Bay. He gazed up at the beautiful blue sky, anticipating the glorious day to come. The owner of the company that provided the generators stood next to him.

"You see that, Davis?" Tremblay said as he stared up at the heavens. The generator operator was not sure what Tremblay was talking about. "A perfect day, my boy, a perfect day! Now, why don't you tell me again how these generators—these *new* generators—won't fail like they did last night? Hmm?"

"Mr. Mayor, what happened last night wasn't the generators' fault. We can't be blamed for that incident."

"An incident regardless of who is at fault is still an incident. Is it not?"

Davis opted out of responding. He could tell arguing any point against Mayor Tremblay was moot.

"Tonight is our most important night of the year. I don't need to tell you that. *You*, on the other hand, need to tell *me* what steps you've taken so that if a single generator goes out, the entire park won't lose power."

Davis cleared his throat. "You now have multiple backup generators, Mr. Mayor. If one were to go out, even though that is highly unlikely . . ."

"If this weekend has taught me anything, friend, it's that *anything* is likely around here."

"Mr. Mayor, last night was a freak accident. A one-in-a-million chance. You can't expect my generators to break down that frequently, can you? A man lost his life, sir. I think that's the bigger issue."

Tremblay scowled. "The man was a drunk and a fool. I resent your comment. *Tonight* is the bigger issue."

Davis gathered his composure and pressed on through clenched teeth. "We have three backup generators. Two of the main ones are securely assigned to different sections of the park. That's double what you had going into the weekend. So I can assure you, there is no chance—not a one—that any of them will fail."

He was about to say something else but Tremblay took a sudden step in the opposite direction. His attention had shifted. "Sir?"

Tremblay held his hand up to silence him. "You hear that?"

The other man was oblivious. "No . . ."

"Sounds like a child. Whistling."

Tremblay wandered off, following the sound. He took a step into the pit that used to be Cape's Side Bay and walked halfway through it before the music stopped and he found himself staring up at the cave high above.

Now Davis was both curious and nervous. Tremblay's personal driver/bodyguard exited the car and watched on with suspicious eyes.

"Uh . . . Mayor Tremblay?" The words stumbled out of Davis's mouth. "Everything all right?"

The mayor spoke not a word; his vision was fixed on the cave. He removed his hat and dropped to his knees in the dirt.

This pushed his bodyguard past the point of minor concern. He rushed forward. "Mayor Tremblay?"

Tremblay remained on his knees, motionless, his head lifted and his eyes fixated on the cave.

"SIR?"

Jarred back to reality by the shout, Tremblay spun around to look in his driver's direction. The mayor's eyes were bloodshot. He opened his mouth; when he spoke, his voice sounded strained and older than the man it belonged to.

"But before they lay down, the men of the city, even the men of Hillsbury, compassed the house round, both old and young, all the people from every quarter: And they called unto Bruce, and said unto him, 'Where are the men which came into thee this night? Bring them out unto us, that we may know them . . .'"

Then Mayor Tremblay collapsed.

MONDAY EVENING

HENRY STOOD IN front of the mirror in the men's restroom on the second floor of St. Joseph's Hospital.

Two grays.

He was certain if he spent any more time in there he would find at least a dozen more. He turned on the tap and washed his face. Minutes earlier, the staff had informed him that Jill was recovering; a slow recovery, to be sure, but a recovery nonetheless.

Henry was a little puzzled to find the Burtons waiting for him outside the restroom. If they were there to decline his offer of dinner or a hotel room, they could have easily just texted him and left.

"Yeah?" He supposed it was only fitting he had the first word.

Mr. Burton cleared his throat. "We understand you feel as though you owe us or the kids something, but I can assure you—"

Henry cut him off with a quiet laugh. "Owe you? No, not at all. I want to. As a gesture of thanks."

"You have nothing to thank us for," Mrs. Burton said. It was the first time she'd spoken since arriving in Leafsview.

"My son is here. He's safe. I have a *lot* to thank you for." She took a deep breath. "Please tell me you'll at least come to dinner."

"We just . . . we couldn't impose."

"Impose? Nonsense. No imposition whatsoever. Rachel and I would be more than happy to take you and the kids out. Heck, I've been with Morgan all summer, he's practically family. Now, come on; I know a great little Italian place. You like osso buco?"

"I don't think I know exactly what that is."

Henry put his hand on Mr. Burton's shoulder and grinned. "You're gonna love it!"

Tremblay lay on a gurney in the back of an ambulance parked at the rangers, headquarters. He raised himself up into a sitting position as Ava ran toward him.

"I'm quite all right," Tremblay said, even though Ava hadn't asked (nor had the thought even crossed her mind).

"Good." She pretended to look relieved. "So, you gonna tell me what happened?"

"Nothing. Probably just a blood sugar thing. Actually, would you be a dear and grab me a candy bar or a cookie or something? Thank you ever so much." He rested back down on the gurney. Ava rolled her eyes and made her way toward headquarters.

She searched her pockets for loose change and inserted the coins into the vending machine. Knowing he loathed them, she made oatmeal-raisin cookies for Tremblay. When she turned back, the mayor's driver was standing directly behind her. She jumped and dropped the cookies. "Jesus F., you scared me!"

"Sorry." His tone was dry.

Ava glared up at him (he stood a foot taller than her) and bent down to retrieve the cookies. When she stood back up, he was still there. "Yeah, what?"

"Can I have a word with you?" His tone never shifted, still dry and firm.

"Sure."

The driver fixed the collar of his jacket and cleared his throat. "Before the mayor took his . . ." he searched carefully for his next word, "*fall*, he said something. He spoke."

"Ooookay. What'd he say?"

"I'm not quite sure."

"So you just wanted to tell me that the mayor said something before he passed out but you don't know what he said?"

The man shrank back a little. "I know it sounds crazy . . ."

"Was it something important?"

"Well, it sounded more like he was quoting something. But also, it didn't quite sound like him. It sounded like . . ."

Ava's foot tapped impatiently on the wooden floor. She had a job to get back to. "Like what?"

"My mother's a Christian. I never really got too into it. But what Tremblay said sounded like something I recognized from being in church as a kid. Like gospel, or something."

"Gospel?"

"Yeah. Biblical."

"Biblical like how?" She felt like she was speaking with a child.

"I don't know. He was calling for the men of Hillsbury to come down so someone could know them."

This was beyond odd. Hillsbury was a Christian town, to be sure, but Tremblay wasn't exactly a devout churchgoer. He showed up for holiday masses and special occasions, but his presence was more for show than anything else. The mental image of him quoting scripture was so out of character that it was almost laughable.

Ava stared up at the driver with confusion . . . then a realization struck her. She shoved the cookies into the driver's chest and said, "Give those to the mayor," before rushing off.

"What? Wait! What should I tell him?"

Ava grabbed a handful of her uniform and gave it a little wave, as if the driver had no idea what it was she did. "To eat these and drink plenty of fluids? I don't know! I'm a ranger, not a doctor." Then she entered Henry's office, shut the door and called Henry's cell phone.

"Pick up, pick up, pick up."

"Hello?" Henry's voice crackled over the line.

"Henry!" she blurted out, excited to hear his voice and nervous as to what she was about to tell him. "Genesis!" she said. "He quoted Genesis!"

"What? Who?"

"Tremblay. He passed out earlier today while scouting the new generators at Cape's Side, and before he went down, he quoted something from the book of Genesis."

"My God."

"Yeah. That's the idea, Henry."

"Very funny. What verse?"

"I don't know, I wasn't there. His driver just told me. What the hell's going on?"

Henry paused. He knew things in Hillsbury were going south, but he wasn't sure just how bad they were about to get. "I wish I could tell you. Or . . . maybe I don't. Who knows? So you don't know exactly what he said?"

"No, his driver just told me he quoted Genesis. This can't be good, Henry, not after what Corbin was saying. About God and aliens and . . . shit, I . . ."

Henry tried to calm her down. "Take a breath. It's okay, it's all right. You're all right."

"Corbin won't return my calls, Henry."

Henry was quiet for a long while.

Ava wasn't sure why she'd blurted out Corbin's name. She'd thought about him all morning, ever since hearing the mysterious whistling at the bay; it had seemed like the kind of thing that would have fascinated Corbin Mench, (as well as the kind of thing he would have had an explanation for).

Henry knew that Ava and Corbin had shared more than a few personal moments that might have blossomed into something else. She hoped Henry wouldn't chastise her for bringing Corbin up now, like some lovesick schoolgirl pining after a lost crush. Thankfully, her boss's tone was gentle and soothing.

"Look, Ava, I'm sure there's nothing to worry about. You know what they say: moments before death, even the biggest sinners, atheists, whatever, find God. Maybe Tremblay found God before whatever happened to him."

"Yeah. Maybe."

"Ava, I've gotta go. I . . . kinda promised the Burtons I'd take them to dinner. But any development, gimme a call. All right?"

"Henry . . ."

"You're gonna be fine. Everything's gonna be fine. I gotta go."

"All right." Her voice sounded as though the life had been stolen from it.

"Have a good night."

Ava opened the top desk drawer and found the bottle of scotch Henry kept hidden under a pile of old paperwork. It wasn't the best scotch you could find, but it would be enough to take her edge off. And she needed that right now. She poured the scotch into her coffee cup and took a swig, then slammed the mug down on Henry's desk so hard the handle broke right off. Her injured finger was pricked by the sharp edge of her mug. Swearing, she stuck the finger in her mouth and retreated for the bathroom.

For what felt like the millionth time that weekend, Ava ran her finger under cold water and watched the blood pour out. That was when she heard the whistling again.

She couldn't properly identify the tune. Was it even a familiar one? It was hard to tell. But it was there, and it was real. She could hear it, clear as day.

Ava followed the whistling until—before she knew it—she was standing at the mouth of Cape's Side Bay again. *Unusual,* she thought, as she realized she was standing in the spot where Tremblay had had his episode, and where she'd first been led by the ghostly whistles that very morning.

Ava looked around at the pit that was the old bay, then at the cave where Bruce Archer had allegedly fallen to his death. She thought of all the stories she used to hear about this place, and a shiver crawled down her spine. She felt uneasy and wanted to leave, but it was as though something was keeping her there, forcing her to look upon the crater against her will.

Then, as if by design, the whistling returned. Her wounded finger pulsated; she could feel the blood rushing up to its tip. The pain was excruciating, as if someone was cutting off her circulation.

She held the hand up, grimacing, the pain so severe she couldn't even scream. Blood dripped down her palm and arm, soaking her sleeve with crimson. She gripped the wound as tightly as she could, but to no avail. Nothing could alleviate the pain.

Nothing could stop the bleeding.

Lights filled the sky, blinding her. Three sets of four pod lights circled above. When Ava's vision returned, she saw a shape in the distance. A shape in the form of a person.

"Joel?"

Tremblay signed a piece of paper and watched as the ambulance drove off. He dusted off his suit and rolled his eyes as Bentley Trundle approached him.

"I heard you had quite the afternoon," Bentley teased.

Tremblay glared at the deputy sheriff. "I would have been fine if you'd done your job and secured the bay last night. What in God's name was Bruce Archer doing out there so late, anyway?"

Bentley shrugged his shoulders, feigning ignorance. He felt it was in his and everyone else's best interest to keep any information regarding Bruce Archer and Corbin Mench away from Mayor Tremblay.

"Maybe you should take the night off. I can emcee the festivities in your place?" This irked the mayor, as Bentley knew it would.

"Like hell, you will. I've worked too hard to miss out on tonight. My face must be seen. It would take certain death for me to miss out on the grand finale! You of all people should know that."

Bentley could hardly care less. "Just looking out for your well-being, Mr. Mayor."

"Well, you can sleep soundly, Trundle, because I'm fine."

"If you say so. If you need anything, you know where to find me."

Tremblay glanced sideways at him, lip curled in a lewd sneer. "Yes. Somewhere off with the assistant ranger, no doubt." And he walked off without waiting for a response.

Bentley watched him go, muttering under his breath. "Asshole."

Sunset was Henry's favorite time of day. He remembered how he and Jill would rush out after supper and play hide-and-seek with the neighbors' kids every night during the summer, warm evening air embracing them as they snuck under Old Man Joe's 1947 Ford pickup. Back when he was small enough to actually fit underneath a vehicle. The thought made Henry laugh.

They had just pulled up to Giovanni's, an Italian eatery located in the old house of Giovanni Tufo. The family had immigrated to Leafsview in the early sixties, buying the house with Giovanni's meager factory salary. As he grew older and the workload became more strenuous, Giovanni's son suggested they reconstruct their house into a restaurant and earn their living via hospitality rather than manual labor. An idea Giovanni believed ridiculous. Years later, Giovanni's was one of the finest Italian eateries in the whole county.

The Burtons seemed unsure of what to think of the place, but Henry assured them the food was great. They were seated at a table toward the back, next to a window, in what had once been the Tufos' living room.

The waitress came by and poured red wine for the adults and water for everyone else. Mr. Burton gave the menu the briefest of glances before stating that he would "try the osso buco," with a pronunciation that almost made Henry laughed out loud though he appreciated the attempt.

"So, are you both still expecting to head back tonight?" Rachel asked the Burtons.

Mrs. Burton lowered her menu and glanced at her husband. Claudia and Morgan were silent, but Jeffrey knew they both hoped the kids could spend another evening in Leafsview.

"Well," Mr. Burton said slowly, "I think so. Yes."

Claudia couldn't help but sigh with displeasure. Her father looked over at her. "Claudia? Something the matter?"

"No," she said hurriedly.

"I thought you'd want to see the fireworks?" her mother inquired. Claudia just shrugged.

"Morgan?" Mr. Burton asked. "What about you?"

"Yeah. I dunno. I spent all summer at the park."

"And you don't want to see the big fireworks show the mayor promised?"

Morgan also shrugged. "They're just fireworks, Dad. It's not like the mayor's gonna walk on water."

Now Mr. Burton turned to his wife. She herself had no real interest in watching the fireworks either. But she also had no desire to spend the night in a hotel room when she could easily return to the comfort of her own home. But she could read the expressions on her children's faces; she knew exactly what *they* wanted.

"I guess we're staying in a hotel tonight," she said.

Morgan couldn't contain his excitement. He slammed his palm down on the table, upsetting his water glass. "Sorry."

Henry smiled, holding out his wine. "A toast," he said, relief pouring through his words. "To friends."

The toast was returned in kind. "To friends!"

The last orange sliver of sun was disappearing over the horizon. The park had reached a new record in attendance, something that filled Mayor Tremblay with an almost obscene amount of glee. He was certain that after the success of that evening, there was no way he wouldn't be reelected; after all, it had been his vision that brought the carnival to Hillsbury, that transformed the great fireworks display into a weekend-long extravaganza, even in the face of naysayers and nonbelievers. All of the credit was his for the taking.

Tremblay checked his watch. It was nearly time for his speech.

Grinning at a sea of voters, Tremblay approached the podium.

Room 249 was silent. Steve had stayed the night, even after the woman's family arrived. Henry had graciously given him permission to remain at Jill's side. For whatever reason (and in spite of the fact that her family had come to her), Steve still felt responsible for Jill's safety, as long as she was being hospitalized.

The sound of harsh, beeping alarms jarred Steve from a half-accomplished nap. He rushed to the bed, where Jill was convulsing and foaming at the mouth.

"Jill?"

Nurses surged into the room, asking what happened. As was the case for the entire weekend, Steve was bereft of answers. He was quickly escorted from the room, the door was shut, and he could see no more of Jill Carter.

MONDAY NIGHT

HENRY WAS DOWNING the last dregs of wine when his cellphone vibrated. The display informed him that it was St. Joseph's Hospital.

Tremblay stared out at his adoring public. The grin he wore couldn't possibly be any wider. He tapped the microphone twice—much to the chagrin of the audio operators—and spoke. "Test, test. Is this on?" He knew full well it was, but doing so had captured everyone's attention without him actually having to ask for it.

All those in attendance turned to face the podium. The crowd hushed.

"Greetings!" Tremblay called out. "And welcome to Hillsbury Park!"

The crowd erupted in applause. Tremblay raised his arms for silence.

"Hillsbury truly is the best town in the world! All of this . . . the vendors, the games, the rides, the magnificent fireworks we're about to witness together . . . I brought to all of you this year because I believe—heck, I *know*—that you all *deserve* the best!"

Another loud cheer erupted from the crowd. Tremblay had them eating out of his hands. Everything was going perfectly.

Rachel dropped Henry off at the front doors of the hospital and went to park. He ran up a flight of stairs, taking them two at a time, until he reached the second floor, where a young woman with a clipboard was waiting for him. She was not dressed in scrubs and didn't look like any of the nurses he remembered seeing.

"Mr. Carter," she said.

"What happened? How is she?"

"From what we could tell, your sister suffered a massive seizure."

"How . . . how is that possible?"

"At this time, we don't know what caused it. Jill seemed to be in full recovery, and now . . . well, to be perfectly honest, now she's regressing."

"Regressing how?"

"Your sister is dying, Mr. Carter."

Henry couldn't believe what he was hearing. "No." He barely even noticed that he'd started crying. "No, that's not possible."

"I'm very sorry. There's nothing more we can do aside from making her comfortable. At this point, we'd urge you and your family to say your goodbyes."

"But she just . . ." Henry couldn't string together a full sentence if he tried. It was unfair; seven years he longed for an answer to his sister's whereabouts. *Seven years.* To finally get her back just to lose her all over again . . . it was devastating.

"She is awake." The young woman said gently. "She's aware of her surroundings. She might not be able to carry a conversation with you, but she'll understand you."

Henry wiped a tear from his eye. The woman apologized again and walked away to give him some privacy.

After several deep gulps, Henry entered room 249.

His sister's neck was slightly raised on the bed, her eyes open. Henry could see just how painful each breath was. Where had she been? What caused the lacerations in her throat? Where was Marcia? It was all just as confusing as everything that was going on back at the bay.

The bay!

Henry immediately retrieved his phone and skimmed his contacts for Corbin Mench.

"Now, the moment you've all been waiting for has arrived," Tremblay announced, arms raised dramatically. "Ladies, gentlemen, dear friends, I give you . . ." He trailed off, filling the night air with silence. A few confused whispers slithered through the crowd. If this were a dramatic pause, it certainly was a long one. And why did the mayor look so perplexed?

"Who is that?" Tremblay asked into the microphone. "Who in the blazes is making that sound?"

Bentley Trundle was watching the speech from the back of the crowd, making sure all was well, and as soon as he heard Tremblay bring up a nonexistent sound, he recalled the events of that morning. Nothing good could possibly come of this. Bentley rushed up to the podium and escorted Tremblay down.

"Get off me!" Tremblay shouted. "You don't hear it? How could you not hear it?"

"Nobody hears it, sir." Bentley's tone was gentle; he didn't want to insult this easily excitable man and make matters any worse.

"Well, trust me! I'm telling you, somebody is out there ruining my night with that horrendous tune!"

"What tune, Mr. Mayor?"

"The damn whistling!"

Bentley looked around at the fireworks crew and some of the event staff and carnival workers, who all wore similar expressions of confusion. Clearly, none of them heard any whistling.

"Where's it coming from?" Bentley asked.

"Over there somewhere!" Tremblay pointed in the direction of the woods.

"All right. Why don't we go take a look?"

Furious at the interruption and determined to prove he wasn't losing his mind, Tremblay nodded curtly. "Yes," he growled, "let's."

"The disappearance and reappearance of your sister were not coincidences," said Corbin. "But sometimes things are better left unresolved."

Standing just outside Jill's hospital room, Henry resisted the urge to squeeze his phone into a metal pulp.

"Excuse me? Unresolved? What in the hell is that supposed to mean? My sister is lying in the room next to me, dying. We had a basilisk living in my park right under my nose without me having any clue about it for God knows how long. And

Bruce Archer and Victor Marchman are dead. Not to mention we have three mutilated boys and one still missing." Henry kept his volume to a minimum; he did not want to draw attention to himself, or to his grim conversation.

"You're forgetting your sister's truck appearing out of the blue. Why do you think that was, Henry? Why, after seven long years, did Jill's truck suddenly reemerge at the bottom of Cape's Side Bay?"

Henry was stumped. He took a deep breath. "Corbin, for God's sake, what are you not telling me?"

"I've told you plenty, Henry. And from what I gather, you've been listening. You're still in Leafsview. You managed to get your son there, and his girlfriend, and *her* family. You've even put them up in a hotel room for the night."

"How on earth could you know all that?"

"When it comes to my cases, I know everything. I'm a smart guy, remember?" He chuckled mirthlessly. "Everything happens for a reason, Henry. Everyone serves a purpose. Your sister's purpose was to save you. Had she not gone missing, you would be in the park tonight. Enjoy the last few hours you have with her. Tomorrow, the doctors will discover that her cause of death is large tumors in her lymph nodes."

Henry fought back tears. "Jesus, Corbin . . ."

"I'm sorry I couldn't do more, Henry. I really am. For what it's worth . . . I hope our paths never cross again."

Corbin ended the call.

Henry let his phone drop to the floor. He took a few deep breaths, then gathered himself and walked back into Jill's room.

"Hey, Jill." He tried to smile. It was a losing battle. He could tell from her eyes that she was glad he was there. Henry sat, resting his palm on hers.

"We've really missed you. A lot. Jeffrey's here. I don't know if you were awake earlier when he came in to see you, but he's here. And we have a new one. Well, she isn't so new anymore. She's six. Sarah. She's asked about you a lot."

A tear trickled from Jill's eye.

"You'll meet her soon, I promise." He tightened the grip on her hand. There was a faint sensation of her squeezing back, finally prompting Henry to smile.

Tremblay and Bentley stood over the mouth of the bay in awe of what they were seeing. Bentley thought Trundle and Ava had been losing their minds, but when they followed the alleged sound toward the bay, all of that changed.

Because Joel Liman stood in the center of the bay, stark naked, his hands covering his genitals. Whistling.

"Joel?" Bentley was flabbergasted. He tried to keep his tone light and friendly, to not spook the boy. He took a step forward but Tremblay held him back.

"Careful, Bentley."

Careful of what? Bentley thought. He pushed past the mayor's outstretched arm and kept walking. Every step he took kicked up a little cloud of dust; the bay was more arid than it had ever been.

"Joel? It's me, Bentley Trundle. Deputy sheriff. Everything's going to be all right."

Tremblay watched from afar with trepidation. Then, a few moments later, his worst nightmare came true.

A multitude of gasps issued from behind him. He turned to see nearly a thousand people wearing expressions of shock and horror. The crowd from the carnival had followed them on their abrupt departure into the woods. Now, practically all of Hillsbury was witnessing the abrupt and disturbing return of the missing Liman boy.

All thoughts of fireworks were forgotten.

Bentley removed his jacket and swung it over the boy. Joel looked up at him: his pupils were completely dilated. "It's okay, Joel. Everything is going to be—"

As if on cue, blood began to run from the boy's eyes.

Bentley nearly jumped out of his skin. "Christ! Someone call an ambulance!" The crowd continued to gawk, stunned. No one moved. "Someone get me a goddamn ambulance! NOW!"

Hundreds of attendees reached for their phones. Some called for help. Others decided it would be more prudent to snap photographs.

Unable to sleep, Patty Liman had spent the majority of the weekend sitting on her porch, waiting desperately for her son to come wandering down the street at some late hour. As each night passed, she took to her porch-side vigil with less and less hope. Tonight, drained and exhausted but still adamant, she'd parked herself in her chair at sunset and sat, waiting, ignoring the futility that threatened to close in all around her like a tidal wave. She'd expected the street to be bathed in the distant colorful glow of the mayor's fireworks.

What she *hadn't* expected to see were the lights of a police cruiser screeching to a halt in front of her house.

The driver of the cruiser rolled down the window and called out to her. "Patty!" His tone was frantic.

She squinted into the car's dark interior. "Officer Dingwell?"

"I need you to come with me."

"I don't—"

"It's about Joel."

Patty Liman crossed the yard and entered the cruiser in a record number of strides.

By the time Patty arrived at Hillsbury Park, it was already swarming with emergency response vehicles. The deeper into the park they drove, the more nervous she became. Eventually, Dingwell had to stop: there were so many onlookers surrounding the bay that it was impossible to go any farther.

"We'll have to walk from here."

"Officer, could you please explain to me what's going on. Please."

Dingwell gave it a serious amount of thought before blurting out, "Joel is in the bay."

He said no more. He didn't need to.

At first they struggled to shoulder their way through the crowd, but eventually people began to recognize Patty Liman and slowly parted to create a path.

As she approached the mouth of the bay, Patty stopped and gazed upon her lost son.

He was clothed only in an adult's jacket, his face smeared with blood. Patty's quaking hands flew to her mouth. Dingwell took her hand and guided her toward Joel.

Patty came face-to-face with her son for the first time in three days. She fell to her knees and wrapped her arms around him. Her fingers moved over his hair, his cheeks, his shoulders, as if testing to ensure that he was really there. When she tried to take Joel's hand, though, Patty found that she couldn't. Neither of his hands would budge.

"His hand . . . why can't I grab my son's hand?" She stared up at Dingwell, who looked nervously to Bentley.

Bentley knelt down so that he was eye to eye with Patty. "Mrs. Liman, it's . . . I'm afraid . . ." He was having a great deal of trouble speaking. Every word sounded painful. "His hands are . . . they're attached to him."

Patty's eyes narrowed, every so slightly, but otherwise she remained as still as a statue, as if she feared that any kind of movement might make things worse. "Attached? What does that mean?"

"They've been . . . sewn to his genitalia, Patty."

Patty had no idea how to react. Her worried mind had conjured up hundreds of terrible possibilities over the last few days, but even her wildest nightmares had never been this . . . *unique*. For a long while, she was at a loss for words. "Well . . . *un*-sew them!" she finally blurted out.

"We can't."

"Get scissors! Someone has to have scissors!" She was bawling now, her voice heavy and almost animallike. Bentley tried to reach for her hand, but she pulled away.

"We tried that," he explained. "We're going to take him to the hospital, and they'll see what they can do."

"What do you mean? What does that mean?"

"The material used to bind his hands is the same as what we found on the other boys."

Patty tried to say something else but found that she physically couldn't. Instead, she tightened her grip on her son until the paramedics arrived to haul him into the ambulance. As soon as one of the responders touched Joel's arm, the boy looked up at his mother, as if only just noticing that she was there.

"Mom." His voice was soft and cold, the voice of someone who had been through so much they barely had the energy left to work their own vocal cords.

Patty wiped tears from her eyes. "Yes, Joel?"

He looked straight at his mother, as if staring into her soul. "Dad'll be home soon," he said.

Patty's heart raced. She had told Joel stories about his father, but he never knew him, and she never once fed him false hope that Bill would ever return.

The paramedics lifted Joel out of Patty's arms and placed him on a gurney. He did not speak, and he remained expressionless. Patty followed, keeping one hand on the gurney as they wheeled him toward the ambulance. The crowd watched in stunned silence.

Until a loud scream from above stole their attention.

A figure was standing at the mouth of the cave, high above Cape's Side Bay. It was Ava Trillium, covered in blood. She was shrieking in utter horror. Nobody present had any idea how she had gotten up there or what was causing her so much distress. All they could do was stare, slack-jawed.

Then a set of four blinding lights appeared, surrounding the park. Ava's head flung upward to face them. The engines of the emergency vehicles shut off. The wind stopped shaking the leaves. Everyone ceased to breathe. For a brief snippet of time, there was the kind of silence only death could bring.

Then a tremendous boom shook the heavens.

The onlookers down below flinched, squeezing their ears and eyes shut. Some of them screamed or dropped to all fours or clung to total strangers for support.

Just like that, it was over. All was back, as it had been before. The park plunged back into the dark of night.

The lights—and Ava—were gone.

The backup generator kicked in and power to the park was restored. Deeply disturbed by what they'd just seen, the crowd scattered, rushing to return to the relative safety of their homes and cottages.

Tremblay stood among the chaos, assuring everyone that things were fine and that the festivities would still take place as scheduled, but it was like trying to reason with a hurricane; no one cared. The surging crowd was so thick, the ambulance couldn't even pull away to take Joel to the hospital. Bentley entered the ambulance with Patty and held her for protection. Patty sat in the ambulance, looking out at her son.

Then another sound rang through the night air, slowly causing the less hysterical people, one by one, to stop what they were doing and look up. Tremblay seized handfuls of his thinning hair, wondering what on earth could possibly go wrong next.

A propeller plane was soaring through the night sky. Everyone stared in amazement. For as long as many could remember, planes *never* flew over Hillsbury. Not since . . .

"I know that plane." This came from Patty, who stared wide-eyed at the dark, moving shape overhead. "That's Carl's plane!"

"Carl?" Bentley asked.

"Yes. He . . . he and Bill used to go on business trips in that thing. But . . . how . . . ?" She watched as the plane circled the bay. It was flying awfully low, its nose pointed toward the cave.

Tremblay began shoving people out of his way, determined to be as far from Cape's Side Bay and Hillsbury Park as possible.

Carl's plane continued to lose altitude. As people clued in to what Tremblay had already surmised, panic struck the park again. The people stampeded their way away from Cape's Side. Men, women, and even children were trampled underfoot without second thought. Nobody who ran had any care save for their own personal safety.

With a spectacular rending noise, the plane collided nose-first into the hills of Cape's Side Bay.

Red-hot debris flew everywhere, killing hundreds. Fire erupted from the remnants of the engine, immediately spreading to the nearby woods, which—like the bay they surrounded—were dry as a bone.

Bentley stood among the hordes of fleeing onlookers and watched the fire inch closer and closer to the cluster of power generators. It dawned on him, then and there, that there would be no escaping what was about to happen. Mayor Tremblay had unknowingly created a death trap.

Bentley thought of Elise, of the life he had given up. He thought of the mistakes he'd made, of the many regrets that dominated his life. A propeller careened into view, smashing into a generator just as the fire reached it. He shut his eyes, exhaling.

The resulting explosion disintegrated Bentley Trundle, Patty Liman, and everyone standing around them. The next generator in line reacted with an explosion of its own, then the next and the next, in a hellish domino effect that would bring an end to the great town of Hillsbury.

Those who had made their way out of the park in time were still running for their lives. But the flames ran faster. Hillsbury had grown so dry over the past twenty-four hours that the fire spread with alarming ease. It caught up to the carnival, eating away at the whack-a-mole, the basketball games, the Skee-Ball, the beer tent. Everything.

Loyal to the end, the mayor's horror-struck driver had the engine running, waiting for his boss to dive into the car so they could make their escape. He could just make out Tremblay's form huffing and puffing across the fiery fairground.

A collapsing support beam from a tent barred the mayor's path, nearly crushing him as it toppled. He staggered back with a yelp and fell over, hitting the grass hard. With a groan, he sat up, noticing a large shape to his right, so close he could reach out and touch it.

It was three perfectly organized rows of hundreds of unlit firecrackers.

A smoldering piece of debris rocketed down from the sky like a rogue comet, wreathed in flames, whistling with an almost sentient fury. Tremblay's shoulders sagged. "Oh God, no . . ."

When the debris struck the firecrackers, the ear-splitting inferno that swallowed up the mayor was every color of the rainbow.

Near and far, people were being reduced to ashes. Jett's shop was next to go. Then O'Leary's Donuts. Then all of Main Street. Whether caught on foot or trapped in cars with their families, no one was safe from the blaze. And as Corbin had observed, no one deserved to be. The affluent visitors who frequented the cottages had earned their means by being ruthless, selfish, and unkind. By stepping on those beneath them to get to the top. By ruining lives to better their own. Hillsbury had become a veritable melting pot for the worst kind of people imaginable.

The experiment of Earth had no place for such people. An example had to be made. Hillsbury would be that example, a reminder that a greater power watched down from the cosmos, judging all it saw.

And so Hillsbury burned.

By the time the helicopters came to put out the fire, it was too late. There was nothing—and no one—left to save.

A giant banner hung across Main Street, reading *Bigger and Better than Ever!* It faded into ash, the final remnant of a town leveled by judgment.

Jeffrey stared into his aunt's eyes and took a small bit of comfort in the fact that she was staring right back into his. "I missed you," he whispered.

Jill could not answer verbally but gave him the slightest of nods.

Henry lifted Sarah so she could see her aunt for the first time. "Jill, this is the newest member to the clan: Sarah. Sarah, meet your Aunt Jill."

Shy and nervous, Sarah smiled. Even though her mother had done her best to explain the situation, she couldn't help but feel a bit scared of the strange-looking woman lying in that bed, covered in cuts and bruises.

Jill reached out slowly, stretching an arm. After some gentle prodding from her parents, Sarah returned the gesture, and their hands touched. Henry's heart raced with happiness. He imagined—and hoped—that Jill's was doing the same.

Suddenly the door swung open and Mr. Burton came running in, red-faced and sweating. He looked mortified. "You have to see this!" he said.

The TV in the waiting room was cranked to full volume. Every employee and visitor stood staring in horror at the images being transmitted live via a news chopper, the images of Hillsbury burning to the ground.

"What happened?" Rachel asked. She was trembling from head to toe.

"No one really knows," said Mrs. Burton. "I think something went wrong with the fireworks, or . . . I don't know. Everything's . . ." She couldn't say another word. She covered her mouth and cried. Mr. Burton wrapped his arms around her. Their entire lives had been lived in Hillsbury. Everything they owned, every memory they had, was gone.

Henry held Rachel tight, grateful that she was with him. While he'd known *something* bad was going to happen in Hillsbury, he never could have imagined anything of this magnitude.

His phone dinged. He checked the screen; it was a text message from Corbin Mench.

I'm sorry for your loss. Truly, I am.

Tears filled Henry's eyes. He really wanted to hate Corbin for not giving him more information, but it was very possible Corbin didn't know the full consequences of the basilisk's presence, either. The astrobiologist may have been a genius, but even he had never been able to stay ahead of the mystery unraveling in Henry's town.

Another text came through: *Within the next forty-eight hours, there will be a position opening for a new head ranger in Tuncton Park. Not as illustrious as Hillsbury, but a fresh start is a fresh start.*

Before Henry could respond, a final text message came in.

Goodbye, Henry.

Henry slid the phone back into his pocket. There'd be time to worry about new jobs later.

Henry looked at the Burtons and their children, then at Rachel. Their lives would never be the same. The pain of losing everyone and everything they'd ever known would never disappear completely. It would test them to their limits. But as he'd learned over the past couple of days, life itself was a test; an experiment concocted by a greater being. A being *he* knew as God, a being others knew as . . . well, as whatever they wanted. He had no idea how to cope with all this new information. He only knew that he would do whatever he could for his family. His life—his whole life, from this point forward—was for them.

He glanced over at room 249. Jeffrey was holding Sarah, and the two of them were speaking to their aunt.

An aunt who had effectively saved their lives, though they would never know it. An aunt who was slowly dying. Henry was positive that, knowing the outcome of it all, Jill would accept the responsibility for the good of her family. And, Henry thought with a swell of emotion, so would he, if presented with the choice. And perhaps that time would come. Perhaps this weekend would not be the last extraordinary, otherworldly event Henry Carter would be present for. He wondered what the odds were of that happening. Then he found himself grinning as he imagined Corbin telling him *exactly* what those odds were, right down to the very last decimal place.

The sound of the TV and the commotion of the hospital faded away into a serene silence. Henry's attention fixated on Jill's room, where a small team of nurses had just entered and asked his children to step out.

Henry approached Jeffrey and Sarah, knelt down, and held them close. He had nowhere to take them. He didn't know what to do next. But fate was impossible to escape. Whatever was to happen would happen; over time, he would make peace with that.

Gently, he guided his children's attention away from their aunt's room. He wiped a tear from Sarah's eye and gripped Jeffrey's shoulder before smiling and saying to them both:

"I love you."

THE FOLLOWING IS AN EXCERPT FROM THE DISSERTATION OF CORBIN MENCH

THE EVENTS OF Hillsbury Park and Cape's Side Bay were no coincidence or random act of the greater power. Over the last year, since visiting the now nonexistent town of Hillsbury, I have made several discoveries. While it is uncommon with these cases for me to go back and rewrite my papers, I felt that in this particular case it was necessary.

Hillsbury Park was an average park until forty some-odd years ago. It was during this time that one Orville Liman made a pact that would seal the town's fate.

As a child, Orville was ridiculed for being an outcast. As a child, he dreamed of being a scientist. He was picked on, beat up, and teased regularly. As he grew older, he fell out of love with this dream. His father wanted him to be a hunter and forced the skill upon him. Orville hated the idea of killing a living creature for sport.

While he put on a façade of enjoyment to please his father, he stuck to reading and studying in his spare time. As he grew older, he became more and more interested in politics. He would eventually rise to the position of mayor of Hillsbury. Over time, many would consider him to be the greatest mayor the town had ever seen.

But his ascendancy to power was partially unjust. Orville prayed regularly to get the position so he could infuse Hillsbury with the greatness he knew it possessed. Back when he'd been a child, Hillsbury was not a well-known haven full of million-dollar cottages; it was simply a small town with a coffee shop and a few other local shops.

Once elected mayor, Orville set his sights on the future. He envisioned the cottages, the firework festivals, all of it. The dreams he envisioned for Hillsbury were, in retrospect, positively prophetic at times.

It is my understanding that through his prayers, Orville was given instructions by a higher being. He was tasked with finding the egg of a serpent living within Cape's Side Bay and leaving it for a rooster to hatch. This would bring Hillsbury good luck. This was a trick, for the beast he'd been asked to create was an unholy one, one that would supposedly guard Cape's Side Bay from wrongdoers.

Orville did as instructed, and thus the basilisk was born. This was the seventh of the deadly sins. This act was the one I could not pinpoint, the creation of the blasphemous creature was the act of sloth. The basilisk was never intended to watch over and guard Cape's Side Bay, as I once believed.

While I cannot confirm the identity of the higher being who communed with Orville Liman, I *can* confirm that Orville was betrayed. He bred the basilisk, and nurtured it, until one day the creature stabbed Orville with its talon. A quill injected a deadly virus into his veins. While the cottages were being built and the festivities organized, Orville passed away. He never lived to see what Hillsbury would become.

The basilisk lurked within the park for years. Only one soul, Bruce Archer, knew of its existence, and even he was not fully aware of what the creature was.

As the decades passed and the residents of Hillsbury grew more and more nefarious, Orville Liman's bloodline was used to put an end to the town.

We are the grand experiment. If we falter or become what we are not meant to be, we are punished. These acts of grand disaster present themselves clearly in the Bible, and while acts of such proportions have not been recorded for thousands of years, Hillsbury was used as an example. It was an incredibly fitting one. Hillsbury thrived on the evil deeds the vacationers earned their livings from. The town was almost literally built upon a foundation of sin. Fear of one's existence must be present in our day-to-day lives.

The people were given ample warnings. The disappearance of Jill Carter and Marcia Richter, for one. And the sudden vanishing of Carl Reeves's airplane. The final warning came in the form of Joel Liman's friends. Most laymen are aware of the three wise monkeys: see no evil, hear no evil, and speak no evil. There is a fourth monkey. One I learned about during my initial research while in Hillsbury.

DO NO EVIL.

This monkey is described in the Yezhuan Scrolls and one of the unofficial pages of the Rig Veda as being depicted with his arms crossed along his body, hands covering his genitals. This was Joel Liman.

The crop circle message was initially meant to deceive, and it is my professional opinion that the being who first communicated with Orville Liman was personally responsible for it. At first glance, it looked to warn of plagues, but plagues can be avoided or prevented. As I deciphered the message further, I discovered it to be a mosaic look at the events in Genesis 19:

Sodom and Gomorrah. By uncovering this message, I learned of the fate that awaited Hillsbury and its people.

Jill Carter went missing in order to be returned to Earth and used to draw Henry Carter and his family away from the Hillsbury massacre. Whether or not the Carters were somehow "above judgment" is an argument for another time; at present, I believe it is safe to say that a message is much more effective when there is someone left alive to learn from it.

What I have taken away from these events is that life must not be taken for granted, nor should one interfere with the path they are set on. There is a greater story at play, always, and we are a small speck in the grand spokes of an even grander wheel.

While the strange case of Hillsbury Park and Cape's Side Bay was one of tragedy, it was a necessary one, for it has brought us several steps closer to understanding our purpose in the great cosmic dance of the universe.

GRAND PATRONS

INKSHARES

INKSHARES is a community, publisher, and producer for debut writers. Our books are selected not just by a group of editors, but also by readers worldwide. Our aim is to find and develop the most captivating and intelligent new voices in fiction. We have no genre—our genre is debut.

Previously unknown Inkshares authors have received starred reviews in every trade publication. They have been featured in every major review, including on the front page of the *New York Times*. Their books are on the front tables of booksellers worldwide, topping bestseller lists. They have been translated in major markets by the world's biggest publishers. And they are being adapted at the biggest studios and networks.

Interested in making your own story a reality? Visit Inkshares.com to start your own project, connect with other writers, and find other great books.

Printed in the USA
CPSIA information can be obtained
at www.ICGtesting.com
JSHW020553260923
49094JS00030B/14